STARGATE ATLANTIS™

THE FURIES

Book four of the LEGACY series

JO GRAHAM

FANDEMONIUM BOOKS

An original publication of Fandemonium Ltd, produced under license from MGM Consumer Products.

Fandemonium Books
United Kingdom
Visit our website: www.stargatenovels.com

STARGATE
ATLANTIS™

METRO-GOLDWYN-MAYER Presents
STARGATE ATLANTIS™
JOE FLANIGAN   RACHEL LUTTRELL   JASON MOMOA   JEWEL STAITE
ROBERT PICARDO and DAVID HEWLETT as Dr. McKay
Executive Producers BRAD WRIGHT & ROBERT C. COOPER
Created by BRAD WRIGHT & ROBERT C. COOPER

MGM

Print ISBN: 978-1-905586-57-8   Ebook ISBN: 978-1-80070-003-1

For my sister, Elizabeth

Let us roll all our strength and all
Our sweetness up into one ball;
And tear our pleasures with rough strife
Through the iron gates of life.
Thus, though we cannot make our sun
Stand still, yet we will make him run.
— Andrew Marvell

CHAPTER ONE

The Prisoner

JOHN Sheppard woke in darkness, unable to move, held upright by the thick fibers of the Wraith bonds. He could see nothing. The corridor was dim, and the alcove he was held in stood in deep shadow. If he could have leaned forward, perhaps he could have glanced up and down the hallway, but the bonds across his chest and throat were so tight that the slightest forward movement threatened to cut off his breath.

There was no sound. Either he was alone, or the other humans imprisoned here must be beyond speech.

A faint vibration through the soles of his feet did tell him something. This was not a planetary base. He was on a ship, each moment traveling further and further from anywhere his team would look for him.

Because he was stupid, and possibly terminally stupid. He'd been so sure that the message that had lured him to Gaffen was from Rodney McKay, his friend held captive by the Wraith and the subject of a terrible transformation. He was so sure that somehow Rodney had slipped out of the programming his captors had used on him and sent a cry for help. John had walked into the trap open eyed, going to the gate address Rodney had specified, only to wind up in the middle of a culling.

Which shouldn't have been a surprise. Teyla had said she thought it might be a trap. Were she and Ronon here too, perhaps bound a few meters away? Or…

"Teyla? Ronon?" His voice came out as a rough whisper.

There was no reply. Which meant either they weren't here, or they were unconscious. Or they'd already been taken to be fed on, some horrible part of his brain said, readily supplying the pictures.

No. He wouldn't believe that. They'd never go without a

fight, and if there had been a fight in the corridor he would have known it.

Besides, John thought, conjuring up the scene on Gaffen just before he was taken, Ronon and Teyla hadn't been anywhere near him. They'd been back in the market, a long way from the gate. They'd gone to ask the locals if anybody knew anything. John had thought that was unlikely. Rodney wasn't just going to walk up to people and say hi, especially since he looked like a Wraith. It was more likely he was hiding in the woods behind the gatefield, keeping an eye on the Stargate and the DHD, knowing that was where the team from Atlantis would arrive. He'd been checking out the woods with a Marine team when the gate had opened again and three Darts come through. It was more likely that some of the Marines had been picked up than Ronon or Teyla.

"Simmons? Hernandez? Anybody there?"

Silence.

John swallowed hard. He'd wondered how the Wraith had done this to Rodney, how they'd messed with him so thoroughly. Now he was probably about to find out. If he was lucky he'd be experiment number two, and at least he'd find Rodney. Maybe together there was a chance one of them would remember who they were and plot an escape. If he wasn't lucky… He'd be lunch, and that would be the end of that.

How long had it been since he was captured on Gaffen? He had no idea. Scooped up by the culling beam of a Wraith Dart, he could have remained in the pattern buffer for days. And there was no way to tell how long it had been since he was strapped here. Hours? Not more than eight or ten, probably. Unless the enzymes the Wraith used affected his metabolism significantly, he'd be hungry and thirsty. Well, he was hungry, but not starving. A dinnertime kind of hungry, not an imprisoned for days kind of hungry. There was an energy bar in one of his pants pockets, but he couldn't get to it, couldn't move his arms or bend enough.

And that was not good. This situation was going to get old really fast.

It wasn't the first time he'd been in prison. It wasn't even the worst. That had probably been Kolya's prison, waiting for his time to run out before Todd drained the life out of him. What had he done then, other than lie against the wall and breathe each time after the Wraith ripped more years of life out of him?

There were things to do, mental tricks to keep yourself in one piece. Some of them weren't very orthodox, but they worked. They were better than going crazy, getting yourself in such a lather that you couldn't do something useful when an opportunity came.

Breathe, and let each breath take you somewhere, take you through the corridors of memory to other places and other times. There were paths he could walk in his sleep, in memory. Breathe, and one pattern took him across the flight lines at Al Kharj Prince Sultan Air Base, the tarmac laid out in concrete squares, across the blowing red gold dust of the areas around the buildings, nearly twenty years ago when he was young and wondered if he'd live through the first days of Operation Instant Thunder.

Breathe, and another memory took him elsewhere, through the underground corridors of Crystal City, when back from Afghanistan he'd spent his days wandering aimlessly, anything to get out of the tiny apartment he shared with Nancy, through mall and metro tunnels, under the glass skylights and potted rainforest trees.

Not a good time. Not a good memory to get lost in, not if he wanted to be ready when the Wraith showed up.

Atlantis, then. He could walk in his mind through the corridors of home, through light-washed streets with floors of burnished tile, stained glass making patterns of light across his skin like the city's own brand. From chair room to mess hall, pier to gate room, he could walk the city in memory. Doors opened in front of him and slid softly closed behind him to the touch of his mind. Towers glittered with ice as he'd seen them last, and his favorite balcony stretched under the tropical sun of a world left behind a year ago. Power substations crackled with blue fire, as though storms swirled around them again, rain dashed in his face. Above it all in dreams the shield made a hemisphere of sky, tinted by dawn through bombardment. He looked down on space below from a terrace pressurized by its fragile skin, slid in his mind into the chair's embrace and felt the stardrive flare beneath him, engines answering to his thought.

"This one."

When words came he had almost stopped expecting them, drowsing in his bonds, his mind far away. John Sheppard looked up.

The Wraith was young, or at least he thought so, with long white hair held back in a bronze clasp, his face rounded and smooth beneath a swirling tattoo that curved from his hairline down the side of his face to his collar like tendrils of vine, and his eyes were dark and cruel. "This one," he said, and he tangled his fingers in John's hair, the claws of his other hand tearing the bindings away enough to expose throat and chest.

Not the transformation then, John thought. Not that. Just the other bit. Well, it shouldn't take long. He steeled himself for the kiss of claws, for the pounding in his ears of his own heart as the feeding began...

But the Wraith was looking at him, turning his head toward the light, as though he wanted to see him better. He could lean forward a little now, and the light stabbed his eyes as the Wraith jerked his chin up.

"You," the Wraith said, "What is your name?"

"Han Solo," John said.

The Wraith snarled, tilting his head toward the light again as though trying to see the color of his eyes.

I'm nobody, John willed him to think. Nobody. Nobody worth trying to get intelligence out of, nobody worth taking to the queen. And at the same time a kernel of an idea sprouted inside him. This wasn't Rodney's doing if this guy had no idea who he was. If he did know, he wouldn't waste time. But if he didn't, if it was only that John looked familiar and he was trying to place him...

The steel claws released him. With a snarl and a backward

glance the Wraith paced away down the corridor in a swirl of black leather.

"Crap," John Sheppard said.

The voice of the drone at the doors was loud in her mind. *My Queen, Bronze would speak with you. Shall I admit him?*

Of course, Waterlight replied, and sat up straighter in her chair, arranging her hands in her lap. Her mother would have told her to sit up straight, to insist upon every courtesy, even with Bronze, who might be her pallax someday, might be her Consort. There was little enough choice. Twelve blades remained to her, and one of them was Thorn, who might never aspire to that role. Twelve blades and seven clevermen, twenty six drones. And Waterlight.

She lifted her chin, her face pale as her white dress in the ship-light, a bluish tint cast by the lights above. Her hair was dark, rising from a sharp widow's peak in the front, falling in a river down her back, held back with the silver combs that had been her mother's, and her small hands were covered by glovebacks of fine white stones set in silver mesh. Too large for her. They did not flex as they should, but rather rang and clattered when she moved her fingers.

You will grow into them, the Consort Thorn said at her shoulder, and Waterlight glanced up.

His face was tight as always, pinched even though he had fed recently. The strain told on him, and she was sorry, sorry once again that she was not more ready...

You are young, he said, catching at her thought like wind, *and youth is not a flaw.* In his mind she saw herself as he did, at rest on some world she did not remember, breaking from his arms to run toward the waves that crashed on the shore in crests of bright foam, her laughter sparkling like light on the water.

I am not that child, she said, mind to mind and heart to heart. She must not be. A fruit-fed baby who trusted all... She must be queen. There was no other choice.

The door irised open, and she schooled her face to bland calmness as Bronze approached, his every movement sharp and keen. He was not so much her senior, and though she did not burn as she would, she could not help but admire the way he moved, his slender form in its leathers graceful and quick, the tenor of his mind bright. If the day came that he were pallax, she would not regret it.

What bring you, my blade? she asked, her voice cool.

He sketched a deep bow to her, a quick nod to Thorn, his mind voice all but bursting with excitement. *My Queen, I believe we have captured the Consort of Atlantis!*

Thorn's voice was dry. *And how would such a miracle have occurred? We have seen nothing of the Lanteans, and have stayed far away from their allies this last dreamcycle. Besides that, he is a warrior, and always accompanied by full many blades.*

Bronze did not back down, his eyes darting to her though he spoke to Thorn. *Nevertheless, I think this is he. He gives another name, of course, but he is very like to the images the Genii circulated. I would stake my life that this is the same man!*

Thorn did not believe. She felt his skepticism at her back. Bronze would do much for attention, much to draw himself to her as she grew older.

And yet she was not a child, and a small, tight-packed bubble of defiance rose in her. If her blade brought something to her, should she not hear him out? Waterlight lifted her chin. *Show me,* she said.

His mind was golden, like the reflecting metal of his name, and the picture was sharp — one of the images the Genii had made, a dark haired human, rather ordinary looking, eyes a muddy shade between brown and green, like thousands of others. The second picture… The human rested in their feeding pens, a film of hair upon his chin rendering him more bestial, his hair threaded silver a little at the temples, but those same eyes, the same expression of fearlessness, as though he knew what was to come and did not surrender. *It might be?* she said, and did not like the uncertain sound in her own voice.

Thorn bent his head, a small flash of interest as he studied the images Bronze showed him. *Possibly,* he said grudgingly, *if this one does not distort them.* Bronze might, might in his eagerness make the pictures seem more alike in his mind than they were, exaggerate this man's likeness to the Consort of Atlantis. *Where did he come from?*

From my run upon Gaffen, Bronze said proudly. *Everwind and I brought eleven, food to keep us some little time.*

Eleven, Thorn thought, and it was there in his mind — darts by the hundreds streaking across the sky, thousands scattering before them, great plazas full of panicked crowds swept clean in moments. Such had been Sateda, in the old days. Now they hunted on the fringes, poaching here and there where it would be little noticed.

Eleven, Bronze said, and his back was steel. *I go and fetch the food we have, not brood in solitude!*

Thorn snarled, and she felt his anger and at the same time knew the truth of his words. If all had not gone so badly, if her mother lived yet…

I am Queen, she said to both, her voice clear as crystals. *And I will have no quarreling, my blades.*

It was her prerogative to call the Consort to order, but she had never done thus. She did not know if he would take it. If he did not…

Possibly it is the Consort of Atlantis, My Queen, he said. Pride blossomed bright in his mind. She was growing. She would not be easily ruled, a weak queen who was nothing but her consort's mouthpiece.

It made her bold. *See that this man is taken to a cell and given food and water. If it is not the Consort Guide, it will do little harm to keep him alive some few more days. And if it is…* She raised her eyes to Bronze, whose heart leaped. *We have a great prize.*

He expected to be taken to the Queen. Wasn't that always how this worked? They'd come and get him, drag him in to where the Wicked Witch of the West was waiting, and then she'd start with the whole 'kneel puny human' routine. So when two Wraith came to get John, he thought he knew the drill. One of them was one of the big masked guys, and the other was the young one he'd seen before, the one who'd asked his name.

The big one prodded his back with a stunner, and John briefly wondered if he could goad him into firing. If he stunned him it would probably be a little while before they got back to the going to the Queen part. It might buy a little more time before she turned his mind inside out.

But no. This guy would probably just pin his arms or punch him. He was built like a brick wall, and wouldn't actually need to stun him to assure his compliance.

To his surprise they went to an ordinary holding cell, the twin of the ones he'd been in before, a bleak little room in semi-darkness, the front wall a sliding grate of irregularly shaped bars. On the floor on one side was a metal dish piled with four or five pieces of fruit, while a metal pitcher held water. John looked at them dubiously.

The young one was already preparing to leave. "What's with the fruit, Frank?" he asked. "Can I call you Frank?"

The Wraith ignored him and stalked off, not even glancing back.

"Ok." John sat down next to the pitcher, glad to at least to be in a different position. "Planning to keep me a while then." He wasn't sure whether that thought was reassuring or not.

It may be, Thorn said grudgingly, studying the likeness of their prisoner against the one circulated by the Genii long ago. The man who called himself Han Solo did not waste time pacing his small cell. Instead he leaned against the wall, his face upturned and his eyes closed, apparently hibernating. This one had been a prisoner before. He did not waste energy weeping or pleading, or throwing himself against things that would not yield.

And if it is the Consort of Atlantis? Waterlight asked. She looked up at Thorn, her head to the side. *What then?*

Then we have a worthy trade, Thorn said, and though he did not wish it she could see the shape of the fears in his mind. Queen Death had little tolerance for lesser queens unless they brought her something of surpassing worth, and Waterlight had nothing. She was nothing by Queen Death's reckoning. A few tens of men, a battered ship — she would be dead already, had it even been worth the time to send men to kill her. The day would come, inevitably, when their poaching trespassed upon a greater hive, or when Promised Return chanced upon one of Queen Death's ships. There was no need for Death to seek out Waterlight. In the end, it would all be the same.

I am not afraid, Waterlight said, and hoped that it did not show that she was.

It was there in the mind of the one she called Father — the Consort of Atlantis might be worth her life in trade. If this human were he, perhaps Death would take him as gift, and leave Promised Return alone. Perhaps his life might buy a few more years for Waterlight.

And if it is not? Waterlight asked. *Will we not then look foolish? And moreover call her attention to us?*

It is a gamble, Thorn admitted. *But perhaps we may first speak to one of her counselors who has seen the Consort before. If this is some other who only resembles him, we will know before Queen Death ever hears of it. Be still, and I shall contact those blades I know who might study this likeness and tell me if it is or not. I think there are those who can tell me with little risk.* He looked at Waterlight, his teeth bared in a mirthless smile. *I am not entirely friendless yet.*

I did not say you were, Waterlight said, trying to keep the color of her mind from shifting with embarrassment. In truth she did not blame him for their predicament, much as some might. He had been Consort. It had been his duty to protect the hive, to protect his Queen with his very life. To have lost her and survived was not something a man might live down. He should have died for her, rather than live for their daughter, even if his Queen had wished it otherwise.

Then with your permission, My Queen, Thorn said sharply. *I will contact those blades I know now in her orbit who may be able to identify the Consort of Atlantis. If we have that one, then perhaps our fortunes will change.*

CHAPTER TWO

Holding the Fort

A COLD wind scoured the whitecaps crashing against the piers, but Sam Carter thought it wasn't as cold as it had been. Atlantis was beautiful in the weak winter sunshine, as always. They were a week past the winter solstice here, and soon the days would lengthen noticeably. They might even get warmer. Sam could appreciate the astronomical elegance of the seasons, even while nearly freezing to death in her flightsuit, waiting for Steven Caldwell on this chilly balcony.

"Sorry about that." He came out through the glass doors to the control room and rubbed his hands together. "Cold out here."

"Yes," Sam said. There wasn't really any other reply to stating the obvious.

"We've got a problem," Caldwell said.

Which was again stating the obvious. Sam settled for looking attentive. She'd had plenty of practice at that.

"With Sheppard missing and Woolsey stuck on Earth, that means the Chief of Sciences is in charge in Atlantis. Dr. Zelenka." Caldwell leaned forward on his elbows, looking out over the sea.

"While McKay is gone," Sam agreed.

Caldwell shot her a sharp look. "You know we're never getting McKay back. Let's be practical. Sheppard may turn up, may actually survive whatever crazy scheme he's playing, but McKay? And who the hell knows what's going on with Woolsey."

"The IOA," Sam said. There was a wealth of information in that statement of fact. She knew Caldwell had rarely seen eye to eye with the IOA, and he knew how she'd been relieved in Atlantis.

"They might send him back. They might send God knows who." Caldwell spread his hands, the light around the corner of the building just touching them.

"Or they might take three months to make up their minds," Sam said. She leaned forward on her elbows beside him. "We've been off the grid for nineteen days. General O'Neill will have recalled *Odyssey* by now. It will probably take *Odyssey* weeks to get back to Earth with its ZPM, but the minute it does we'll have Colonel Mitchell and SG-1 blowing in here locked and loaded." There was a good deal of comfort in thinking of that. It might look like she and Caldwell were hanging out to dry, but Sam knew they weren't. Millions of lightyears away Jack and Cam were moving heaven and earth.

Caldwell nodded as though he found that thought comforting too. "Look, Sam, we know there's nothing here we can't handle. But they don't know that. If it looks like there's too much of a crisis the IOA is going to panic."

"And what? Order Atlantis back to Earth? We haven't got the power to go around the block, much less back to the Milky Way."

Caldwell looked at her sideways. "And scrap the project."

"They wouldn't do that," she said.

"They wouldn't?" Caldwell's eyebrows rose. "In case you didn't notice while you were fitting out the *Hammond*, there's a global economic crisis at home. How much do you think this expedition costs? And how much do you think they're recouping?"

"It's not about immediate cash," Sam said. "It's about the long term opportunities. The scientific advances. The technologies we're discovering are priceless."

"Right now what they are is expensive and useless," Caldwell said. He shook his head. "You scientists get all hot and bothered about things that might pan out sometime, but the math on Earth is this — is it worth any money?"

"We're not a bunch of conquistadores out looking for treasure," Sam said. "This isn't about finding nifty stuff that can go on EBay."

"Or opening new markets?" Caldwell snorted. "Not a lot of new markets here, Carter. Just a lot of people needing humanitarian aid and a whole ton of Wraith. It's costing a lot of money and a lot of lives for a lot of nothing."

"What are you saying?" Sam straightened up. "We can't just pack up and go home."

"And we won't," Caldwell said. "The Air Force has a big investment in ships and we're getting our money's worth in technology that gives us superiority at home. We're not going anywhere. But the Atlantis expedition isn't cost effective. If it starts looking like a liability, the IOA will pull the plug."

"If we don't have a base, we're screwed," Sam said bluntly. "Right now. Today. The kind of damage the *Hammond* took…"

Caldwell looked at her sideways. "How much did you massage the report?"

"I massaged the summary," Sam said, reaching up to push an errant lock of hair back behind her ear. "The devil's in the details, but the IOA won't read them unless O'Neill gives them the full version. Which I doubt." Which she'd stake good money on. The *Hammond* didn't belong to the IOA. They'd never know how close she'd been to losing it with all hands.

Caldwell shrugged. "Mine too," he said. He straightened up. "We can't stay out of communication like this until *Odyssey* gets back to Earth. If the IOA has two solid months or so to stew, they'll eat Woolsey alive and pull the plug on the whole thing. I need to get back to a Milky Way gate and dial in. Those reports aren't doing any good sitting on our hard drives." He let out a deep breath. "The *Hammond* is still under repair. That last series of shots took the Asgard drive out. *Daedalus* needs to make the run. And I feel better about leaving the station with you here to hold Zelenka's hand. He's an ok guy, but not who I'd want in charge in Atlantis."

"I'm sure he feels the same way," Sam said. Something about Zelenka clinging to her arm and expostulating had clued her in.

"You know the ropes and you're better qualified to hold the fort than anybody," Caldwell said. "I'll leave Hocken and the 302 wing here with you. I don't need it to run six days down to the first Milky Way gate and you might need it here."

"I hope not," Sam said. Which was an understatement. With

the *Hammond* severely damaged and Atlantis with no shield, Lt. Colonel Mel Hocken's 302 wing was the only defense they had if the Wraith showed up while *Daedalus* was gone.

"I hope not too." Caldwell gave her a grim smile. "I may turn around and come back or proceed to Earth, depending on orders." He plunged his hands into his pockets against the cold. "Give me six hours to get *Daedalus* squared away and we'll get a move on. I'll take your severely wounded aboard and send them through to the SGC at the first gate."

"That follows," Sam said. There were a couple, especially Joyner's third degree burns, that she'd like out of here if possible. Keller and Beckett weren't a burn center, try as they might.

"Find Sheppard," Caldwell said. "He does this crap. Sheppard's been missing more times than any guy I know and always turns up again."

"Not more times than Dr. Jackson," Sam said.

"I don't think Sheppard's actually been dead," Caldwell said.

Sam couldn't help but laugh. "You know, we see some weird things in our profession."

Caldwell grinned. "Never a dull moment. Except the six days in hyperspace."

"Except for that," Sam said. "I've got the easy part, holding Atlantis. You've got the hard part."

"The IOA," Caldwell said.

September 20, 2009
Dear Jack…

Sam paused, staring down at the email form in front of her, then frowned and started typing again.

The Daedalus is leaving in two hours, so this is my last chance to put another letter in the databurst that they'll send six days from now from PX1-152, the first Stargate on the edge of the Milky Way. It will be full night in Colorado Springs then, but I imagine Walter will be there. He'll sort out all the personal emails and send them on, so on Sunday morning, September 27, you will wake up in your apartment on Massachusetts Avenue to see twenty emails from me, everything I've sent in the last twenty three days, since as far as you're concerned I vanished completely.

She could see just how he would look, unshaved and muzzy with sleep, sloshing the hot coffee over his hand as he bent over his secure laptop open on the dinette table in the alcove with all the windows, a golden morning view eastward toward the Capitol dome just visible over the offices between from his eighth floor apartment. He'd spill the coffee and swear, but he wouldn't clean it up, not until he'd opened the last one, this one.

I'm ok.

That was the thing he'd look for first.

I'm fine. Not a scratch on me. The Hammond *has a few dings, but she's in one piece too. You've got all the reports. They're probably sitting in your email right now. Walter's good that way.*

No need to tell him that. He would have the reports, pages and pages of them. Hers. Caldwell's. Sheppard's. He'd have a hundred pages of reports. So no need to rehearse everything in them. No need to even hit the highlights. He would read them all, know every word in them by noon, drinking cup after cup of coffee, sitting there in boxers and a t shirt while the sun rose high, slanting stripes of gold across the carpet, visualizing the endless dark of space, the flare of shields in the void.

I wish I was there.

He would read that, one eyebrow quirking, say out loud in the quiet apartment, "Carter, that's a lie." And it was. She didn't really wish she were there, not for more than a moment really, imagining a quiet Sunday morning at home.

I wish you were here.

Yes, kind of. And not. Or only a little. He'd smile at that. "No, you don't, Carter," he'd say. He knew her way too well. And he'd take that for all the things she wouldn't say, all the things she wouldn't put in a databurst that would go through Caldwell and Walter and Hank Landry and God knows who else before he read it.

I don't know when I'll be back, needless to say. Caldwell made the call that Daedalus *was making the run because we're still under repair. Since I have no idea what the situation there is…*

How to phrase this bit? With Woolsey and the IOA, with the politics, with the movements of other ships… How long would *Daedalus* stay on Earth? Who would it bring back? When would it come? She had no way to know. She just knew that she'd keep it together until whenever.

…I'll be here.

Maybe they'd get their hands on another ZPM and they could call Earth any time they wanted. Or maybe not. If a hive ship showed up it was going to get very interesting.

Caldwell is leaving his 302 wing with me, as he details in his report. Hocken is good, and they did an exemplary job in our last engagement. I've included commendation paperwork for Captain Dwaine Grant, whose conduct was above and beyond the call of duty.

There was no need to reiterate that. But he'd know that she meant it, would take a closer look and remember Grant's name, read over it carefully seeing the crippled 302 in his mind's eye, a plume of oxygen venting from his wing tank as he dove between the hive ship and the *Hammond*, taking the burst on his shields instead of the now unshielded bridge windows. Jack would read the formal, stilted words that Hocken and Caldwell had written, her formulaic endorsement, and he would see.

Anyhow, I've got to go. The taxi's waiting. He's blowing his horn.

He'd fill in the rest of the lyrics. Peter, Paul and Mary was his cup of tea.

Carter

CHAPTER THREE

Guide's Play

THE MOMENT Guide saw Ember, in the pilot's lounge just off the dart bay, he knew there was something wrong. His face was smooth and well-fed, his dark blue silks immaculate, embroidered in copper with their pattern of whirling atomic particles, but tension showed in every line of his body. He radiated it.

It was enough that Guide let the rest of the party go ahead, allowed himself to be drawn aside as though on personal business that would not wait, his hand on Ember's wrist so that they might speak mind to mind without being overheard.

"Is it McKay?" he said.

"No." Ember's voice was bright and rueful. "That one… I do not know. Sometimes I think there is a spark there, that he remembers. And then I do not. All is the same. Nothing has changed with him, and so we continue."

"Then what is wrong?"

"You may recall Thorn, he who was Consort to Firebeauty?"

"I do, but she is gone," Guide snapped. "Come to the point, Ember."

Ember would not be hurried. "He stands now as guardian to Waterlight, who calls him Father. She is young, she is nothing, and the Queen has not seen her. But now Thorn has contacted us and said that they have captured the Consort of Atlantis!"

Guide took a long breath. "Have you seen the transmission?"

"I have," Ember said. "It is John Sheppard."

Guide did not ask if he were certain. That was useless. Of course Ember was certain. "And you said?"

Ember's eyes shifted. "I said I did not know. I did not think it was he." He shook his head. "It was Ardent who had the watch, and he did not take it to the Queen, saying that he would not waste her time on trifles."

"Still," Guide said contemplatively, "Thorn will call again. He must hope to make a trade, and he will call if his words are not responded to in due time. I take it he left coordinates so that the Queen may speak with him of this if she wishes?"

"He did," Ember said. Fear was bright within him. Sheppard knew too much. He knew too many plots within plots, and most of all that Guide had told him where to find Bright Venture. The damage to the Queen's favorite ship still rankled within her. The example she would make of Ember and Guide…

"Coldly," Guide said, his mind working furiously. "Be cold, Ember. He is not in her hands. You have done well to throw doubt upon Thorn's words."

"He will call again," Ember replied.

"Yes. But it will be some time." He turned about in a swirl of leathers. "I must return to our ship. Say that I have urgent business, for I do."

"What do you go to do?" Ember asked.

Guide shook his head. "If you do not know, it cannot lie uppermost in your mind. Stay your thoughts, Ember. And know I will manage."

"I do," Ember said, and there was no doubt in his eyes.

"Colonel Carter." Todd's face was slightly distorted by the poor transmission, but she thought he was taken aback. "What an unexpected surprise."

"It's nice to see you too," Sam said, leaning over Zelenka's shoulder to the camera above the viewscreen in the control room.

"I do not see Colonel Sheppard with you," Todd said.

"He's busy at the moment," Sam said pleasantly. "I'm afraid you're stuck with me." It had occurred to her that Todd always seemed more cooperative with her than with some — maybe because of the battle with the Replicators. If so, she was ready to take whatever advantage it gave her.

"You mean he is missing and the prisoner of a certain hive," Todd said. "I would like to know what you would give for your consort's safe return."

Zelenka started to say something, and Sam put her hand on his shoulder, hopefully out of range of the camera. "Sorry. I don't know what you mean."

"You do know what I mean, Colonel Carter," Todd said. "And I am prepared to tell you where Sheppard is while it is still possible for you to recover him. If you hesitate, he will be in Queen Death's hands."

"And then she'll know you're double dealing," Sam said with a cheerful smile. "So I don't think I'll need to give you anything for the information."

She thought that he would hiss and spark, but instead Todd smiled. "What have you done with Woolsey, Colonel Carter?"

"He's on Earth right now," Sam said truthfully. "Tending to some business. Like I said, you're stuck with me."

"Indeed I am," Todd said, and bowed his head slightly with what she thought was an expression of amusement. "Then I will tell you that he is the prisoner of a very young Queen named Waterlight, aboard her hive ship at these coordinates. Waterlight is not yet a member of Queen Death's alliance, but she hopes to be so. She will trade Sheppard to Queen Death for favorable terms. Mind you, I do not think it is an alliance she wants, but these are difficult times. We must all make what compromises we can."

Teyla hurried into the control room and stopped, but not far enough back.

Todd could apparently see her on camera, for he nodded pleasantly in her direction. "I see the Young Queen is with you still, Colonel Carter."

"Teyla's a valuable part of the team," Sam said, not certain what that was about.

"Indeed," Todd said, grinning wolfishly. "You choose your proxies well. But you must act quickly. Once Sheppard is in the hands of Queen Death's men, there will be nothing you can do."

He cut the transmission, and it dissolved into a burst of static.

Sam let out a long breath, suddenly aware that her hand was still on Zelenka's shoulder. Her eyes met Teyla's. "Not good," she said.

"I did not hear the beginning," Teyla said.

"I'll recap." Sam glanced along the control panels at Airman Salawi in the far seat. "Airman, will you ask Doctors Beckett and Keller to join us in the conference room? Also Colonel Hocken, Ronon, and of course you, Dr. Zelenka?"

"Of course," Radek said, getting to his feet. "This is very interesting." He pushed his glasses back up on his nose. "Are we to recall the *Daedalus*?"

"That's one of the things we need to talk about," Sam said.

Theoretically, Radek was in charge, Teyla thought. But he took his usual seat along the side of the conference room table, looking at Sam expectantly. Old habits were hard to break, and she had been in charge here once. She hesitated, looking at the chair at the end of the table. By rights it was John's place, but he was missing. Leaving it empty was perhaps too stark. Sam slid into the chair at the end as Colonel Hocken and Ronon came in.

Ronon sat down beside Teyla. "What's going on?"

"Todd has called," she said. "He told us where he thinks John is."

Ronon blew out a long breath. "Another of Todd's deals," he said.

"Yes. And we do not know what it portends."

Jennifer and Carson came in together, sitting down beside Radek across from her, while Hocken took the seat on the other side of Ronon, leaning forward expectantly in her crisp flight suit.

"We've had a communication from Todd," Sam said, and hit the playback to the wall screen to let it speak for itself. When the transmission finished there was a long silence.

"We go get him," Ronon said. He put his hands on the table and looked at Hocken, who was frowning. "That's what we do."

Sam's brow creased. "How?"

"What do you mean?" Ronon asked.

"I'm not saying we shouldn't," Sam said, one finger tapping on the table. "What I'm asking is how. The *Hammond* isn't capable of hyperspace travel and won't be for six or seven days at least. The 302s have no hyperspace capability, and there is no Stargate near the coordinates Todd gave us. It's the same problem with a puddle jumper. We don't have any way to get there."

"*Daedalus*," Radek said. "We could recall *Daedalus*. Colonel Caldwell—"

"The *Daedalus* left three days ago," Sam said. "Right now it's between galaxies and out of communications. Even if we could recall Daedalus, it will take Daedalus at least three days to get back here. By that time Colonel Sheppard may be dead or traded to Queen Death. And if you've got a way of reaching the *Daedalus* while she's in hyperspace, let me know. That's the scientific coup of the century."

"We can't just do nothing," Ronon said.

"We could try to contact the Travelers," Jennifer said. She looked across at Teyla appealingly. "They like Colonel Sheppard. They loaned him a ship before."

"I'm comfortable with trying that," Sam said. "The problem is that the last time we did that it took weeks for them to get the message. We can't count on their help in time."

"There's no other ship that's hyperdrive equipped?" Hocken asked. "What about that warship the Genii have?"

"I'll try flying the damned thing," Carson said, putting his hands on the table. "No promises, now. But I'll give it a turn."

Time, Teyla thought. Time. Time to contact Ladon Radim, to hope that he could be persuaded, as unlikely as that seemed. Time to get the ship here and then get there. Time was slipping through her fingers like a fistful of water.

"Thank you, Carson," Sam said. "I think it's worthwhile to ask the Genii. I don't know that they'll cooperate. Or what they'll want in return." She looked at Ronon

"Sateda," he said.

"Maybe." Sam steepled her hands in front of her mouth. "That's a pretty stiff price."

Teyla closed her eyes. A ship. There must be a ship. Some way of reaching the coordinates in time, before the Wraith… Her eyes sprung open. "There is another ship," she said. "Another ship here in Atlantis."

Sam blinked. "What other ship?"

"The Wraith cruiser," Teyla said. She looked down the table at Mel Hocken. "You took out the life support and made a hull breach. But its hyperdrive was intact, was it not?"

"Yes, so?" Hocken looked confused. "It's a Wraith ship. Nobody can fly it. It's adrift in a decaying orbit."

Sam had been here two years ago, and she sat bolt upright in her chair, a smile breaking over her face. "Nobody except Teyla."

"I can fly it," Teyla said with a voice that sounded more confident than she was. "I have flown a hive ship before. I can use the interfaces. If the hull breach can be repaired and the systems restored, I can fly it."

"We will have to see how bad it is," Radek said. "But unless it is very bad indeed, it will be much easier to seal off compartments and isolate the breach than it is to rebuild the *Hammond's* Asgard drive. That is not easy." He looked at Sam.

"No," she said, "it's not."

"I will have to go aboard and see," Radek said. "But unless it is very bad it should be possible in a day or two, working around the clock."

"So we go get Sheppard in the Wraith cruiser," Ronon said. "Sweet."

"It's a cruiser," Sam said. "No dart bays. No place to put 302s. And you can't shoot it out with a hive ship. This isn't that kind of mission." She looked at Teyla. "If it is a mission. Let's get Dr. Zelenka up there to see what kind of shape the cruiser is in, and then we'll talk about it." She looked down the table, making eye contact with Carson, Ronon and Jennifer in turn. "We can't strip Atlantis of our defenses. This might be a trap. Todd has played us before."

"Yeah," Ronon said grimly.

"What if this is a ruse to lure you and our air cover away, to get our teams out in the field while they attack again?" She shook her head. "We can't risk it. With Major Lorne unable to walk at present, and our shield inoperable, you're not going anywhere."

"Teyla can't do this alone," Ronon said. "Sheppard…"

"Ronon." Sam said quietly, and to Teyla's surprise he stopped, his hands closing in frustration. "Let's see where we are after Dr. Zelenka has a look at the ship. If it's not repairable, it's all an academic question."

"Then I had best get going," Radek said, getting to his feet. "Carson, will you take me up in a jumper? And I will want a team together. We will need suits. Teyla, will you come?"

"Most assuredly," Teyla said.

Of course they could not strip Atlantis' defenses. It might be a trap. She did not think it was, did not feel it in her bones, but the one they called Todd had never been entirely honest, even when she had played his Queen to assist him in his plan. When she had been Steelflower.

And in that moment an idea blossomed.

Ronon and Jennifer walked out together, he bending his head to speak with her, Radek bustling around them in conversation with Hocken about comparative ship technology. Teyla rose to follow them, then stopped.

Sam closed her laptop, looking uncomfortable. "Teyla, you know if there's a way to make this work…" she began.

"There is a way," she said, and though cold dread settled in her stomach she spoke on. "A way that is certain, and risks no lives except my own."

Sam frowned. "What's that?"

"Dr. Keller can transform me once again into Steelflower," she said. Teyla lifted her chin. "She is…I was…Todd's Queen, a person of note. I cannot even begin to tell you what it means among the Wraith to be queen. I cannot explain how it feels, how a queen holds sway. What the mental bonds feel like. But if this Waterlight who has John is young and untried, I can push her. I can compel her men. I can make them release John to me."

"And if they see through you?"

"No one did before," Teyla said. "And I was many days among them. Why should they in the course of a single meeting or two, when I come with my own cruiser? I can demand their compliance if nothing else."

"If they don't buy it?"

Teyla took a step closer. "It is only my own life at risk."

Sam's eyes were very blue, and met hers frankly. "That's not nothing."

"If it were General O'Neill, would not you do it?" she asked.

Sam's gaze slid away, and she smiled ruefully, as though shaking her head at herself. "I have," she said. She picked up the laptop and looked at Teyla. "Ok. If Dr. Keller is comfortable with the procedure and the ship is flyable." She smiled again. "It's not like I can order you not to, right?"

"That is true," Teyla said. "I am a contractor, and I can quit."

"I don't think that's necessary," Sam said. "But you'd better go talk to Keller now so you'll have time to suit up if Zelenka needs you upstairs to initialize systems on the cruiser. Unless you were planning for Torren to do that."

"Torren is on New Athos, and can stay there until I return," Teyla said. "It is best. And I will speak to Dr. Keller now."

CHAPTER FOUR

Quicksilver

THE VISIT to Gaffen had been delayed and delayed again after the loss of the queen's cruiser, but finally Ember had managed to convince someone that it was a priority if they were to make use of the stolen ZPM. What had proven impossible was to convince anyone that Quicksilver should accompany them. Quicksilver snarled silently at the memory. Even Ember had refused — you are too important to risk, he had said, which was probably true, but not really an adequate excuse. Nighthaze had tipped his head to one side, perplexed — your men can't handle this on their own? — and he had not dared take the matter further.

Which meant he was stuck here, on the hive, while Ember and the others were on Gaffen, and there was no way he could ask them to investigate the last few addresses in the DHD's buffer to see if Atlantis had dialed there. He had almost convinced himself that he was mistaken, anyway, that he was truly Quicksilver, brother of Dust, senior cleverman in the hive of Queen Death, but the decision to send his men to Gaffen wakened all his previous doubts. And now he would never know.

He snarled again, pacing the length of the chamber he shared with Ember, as much at his own melodrama as at the situation itself. He would find another way to test his hypothesis, of course — if it was impossible, he was the man to do it — but that would mean starting over again. And there was no way to predict when the queen would order another attack on Atlantis's blocked Stargate. If he were McKay in truth, that ought to please him, but at the moment, it was only more frustration.

At least Ember's absence gave him a chance to search the other cleverman's files. He had been through them before, but always in haste, always with one eye on the door, for fear that Ember

would return and catch him at it. This time he would have time
to work without fear of being interrupted.

He went to his own console, entered a query. The screen
pulsed for an instant, then displayed his answer: Ember's shuttle had left the hive. And that meant it was time to get to work.
He turned to Ember's console, entered the codes he had stolen,
and watched as the system unlocked itself. He would need to be
careful, do nothing that could not be erased, but he would at least
have a chance to look at Ember's files on him. He was typing the
query even as he thought, scowled as the system returned a null
result. All right, maybe Ember didn't keep a file on him — that
was a point in favor of his being Quicksilver — or maybe it was
just better hidden.

At second search, there was a hidden portal, secure storage
reached through a second set of codes. Quicksilver stared at the
screen for a moment, then entered a code he knew Ember kept
in reserve. The subsystem opened obediently, but the screen was
blank. Quicksilver narrowed his eyes at the screen. That made
no sense; he was sure there was something here, something
hidden — the numbers didn't match, there was something in
the volume in spite of the void. He considered it for a moment,
then entered another code. The screen shifted, and a gameboard
swam into view.

"Oh, please," he said, irritated. If he'd wasted time on Ember's
secret plan to win at towers… And then the pattern registered:
not a plan, but a problem, and in the moment he identified it, he
saw the solution. He moved the silver blade, and the image dissolved, revealed a tiny list of files.

None of them had anything to do with him, either. One was
communication codes — Ember was more loyal to his commander than to his queen, it seemed — and the rest were short
notations, work on the ZPM and the new hyperdrive, nothing
to do with him. But the last…

He caught his breath. The last was a video file, captured from
the hive's communications system — perhaps even excised from

it, from the codes, and that was worth seeing. He triggered it, leaning close to capture every nuance.

A stranger looked from the screen, an unfamiliar older blade. "Old friend, I seek to confirm or deny a — possibility. In culling Gaffen this last ten-day, my queen's blades took one who greatly resembles the Consort of Atlantis. I know you have seen him yourself, and so I set his image before you. Is this the human himself, or merely one similar?" He paused. "If it should be so, we may wish to treat, my queen and I, that we may come to some agreement with your lady."

The screen brightened, filled with a human shape: a man sitting against the wall of a holding cell, his eyes closed, head tipped back against the cell's wall. The camera zoomed in, focusing on the face, shifting slightly to get the clearest view. The man opened his eyes as though he'd heard something, stared into the camera as though he sensed its presence: a dark-haired man, ordinary enough, a few days' growth of beard on his chin, hazel eyes that stared defiance.

Quicksilver closed his own eyes, his stomach roiling as though he were in freefall. He knew the man — knew him with a certainty he had not felt since before he was captured, could put a name to him, a human name. John Sheppard — Consort of Atlantis, indeed, commander of the Lanteans; the man who had led the attack on the hive, who had tried to capture him. Tried to rescue him…

Tried to answer his message. The stranger had said Sheppard had been taken on Gaffen. And that meant that his own message had been received, and answered: Sheppard had come for him — had come for McKay, and he was McKay in truth. And, unwittingly, he'd led Sheppard into a trap.

His heart was racing, painful in his chest. He was Rodney McKay, except he'd been turned into a Wraith — but that wasn't the important thing right now. Atlantis knew that, Sheppard knew that, and they'd come for him anyway. Except Sheppard had been taken prisoner.

"All right," he whispered. "All right. Think."

First of all, this message was old — for all he knew, the team might have rescued Sheppard already. At the worst, he wasn't being held by Death, because everyone in the hive would have heard that news, so Sheppard was still with this other blade's queen, whoever she was. And that made rescue or escape a whole lot easier. Sheppard would escape. He always did.

Second — the thought was a sharp as a knife to the heart, but he faced it anyway. Second, even if Sheppard was a prisoner, there was nothing he could do about it. He had to keep his counsel, hide what he knew, and wait, either for rescue — because Sheppard wouldn't leave him behind — or for a chance to escape on his own. Sooner or later, there would be a chance. There had to be a chance. Sooner or later, someone would come.

He took a shuddering breath, feeling his heart steady a little, extended his hands to see them shaking. They looked alien, suddenly, frightening, with their heavy claws badly tended, and the thick vein that wound around his feeding hand. He curled his fingers to fists, and looked away. Ember had hidden this file, cut it from the ship's record and concealed it: the cleverman was playing a double game, at least, or maybe even triple, and that was something he could use.

And in the meantime, he would back himself out of Ember's systems, shut everything down very carefully. He frowned at the keys, suiting action to thought, watching the file fade, the empty subsystem reappear. He would pretend he had never found any of this, never doubted what he was told. And when Ember returned…

His feeding hand flexed. He would get answers this time.

CHAPTER FIVE

Rain

THE IOA preferred to meet at Homeworld Command rather than at the SGC. There were many more five star restaurants in Washington, Jack thought cynically. And besides, it was the least he could do for Hank Landry. Keeping the IOA firmly in DC and out from under the feet of the Stargate program was worth a good deal.

Also, when you met at the SGC something unexpected might happen. And it was almost never good.

The downside was that in DC they tended to meet and meet and meet. Their meetings in Colorado Springs were shorter. They were all in a hurry to blow this taco stand and get home. In DC there was no reason not to just go on meeting and meeting.

Especially when there was fun to be had. Crucifying Dick Woolsey was a blood sport.

He'd been their darling and he'd disappointed them. It wasn't enough to fire him. They were going to get their full money's worth out of seeing him fight hopelessly for his job first. Clausewitz, or whoever it was, was right. Politics was crueler than war.

They sat around Homeworld Command's tidy conference table, coffee and tea and water continually resupplied by a nearly invisible lieutenant with enough security clearance to go to the moon, in their fifth hour today of savaging Woolsey. Lesser men would have already resigned. It kind of made Jack O'Neill feel sorry for the poor bastard, for all that Woolsey had been a thorn in his side enough times.

Roy Martin, the new American representative, wanted to go over everything in tortuous detail and wanted hard copies of everything, 'not these fancy electronic files.' Another job for the highly cleared lieutenant, running out to the printer like the model of twenty four year old efficiency. Next month she'd be training to be on an SG team. If she didn't wash out, she'd be past getting the coffee. But as it was, Anderson (he thought her name was Anderson, he'd look when she came back in) was taking the opportunity to impress rather than sulking about being a glorified copy girl. There was something about her ramrod straight posture and the quick click of her heels that reminded him of somebody.

"Is that not the case, General?"

Everybody was looking at him. And he had no idea what the question was. "It might be," Jack said.

Woolsey looked exasperated. "It might be that it is our policy to require an IDC before we drop the shield or open the iris on the Stargate? Hasn't that been hard and fast for the last thirteen years?"

"It is absolutely our policy," Jack said decisively. "But there are always exceptions. For example, if the incoming traveler sends a video message providing positive identification in the absence of the equipment to transmit an IDC properly."

Woolsey looked at him like he was needlessly muddying the waters. Which he was. Jack shut up.

"And so we did not lower the shield when the message came in from New Athos. We responded by radio with assurances that a team would be on the way until the transmission ceased on the other end," Woolsey said.

"And why did you provide them with the vital information that we were about to send men through the Stargate?" Shen asked.

Woolsey's mouth twitched. "Because," he began.

S.R. Desai, the Indian representative, folded his hands on the table before him. "I don't believe that our new colleague, Mr. Martin, has actually heard the message in question. Perhaps it would be instructive to play it for him so that he can better understand the decisions that were before Mr. Woolsey in the moment."

Shen pursed her lips. "We all have a transcript," she said shortly. "I don't see that we need to waste…"

"It's a proper request," Desai said mildly.

"I'm happy to provide that if it's necessary," Jack said, not looking at Desai. He thought he understood what he was up to. He glanced at the officer at the back of the room. "Colonel Davis, would you play the sound file in question?"

It only took Davis a minute. He was good.

"Atlantis, you have to help us!" A panicked voice, a young man, his voice breaking on the edge of terror. "We have Darts… I don't know how many! They're… " A sob, a scream as though someone in the background cried out in mortal terror. It echoed through the gray and white conference room, cutting like the stench of blood. LaPierre's hands clenched on the arms of his chair, and Anderson, silent beside the coffee service, raised her chin. "Please! You have to help us! Atlantis…" It faded in a burst of static. The Atlantis controller's calm voice could still be heard. "New Athos? New Athos? Can you hear us? New Athos? We are sending a team with all possible dispatch. Can you hear us?" An accented voice, quiet behind hers, Dr. Zelenka. "I do not think they can. Bùh jim pomoz."

Davis turned off the recording.

"Perhaps that answers your question, madam?" Desai asked Shen. "I think it is helpful, do you not, Mr. Martin?"

"Very helpful," Martin said. He frowned down at his briefing book as Anderson silently refilled his coffee, decaf, as he'd said.

Nechayev's eyes met Jack's, a flash of amusement there. "So now that we have established why New Athos was informed that our gate team was coming, let us move to what happened when they arrived…"

Lt. Colonel Davis was doing a good job of showing the IOA members out, and Jack smiled and let him do it. That was what they paid Davis for. Woolsey was last, his leather briefcase in hand, raincoat over his arm, hanging back. Outside the full glass windows the evening rush hour traffic crept up Massachusetts Avenue toward Columbus Circle, red tail lights bright in the gathering dark.

"You ok?" Jack asked Woolsey quietly.

Woolsey gave him a sideways glance. "I think I'd rather be interrogated by Replicators again, frankly."

"I hear you." Jack looked at the retreating backs of S.R. Desai and Aurelia Dixon-Smythe as Davis herded them past the security desk.

Woolsey took a deep breath as they disappeared around the corner. "I was thinking… Do you want to go across the street to Capital City Brewery and get some dinner?"

Which translated as let's spend three hours with you holding my hand while we rehash every word of the hearing. Jack thought another fifteen minutes would have him screaming in a decidedly un-Air Force way.

"Actually, I've got a lot of paperwork to catch up," he said. "This has eaten my whole day. I should probably just take the laptop home and nuke something rather than go out, Dick."

"Sure," Woolsey said. He looked kind of crestfallen, and for a moment Jack almost said to hell with it. But three more hours of how the IOA sucked?

"Another time," Jack compromised. "They've got good steaks."

"Yeah." Woolsey nodded and squared his shoulders. "I should be getting home too. Not that I've got paperwork from Atlantis…"

Before they started another round of speculation there, Jack headed for the glass conference room doors. "I've got to run by my office and get my laptop."

"Ok. See you later." Woolsey looked out the window. "It's stopped raining."

"Good," Jack said.

There was the distant rumble of thunder off to the west as Jack left the building, putting on his cover absently while glancing up at the sky with a lifetime's force of habit. Thunderclouds building again to the northwest, catching the updrafts over the edge of the Appalachian front beyond the horizon, away from the microclimate of the river. Thirty minutes, forty. Plenty of time.

It was only eight blocks to his apartment, two rooms whose rent at three times the price of his mortgage in Colorado Springs was supposedly justified by granite countertops. He wouldn't miss this when it was time to retire. Eight blocks, enough to provide a little aerobic exercise. Something he got less of now that he ended fewer reports with 'we retreated to the Stargate under fire.'

He changed clothes and put some random dinner something in the microwave, then opened the fridge again. Why not? He pulled out a beer and popped it open just as there was a huge crash of thunder and the lights went out.

"Aw, crap."

He went over to the floor to ceiling windows in the alcove with the dinette table and looked out just as the first spray of rain dashed against them, the fall thunderstorm he'd seen coming breaking over the city. Horns honked eight stories below, the swirling raindrops illuminated by the bright headlights of a big red Circulator bus, opening doors between stops to let two dashing women with their purses over their heads onboard. The traffic lights were out, and the lights across the street, but up toward the Hill the lights were on, streetlights two blocks away. Just the local transformer then. Well, he could wait for dinner.

Jack sat down at the dinette table with his laptop and opened it, behind glass as microdrafts threw rain horizontally against the window.

September 22, 2009
Hey, Carter…

…you've been missing for twenty six days now. Well, not missing missing. Not MIA. Just disappeared. You're probably perfectly fine. You, and your ship and Atlantis. Everybody's perfectly fine. It's probably just something wrong with the Atlantis gate or something, so that you can't dial in and send a databurst.

It's probably not that it's been destroyed. That the *Hammond's* been destroyed. I'm sure everybody's ok.

We had Woolsey's second hearing today.

And there wasn't much to say about that. There wasn't much he could tell her that wouldn't look like stuff above her grade level when it went through Landry and Caldwell and everybody else, wasn't stuff Walter needed to know for water cooler gossip at the SGC. And if she never read it…

He wasn't going there.

It was pretty interesting. Don't know how it will all come out.

Translation: it sucked, and they're probably going to sack him. Jack took a long drink of his beer. Probably he should have gone to dinner with Woolsey. He'd get some dinner that way.

But he might also kill him, which would be bad. He wasn't sure who he could really stand to see right now.

It's raining here, a hell of a thunderstorm. The power's out, but I'm on the laptop. Dick says to give you his best.

Well, he would say it. Although he'd probably say something like "Do you think they're all right?" and Jack would have to say, "Sure, of course they are. Just because they disappear for a month or so doesn't mean a thing. This is Carter and Sheppard. They're fine."

We've recalled Odyssey *and Mitchell is champing at the bit to dial in when they get back to Earth with their ZPM.*

As soon as they could dial Atlantis, they would. And Mitchell would be the first one through the gate, Mitchell and Teal'c and Daniel and Vala…

There was a loud pounding on the apartment door, and Jack reached for the sidearm that of course he wasn't wearing. This was Earth. Not that it was always safe. And usually people rang the bell. Of course the power was out, so they probably couldn't.

He was nearly at the door when a familiar voice called through it. "Jack? You there?"

"Oh for crying out loud." He opened the door on the tall, hooded and dripping wet specter outside.

"Hi, Jack," Daniel said.

"Hi, Daniel."

Daniel pushed back the hood of his rain jacket and shook his wet hair like a dog. "The power's out," he said.

"I know."

"I walked up eight flights."

"Good for you," Jack said.

"I was in the neighborhood," Daniel said. Fifteen hundred miles from Colorado Springs. "What are you up to?"

Jack glanced back at the glowing laptop, the only light in the apartment. "Oh. I was just emailing Carter."

"That's what I figured," Daniel said, his head to the side. "But it's dark in here. Come get some dinner with me. There's an Irish pub up by Columbus Circle that's really good, and we won't have to catch a cab in this haywire traffic."

"We'll get soaked," Jack said.

"I'm already soaked." Daniel said. "Hot boxties. Guinness."

"Ok." Jack went back in to look for a jacket that wasn't his uniform overcoat while Daniel prowled over to the window, looking out at the traffic while carefully not glancing at the laptop screen.

"They probably blew their gate up again," Daniel said. "That happens."

"Yeah."

Daniel looked at him squarely. "We'd know. This isn't it."

"It never feels like it," Jack said. "It likes to catch you like a gut punch. It never plays fair."

There wasn't anything to say to that, so Daniel just shrugged. "I thought I'd stay until *Odyssey* gets in."

Jack let out a long breath. "I've got a flight to Peterson the day before."

"I'll come back with you then. Mitchell will kill me if I'm not there the second *Odyssey* arrives."

"Right." For a second he thought Daniel was going to say something. He'd probably rather not hear it. So he put on his jacket instead. "Pub by Columbus Circle, huh?"

"Yeah." Daniel smiled. "It's good."

Jack made sure his keys were in his pocket, came out and pulled the door shut. "Woolsey got massacred today."

"Tell me about it," Daniel said, and he did, for eight flights down.

CHAPTER SIX

Disguises

JENNIFER shook her head. "Teyla, I don't know. Are you sure about this?" The cup of coffee she'd brought back to her desk was going cold, and the file she'd just opened on her computer was sitting untouched. When Teyla had come in, she'd expected — well, she didn't quite know what she'd expected. A request for aspirin, maybe. God knew the last few weeks had been one big headache. But not this.

"It is the only way," Teyla said seriously. "I cannot attack a hive ship with a cruiser. I must persuade Waterlight that Colonel Sheppard is not worth winning the anger of Steelflower, and sway her with the Gift if she will not see reason. For that, I must be able to speak with her as an equal. As a Wraith."

Jennifer nodded. "I can't say I love it, but it makes sense," she said. "I just wish I knew the long-term effects of doing this to you again. If there are any. When we first came up with this procedure — "

"You assured me before then the procedure is completely safe, and completely reversible," Teyla said, sounding a little frustrated. "Is that not still true?"

"Yeah, but at the time I thought it was a one-time thing. I didn't think I'd be turning you into the Michael Jackson of the Pegasus galaxy." At Teyla's puzzled look, she winced. "Really famous singer with a *lot* of plastic surgery. Who died recently, so that was a pretty terrible thing of me to say, actually — "

"Will you not help me?" Teyla asked. "I do not wish you to do things that you believe to be wrong, but time is limited, and Colonel Sheppard's life is at stake."

Jennifer raised her coffee cup to hide her frown. She knew Colonel Sheppard would say he wasn't worth what she was about to do, but she also knew that it was Teyla's job to put herself in harm's way. She was getting used to patching up soldiers so that they could go out and get hurt again the next day, treating their wounds and their symptoms until they'd used their bodies so hard that she had to send them home.

And if she was starting to have doubts about whether that was what she'd taken the Hippocratic Oath in order to do, this wasn't the moment for them. "All right, then," she said. "Let's get busy turning you into a Wraith."

The anesthetic looked like water as it dripped down the tube, colorless and harmless. But then, vodka looked like water, too, and Jennifer had had enough bad hangovers in college to know that appearances were deceptive. Too many drinks at too many frat parties she'd been way too young for, all in the name of trying to fit in when she was a junior in college at sixteen. If she'd known she'd end up standing here in an alien city in another galaxy about to turn one of her friends green, maybe she wouldn't have bothered trying so hard to be normal. Maybe she would've been friends with guys like Rodney, like Dr. Zelenka, the ones in the anime club, who'd hung around the science hall wearing superhero t-shirts.

It was all too easy to imagine Rodney as he must have been at eighteen, pudgy and unshowered in a faded Batman shirt, and she closed her eyes as pain pricked, sharp as the hypodermic in her hand. She couldn't afford thoughts like that now, not in surgical scrubs and mask with Teyla unconscious on the operating table. Not with so much at stake.

Jennifer took a deep breath and counted slowly as she exhaled, grounding herself firmly in the present, feeling the weight and pull of her hair fastened into a bun at the base of her skull, the slight pressure of the elastic holding her cap and mask in place. This wasn't the time for anything else. Not her life outside. Not her feelings. Not even her patient, because you can't operate on your friend or a five-year-old or a man who looks like your father or a young mother of two. There was only the procedure. Only each precise action in the silence.

It was harder working without Todd's input, but she had extensive notes and photos from last time. The facial surgery was first, and, like last time, it made Jennifer wish she'd paid more attention during her plastic surgery rotation. She'd done well, but at the time, she'd hated the idea of spending her life doing nose jobs and facelifts instead of actually saving lives. She hadn't imagined she'd wind up needing the same skills to turn beauty into a beast.

Even without much experience, though, it was simple to find the hairline scars left from last time and re-open the incisions in order to insert the silicone implants that gave Teyla's brows the bony contours of a Wraith's. The sensor pits on either side of her nose were trickier, requiring dyed silicone and skin adhesive and some swearing beneath her breath, but by the time Jennifer was finished, they looked the same as last time.

The hand surgeries were more difficult, requiring an hour each to put implants in each finger to lengthen them and more silicone to give her knuckles the bony ridges of a Wraith. The fake feeding slit was a challenge as well, constructed similarly to the nasal pits but ringed by temporary tattoos to simulate lips. But the moments blurred, faded, and while she was dimly conscious of the beeping monitors showing Teyla's vitals regular and steady, of her own knees and feet that wanted a rest, those things seemed insignificant. Like only her eyes and hands were alive.

While the adhesive on Teyla's hand set, Jennifer turned her attention to her teeth, using strong dental adhesive to attach the fanged caps. She'd never wanted to be a dentist, either. Too messy, and nobody liked you, a lifetime of bad breath and crying kids. She'd thought about oncology because of her mom, but she hadn't wanted a lifetime of that many dying patients, either. But surgery— surgery wasn't about the patient, not while she was in the operating room. It was about fixing a problem, and it was only afterwards that the person became real again.

After the teeth, the rest was easy. She'd worked out the right drugs with Todd's help last time. The first was designed to engorge and darken her veins, making them stand out black against her skin. The second spread throughout her body quickly, bonding to the melanin in her skin and giving it a greenish cast. Jennifer wasn't sure how she'd have done the same to someone paler, and was glad she didn't have to figure that out. The last IV push was the drug to send Teyla's oil glands into overdrive, making her skin look slick instead of soft.

A glance at the monitor told her the drugs had made Teyla's blood pressure spike, a known risk. Teyla usually ran somewhere around 110/70, ridiculously healthy, and she wasn't in an immediately dangerous range now. Even so, Jennifer made a mental note to keep an eye on that.

She stepped back and pulled her mask down, breathing the cooler, drier air with relief. The band of her cap was itching, too; fully back to herself now, back in her own skin, she noticed that as well as her aching back and thirst. Teyla was stable and not likely to wake for at least an hour yet, so Jennifer took a moment to snag a bottle of water and sat down by Teyla's bedside, her eyes on the monitors.

All that was left was cosmetic, putting in hair extensions and dying Teyla's hair black, and applying and polishing long, clawed fake fingernails. Not exactly doctor's work, but Jennifer had done her own experimentation with hair dye and fake French tips in college, and you could find instructions for just about anything on the Internet. You could buy just about anything online, too, like the cat's eye contact lenses they'd had sent over from Earth last time.

The hair would have to wait until Teyla could sit up, but the fingernails would be easier while she was unconscious. She applied the acrylic nails she'd carefully filed to sharp points and waited for them to set, shaking the bottle of green nail polish. Green-wich Village, the label said. There was probably a college student wearing the same nail polish sitting in a New York coffee shop right now, some girl with Teyla's eyes who had never heard of the Wraith.

Teyla's skin was already beginning to change color as Jennifer took her hand and gently stroked color on her thumbnail. Her skin felt smoother, too, and a little cooler, its normal brown changing quickly now to a black-marbled green. The nail polish really was her color, Jennifer had to admit. For a moment she imagined a Wraith queen frowning at bottles of nail polish, trying to choose a shade of green to match her skin. Maybe they did.

Jennifer's gaze fell back to their hands as her thumb lightly stroked along Teyla's knuckles, careful of the IV. Her tired eyes made Teyla's hand blur when she blinked, and it was easy to imagine it bigger, squarer.

She closed her eyes as they started to burn in a way that had nothing to do with fatigue. It was so easy to imagine that they'd just rescued Rodney and she'd found some way to turn him back to a human as he slept. She'd sit by his bedside just like this, holding his hand and waiting for him to wake up and know her. Waiting for everything to be fine.

She knew better. It wasn't going to be easy to return Rodney to anything like human, if it could be done at all. Whatever she did when they got him back, whatever treatment she tried in her attempt to even keep him alive, it wouldn't make it like this had never happened. And that was what some part of her wanted, the part that was still a little girl hearing her mother saying *Honey, I have cancer,* saying in her own small voice *But you'll be okay, right?* She remembered curling up in bed that night, closing her eyes and praying she would wake up in the morning and have it all be a dream.

Make it not have happened, she thought, her eyes stinging, but she was too old to believe in magic, and she hadn't prayed and meant it in a long time. Teyla's hand was warm and limp under hers, and she tried not to hang onto it tightly enough to smear the drying nail polish. *I can't cry,* her mother had always said briskly. *I'll ruin my makeup.* She'd worn it to the end, touching up her lipstick in her hospital bed with shaking hands and making a face at her reflection in the compact mirror.

Jennifer startled when Teyla's hand twitched, then slowly turned in order to curl around her own. She looked up to see Teyla watching her. Teyla's lips twitched in the closest she could get to a smile. "Do I look that bad?" she asked, voice still a little thick from the anesthesia.

Jennifer straightened her shoulders, trying to find her professional voice. "Everything went just fine," she said. "How are you feeling?"

"Jennifer."

"You look … probably a lot like Rodney looks right now," Jennifer said, glancing up at the monitor because it was easier than meeting Teyla's gaze.

"If there is any way," Teyla said, "you know that we will bring him home."

"I know," Jennifer said, but she couldn't bring herself to add that that wasn't even going to be the hard part.

Jeannie scanned the tables for familiar faces but, this early, there weren't many people eating yet. At last she spotted Radek in the far corner, reading something on his laptop as he ate, and made her way over. "Hey, Radek. Mind if I join you?"

He looked up, blinking at her behind his glasses. He definitely had the perpetually startled absentminded genius thing down, reminding her of her favorite physics professor from grad school.

"Please," Radek replied, nudging the laptop aside as Jeannie sat, arranging her tray. "You have been working on the computers?"

"If you can call it working," she said, her mouth full of sandwich, and then shrugged, amending that. "Well. I think I've made some progress on that problem I mentioned yesterday, the safety protocol he buried in the controls for the underwater lights."

"Good." He nodded, spearing pasta with his fork. "And the override of the locking mechanisms coded into the translation program? Have you gone further with that?"

"Not yet. The encryption is — "

"You do not have to tell me." He smiled. "Why do anything

simply if you can instead make it incredibly complex? That is the way of Rodney McKay."

Jeannie laughed. "Incomprehensible to mere mortals. I know." She shook her head, taking another bite of sandwich and wondering what the spicy blue stuff in it was. "How's the Wraith ship coming along?"

Radek waggled his head from side to side, chewing. "It is coming," he said. "More slowly than I would like, and more like surgery at times than engineering, but...it progresses."

"I don't suppose you can give it a truckload of aspirin and hope for the best?"

"I have considered it." He returned her smile. "But it will not be much longer, I hope. What is interesting me more at the moment is this," he said, turning his laptop so that she could see the screen. "It is hard to notice from here — it is a bad angle for our sensors, even when they are working properly with all this ice — but from orbit, see? We have picked up some anomalous energy readings from an island in the southern hemisphere."

Jeannie pushed her tray to the side, leaning closer. "Wow," she said appreciatively. "That can't be anything natural, can it?"

"This galaxy is full of strange natural phenomena, but I think that is a long shot. The power signature is too close to the technology used in the city itself. I am almost certain that whatever we are picking up was made by someone, and very possibly by the Ancients."

"Those Ancient guys certainly got around."

"Basically this galaxy was a big laboratory for them," Radek said. "It could be they were interested in the effects of a colder climate. Although if they seeded a group of humans on this planet, it seems they did not survive."

"Not much question about why," Jeannie said. Outside it was sleeting, ice rattling against the windowpanes. "But if they intended this to be a human world — "

"You would expect to find a Stargate, yes, I am way ahead of you," Radek said. "That is part of why it is interesting. What would the Ancients put on a planet that didn't have a Stargate?"

"I don't know," Jeannie said. "Unless when the original inhabitants discovered that, big surprise, you can't farm ice, they moved the Stargate somewhere else? Those things can't have been exactly cheap and easy to build."

Radek spread his hands. "Who knows? But I am requesting a flyby this afternoon to get some sensor readings. Come up and take a look?" He shrugged with his eyebrows. "I will not be there, as I must get back to the repairs on the Wraith cruiser, but for you it would be something different than Rodney's code, at least."

Jeannie nodded. "Please. I'm telling you, when we get Meredith back …" She couldn't quite maintain the exasperated tone she was going for.

"When we get Rodney back, he will owe us one," Radek said.

"For this you need a surgeon, not an engineer," Radek muttered, trying to get the clumsy fingers of his vacuum suit to pick out the tiny strands of what he supposed was the Wraith cruiser's neural network so that he could splice them. Not electrical cables, but the biological equivalent, they were slippery with the mucous that coated them. And it did not help having to work in the equivalent of big, sloppy mittens. But until the hull breaches in this section were fully sealed, he had to work in a vacuum suit.

This breach was only about ten centimeters long, perhaps made when a piece of superheated shrapnel had sliced through the ship's skin. If that were the case, the edges should have been charred. Instead, they were pinkish white, thick and webby.

His radio clicked, and Colonel Carter spoke in his ear. "Dr. Zelenka, how's it going?"

"It is going," Radek said. He did not look up from the tiny strands in his hands. "And it is fascinating. You should see. I think the ship has begun to heal itself."

"Come again?"

"The ship is healing itself," Radek repeated, putting aside the strands. He might as well talk first. "The hull breaches are not so large as they were at first. The small one aft and port has already closed, though the skin is very thin there and you can see where it was."

"They do that?" Carter sounded excited.

"To a certain extent at least," Radek said. "What I am doing is splicing and reconnecting the bioelectrical systems, much as Carson does when he does surgery on a wound. But the ship, like a patient, is already healing itself and will do so to a certain extent whether we intervene or not. It is better if we do, I think, just as it is better that Carson set a bone right."

"That's incredibly nifty," Carter said. "I wish I could come up and take a look."

She couldn't, of course. With him up here, Carter and Kusanagi were working on the Hammond's systems. "You would find it fascinating, I think," Radek said.

"Anyway, I was going to tell you that Dr. Keller and Teyla are on their way up to you. You have the forward sections repressurized?"

Radek nodded even though he knew she could not see him. Habit. "Everything is repressurized except the port drive sections and the ventral landing array. I do not know what can be done about that. The bays that hold the landing gear are open to space with their outer doors entirely gone. But fortunately they are sealable to withstand vacuum. However, there is no landing gear. Teyla must not try to land on a planet."

"Tell her that," Carter said.

"I will," he replied. He tried for the fortieth time to push his glasses up on his nose, an impossible task since his glasses were inside his helmet and his mitted fingers were outside. "I am connecting tissues, but I cannot initialize any systems nor make much sense of the controls. Some of them are designed for ease of use, but the diagnostics seem to involve the same kind of telepathic interface that the guidance systems do. Perhaps Teyla can make sense of them."

"She'll be there in a few minutes," Carter said.

"Then I will come out of the port drive section," Radek said.

And get out of this suit, he added to himself. While he was not particularly claustrophobic and the suit itself did not bother him, the clumsiness did. He went methodically into the next chamber, which they were using as an airlock, and patiently waited while it pressurized. It seemed to take much longer than one of their airlocks did, five to seven minutes, but there was no doubt that it worked. By the time he had removed the vacuum suit and neatly stored it, all systems inactive, and opened the door to the section beyond, Dr. Keller and Teyla had already come aboard.

Dr. Keller looked a little nervous, glancing around at the dark and seamed walls as though expecting a hull breach any moment. Or perhaps it was just that the Wraith ship was disconcerting.

Though not nearly as disconcerting as Teyla. She turned, and Radek's breath caught in his throat.

She was no taller than he, but she seemed to fill the chamber entirely, green tinted skin stretched tight over sharp cheekbones, sensory slits to either side of her nose flaring slightly. Long black hair caught up in black combs fell to her waist, and a tight bodice of dark emerald material embroidered with black clung to the contours of her body. A long black coat was the same length as her divided skirts, which fell in wide folds to tightly laced leather boots. She lifted her chin and gave him a smile that penetrated to the bone, for all that Radek saw the artifice of it.

What these nuances might mean in Wraith culture he didn't know, but he knew what they meant in his, every trick of posture and stance meant to convey dominance and power. And oh yes, unmistakable allure. For all that his own personal tastes did not run that way, Radek could see that it was well done. If the Wraith were anything like many men of his acquaintance, they would be lining up to kiss Teyla's feet.

Teyla smiled, and this time her face lit like a delighted girl who has pulled off something she was not certain of, which only made the contrast still more intriguing. "Does it work?"

"It works splendidly, my dear," Radek said, coming forward and taking her hands like a partner in a dance, looking her up and down. "I should be trembling in terror."

"I thought," she said, glancing down at the dark emerald bodice, "about how we think of color. Skin tones are innocent, but darker versions of those colors are…"

"Are sex." Radek nodded. "Very clever. And the green does look well on you." He smiled. "It suits your complexion?"

"I hoped it would." Teyla retrieved her hands gently. "Now let us see if the ship will fly."

"You cannot use the landing gear," Radek said, following her toward the control room. "Because it is not there. And I have nothing to replace it with. So you must not land on a planet. Other than that, the unhealed breaches are in the port drive section, which hopefully you will not need to enter. If you do, there is a suit in the airlock with nearly six hours of air in the tank."

"I hope I will not need to," Teyla said. She stepped up to the command podium, its few lights blinking fitfully amber, sliding her hands into the grips, her eyes closing. For a moment Radek was forcibly reminded of John, of the way he looked in the chair interface. There was that same expression of concentration and transport.

The main viewscreen came to life, yellow letters scrolling up the side of a heads up display of curving lines that it took Radek a moment to interpret as a map of their solar system. Deep within the ship there was an almost subsonic purr, the main engines coming online. His hands flew over his laptop and its sensors. Yes, that was it. Main power. A mist was rising from vents near the floor, the ship's ventilation systems restoring what they must interpret as a dangerously dry atmosphere.

Dr. Keller shivered.

"Are you all right?" Radek asked quietly, his eyes still on Teyla who swayed slightly, her head tilted back.

"I'm fine," Keller said. She frowned. "But she shouldn't be up yet. The cosmetic surgery is completed, but I'd be more comfortable if she waited a day before she exerted herself. She's only been out of anesthesia about ten hours."

Radek shrugged. "We have time constraints."

"I know." Keller pursed her lips. "That's why I'm not putting a hold on this." She let out a sigh. "It's purely cosmetic. She can't actually use that feeding mouth on her hand to feed. It doesn't connect to anything. And any kind of careful examination will show that her lymphatic system isn't Wraith."

"If she is subject to that kind of examination, she will already be caught," Radek said.

"I know that too." Keller shook her head. "Fortunately, her telepathy is real and natural. She's going to have to rely on that."

"That, and sheer balls," Radek said. He smiled, looking at the expression on Teyla's face, the slight sway of her body in time with the ship's rumble, skirts whispering. "Fortunately, she has plenty of that."

Steelflower drifted in shiptrance, the cruiser ready and eager beneath her hands. It was relieved, soothed. It had been frightened, alone in space, injured, its people dead. Now there was a queen, and her hands were on it. Her mind was strong and clear, and she spoke to it. There and here, she said. Now and again. It would serve her. Masterless, it had limped in a decaying orbit, hardly caring to repair itself. Now it must. She willed it, and it would please her.

She gave it coordinates, her hands steady on the controls, asked if it were capable. Its eagerness was like a quiver through its systems. It would do as its queen desired. It was born to do so.

"I am ready to go," Teyla said, sliding her hands out of the grips and turning around.

"If you are certain," Radek began.

"I am certain," she said, "Go on. All will be well."

He looked as though he had other things he wanted to say, but he did not, just gave her a quirky sideways smile as he followed Dr. Keller out. "Good luck."

"Thank you," she said, and turned back to the command console. A deep breath. It was not done yet, not too late to stop this. But if she did...

No, Teyla thought. It was too late. She was Steelflower, and now she must dig deep, find the core within her, the fragile, tangled strands of her ancestry that held the power. A Wraith Queen stood among her foremothers. Steelflower was of the lineage of Night, or so Guide had named her when he had given her the name and likeness of a young queen lost long ago. But it was not her real lineage, that precious link to the past that the Wraith so valued, kinship and genetic variation in one. For the first time she wondered who she had been, that queen whose son had done unspeakable experiments on humans, the one whose son created her Gift, mingling his own DNA with that of his captives.

Once, long ago, when she had first learned of her Gift, she had dreamed of an Atlantis overrun by Wraith who saluted her as their queen, and now, half caught in shiptrance, she saw it again, blades bending before her, hair flowing down like water. 'Osprey queens are always the most beautiful.' She had dreamed true before when she had dreamed of her Gift. Osprey, she thought. The white bird, the white ghost, drifting insubstantial as mist through the shadowed woods... Wraith. Was that what they had meant, once? Once, when long ago they were hunted? Was there one who moved like fog, hiding her presence in clouds that sent shivers running up the spine?

Beneath her hands the ship quivered, ready and waiting. *Go*, she said, and saw the hyperspace window open before them, needing no viewscreens or monitors. Her hands in the control grips, she could see what the ship saw, her touch giving her access to all its data, quick as thought. *Go*, she said, and they went.

CHAPTER SEVEN

A Game of Queens

"THERE is another ship."

In the darkness, John Sheppard woke from a light doze, but he knew better than to move. One of the Wraith had paused outside his cell, the young one, speaking to another. Better to be still and have them assume he was still sleeping.

"What other ship?" The second Wraith was older, and John could hear the sound of irritation in his voice.

"It says it is the cruiser Eternal, bearing a queen aboard, and that she will speak to our queen immediately about the Consort of Atlantis." The younger Wraith glanced toward John, and it took an act of will to be still. "You must come."

"Of course," the other said, and hurried off.

When they were gone John sat up cautiously. Not good. So very not good. He scrubbed his hands across his chin and looked around for the water pitcher. From his growth of beard he thought he'd been a prisoner of the Wraith for four or five days — certainly not more than that. They'd fed him. Well, raw fruit and nothing else, but he had the impression that they didn't have much idea what humans ate, the way that a kid who's just found an injured rabbit gives it three or four carrots. Not nutritious, exactly, but he wasn't going to starve quickly that way.

Another queen. He could make his bets there. Queen Death had Rodney, and if she hadn't been successful in getting everything she needed out of him, John would be the next best thing. He'd had a few days reprieve, but this was still going south as fast as it could.

In the last few days he'd had plenty of time to examine the cell and the door. Without tools or even a knife there were no opportunities there. But they'd have to transfer him. If Queen

Death wanted to claim him, she'd have to have him moved to her ship. That would involve getting out of the cell and presumably being escorted to the dart bay or to a docking port.

John got up, stretching carefully. That was the moment. If he could stumble and seem sick, maybe he could get a weapon. One of the big stunners the masked Wraith had would be perfect. Let the guy get in close and shove him, then whip around. It might work.

He rinsed his mouth with water, took several small sips. Get ready. Be prepared.

It seemed like forever before he heard footsteps again. Too many. Not just the couple of guards he expected for a prisoner transfer, but six or eight. Maybe ten. Way too many.

Two masked ones. The young Wraith with his tattoos of vines, the one he'd called Frank. An old one with a sharp, bitter face. Another soldier in leathers, looking impatient. A girl, young as Ellia had been, small and slender, her steps quick and light between another two masked guards. Beside her another queen.

John felt his heart hesitate in his chest, and it was all he could do not to move.

The sharp one spoke. "Is that it? Is that the Consort of Atlantis?"

She raised her head as the door slid back, mottled patterns of light crossing her face, smooth and impassive, her long coat sursurrating with the whisper of leather on silk as she took a step forward, and his hands tightened at his sides. "It may be," she said, her eyes sliding over him calculatingly. "I will take it from his mind if he is."

Queens had touched his mind before, seized it, pushing and tearing and prodding, sending him burning in pain before them. And yet there was no touch. Nothing. She might as well not exist.

The young queen looked at her, her eyes filled with what John thought might be admiration. "Can you truly take it from him so easily?"

"Of course," she replied coolly but not unkindly. "It is just a matter of exerting your will."

Her eyes flicked to his for a fraction of a second, slitted pupils wide, and then she raised her hand, feeding mouth open, lips purple in the dim light. Her voice was like a lash. "Kneel before me, puny human!"

John swayed, shook as though struggling with every fiber of his being, teeth grinding.

"Kneel!" she commanded, and his chin snapped up as though she had slapped him.

His legs crumpled and he fell to the floor before her, his forehead against the toe of her boot.

"He is the Consort of Atlantis." Steelflower's voice cut coldly through the silence, broken only by the harsh breathing of the human who knelt at her feet. "I will take him."

Thorn, who stood in the place of Consort to Waterlight, shook his head and stepped forward, though it was not his place to speak when Steelflower spoke queen to queen. "We cannot allow that. If Queen Death hears that we have given such a prize to you instead…"

Steelflower turned, the leather skirts of her coat brushing over the groveling human, her eyebrows rising ominously. "And why should she hear of this?"

Thorn's eyes dropped. "We have already sent word to her twice, though she has not responded. If she does, and we say that we have already given him to you…" He let his voice trail off.

Steelflower turned about again, her eyes this time seeking Waterlight, and her tone was not imperious. "Are you afraid of her?"

Waterlight met her gaze, golden eyes to golden, and then she nodded a fraction. "Yes," she said simply.

Steelflower shook her head, reaching out her hand to rest upon Waterlight's arm. "Little sister," she said, "why should we fear her? Are we not queens together?"

"Perhaps because she has forty ships and we one," Thorn said dryly. "Or perhaps because thousands of blades answer her call, not a dozen."

Steelflower shot him a look, quick and angry. "Does he speak for you?" she demanded of Waterlight.

The girl swallowed, her pale throat working in the shiplight. "He stands as consort until there is another," she said softly.

Steelflower's fingers touched her chin, lifting her face not unkindly. "We are queens together," she said. "And it is true that Death has ships. She has many men at her call. But perhaps she has more than her fair share. That is not the way of things, that all queens should bow to one! To each her hive, to each her blades and clevermen, to each her drones and her children in the chrysalis. It is not right that we should all bow to one, that many should serve an absent mistress. It is not right that we should slay one another instead of respect one another as sisters should."

"You call me sister but you are of Night and I of Osprey," Waterlight said. "We are not kin in bone and blood. How should I know that you do not betray me?"

"If I intended you harm, should I come before you like this? Without even a single blade to defend me?" Steelflower asked, and her eyes lingered over Waterlight's face. "Besides," she said carefully, "My mother's Consort was a blade of Osprey, and so I may count you kin if I choose."

"By the old ways of counting, perhaps," Thorn said.

"I hold to the old ways," Steelflower said, but her eyes did not leave Waterlight. "In some things. And in others we must find new ways." Her hand reached down and seized the human's hair, twisting his neck up to her. "I have many uses for this one. If you give him to me, I will give you my word that Death will not revenge herself upon you for it."

"You will stand with us against Death?" Thorn said, and his voice was tinged with skepticism.

"If it is necessary," Steelflower said sharply. "But you have said yourself that she has not responded to your messages. Perhaps she does not believe you. If she does, we will stand as allies."

"Allies." It was the young blade, the one they called Bronze.

"Our sensors show your ship is unmanned. What allies do you bring?"

"And need I blades to fly my own ship?" Steelflower's voice was cool. "Will boys like you show me how to do it?" A note of amusement crept into her voice, and her eyes raked him from toes to hair, as though he were very pretty indeed. "You are beautiful, but not yet wise."

Bronze gulped, his skin darkening with his reaction, while at her feet the human made a strangled sound.

Steelflower turned to Waterlight, her voice light. "He is very pretty, this one of yours. Will you make him pallax someday?"

Waterlight tossed her hair in a fair approximation of Steelflower. "Perhaps," she said. "If he continues to please me."

"Very pretty," Steelflower said as he flushed beneath her gaze. "You have good taste, sister."

"Thank you," Waterlight said. She looked down at the human on the floor. His form was bestial as Bronze was graceful, and yet he too seemed affected, a fine layer of moisture standing on his skin. "I am minded to give him to you, if you stand as ally with me."

Thorn hissed, but she turned to him. "We must have allies," she said quietly. "And this is better than all else that is before us. I should rather an elder sister than an overlady."

"You are like to have neither," Thorn began, but he did not finish. He would not speak so before Steelflower. It would be more than unseemly. Open disrespect of his queen would make him despised.

"Then this one will accompany me to my ship," Steelflower said.

Bronze blinked, putting himself forward. "But is that not dangerous, my queen? He is an animal, and not a tame one. What if he should harm you?"

"This one?" Steelflower said contemptuously. "He has not it in him. His mind is open to me, and he can no more raise his hand to me than you to Queen Waterlight." She turned the human's face up to the light, her dark green nails biting into the skin of his face, turning it this way and that. Her eyes were on his, and she smiled a thin, cruel smile. "You are mine, are you not, human?"

"Yes," he whispered as though it were dragged from the core of his being, his body swaying forward as though the touch of her skirts were balm.

"Then make your abject obeisance," she said, and released him.

He bent, graceful as a blade, his head to the floor, his lips to the toe of her boot. "I yield," he said.

Steelflower smiled. "You see?" she said to Waterlight. "He is quite tame. I have no fear that he will harm me. I hold him entirely with my mind."

"I have never seen a human who was not hand-reared behave thus," Waterlight said, and her eyes were shining. "You are very strong."

"Yes," Steelflower said simply. "We will go to my ship."

"Will you not stay and talk with me a little?" Waterlight asked. "Surely if you name me sister…"

Her head whipped around at the same moment as Steelflower's, both their ships registering surprise at the same moment, Thorn's a millisecond later.

"There is another hive ship coming out of hyperspace," Thorn said. He turned to look at Steelflower, his voice as dry as ever. "Perhaps it is Queen Death, and you may show me your alliance."

Waterlight gulped.

The third blade reported very correctly. "There is a transmission coming in. Shall I put it on the screen here?"

"Yes," Waterlight said, her back straight as Steelflower's beside her, the human crouching at her knees, almost touching her leg. "Sister," she said.

"I do not fear her," Steelflower whispered. "And neither must you."

The image on the screen resolved. Not Queen Death as she had feared, but an older blade, his face seamed with age, a star tattoo about one eye. For a moment, a moment only, he hesitated, seeing the queens together. "My beloved queen," he said, dropping his head in deep respect. "I have come to rendezvous with you as you directed. It is my honor to serve you, and my pleasure to see that you are well."

Steelflower did not blink. "My dear Guide," she said evenly. "You are as always the model consort."

"Four hundred men," Thorn said tightly. "We are reading four hundred men aboard your hive, and shields are raised. Is this how you bring alliance?"

"Guide is tender of my safety," Steelflower said. "And sometimes overzealous. Guide, drop your shields immediately so that Queen Waterlight may see that I intend no betrayal." So intent was she upon her consort that perhaps she did not even notice that the human's hand had tightened on her ankle.

For a moment Guide hesitated as though he would not obey, but then he bent his head in deep respect again. "As Queen Steelflower requires," he said.

"Shields are dropping," Bronze said at the sensors.

Steelflower looked at Waterlight. "I thought it best if I came to talk to you alone, rather than with Guide and a full hive. I thought that would seem as though I wished to intimidate you, rather than speak as queen to queen. And so I asked my consort to follow after. But I fear he values me rather too much, and did not wait as long as I said."

Waterlight's eyes were shining. "What other would do as you do?" she asked, "To come alone and speak with me as kin, when you might have had me beneath your guns and simply demanded my compliance?"

"That would be the act of an enemy, not a sister," Steelflower said.

"Then gladly I name you sister and ally," Waterlight said.

"As I name you," Steelflower replied.

"My Queen?" Guide said. "Will you not come aboard your ship?"

"I would prefer to travel aboard the Eternal," Steelflower said coolly. "Come to me there and make your report."

"As my queen wishes," he said, and the transmission ended.

"I must return to my ship," Steelflower said to Waterlight. "I would hope that we may yet speak further, but it seems my consort is eager to speak with me. No doubt some matter has arisen he feels needs my attention."

"Of course," Waterlight said.

Guide met them in the corridor outside the docking port, and there were many expressions of respect all around, Thorn to Guide, Waterlight to Steelflower, before the portal closed and they stood within the skin of the cruiser Eternal, Steelflower, Guide, and the human John Sheppard.

Guide watched as the portal iris closed, and the cruiser disconnected from the Promised Return, floating free between the two hive ships.

"What in the hell is going on here?" Sheppard demanded.

"I was about to say the same thing," Guide echoed.

"I am surprised you ask," Teyla said, turning to Guide, her long coat like a blade's swirling around her. "Since you are the one who told me where Colonel Sheppard was."

"This was not what I had thought Carter would do," Guide began. "It is…"

"Wait." Sheppard held a hand up. "Todd, you told Teyla where I was?"

"I told Colonel Carter where you were," he corrected. "Though I had no doubt that she would share that information with the Young Queen. And that she would take steps to insure your release." He swung back to Teyla. "What are you playing at with Waterlight and Thorn? Do you have any idea the stinger's nest you are getting into?"

"Wait," Sheppard said again.

Guide stopped, his eyes on his face. "Yes?"

"Thanks." Sheppard was disheveled and dirty, but his back was straight and his eyes level. "I appreciate it."

Guide huffed, almost a laugh. "It was nothing, I believe the expression is." He shook his head, turning back toward Teyla, looming a foot over her, and yet she looked as though it didn't even occur to her to step back, unarmed and inches from his feeding hand. "But this masquerade is unexpected, and throws all into disarray." He shook his head again. She was Steelflower to the core, and though he knew it was false he could not fail to respond to her as though she were the Queen she pretended. She might wear a human body, but there was no mistaking the strength of mind that dwelled within. Were she Wraith indeed, she might have been a great queen. "I do not know what you hope to gain."

"Besides Colonel Sheppard's release?" She lifted her head, her beautiful hair rippling at the movement in the soft shiplight. "We have tried and failed to gain access to Dr. McKay. Perhaps Steelflower can prevail where Teyla Emmagan failed."

"Not now that you have now branded yourself enemy to Queen Death!" Guide snapped, not disguising the fear in his mind, not from her. "And myself as well! Do you not see that this is the cruiser Eternal, and now Thorn knows so as well, he and all his crew? This is one of Death's ships."

"Not any longer," Teyla said, her chin rising proudly. "It met with an accident."

"And I shall have to explain to Queen Death why my queen is raiding her scoutships!" Guide exploded. "She will hear of it, and then she will want your head!"

"She can come and get it," Teyla said.

"And she will not have to look far for mine, or that of my men!" Guide snapped. "But that is nothing to you. We are Wraith. If you were Steelflower, you would have a care for the men of your own that you thus condemn to death." He stalked away, finding some respite in motion that took him away from her. "You will disappear again, and I shall dwell with your folly. I gave you all you needed to do this cleanly, as I did with McKay!"

"You didn't tell us McKay was Wraith," Sheppard said.

"I did not know that," Guide snapped. "Do you think that I am Death's Consort, to be privy to all her secrets? I have gone too far as it is."

"And not far enough," Teyla said, taking a step after him, her hand rising as though she meant to take his wrist. She glanced back at Sheppard, her golden eyes inscrutable. "We cannot be half allies, Guide, as we have tried to be."

He swung around wondering what madness she and Sheppard had concocted between them, but Sheppard looked as baffled as he.

Her hand closed on his wrist, her mind touch firm and strong as a queen's, intimate as a lover's, not compelling but simply persuading him of her honesty. "We must be allies or enemies, Guide." Her eyes held his. "Queen Death will destroy us all if we do not stand together against her."

"Allies?"

"All of our counters unmasked on the board," she said.

He looked at Sheppard behind her. "And you think I will believe that you will put all your counters on the board?"

"As much as you will," Sheppard said.

"John," she snapped, though she did not look around. "Can you not see that we cannot do this without him?"

"Get McKay back or defeat Queen Death?" he said.

"Both." Teyla spared him a glance over her shoulder, her hand still on Guide's wrist. "She will crush us both if we do not act together, and then she will destroy all civilizations in this galaxy that have any technology."

"She would take us back to the days after the First Armada," Guide said, and the taste of the words was bitter in his mouth. "What lovely promises we had in those days! Once the Ancients were defeated, we should have plenty. Once cities lay in rubble, we should feast. But you know what came, John Sheppard. When the predators outnumber the prey, they turn upon one another. When the prey are hunted to extinction, what then shall we feed upon? You did not believe me before when I spoke of husbandry, but this one did. Teyla Emmagan has lived as a predator in the woods and fields, and she knows."

She nodded. "We do not overhunt, because if we do in time

to come we will starve."

"Queen Death overhunts, and in destroying she will render us starving in no short time unless we find your Earth. But it will not be easy pickings if we find it, and if we do not, then we will starve." He gave Sheppard a mirthless smile. "I believe it is intended to be motivational."

"Burning your ships on the beach so you can't retreat," Sheppard said. "Nice."

"In the years after the war your numbers dropped until you were almost extinct," he said. "Groups of wanderers making brief shelters in broken buildings, in caves, flirting with genetic viability. And we starved too, knowing that if we took too many we might eat today, but there would be none tomorrow. And how should there be? Your kind take many years to reproduce and to grow to adulthood. If we cull more often than once a generation, soon the numbers will begin to drop and then there will be none." Guide paced away from her, from her hand on him. "And so the long hibernations were born, to sleep through the years between one culling and the next, waking for a year or three in twenty, and then sleeping again. In each interval our prey might reproduce, and in time replenish the ecosystems."

"And that is the core of it," Teyla said quietly. "You need us. And we need you. The peoples of the Milky Way will keep you from Earth. That is assured. But I am not of Earth, and there is a limit to what they will do here, a limit we have very nearly reached. The people of Earth will not send enough ships to defeat Queen Death, and we will die."

"Teyla," Sheppard began.

"Truth for truth, John," she said, her eyes on Guide's. "They have neither the power nor the will to conquer this galaxy. They will leave us to you, and you have already seen where that will end."

Guide took a long breath, perhaps the longest of his life, very long and very strange indeed, his eyes upon this one with the seeming of a young queen but who was not. She was kine. Or half kine, the product of a twisted experiment which had given an animal the semblance of a person, the mental voice of a woman. His answers should be clear, and yet they were not.

His true queen would speak thus, once and away.

His eyes slipped past her to Sheppard. "And when we are done, Sheppard? When we have defeated Queen Death together?"

Sheppard put his head to the side as he had done once, escaping Kolya's prison together. "All bets are off."

"All bets are off," Guide said gravely.

CHAPTER EIGHT

The Last War

SAM SLEPT aboard the *Hammond*, no matter what was going on in the city. To do anything else would give the wrong impression to her crew. It was one thing to use the office above the gateroom in Sheppard's absence. That was a matter of convenience. But she slept shipboard. She might be the senior officer on station in Atlantis, but she was the commander of the *Hammond*.

Besides, that office was borrowed. This was home.

Her cabin was the largest on the *Hammond*, nice enough if you didn't mind having your feet in the shower to brush your teeth. There was a small single bed built into the wall, storage space beneath it, the other wall occupied by a metal desk similarly bolted down. The chair wasn't, as that would be really annoying. The wall between the door and the desk held a closet ten inches wide and a bolted on mirror. Above the bed a framed picture of the *Hammond* was likewise screwed in with four big screws.

Her laptop was on the desk, sharing the cramped space with her mp3 player and its mini speakers, currently blasting ABBA at the top of their tiny voices, *When All Is Said and Done* from one of the late albums, her email open on the desktop. There was nothing new from outside Atlantis, of course. It had been nearly a month since the last databurst. There was nothing she hadn't read twenty times, nothing she hadn't replied to.

But still.

September 24, 2009
Dear Cassie,
Sam looked up at the pictures held to the wall above her desk with magnets. There was Cassie smiling back at her, her mortarboard on her head, Jack with his arm around her grinning

like a loon. Cassie had a bottle of champagne in her hand, and was holding on to her mortarboard with the other hand, a smile that ought to light the world on her face. Yellow letters printed across the bottom of the picture proclaimed 'Congratulations Class of 2009!'

It was hard to believe that the young woman in the picture was the mute child they'd rescued so long ago, the one who had clung to her in the darkness waiting to die. Now she was the assistant's assistant for an organization that helped refugee children around the world, the kind of starting position that a liberal arts degree got you these days. Mostly, she answered the phone.

I hope you're doing ok, and that work isn't too boring. It probably is, but it's a start. There aren't many jobs where you get to save the world at twenty two.

Sam hoped that didn't sound too sanctimonious, or like the kind of letter Jacob had sent her when she was twenty two.

When she was twenty two she'd been in Saudi Arabia, part of the build up called Desert Shield. Her top ten class rank at the Air Force Academy had at least won her that. Not a top posting to a top squadron, not F-15s or F-16s, the best of the best, even though she had more than earned it, but at least she could shuttle a Warthog around behind the lines. Congress forbade women to fly in combat positions. It didn't matter how much she deserved it or how well she had done, or even how much her superiors wanted to give her the chance. Congress said that her uterus disqualified her. The American public would not stand for women being killed.

She'd been bitter. Of course she had been. Bitter, and certain that it would not be long before that asinine rule was overturned.

Nineteen years later it was still here, ignored more than obeyed, gotten around by a generation of Air Force commanders her age who came up with baroque excuses to avoid saying they were actually sending women into combat, actually letting them compete on a level field with men. Congress hadn't budged. But more and more positions were open to women, at least in her service.

Technically, captaincy of the *Hammond* wasn't a combat position. Technically, the *Hammond* was a research vessel. Of course officially the *Hammond* didn't exist, which made it much easier to ignore that its captain was a woman.

Mel Hocken was in the same position. It wasn't technically prohibited for a woman to fly a 302, because technically they didn't exist. And if they did exist, they were technically a research project into high altitude aircraft. Which certainly did not involve engaging in air combat with alien spaceships.

Sometimes she thought that the sheer dishonesty involved negated the honor they were supposed to embrace, but then Congress couldn't be expected to be as progressive as the military.

All of which was not Cassie's problem.

I hope you're finding the work rewarding. I know that when you're in a starting position, not directly in the field yourself, it may seem like you're not really doing anything. But you are, even when you can't see it yet. Even if you're not the one out there working with kids directly, the work you do makes the field work possible. There's nothing wrong with learning the ropes in a support position.

Ok, she had more or less bitten Jacob's head off for saying the same thing, back when she was flying a Warthog around Saudi Arabia while Rotsy boys like Sheppard who barely graduated from state universities were flying vipers under enemy fire. Why yes, Dad! I should totally appreciate the chance to back up guys with half the brains and half the hard work because they're men.

Jacob had been reasonable then, even if he'd overestimated Congress too. Just a couple of years, Samantha. Just a couple of years, and you'll rise to the top. You'll pass them and leave them in the dust.

Now she was a full bird colonel with the *Hammond* in her hands, and Sheppard saluted her. She'd make field grade, if she wasn't killed, and he never would.

I know you want to make a difference, and you already are even if it doesn't feel like it yet. You are, and you will. And as far as the conventional wisdom that an undergrad anthropology degree doesn't lead anywhere, look at your Uncle Daniel. Sometimes you can't imagine the places things can lead you when you begin.

Of course Sheppard didn't want to make field grade. The last thing he wanted was a star on his shoulder and an apartment in DC, a desk job far away from Atlantis. He might not know it yet, but this was his last post. If anyone was ever stupid enough to try to transfer him out, he'd resign first. She'd make sure nobody was ever that stupid, if she could.

We've got a lot going on here, as I'm sure you can imagine. It's gotten kind of hairy, but nothing as bad as we've seen.

That was circumspect enough. It sounded like she was in Iraq or Afghanistan, which she reasonably might be.

I want to ask you a favor, seriously, Cass. I know you've got a lot going on with your friends and your life, but can you look in on Jack for me? Drop in on him and keep him busy? Get him to help you with something. There could be something wrong with your car or your apartment or something. Give him somebody to take care of. I know you can handle that stuff on your own, and that you're grown, but it's good for him to be needed.

If she knew Cassie, her car barely ran and her shower had water leaking in the ceiling from the upstairs neighbor. Nonprofits paid receptionists even worse than the Air Force paid second lieutenants, and Cassie was sharing a falling down townhouse with five roommates in a fairly terrible neighborhood of DC. But she'd never ask Jack for help unless she thought it was for him.

Sam smiled, imagining Jack with his shirt sleeves rolled up, fixing the showerhead in a mildewy bathroom, while Cass sat on the edge of the sink and told him all about refugee kids in the Sudan, both of them feeling so good about helping each other. Then he'd take Cassie out to dinner somewhere she couldn't possibly afford, smirking as everyone looked at his gray hair and three stars and the radiant girl with him. Dirty old man, they'd whisper, and Jack would soak it up until Cass said nice and loud, "Dad, this is just so swell of you!"

Take care of yourself too, and be careful. I wish I could say I'll see you at Thanksgiving, but I probably won't make it home by then. Maybe, if I'm lucky, and everything calms down here. It would be nice.

It would be nice, but unlikely. Cassie wouldn't be alone, not unless she wanted to be. She'd have Jack, and maybe they'd go home to Colorado and there would be Daniel too, and Cam and Vala and maybe Teal'c if he made it. And Vala would pocket the rolls and Daniel would get tipsy on one beer and they'd talk about how they missed her. She and Janet would be the ghosts at the feast.

"Absent friends," Daniel would say seriously, his glass lifted, and everyone would say it too, except Jack who never did, just silently touching his glass to theirs.

I love you, Cass.

Sam

It was the best seafood in DC, or at least the best in a place that wasn't pretentious and full of power meetings. Jack O'Neill rolled up the sleeves of his plaid cotton shirt and waved as his guest came in the door, looking around cheerfully before he wound his way among the tables and sat down opposite.

"A fine idea," said Konstantin Nechayev, tossing his jacket into the other side of the booth. "We are cold warriors again, meeting in some out of the way place where we will pretend to be fishermen."

"I never did that," Jack said, deadpan. "I really did work on a trawler out of Gdansk."

Nechayev laughed as the waitress came over. "I will have whatever beer he is having. And I was on a shrimp boat just off Key West."

Jack waggled a finger. "I thought there was something Forrest Gump-like about you, Konstantin."

Nechayev flipped open the laminated menu. "So this is on your expense account or mine?"

"Whichever," Jack said.

Nechayev looked at him over the menu. "It is sad, is it not? The things you do for your country. Dinner with an IOA member — what could be more dismal?"

"Dinner with a system lord," Jack replied. He looked up at the waitress. "I'll have the Fisherman's Platter with the clam strips."

"I will have the same with the shrimp," Nechayev said. "I am yearning for my old shrimp boat days."

The waitress duly sent off with instructions as to baked potatoes, coleslaw and other such, Nechayev spread his hands around his beer bottle. "So what is this about? You know that I cannot dig Dick Woolsey out of the hole he has dug himself. If he had kept quiet for a few months this would have blown over, but he did not. And now we do not know what is happening, which makes everyone imagine the worst." He looked at Jack a little too keenly. "Including you. Are you sure Woolsey even has a command to return to?"

Jack shrugged. "It's a communications problem. Stuff happens. You know that as well as I do. Civilians panic."

"Yes, civilians. And we are old soldiers, you and I. I do not think this expedition is safe or will be accomplished without a great many casualties. It's part of the cost. But most of the member states are not willing to explain how they even lost five men, much less many more. We will lose thousands if we see this through. And that is the thing you cannot say, not even to your president."

Jack carefully examined the label on the beer bottle. "I don't know."

"You know as well as I that there is no such thing as a cheap war." Nechayev took a long drink of his beer. "Nor should there be, in my opinion. It is when people think it is cheap that they get cavalier. Why not do it, if it can be accomplished with so little risk? Why not do it, if all it will cost is a few dozen sons of the poor?" He put the bottle down. "Or if it can all be kept secret."

The waitress returned balancing a tray full of fried seafood, and it took a few moments to sort it all out.

Jack shook the ketchup over a spare corner of plate. "I won't deny Dick's dug himself a deep hole," he said. "There may not be a way out."

"So now we come to it," Nechayev said, picking up a calabash shrimp and popping it in his mouth. "Will I support your candidate to replace him? Your Colonel Sheppard, I assume?" He chewed thoughtfully. "He seems like a good man, and I've no doubt he's a good soldier, or they would not have held so long. But he's military. They will not do it, not most of the other IOA members. They did not like Carter, and they slapped down the idea of Caldwell as though it burned them. They won't buy Sheppard, no matter how you paint him." Nechayev looked at him keenly. "They only swallowed Carter because they were terrified of the Replicators."

"And fired her as soon as she cleaned them up." Jack didn't look up from his plate.

"Yes, well." Nechayev shrugged. "That is the way it goes." He took a long drink of his beer. "An entire sentient race wiped out."

"They're machines," Jack said. He looked at Nechayev across the table. "Sophisticated machines. No different than blowing up a tank or taking out a satellite."

"Not people. Not possessing an immortal soul." Nechayev shrugged. "I am not arguing that they were. That is the thing about machines. You cannot appeal to their better natures. Failsafe devices and dead men switches." His eyes met Jack's. "We have seen those in our nightmares, yes? The machines that cannot be dissuaded from their programming, locked in a firing routine long after all those they protect are dead." He took another long drink of his beer. "We are old cold warriors, you and I. There is no reasoning with the machine. It is as well that Carter destroyed them utterly."

Jack didn't reply, only turned the beer bottle around in his hands, reading the label.

"I only mention it to point out that I doubt she would have been so quick to annihilate them completely with no quarter asked or given if it had not been for her own experiences with the Replicators in the past. Taken prisoner and tortured terribly, was it not?" Nechayev shrugged again. "But then we are all what life has made us. We all have those we cannot forgive."

"True enough," Jack said, still turning the beer bottle around. He put it down and raised his eyes. "I know the IOA won't have Sheppard or Caldwell. I had a civilian candidate in mind. Dr. Daniel Jackson."

Nechayev whistled. "That is a game changer," he said quietly.

"I thought you'd think so," Jack said, spearing a clam strip. "How about it?"

"No one can say he's not qualified," Nechayev said. "He's eminently qualified. One of the foremost experts on the Ancients in the world, active at the highest levels of negotiations for a decade. A close friend of yours, of course, but that is to be expected. You would hardly recommend someone you didn't trust."

Jack smiled pleasantly. "No. I wouldn't."

"Shen won't buy it."

"Of course," Jack said. "She wants it herself."

"When pigs fly, as you say," Nechayev replied.

"We're paying the bills. It's an American." Jack speared another clam strip and twirled it in the ketchup. "You know the saying, you've got to dance with the one that brung you?"

"I do know it," he said. "And I will tell you something that you already know as well. Our interests are far more in the Milky Way than Pegasus. Not nearly so far, and much more friendly. There are many opportunities among the Jaffa alliances and others that do not involve going nearly so far, or encountering quite so many life sucking aliens. We want our hand in, if there is a hand in Pegasus, but frankly if the IOA closed down the expedition tomorrow we would not weep." Nechayev took a long drink of his beer. "You are overcommitted, O'Neill. You know it. You are overextended on Earth and…" He cocked his head to the ceiling. "Now you are looking down the barrel of a sour economy and an isolationist population dreaming of a solution that will make everyone else's problems not their problems. You hate the

IOA, but we are your best chance at not having to fold your hand completely. Perhaps if you can shoehorn some of it off onto us or those hungry boys who are pretending they are building weather satellites for Ariane just outside Warsaw, you will not have to turn over the City of the Ancients to the Chinese."

"The Austerlitz is eighteen months from completion," Jack said quietly. "And it's only the communications systems that are being assembled in Poland. The hull is being built in Clermont Ferrand."

"And then the EU will have their own warship, and we are three years from replacing the Korolev," Nechayev said. "And you've suspended work on your new vessel indefinitely."

"Money," Jack said.

"There is no such thing as a cheap war." Nechayev shrugged. "Very well. I will back Jackson. But you…"

"I know," Jack said. "I'll owe you through the nose."

"I was going to suggest a less polite part of your anatomy," Nechayev laughed. "But I will take your nose if it is what is offered."

CHAPTER NINE

Sheppard and Guide

"WE HAVE much to discuss," Guide said. "If you do intend to make an alliance in truth." He looked from Teyla to Sheppard. "There are other things besides the location of Dr. McKay that may prove of interest to you."

"And I'm sure there's a lot of stuff you'd like to know," Sheppard said pleasantly. "We'll see."

Guide snorted. "I understand if you must consult with your Colonel Carter first. After all, you are her consort, and doubtless she will want to hear of your safety first and foremost."

Sheppard frowned. "What?"

"Do you not think she will have a care for your safety?" Guide baited. He had seen such before, a blade trying to play old queen and young queen both, a dangerous game, and one that usually lost a man his life. "Are you not her lover?"

"Carter's?" Sheppard's eyebrows rose, and the bewilderment in his voice was genuine. "You think me and Carter? No. Not at all. She's been with somebody else for a long time. We get along really well, but not that way at all."

Teyla looked amused. "Though I am sure she will be glad to hear he is safe and well."

Guide nodded inwardly. Better. That was safer, if Sheppard was not playing some dangerous game of his own. Better if he were Consort to She Who Carries Many Things in name only, a reliable man that a queen might choose to represent her in the absence of her own consort of many years, some older blade who doubtless protected their interests elsewhere. Such a man might be valuable to a queen. "I must have misunderstood," Guide said smoothly. "Your pardon," he asked of Teyla.

"Of course," she said, and Sheppard tipped his head to her, as if wondering what that exchange were about.

"If we have much to discuss," Guide said. "Will you come aboard my ship?"

They exchanged a look, but this time it was Teyla who spoke. "No. But we will give you coordinates where you may meet us, and there we will talk."

"And if it is a trap?"

"How should it be?" she asked. "I did not know you would come here, so how could I have arranged with any other to ambush you? And if I did give you the coordinates for a rendezvous with the *Hammond*, the hive ship and the *Hammond* would be well matched, and you would come out of hyperspace with your shields raised."

Which was of course true. Guide sighed. "Very well," he said tersely. "Give me your coordinates. I will have my shuttle return me to my ship, and we will follow you to this location. I hope you appreciate that doing so is an unprecedented act of trust."

"Not so much," Sheppard said. "We'll be talking under your guns." He still looked doubtful.

"I will speak with my ship first," Guide said, and stepped away, lifting his communicator to his mouth. He did not speak into it, only turned his back and listened, wanting to hear whatever passed between them. It would tell him a great deal, what was said and not said. If this were an ambush, there would be no need to say anything.

"We must do this, John," she said quietly, her tones too low for another human to hear at this distance.

"You really think this is the best shot of getting to Rodney?"

"I do not think we will ever have a better. And what do we lose by talking? Let us take the opportunity we have. It may not come again."

There was a long pause. "Ok." Guide did not turn, but he heard Sheppard's voice change. "I didn't expect you to come."

"Did you think that I would ever leave you?"

Guide closed his eyes.

Did you think that I would ever leave you? She had said it softly, mind to mind, her fingers where the pulse jumped in his wrist, half turning her head to look at him sideways, red hair rendered dawn colored in the shiplight.

You should have, he had said, and the smoke wreathed them, smoke and the scent of burned shipflesh. *It would have been wiser.*

Snow said nothing, but in her eyes he saw her demurral. *Never.*

Guide spun around. "I will meet you," he said sharply. "But know that if this is a trap I will never treat with you again under any circumstances."

"It is not a trap," Teyla Emmagan said.

He turned and strode off to the airlock where his shuttle waited. At the door he turned and glanced back to see them standing apart, silhouetted against the light behind them, her dark skirts and tight laced boots, Sheppard's tall, lanky shape as he bent his forehead to hers.

Hyperspace cradled the cruiser Eternal, blue streaks shifting in endless patterns past its windowless hull. John finished every last morsel of the cheese and crackers from his MRE and opened the brownie. "You know, I'd forgotten these were good," he said.

Teyla looked amused. Or at least he thought she did. The curves of her face were different. "You sound like Rodney," she said.

"I've been eating nothing but fruit for days. Cold beef ravioli started looking pretty good." John looked up at her. "You're not eating."

"I cannot," she said and shrugged. "Just the protein shakes and energy drinks. There is too much plastic surgery in my mouth for me to eat anything solid." Teyla reached for the thermos beside her. "Jennifer has tried to make it palatable. But it is terrible all the same. I will be fine for a few days," she assured him. "It is just that I think the beef ravioli has begun to look good too."

"I'm sorry."

"Don't be." She took a drink and grimaced. "We will hear what

Todd has to say. I think it is important, from the shade of his mind."

"'That's kind of creepy." John looked down at his brownie. "You reading his mind."

"John?" Her voice was low, and he glanced up, meeting narrowed yellow reptilian eyes. "You know that I cannot really touch your mind. Not yours, nor any other human's. It does not work that way."

"I know," he said, seeing the way she turned her hand over on her skirts, hiding the feeding slit in the folds of cloth. "Hell of an act."

"You made it work," she said. "I could only hope that you would have presence of mind to play along. I did not realize you would do so quite so thoroughly." There was a mischievous note in her voice.

"Yeah." John carefully flattened out the brownie wrapper, like it was important. "That was…disturbing."

"Yes," she said, and he didn't think he imagined the tremor in her voice. As disturbed as he was, she must be ten times more so. He didn't look away from her yellow eyes, from the night dark fall of hair, pale greenish skin against the dark lines of bodice and coat, from the way she twisted her hand in her skirt as though to hide it.

He reached down and took it, turning it very deliberately palm uppermost. It was a good job from Keller, he thought. Her small fingers were elongated, rendered more so in illusion by the long dark green claws shining with emerald lacquer, the lips of the feeding slit open and slightly moist, a little purpled at the edges. Very deliberately he bent over her hand, kissed the base of her palm and watched her shiver.

"John," she said, and her eyes were shadowed. Strange, yes, but the expression in them wasn't.

He was no good with words, never had been. "Teyla," he said. "It's you."

"It is all me," she said sadly. "This is not entirely an act. This is part of me. It is part of who I am."

"I know."

She lifted her head to the ceiling, blinking, her hair falling back. "I wish I could say that I am pretending. That I am very clever. But it is not all pretense. I am this person. She is part of me. And I do not know if I can live with that."

"I can," he said, closing her hand in his, small and strong in his fingers.

"I am kin to the Wraith. There is nothing that can be said of someone worse than they are like the Wraith. Than that they are Wraith." She blinked again as though she did not want to cry. "And yet this is me. This will always be part of me. I am not pretending, John. I am being something I have always been."

"You're a lot of things," he said, and shifted closer to get his other arm behind her back. "You've always been a lot of things. You're a good trader and you make impossible deals. Remember when you told me that? You're a good fighter, a reliable soldier. You're always good backup. You're a diplomat, and God help us we need one. You're a mom. You're a friend. You're smart and you're tough and maybe the bravest person I've ever seen." He shrugged and gathered her in against his shoulder, his face against the top of her head. "This is just one more thing you are. Really scary."

She gave a strangled little laugh, her hair falling forward so he couldn't see if she was crying or not.

"Hey, you know. Steelflower is kind of hot. In a wrong kind of way," he said to the top of her head.

At that she did laugh, though he thought there were tears in it. "John. You are crazy."

"I know," he said. "But I'm good with that." It sounded starker than he'd expected, truer.

Teyla lifted her face, her eyes searching his.

"I told you that a long time ago. Seriously got a screw loose. That's me. Nancy…" He took a deep breath. "I blew that up pretty badly."

"I am not afraid of you," she said. "And I can live with that." She dropped her head, the side of her face against his shoulder. "I have seen you crazy, when you did not know where you were or who I was. And I did not fear you then."

"Teyla." He shut his eyes against the memory of that day on the planet with the Wraith experiment gone awry. "I shot Rodney. It was just luck that I didn't kill him."

"You did not shoot me. You thought that I was Holland."

"And there's another kettle of fish," John said, his eyes squeezed tight. "Nancy…"

"I am not Nancy," she said, and the urgent sound in her voice made him open his eyes. The corners of her mouth twitched over fanged teeth, an ironic and monstrous smile. "Nancy was not Wraith."

"No," he said. "She sure wasn't." He swallowed. So many words, and so hard to say. His words had died that cold spring in Washington, frozen before summer came into Antarctic ice. "She wasn't anything like you." So many words, poured out on a marriage counselor's silence, words to condemn him, words to cut him to the bone, and no words he could make in return, nothing that would thaw him, frozen in desert night, scoured by raw winds. Antarctica had almost felt good. The icy winds were real.

Golden eyes and a monster's face, her hand in his and her head against his shoulder, her heart beating against his arm, beautiful and deadly, strange and familiar at once.

"We'll just watch out for each other and muddle along. Right?" he said, and watched her eyes spill over at last.

"Yes," she said, and smiled through her tears. "We will just muddle along."

"Todd better not get any ideas," he said. "I mean, Steelflower is pretty hot."

"I can handle Todd," Teyla said, raising her chin. "I am his queen."

"No."

She looked up at him swiftly. "No?"

"You're my queen," John said.

Jeannie drummed her fingers on the conference room table, waiting for everyone to arrive. Radek wasn't actually drumming his fingers, but he looked like he wanted to. Ever since they got the detailed readings from the flyby survey of the island, it had been clear that they couldn't send a team to investigate fast enough to satisfy him.

Colonel Carter was the next to arrive, a smudge of oil on one cheek as if she'd been interrupted working on the *Hammond*. She was just pulling back a chair to sit down when Ronon came in looking as if he'd just come from the gym. He'd said something yesterday about training sessions with the new Marines, which apparently meant teaching them how to survive when a big Satedan tried to kill them.

William Lynn, the archaeologist, came in a moment later. "I'm sorry," he said. "I did want to take a moment to look over these sensor readings, since this is the first anyone's told me that they found any."

Radek cleared his throat. "Yes, well. Now that we are all here," he said, and stood. He tapped at his laptop, and a map of the southern ocean appeared projected on one wall. "While we were working on the Wraith cruiser, we picked up some anomalous energy readings coming from a large island in the southern hemisphere," he said, pointing. "Dr. Cain and Dr. Ikeda did a flyby of the island this afternoon, and the results of their scans are very promising." He tapped a few more keys, and an overlay of power readings at different locations appeared on the map.

Colonel Carter leaned over to see better. "Oh, interesting," she said. Ronon glanced skeptically at William, who shrugged as if to say that he didn't see what was interesting yet either.

"We believe these power readings suggest that there is Ancient technology present on this planet, and, what's more, that some of it may still be functioning." He pushed his glasses up his nose and changed the display on the screen. Now it was showing geological maps, showing their best guess at how the islands and the ice had shifted over time.

"We think this island used to be a lot bigger," Jeannie said. "Now a lot of it is under water, and the rest of it is under ice. But there's room for who knows what down there. Okay, probably not a city this size, but something big."

"Also interesting, Dr. Ikeda took some samples of the ice from the jumper, and we have found trace amounts of naquadah," Radek said. "That is certainly not naturally occurring on this planet. We are thinking now maybe there actually was once a Stargate here, only now it is buried by the ice."

"Or by volcanic activity," Carter said. "If the gate was on a volcanic island, and the volcano entered an active phase, the gate could now be under meters and meters of rock."

"Right," Jeannie said. She was getting more confident as she spoke, falling back into the tones she'd used when she had to present in class. "Can you switch back to the other map, Radek? Thanks. So we noticed that these weak energy signatures fall roughly on a grid, as if they're small devices located in different rooms."

William looked more closely at the map, as if the pattern was starting to seem meaningful now. "The lights are still on?"

"It could be," Radek said.

"And the big one, there in the center?" Carter asked. "You're thinking power source?"

"Maybe even a ZPM," Radek said. "That would be nice to think. Certainly they would have required a power source of some kind. If it is a ZPM, I doubt it is fully powered. The energy signature is too weak for that, even if it is fainter because it is being transmitted through ice."

"Or rock," Carter said. "If the whole thing's been buried in lava, you're not going to get to your ZPM. Still, it's worth checking out."

"I thought you would think so," Radek said in satisfaction. "Unfortunately I am needed in the city right now, but if Ronon could take a team to do a preliminary survey, we can at least see what there may be to find. "

"No problem," Ronon said. "Just don't expect me to figure out what the Ancient stuff does. I can recognize a ZPM, but beyond that I got nothing."

"That's enough for a start," Carter said. "Please don't try to turn anything on, but if you find anything interesting, I'm sure Dr. Zelenka would like some video."

"Definitely," Radek said. "Dr. Lynn, perhaps you can figure out something about what they were doing down there."

"I'll do my best," William said. "I suppose it's too much to hope for that they left an explanatory note."

Radek looked like he was trying not to roll his eyes. "Is that usual to find at archaeological sites that have been abandoned for centuries?"

"You'd be surprised," William said. "People do document their activities."

"I'll take Cadman for backup, but we'll need someone to fly the jumper," Ronon said.

"Someone who is not currently engaged in critical repairs," Radek added quickly,

Carter glanced down at her laptop, probably looking at people's current assignments. "What about Dr. Robinson? She's been training with the jumpers in her free time, and she could use the flight hours. This ought to be as routine as it used to be for someone to run over to the mainland."

"There's a lot of ice," Ronon said.

"And there's going to be, and people are going to have to learn to fly and land in this weather," Carter said. "It's a nice day, there aren't any storms on the radar, and from what the earlier team reported, there's a wide, flat area where you can land."

"I see no problem," Radek said. "This should not be hard."

"Knock on wood," Jeannie said under her breath, but she didn't think anyone heard her.

CHAPTER TEN

Quicksilver

EMBER had been avoiding him. Oh, it was subtle enough, nothing anyone else would notice — if anything, any other man would read it as confirmation of Quicksilver's recovery, that Ember no longer hovered over him like a crèche master. Instead, he worked a different shift, busying himself in the biolabs rather than in the engine compartments, where the ZPM was now wound into its new socket. The tests were proceeding well, the power interface was solid… And Ember avoided him.

Rodney made his way through the corridors that laced the clevermen's quarters, avoiding the main thoroughfare. It had been painful to walk there when he believed he was Quicksilver, and had no idea why the blades looked sideways at him; now it was too dangerous, in case his thoughts slipped, and betrayed what he had found. But he had to talk to Ember, and this was the only time he could approach the cleverman unaware.

A single drone watched the entrance to the holding pens. He stood aside at Rodney's approach, mind blank, and Rodney stepped inside, the door sliding closed behind him. To either side, the cells stretched toward the hive's bow, only a third full now, but… He had not been there since he had regained his memory, somehow hadn't expected to feel anything different, but now — now he recognized the faces that hung in the webs as human, as kin, not kine. He could feel their fear, see here and there open eyes, waiting to see who would be chosen this time. There was a girl of maybe seventeen, fair hair lank about her face, her eyes sliding closed as though in prayer. Two cells beyond her, a dark young man, the web twitching as he tried, hopelessly, to free himself. An older woman, a grey-bearded man, a girl whose eyes were vivid blue: people, all of them, and he shuddered, unable to look at them any longer. He had fed on them — oh, he hadn't done it directly, that was a minor mercy, but they were just as dead, the ones Ember had chosen for him. He was as much a murderer as any Wraith — worse, a cannibal, consuming his own kind…

With an effort, he killed that train of thought, wrenched his mind back to the problem at hand. Ember should be here — yes, there he was, just turning away from a cell. A body dangled, withered, and Rodney shuddered again.

Quicksilver?

Rodney closed the distance between them in a rush, slamming the Wraith against the nearest support. His feeding hand came up, almost without volition, flattened against Ember's chest, claws digging through the layers of his coat to touch flesh. Ember hissed and flailed, got his own feeding hand between them, but Rodney had the advantage of leverage, caught his off hand and bent it up and back, pinning him against the hull.

What—?

They touched skin to skin, off hand to off hand, and Rodney felt the confusion beneath the words, the bright blossom of fear, the moment when Ember realized what had happened. He flexed his own fingers, setting the claws deeper, and Ember hissed again.

Stalemate, Quicksilver. Look down.

Not likely, Rodney said, but he could feel the prick of claws in his own chest, see their position reflected in Ember's mind. They stood body to body, each ready to feed — like enemies, like blades in battle, like lovers.

You cannot kill me, he said.

Watch me, Rodney answered. Ember had lied to him as much as Dust, deserved anything he did to him—

If you kill me, Ember said, *the Old One will fillet your mind, strip out every secret you have ever held, and feed on you laughing.*

The image that came with the words was sharp and shockingly vivid, but Rodney didn't relax his grip. *So?*

You know more of Atlantis's secrets, Ember said. *And I have not pressed you for them.*

You did this to me. Rodney let his fury fill the words, the anguish of seeing himself made monster, and felt Ember tremble under his hand.

I did not, and well you know it. Dust had the idea, some time ago, when Lastlight that you call Michael was made mad. You were his chance to test it, cleverman of Atlantis. I merely maintained what he had done.

And that makes it better? Rodney felt his feeding hand pulse with his anger, ready to strip the life from Ember. There was a warning pulse in his chest, Ember matching him, and he laughed soundlessly. *Really, give me one good reason.*

Because you won't survive if you do, Ember answered.

Rodney snarled, recognizing the truth in the words. *And I should trust you?*

We are in this game together, Ember said. *Whether I like it or not.*

Rodney blinked, another set of pieces slotting into place. Guide — yes, he knew Guide, had indeed worked with him on Atlantis, though that hadn't quite worked out the way they'd planned. As nothing had, when they dealt with Guide.

"Todd," he said aloud, and Ember cocked his head in question. *Guide. He's playing another of his games — is it a triple cross, or is he working up to a quadruple cross this time?*

To his surprise, a kind of wry amusement flicked through Ember's mind. *I wish I knew.*

And Sheppard, Rodney said. He was sure Sheppard had escaped, otherwise the hive would have been buzzing with the news, but he needed to be sure. *You hid the message — and, believe me, if anything goes wrong, I'll make sure everyone knows about that — did he escape?*

You know as much as I, Ember said. *He is not Death's captive, that is certain.*

And that would have to be enough, for now. Rodney said,

What does Guide want from me?

He doesn't want your death, Ember said. *And, believe me, I have urged otherwise! Nor does he love Death. But our queen is missing — as you know.*

And he keeps in contact with Atlantis, Rodney said, slowly. There was something about Todd's queen, something wrong there, but the memory slipped from his grasp.

Just so, Ember said. He paused. *I do not know what Guide plans, nor will he tell me.*

Rodney caught a brief image, memory or fear, he couldn't tell: Ember on his knees before Death, life ripped from him. *But he wishes you alive, and I obey.*

And if you don't — Rodney took a breath, released his claws. A moment later, Ember did the same.

I will keep you so, he said. *For all our sakes.*

CHAPTER ELEVEN

Interfaces

THEY came out of hyperspace in an uninhabited system, just as planned.

John paced around the command podium where Teyla stood, her hands in the grips and her eyes closed. "Are you putting the shields up?"

"Yes, John." Teyla didn't bother to open her eyes. "They are already up. And we are here well before Guide." She heard him cross behind her again.

At least he sounded sheepish as she instructed the cruiser to take up a high parking orbit around a gas giant. "Sorry."

The cruiser complied smoothly. It was, for want of a better way of putting it, feeling better. The hull breach aft had repaired itself, though the skin of the hull was still thin and cold there, and the internal sensors did not work. They needed to be grafted to the neural net of the cruiser, and it had not been done. Teyla was not certain how to do it. Speaking with the ship did not make her an engineer.

Once their orbit was settled she opened her eyes and stepped back, swaying a little as her vision returned to the physical room around her, soft lit blues and grays allowing the screens to be in high contrast. He was watching her, a strange expression on his face.

"What is it?" Teyla asked.

John shook his head. "You look different when you fly. I don't know. You look…"

"I look what?" she asked, her brows rising.

"Happy," he said. "Well, not that exactly. Satisfied. Pleased. I guess I always thought the Wraith tech would be hard."

"It is not hard for Wraith, John," she said, lifting her fingers from the podium. "Why would anyone build an interface that was painful or unpleasant to use?"

"I've wondered that about the Ancient stuff," John said, sitting down on the edge of the platform. "Carson's gotten used to it, but he doesn't like using the chair because it's uncomfortable. And Sam said that General O'Neill found using the chair on Earth really painful. That he said using it hurt a lot. Why would you build something that way? They both have the naturally expressed ATA gene too, even out of the same cluster."

"And you do not find it painful." She made it a statement as she came and sat beside him on the edge of the platform, her heeled boots stretched out before her. "I have seen you when you use it. You look ecstatic, as though you are enraptured."

"It feels really good." John shrugged. "It did the first time in Antarctica. It feels great. I don't even really have any words to describe what it's like." He looked up at the ceiling, as though recalling it minutely. "It's like being totally safe and totally free at the same time. Like letting go absolutely into this zone where you can feel everything and see everything, and at the same time it all makes sense. Like skiing downhill, when the momentum is carrying you and you can't hear anything except the wind and you couldn't stop if you tried and you feel like you can fly. Like you have to let go, and it's the best thing ever."

"But you do let go," Teyla said, ducking her head sideways at him. "Perhaps it is a matter of temperament as well as genetics. I do not think General O'Neill is very good at letting go. He seems to me a man who will not surrender, who cannot in some inner place in his soul."

"You can't control the interface," John said. "You can't. It's too strong. It's not meant to be used like that. You have to slide into it and let it show you. It will do what you want, but you can't make it. It's like I was saying about skiing. Gravity is going to pull you down the hill. You can't make it work some other way. You can just steer how you get there. That's the skill." He spread his hands out, flexing them to shake out tension. "You think he doesn't let go?"

"I do not know him well," Teyla said, "But he does not strike me as someone who can cease struggling. And if it is as you say, the more he fights the more it hurts. Carson wants to make it do things that are not quite the way it wants to, and so he finds it uncomfortable if not actually painful."

John grinned sheepishly. "And I totally let the city top."

She nudged him sideways, laughing. "It seems to work."

He shoulder bumped her back. "Is that what it's like to fly a Wraith ship?"

"Ummm," she said, thinking. "Not exactly. A Wraith ship is designed for a queen. It desires mastery. It expects to serve you. No, not even that. It craves serving you. I do not know how to say it other than that it is designed to feel pleasure when it does what you wish. Otherwise it would not go into battle. It would not do things that will cause it pain, that might even cause it to be destroyed, unless the pleasure it got from serving you were so great that it overrode even self preservation."

"Otherwise the minute you shot a Wraith ship it would get scared and run away," John said. "Too bad it doesn't work that way."

"It does not," Teyla said. "The reward of its queen's or its commander's approbation is so intense that it desires it even at the cost of great pain." She flattened her hand against the floor of the platform. "Eternal would go into fire for me because it is well trained and it wishes to please me above all else."

"Like a cavalry horse," John said.

"What?"

"On Earth up until about a hundred years ago we used horses in war. They would charge straight into cannon fire sometimes, if they were trained to do it and their riders knew what they were doing. You could charge batteries that way, half a dozen guns firing grapeshot. And the horses would do it, if it was a good unit and they had that kind of rapport." He looked around. "Is Eternal as bright as a horse?"

"About the same, I would guess?" Teyla replied. "I have never worked with horses. We did not use them on Athos, but I have seen them. Though I thought they were too small to carry a man on their back in a fight as you say."

John nodded. "All the horses I've seen here are little. Thirteen, fourteen hands. I'm guessing here, but I think maybe when the Ancients brought people from Earth back to Pegasus ten thousand years ago and some of them brought their domestic animals, we didn't have the bigger horses yet. I think they were bred later for height. In 8,000 BC it would have all been little horses. And maybe the Wraith here haven't ever let a civilization reach the point where they could breed warhorses for size." He put his head to the side thoughtfully. "That's not true in the Milky Way. When I was at the SGC for six weeks a couple of years ago we visited this allied world that had been under the protection of the Asgard, and they had regular sized horses. But then presumably they were seeded from Earth in the Middle Ages, not ten thousand years ago."

"That is truly fascinating," she said. "There is so much work to be done, so many mysteries to solve. It will take lifetimes to even begin."

"I hope we have lifetimes," he said.

"I hope that we do too," she said. "There is so much we might be, if we ever had the chance. If we could ever grow without knowing that as soon as we have reached a certain height we will be cut off. There is so much we could learn from you, and so much you could learn from us. So many marvels and so many amazing things, if we could but share."

John looked at her sideways. "You don't believe that we'll contaminate you if we have too much contact?"

Teyla snorted. "John, for us that is nothing but a way for your people to feel justified in deserting us. To make it a virtue to leave us to die. How could those of us who have lost kin, who even now worry about their children, wish that you will go away and leave us to the Wraith? Do you think I wish that Torren did not have access to antibiotics or to surgery if he needed it? Since Sateda fell, we have not had anywhere we could trade for many medicines, and Athosians have died for the lack of them. 'Let us not interfere' is nothing but an excuse for turning your back on people in need, a way to make your selfishness a virtue."

"Yeah, but sometimes ham-fisted help is worse than none at all," he said. "A lot of bad things happen sometimes in the name of being well-meaning."

"And so the answer is to do nothing at all?" Teyla challenged. "One must use judgment, in this as in all things. But is it rational to say one doctor is bad, let us have no more doctors?" She shook her head. "One must care, John, if one is worthy of being called human. That was a thing I knew of you the first day."

"Huh?"

Teyla tilted her head back, looking up at the ceiling of the cruiser. "You had come among us for a day only, and then there were the Wraith. They had culled our people, destroyed our camp, and even then a second wave came down upon us to seek retribution for the Dart that was destroyed. And what did you do? You did not speak of contamination, or of the importance of allowing our culture to develop on its own. You took them all to Atlantis, Jinto and Charin, Kanaan and all the rest. You took them through the gate to your camp, and you shared your food with them. You were beleaguered yourselves, in fear of the shield failing, cut off from your home. And yet you shared with us all you had. Your limited supplies, your fading power. And then you came for the captives."

Teyla leaned back against the step. "I expected to die. How not? We were culled. We were the Lost. A few minutes might pass or a few days until we were fed upon. When the Wraith took Colonel Sumner, I knew I would be next." She shook her head, half leaned against his shoulder. "The last thing I expected was to see you and Lt. Ford sneaking in. You must understand that no one is rescued. No one returns. I stood with my age-mate Halling and knew we would die together. And then you came. Why should I think it would be better if you had not interfered?"

"We woke the Wraith," John said. "It might have been a lot better if we hadn't. A lot of people might be alive today if we hadn't."

"John, we have been dying for centuries. For thousands of years. You have seen what the Wraith did on Sateda, six years before you came. Once they did the same to Emege and the cities of Athos. That is not something you began." She shook her head. "It is a conceit to believe our story begins with you, or that before you came we dwelled in an innocent paradise. The myth of your culpability is just one more way of making the story about you."

"I'm sorry," he said quietly.

"Do not be," she said, leaning against his shoulder. "We know no more of you than you do of us, and is it not human nature to fit those you meet into your story? To find a frame that allows you to reach for understanding? You tell your stories and I tell mine. And both are true, and both are false."

"That makes a weird kind of sense," he said. John looked at her sideways. "I don't know what to do except follow my gut. You know. Do what I think's right. I never claimed to understand it." He squeezed her hand, long green claws between his fingers. "I'm not like Carter or McKay. I wasn't some kid genius who always figured they'd have the weight of the universe on their shoulders. I'm not like Elizabeth, who knew she had what it took to make decisions that affected millions of people. I don't know what to do with that kind of power."

"Follow your gut," she said.

John let out a long breath. "I'm not sure my gut always makes good decisions."

"No," she agreed. "Sometimes it makes bad decisions for the right reasons. You are not wise, and you are a hard man, an expedient man who will do anything for those he loves. But you are not selfish. You do not act out of self interest. You do what you think is best, and perhaps you are wrong. But you do not do it for your own profit." She nudged him sideways. "And you know when to listen to those wiser than you."

"And that would be you?" She could not tell if he were joking or not.

"I am conceited," she said, "and like to think so. It is my great weakness to think I understand all, that I am so very clever and that I understand people so well. And yet what a mess I have made of my own life! I destroyed my marriage to Jorrah long before you came to Athos, and you saw what passed with Kanaan. I no longer speak for my people, no longer fit among those who share my blood. I am Bloodtainted, and I sit here with you as a Wraith Queen." She stretched her hand against his, claws against his skin. "I am Teyla Who Belongs Nowhere, Teyla of No People. I do not know where I can live."

"Atlantis," he said, and she turned her head to look at him. "You belong in Atlantis. It's your home."

"A place between?"

"Yeah," he said. "It's your home too."

She looked down at their joined hands, his big and warm, hers tinted green with veins like twining vines about them. She had said nothing to anyone else. What could she say, lacking proof? "Carson thinks the Wraith began as a failed experiment of the Ancients," she said. "That like the Replicators it was an experiment that went wrong."

John was quiet for a long moment, his head bent in thought, and she knew he was adding it up, all the things they had seen, the experiments left by the Ancients who had played games with human beings, who had made war on their creations.

"It could be," he said. "It makes a hell of a lot of sense, really." He raised his head. "And then they tried to kill them."

"Only the Wraith are not easy to kill."

"The Wraith hunted them down instead." John nodded. "I'll buy that. It makes a lot of things make sense."

"It does," Teyla said. "They are the avengers, seeing retribution from their creators. But you know this is not something people can accept. It is too much. It is too painful. It cuts to the heart of our stories."

"You can't expect people to react well when you challenge them like that," John said. "That's not how it works. You can't destroy what people believe about themselves and expect them to thank you." He shrugged. "Any kind of social change. You've got to do it really carefully, or the backlash kills people. Sometimes literally. And you're talking about something that would rip apart the foundations of every civilization in this galaxy."

"That is why I have spoken of it with no one but you," Teyla said. "And why Carson only spoke to me. We have been too hurt. Our scars go too deep. Your people do not have these scars, and so perhaps they can, some of them, bear to see the Wraith as people. But they have not lost loved ones. They have not lived their lives in terror. They have not seen their children fed upon. They are good men both, but can you see Ronon or Kanaan accepting this?"

John blew out a deep breath. "Ronon," he said. "No, that's not going to work."

Teyla's head lifted at the same moment that a blue light began to blink, and she hurried to her feet.

"What's that?" John asked.

"Sensor alert," she replied. "Todd's hiveship has arrived."

The island looked like a big chunk of ice. As Eva Robinson brought the jumper around looking for a place to land, that was her first thought. It glittered in the sun like a bright proof of Atlantis, almost too bright to look at as every surface glared in the morning sun.

Automatically the windscreen of the jumper responded to her thought, darkening with a gray tint to dampen the glare. That was pretty neat. She wasn't sure she'd ever get used to this many features, but she was certainly willing to try. She'd flown the jumper around the city on practice runs, but this was the first time she'd gone on an actual mission, something she'd never anticipated doing.

Very carefully, Eva set the jumper down on a windswept snow-field on a small plateau overlooking the sea. It wasn't far from where the sensors detected power sources. Nothing on this island was. Maybe it had once been bigger, but it sure wasn't very big now.

She shrugged on her heavy parka as Laura Cadman opened the back gate. Laura had been in her office a couple of times to talk about Carson. It was a little strange to work with the clone of the guy she'd been involved with who didn't remember the last eight months of their relationship before his death. She'd mourned him, finished her rotation and gone back to Earth, thrown herself into her work and gotten promoted, been posted to the *Hammond*. She was over him. And then suddenly she had to work with him. Or with his clone, who didn't remember everything she did. It was a damn good reason to come talk to her, in Eva's opinion. Not at all the kind of adjustment issue you were likely to encounter on Earth!

"It looks like Alcatraz," Laura said, stepping out onto the ramp.

"Alcatraz?" William Lynn hurried down the ramp after her, putting on his sunglasses against the snowglare. "I don't see it. This is beautiful."

"The way it's situated," Laura said, gesturing with the muzzle of her gun toward the sea and the shore of a larger island a short distance away, separated by a bay of frigid water. "The rocks. The shape of the island. The sea cliffs. It would be a hell of a place to escape from."

"Maybe it was a waystation," Ronon said, clomping off the ramp and into the snow. He sunk to his knees. "If you put the Stargate here, you could control access to it. Nobody else on the planet would be able to use it unless you let them." He shaded his eyes with his hand, looking out over the sea. "I'd hate to assault this place."

"It does look quite defensible," William agreed. "I'll look for the remains of fortifications."

"How about we look for the power source?" Ronon said. "That's what we came to do."

"Right." William pulled out his scanner. "I'm reading the energy source in this direction." He pointed away from the sea, toward a rocky ridge that ran the length of the island, gray stones festooned with snow and sheets of ice.

"In the middle," Laura said. "That makes sense."

"This is interesting," William said. "Very interesting."

"What is?" Ronon swung around, looking at the archaeologist bent over his instrument.

"I'm picking up a fairly strong trace of naquadah here. Perhaps this was the location of the original Stargate, or where some of the remains of it wound up."

"Here?" Eva said, looking around. "I don't see anything."

"It's about three meters down beneath the ice," William said.

"Overrun by glaciers?"

"It makes sense." William shrugged. "This island could have changed considerably in 10,000 years. As you know, Earth originally had a Stargate in the Antarctic region which was rendered inoperable by glaciation."

"Do I know that?" Eva said. "How would I know that?"

William looked confused. "I suppose you wouldn't," he said. "It came up in the off world trainings I had with Dr. Jackson. A cautionary tale about not getting fixated on a solution."

"Beg pardon?"

"Colonel Carter — Captain Carter then — found the Antarctic gate by accident when our gate malfunctioned and she and General O'Neill got sent to the wrong one. He was badly injured and nearly died while she tried to figure out how to fix the gate and dial home. Turns out there was nothing wrong with the gate, and if she'd tried dialing any other gate address other than Earth she'd have been home in an hour. But she got stuck on one solution, if you see. She had to make the gate dial Earth. Which it couldn't, because they were already on Earth." William shrugged. "As I said, a cautionary tale."

Laura blew out a breath, steam in the frozen air. "Wow. That sounds like the kind of mistake I would make. I can't believe Carter did that."

"Everybody was young once," Ronon said gruffly, steering

William toward the rock formations that towered over the plateau.

"Except you," Laura said cheerfully. "You're forty going on seventy five."

Ronon looked at her sideways, and Eva thought she saw a spark of actual annoyance there. "I'm thirty one."

"Yeah?" Laura grinned up at him, unabashed.

"Yeah." He looked at her pointedly. "Now how about you help Dr. Lynn find a way in? Unless you'd just like to blow the cliff up."

"I would," Laura said, looking up. "Except I think using explosives would probably start an avalanche. That's a lot of snow and ice right over us."

Eva glanced up. It did look a little menacing as well as pretty. "Jinx," she said under her breath.

Ronon looked over at her as Laura went to join William poking along the cliff base. "Yeah, I don't like it either," he said, raising his face to the beetling ridge above. He gestured off toward the cliffs below. "This was not a good scene for somebody."

"Alcatraz?"

"The Chateau d'If," Ronon said grimly. "Toss somebody off that cliff and they aren't coming back." Eva's eyebrows rose, and Ronon shrugged. "A book Zelenka loaned me."

"I've read it," Eva said. "About a man imprisoned wrongly for fourteen years and how he got his revenge, if I remember."

"Good book," Ronon said. He gave her a wolfish grin. "True to life."

"Are you and Dr. Zelenka friends?" Eva asked. That was an odd couple if she'd ever seen one.

"He's a good man." Ronon nodded, looking over to where Laura was walking along the cliff knocking on it with her fist like she was planning to find a door. "She's not going to find anything that way. The Ancients didn't build like that, like it was some kind of role playing game where you just have to walk up and say the password."

"Maybe we should try Open Sesame," Eva said, following him toward the cliff face. She raised her hands up with a smile.

"Speak, Friend, and enter!"

Beneath the ice a faint tracery of blue lines appeared, spreading up and down and across, limned not on stone but metal. With a faint grinding sound the ice cracked as the massive doors began to move.

"Oh my God," Eva said. Chunks of ice the size of her fist fell away as the panels slid back, twice her height and twenty feet wide.

"Good job!" Ronon clapped her on the shoulder.

"Of course it responds to the ATA gene!" William hit himself in the forehead dramatically. "Why didn't I think of that?"

Everyone except Laura refrained from answering. "Because you were fixated on a solution?" she said.

"Very funny." William turned toward the doors as they ground open. "Now let's go in and see what we've got."

CHAPTER TWELVE

Son of the Ancients

"YOU came to me before when you wished to test your retrovirus," Todd said. He was pacing, and each time he came to the end of the room he swung around, exactly the same number of steps across the control room of the cruiser each time. "Because you needed Wraith subjects, and you needed my help."

"Yeah," John said. "But it didn't work."

"It did not," Todd said, "And if it had I frankly doubt that most of us would have been willing to take it, given the diminishment in capabilities it inflicted." He gave John a look that might have been intended as a mirthless smile, or as something entirely different. "Would you accept a retrovirus that would leave you blind? Or that would make it impossible for you to engage in intimacy?"

"Um," John said, not entirely sure that was translating right.

"The telepathy," Teyla said. She was sitting in the only chair in the control room, her ankles crossed, seeming utterly self possessed. "Without it a Wraith cannot emotionally connect normally."

"Just so," Todd said.

"It didn't work," John said. "We know that. So? Nobody is suggesting we use it again."

"We have been working on our own retrovirus," Todd said.

"We?" Teyla's brow rose. "Queen Death?"

"My own clevermen," he said, swinging around again.

"The retrovirus that has turned Rodney into a Wraith," John said flatly.

"And what good would it do us, Sheppard, to have more Wraith? Why should we want to make more humans like us, to compete for already scarce resources?" Todd glowered at him. "Queen Death may find it amusing or even useful to turn one of her enemies into her pet, but it is of no long term strategic value."

"And yours is," Teyla said, making it a statement, not a question.

"We hope that ours will solve our problems in the long term, yes." His eyes met Teyla's, and John wondered if some other conversation were passing between them, one he couldn't hear. "But we have reached the point where your cooperation would be helpful."

"And why's that?" John asked.

"Ours is intended for humans," he replied.

"Why would we do that?" John began.

Teyla frowned, shaking her head slightly. "Let us hear," she said.

"It is not to our advantage to kill our food source," Todd said. "The process of feeding is almost inevitably fatal for the human, and so therefore it takes an exceedingly large human population to support a hive. It is possible to feed without killing, yes, but only by feeding very shallowly, not enough to sustain one for long, and even so the process is so debilitating for the human that most die anyway, or at least appear greatly aged and are no longer capable of functioning normally."

"That's one way of putting it," John said. He didn't see how this was going anywhere good, but Teyla was still listening, a little frown on her face.

"Our retrovirus is designed to provide humans with an enzyme that reacts with our enzyme during the feeding process," Todd said.

"Like the Hoffan drug," Teyla said.

"Indeed, in conception. But most unlike in practice. What ours does is to provide a strengthening agent for the human, so that the effects of feeding are not traumatic to the human physiology. Being fed upon would leave a human debilitated and weak, but it would not appreciably age them as it does now, and would not, were they healthy to begin with, prove fatal."

Teyla nodded slowly. "And so, in practice, the same humans could be fed upon many times, rather than requiring fresh prey on each occasion."

"Provided there were sufficient time left between. We do not know how long that might be. Months, certainly. Possibly years. But even if it were years, if the humans in question could continue to live and reproduce, we would not find that our herds were depleted so dangerously and quickly." He paced away, turning again at the far end of the room. "A much smaller population of humans could sustain us. We should not have to slay within the populations of our worshippers."

"You could just milk us like cows," John said. The idea was sickening.

"In a word, yes. It is the difference between milking cows and slaughtering cows. If you have a limited number of cattle, the former is more sustainable."

"I can't believe we're going there," John said.

"Do you suffer any long term effects of being fed upon?" Todd challenged, raising his eyes to John's. "I fed on you nearly three years ago, but did not drain you to death. I am sure it was unpleasant and painful, but more so than any other wound you have received? Do you feel any effects of it now, even so much as from that Iratus bug wound on your neck?"

John lifted his hand, rubbing at the raised circle of thick tissue on his neck involuntarily. "No," he admitted. "I don't feel any effects now."

"That is our goal. If it were no more than that, something unpleasant and painful from which one might recover in a few weeks, and feel no effects from three years later, then we might reach symbiosis," Todd said.

"Symbiosis?" John snorted. "Symbiosis is when two species benefit from each other. What do we get from you? It would be better for humanity if all the Wraith were dead."

Todd's eyes sparked. "And do you have the wherewithal to do that, John Sheppard? I think not."

"Not yet," John said.

"Is that what you want then? Genocide? To utterly destroy a

sentient species down to the last one? You are indeed the son of the Ancients, John Sheppard."

Teyla took a quick breath.

Todd looked at Teyla sideways. "Ask yourself if this is what your queen wants. You see her there in the semblance of one of us. She is not entirely a stranger to us, is she?" He met her eyes. "Can you say that you wish all of us dead? That you wish your kindred utterly extinguished?"

John swallowed. "If it would safeguard human lives. People come first."

Todd's mouth quirked. "Is that not always the answer? But who are people, Sheppard? That is the problem. And how much tainted blood does it take to make you not a person? As much as hers? As much as her son's? There are many humans in this galaxy who would kill her in a moment for the blood she bears, who would kill her son without mercy."

Teyla's voice shook. "And would you show any such mercy? You have not before, when you fed upon the children of the Athosians."

"We have killed out of hunger. Not out of fear."

"Sateda looked like fear to me," John said.

"I am trying to find a way that we need not kill you," Todd snapped. "But I see I was foolish to attempt it. You would rather continue your manly posturing about how you will destroy us when it is your people who are on the brink."

"No," Teyla said quietly, "It is my people." She looked from one to the other, her eyes lingering on each of them. "We have been culled to the bone, and Michael nearly finished us. It is my people who will die."

"And so it is your decision, is it not?" Todd asked her, and there was no mockery in his tone. "You may decide, here and now, the fate of humans and Wraith both in this galaxy. It is upon you in this moment, Teyla Emmagan."

He saw it cross her face, the knowledge and the power. The responsibility. Whatever she did, trusting Todd or not, everything that came after would be her burden. Whoever lived or died, she would know it was her choice.

Nobody could live with that. Nobody could live that way.

John straightened up. "You're right," he said to Todd. "We don't have the wherewithal to kill you. It's an academic question. We don't have the means to do it, and Earth doesn't have the will. The Pegasus Galaxy isn't our first or even fifteenth priority. We're not the Ancients. We're just people who inherited some of their stuff." He looked at Teyla. "I think we should hear Todd out."

"I think so too," she said. He couldn't read her expression, not changed as her face was.

Todd nodded slowly. "We have been working on a retrovirus which would allow humans to be fed upon without permanent injury. Unfortunately, we have reached an impasse. Your Dr. Keller's knowledge would be invaluable, as she was working along parallel lines with her retrovirus. If we are to be allies in truth, that is one thing I put before you. We have a possible means of ending random cullings forever. But I would like your Dr. Keller's help."

John took a deep breath. "We want Rodney back."

"He is not mine to return to you," Todd said.

"I know," Teyla said quietly. "But in this guise I think I have a chance of reaching him. And perhaps more importantly I can be a counterweight to Queen Death."

"You have no concept as yet how strong she has become," Todd said. "So many hives have flocked to her and her impossible promises. They are weak minded, lured by the scent of gifts she can never provide!"

"People are like that," John shrugged. "Tell 'em what they want to hear and they'll do whatever without thinking too hard about it."

"People?" Todd's brow rose.

"Um," John said.

"Do you think there are none who would work against her, if another queen opposed her?" Teyla asked smoothly, opening her fingers against the smooth cloth of her skirts.

"It is hard to say," Todd said. "It is a matter of prestige, but it is also more than that. A queen attracts a following by the force of her personality and her allure, her charisma. But she holds it by the force of her mind. I do not know if Queen Death has been challenged by another queen. In the time I have known her she has avoided meeting another queen face to face, preferring to work by proxies or simply kill them at a distance. She is young, and while the force of her charisma is considerable I do not know if she has the strength to defeat one who is not bowed by her allure."

"And why aren't you?" Teyla asked in that same smooth, quiet voice.

For a moment Todd hesitated. "I am very old," he said. "And I have seen many queens come and go."

John looked at her. "What do you think?" he asked, figuring this was about the highest stakes he could imagine, wishing for a moment that the telepathy did work with him. But it didn't. It never would.

"It is not our decision to make alone," Teyla said carefully. "I think that we both see the merit in your plan, but this is a decision that must be weighed by others as well. Dr. Keller must decide whether she will come, and Colonel Carter's opinion must be considered. We will return to Atlantis and speak with them. But either way we will meet you at a rendezvous you suggest afterwards."

John took a deep breath. "It could save lives now," he said. "If fewer people are being killed by the Wraith, that's a good thing. Maybe the best we can do."

"And you will live with that, John Sheppard," Todd said. "Very well."

Laura shone the light on her P90 around the space beyond the doors, William almost jostling at her elbow. There was a cracked floor that might have been concrete and a broad, empty space, high ceilinged and cold.

"Hey, Robinson," Ronon said. "Can you think about lights?"

"I can try," Eva said. On Atlantis she didn't have to think about lights. They just came on at her approach. *Lights*, she thought. *Lights. Lights.* But either that wasn't how it worked or the lights weren't working after all these centuries. It stayed stubbornly dark. "I'm sorry," she said.

"It's unlikely they would work after so long," William said, his flashlight beam playing over the floor and the walls beside the doors, pitted and fractured by ice. "This place is not in very good condition. A lot more like most of our Ancient finds than Atlantis."

"Something still works," Ronon said in the rear. "The power source. Let's find it."

"Straight in, then," William said, checking his scanner. "And down. Perhaps there are stairs."

Laura's light flicked over flaking blue stripes painted on the floor. "This looks like a hanger," she said.

"There are many reasons you might mark symbols on the floor," William began. He stopped short as his light played ahead. "Or it might be a hangar," he concluded. The beam of his light danced over a familiar stubby shape.

"It's a puddle jumper," Eva said.

"A wrecked one," Ronon added. Even from here it was obvious the jumper was in bad shape. The left drive pod was extended, the casing blackened by fire, corroded machinery dangling from it. The hull was scorched above the drive pod, the outer ablative coating peeling back from the metal beneath. As they walked around it, the windscreen was darkened, rendered opaque by fire or time.

"That's too bad," Laura said. "It would be nice to find another one. But I suppose Dr. Zelenka will want to take a look anyhow."

"He can always use parts," Ronon said. "We can't make a bunch of stuff. There might be some parts he can scavenge here. We can bring back a team later to do that."

"Maybe there are more jumpers in here," Eva said hopefully.

Unfortunately, it looked like she was wrong. They checked out the entire hangar bay, a space big enough to have held a dozen jumpers, but it was empty.

"Not even any fire suppression equipment," Ronon said, his eyes examining the corners sharply. "Somebody stripped this place."

"It appears that they left voluntarily and with sufficient time to remove anything of value," William said. "Perhaps they simply closed the base down."

"Maybe so." Ronon shone his light along the far wall. There were two metal doors. He frowned. "Those are pressure doors, the kind we have in Atlantis in the areas that are underwater."

"Maybe this place flooded sometimes?" Laura asked.

"I can't imagine how, from the geological work we did," William replied. "We're far above sea level, and it seems likely it would have been even further away 10,000 years ago."

"Bad weather?" Eva suggested. "It does get really cold here, right?"

"It does," William conceded. "Perhaps that was the reason."

"We should see what's on the other side," Laura said.

It took three of them to pry the doors open with Eva holding the light so the others could work, Ronon on one side and William and Laura on the other.

"Perfectly ordinary hallway," William said. He looked at Eva. "Can you try the lights?"

Frowning, she put her hand to the wall. *Lights*, she thought really hard.

"That's something," William said, and she opened her eyes. A few dim emergency lights had flickered to life here and there, providing some illumination.

There still wasn't anything to see. It looked like an underground version of one of Atlantis' maintenance corridors, just utilitarian metal and stone. Ordinary doors marked its length for perhaps a hundred feet, where it dead ended in a T intersection.

"Let's start trying doors," Laura said.

The air was cool but stale. Ventilation was working somewhere, and Eva said as much.

William nodded, his light playing around the third empty room Laura had opened. "Not uncommon in Ancient facilities. But I must say, this is one of the planer ones I've ever examined, even the much older ones in the Milky Way. No ornamentation, no script… The Ancients liked to make functional things beautiful and elegant. Here it seems they just didn't bother."

Ronon opened the door across the hall. Six niches filled the other three walls, each roughly seven feet long and four feet wide, stacked one on top of the other. "Barracks," he said. "This looks like the crew quarters in the undersea drilling station we found on Lantea."

William nodded, for all that was Greek to Eva, a reference to some mission she'd never heard of. Presumably William had gotten much more classified material to review than she had. "That follows."

"Only here they took the mattresses and lamps with them," Ronon said, looking around. "Didn't leave a thing. They didn't desert this place in a hurry. They shut it down."

"I'd be inclined to agree," William said, backing out into the hall again.

Laura looked out of the door of the room across the hall. "Bathroom," she said. "No frills, just the basics."

"Some kind of military base?" Eva wondered aloud.

"It seems likely," William said. "Just a hypothesis, of course. But this far out in the rim it may have been abandoned early in the war. This is far from all known population centers, and there seems to have been no strategic material here to defend." He shrugged. "Perhaps simply not worth keeping as the Ancients became overextended."

"It's kind of creepy," Laura said.

"It's just a ruin," William said. There was a slightly exasperated tone in his voice. "And not a particularly interesting one at that."

"It'll be interesting if it has a ZPM," Ronon said. "How about we skip all these rooms and go straight for the energy source?"

"Just a quick look," William promised, though by the tenth

room even he was beginning to sound frustrated. "Maybe a kitchen," he said of a long room stripped of everything except for some heavy stone sinks.

"Kitchens, barracks, bathrooms, storerooms," Eva said as she opened the next door. "I wonder what it was all for?"

"A military outpost does seem likely," William began.

Laura looked in. "Or a research facility," she said. "This is more like it."

Banks of metal shelves lined the walls, wires dangling where pieces of equipment had been pulled. A central pedestal held a stripped terminal, empty slots clearly showing where viewscreens had once been installed. Along the opposite wall of the room one way glass partitions separated out two isolation chambers, entirely empty except for a few overhead lighting fixtures, though small holes in the walls here and there suggested where other equipment might have gone.

William ran his hands over the remaining terminal almost lovingly. "This still has power," he said.

"The lights do," Eva replied. "Want me to initialize it?"

Ronon shook his head. "No. Lynn, you just get video, ok? We have no idea what this stuff does, and I've seen McKay nearly blow himself up way too many times turning on Ancient stuff he didn't know anything about. Get some video, and when we bring Zelenka back here he can have a look at it."

"It seems to have operative systems," William said. "I could just…"

"Leave it alone," Ronon said patiently. "Find the ZPM, if there is one. Zelenka can have a look at this stuff and see what it does."

"It might be a weapon," William argued.

"It might be just the environmental controls," Eva said sensibly. "It looks like they took everything else except the lights and the ventilation systems. It's probably the terminal that controls them."

Ronon gave her an approving look. "Right. So let's find the power source."

Laura had been looking at the isolation chambers, trying to

find the way to open them. Now she stopped, her head going up. "Ronon," she said, "I don't think this was a lab."

He came to see what she was looking at, Eva and William at his shoulder. One of the walls was scratched, long gouges in groups of nine, a tenth hash mark across each group tying them together.

"No," he said grimly. "It was a prison."

They went on, down metal stairs that creaked alarmingly from corrosion and stressed joints, past more conventional cells set into the walls, bars drawn back across empty space. There were twenty of them. Eva counted. Twenty, and each had held a single person? Or each had held a dozen prisoners? There was no knowing. Everything was dark and silent, empty and clean, leaving no clues to the original occupants.

"I can smell the ocean," Eva said suddenly.

It was colder here, and there was a distinct salt tang to the air that didn't smell like the ventilation systems.

"I think there is water ahead," William said. Sure enough, when everyone was quiet the faint lapping of waves could be heard. Another pair of pressure doors, these open, and the water was louder.

It looked something like one of the underwater jumper bays in Atlantis, and perhaps it originally had been. Now, with the ice overreaching, it was an ice cavern half filled with water, a pale blue light descending through the ice from the sky above.

"It can't be very thick," William said, looking up. "Not and let so much light through. But I don't see the outlet."

"Underwater," Ronon said. "The ice probably doesn't go down very far in the seawater."

"It's enormous," Laura said, looking off to the right. "Maybe there used to be some kind of energy shield or something and the ice formed over it. When the shield failed, it left this big ice dome."

"It's really beautiful," Eva said.

Ronon nodded. "Yeah."

"Maybe this whole planet was a penal colony," Eva said.

Ronon shrugged noncommittally, his eyes on William, who

was picking his way along the ice that rimmed the cavern, out toward a dark shape on the ice. "What are you doing?" Ronon called.

"Looking at this," William called back. He bent over the whatever it was, his red jacket a bright spot against the white and blue. "Interesting. It looks like one of those squid. Part of a carcass. It might have washed up in here."

"Funny place to wash up," Eva began, and her breath caught in her throat.

"William!" Laura yelled in the same moment, and the archaeologist spun around.

Almost invisible against the ice, an enormous white shape reared up, half again William's height, towering over him with a roar that echoed through the dome. Its ursine snout opened to show sharp teeth, and its forepaws had long claws, like the biggest polar bear Eva had ever imagined.

"Run!" Laura shouted.

"Drop!" Ronon shouted at the same time.

William stood stock still, whether in indecision between two entirely contradictory suggestions or just in sheer terror.

"Hey you!" Ronon shouted, running toward it, angling around the edge of the pool. He didn't have a clean shot with William between him and the bear. "Hey you!"

The bear spun around, roaring, looking at this new, noisier interloper.

"Drop!" Ronon yelled again, and William did, falling to his knees with his head covered. The energy pistol spoke, flaring bright in the blue gray light. One shot, two, three... The bear went over on the fourth shot, toppling with a sound that Eva could hear from across the cavern.

"Oh my God," she said, her heart racing.

Ronon grabbed William's hand, dragging him to his feet. "You ok?"

"Yes." William's voice was a little shaky. "Just fine."

"Let's get out of here," he said. "That thing was pretty tough.

Don't you know any better than to mess with a predator's kill? You see a carcass like that and whatever killed it probably isn't far away."

"Do you think those things can swim?" Laura asked as they drew nearer. She cradled her P90 watchfully.

"Probably," Eva said. "Polar bears on Earth are good swimmers."

"That would explain how it got in here," William said. He dusted the snow off his jacket where he'd lain on the ice.

Laura's eyes suddenly went wide, looking over Eva's shoulder. "And how its twelve friends did," she said.

CHAPTER THIRTEEN

Beneath the Ice

"EVERYBODY back!" Ronon yelled. "Cadman, cover them!"

A pack of the bears—Eva wasn't going to stop and argue with Laura about whether or not there were twelve—were pulling themselves out of the water. The first were already on dry land, rushing toward them at an alarming rate. For a moment time seemed to stop. I'm going to be eaten by a giant polar bear, Eva thought quite calmly. One always wonders how one will die. She'd considered a good many likely scenarios over the years. But somehow giant alien bears had never figured in.

"Get back!" Ronon yelled, grabbing her by the shoulder and shoving her after William. "Cover us from the door."

William hadn't needed to be told twice. He was sprinting for the entrance at a speed that would have looked good in high school track and field.

With a noise that sounded ear splittingly loud, Laura opened up with the P90. The ice dome amplified every sound, and to Eva it sounded like a dozen guns. Laura looked perfectly calm, the weapon cradled against her, as she fired again and again on the onrushing animals. Another thing for the file, Eva thought as she ran past. Laura might come in the office and flail about relationships, but at the bottom of it she was a Marine, the only Marine lieutenant in five years who hadn't come home from Atlantis on a stretcher or in a body bag.

"Woah," William yelled, skidding to an abrupt halt. Two of the bears had somehow come around behind them, or perhaps they'd already been inside the dome, white on white, camouflaged the entire time. However they'd gotten there, they were between William and Eva and the door blocking their escape.

Behind, Ronon's energy pistol spoke again.

"It's not dropping them," Laura yelled to him. It ought to. Even Eva knew that. The bears ought not be taking five or six shots from a P90 to slow them down. Surely not.

Ronon pivoted. "Cover. I'll clear the door." He came tearing back, energy pistol in hand, drawing a bead on one of the bears between William and the door. William had his little 9mm in his hand.

"Tell me you're not going to shoot bears with that," Eva said.

"It's better than nothing," William said.

One of the bears charged. It couldn't have been more than twenty feet away, and Eva stood stock still, remembering some old documentary she'd seen that said the worst thing you could do was run. The seconds elongated. She could see every detail of fur and snout, every tooth. Ronon fired again and again. Three times, four. Five. The bear fell, sliding across the ice carried by its momentum, claws raking almost at her feet.

Behind her, the clatter of automatic weapons fire stopped. Laura had fired the whole clip. And the bears were still coming, still six or eight of them.

At least the way to the doors was clear now. "Go!" Ronon yelled. "Get through to the other side!" He dropped back, dashing around Eva to cover Laura, who had to reload.

Eva ran for the door, William's back ahead of her. He was almost through, dodging around the carcass of one of the bears Ronon had shot. How could every moment take so long? Surely it was only seconds. She was almost there.

Laura shouted something she didn't understand, and in the next moment there was an explosion behind her, loud enough to make her ears ring, strong enough to make her lose her stride.

A grenade, some part of her thought. Laura was out of bullets so she threw a grenade. That ought to stop them…

There was a horrible rumble and cracking sound, blue suddenly splitting to bright gold.

"Oh crap," she heard Laura yell, and then with a single dreadful heave the ice dome above them collapsed.

For one moment Eva saw blue sky above, sunlight streaming down as the enormous chunks of ice fell away. She had presence of mind to put her arms over her head as the pieces fell, huge as appliances or small cars, tumbling her into darkness.

And then there was nothing.

There were voices. It seemed like she ought to recognize them, but she didn't. They were coming from so far away, from a place of pain that she retreated from. Her daughter? Maybe. It might be Desireé, heard through something heavy and muffling. A young woman's voice, swearing and crying, begging forgiveness. Desireé might do that. Though she didn't have anything in the world to blame herself for.

And that was worth coming back for, back from that dark, quiet place. Desireé mustn't worry. She mustn't blame herself.

She couldn't draw a full breath. Something was pressing down on her, the weight against her back, shoving her down on her right side, her left leg on fire. She wanted to say that it was ok. There was nothing to blame anybody for. But she couldn't draw breath for a single sound.

"Hang on, Eva! We're coming to get you!" A man's voice, a strong baritone with an English accent. William. Dr. William Lynn. And with that it came rushing back.

Snow against her face, ice digging into her… She must be trapped beneath the collapsed ceiling of the ice dome.

"Over to the left there. Lift." A bass, roughened by strain as though he were shouldering something heavy. Ronon.

Snow pattered down, small crystals falling around her, touching her face. Not entirely dark. Through the few inches she could see, there was a faint light, one stripe of gold impossibly far away. She couldn't even turn toward it, but it was there.

"Goddammit. Goddammit. Don't be dead." That was Laura, quick and desperate, the voice she'd taken for Desireé's. She'd thrown the grenade that dropped the ice cavern ceiling.

At that she tried to speak, to say that she wasn't dead, but all that came out was a whisper instead of a shout, a low moan.

"I heard something," William said. "I think I heard something."

"Don't stand there," Ronon said. "Careful! The blocks under it will shift."

"Eva! Can you hear us?" That was Laura again. The sound of ice moving, of something heavy being thrown.

Ronon was strong. He would be lifting big chunks of ice. He'd get to her if anybody could.

"Ro…" It was a little louder this time. The weight seemed less. She could draw a full breath, though it sent stabbing pains through her side. Broken ribs, she thought. But she could breathe.

"Take this one. That end." That was Ronon again, calm, unhurried, taking it apart like a puzzle.

"Ugh." William, trying to take the other end. Blocks shifted. Light poured down a shaft that opened, dazzling and bright.

"Eva?" More swearing. Laura sounded like her voice was choked with tears.

"I can see her!" William exclaimed triumphantly. "I can see the top of her head."

"Easy does it." Ronon. "Cadman, move that there."

"I'm here," she said, and this time it came out. Thready, but she could speak. The weight pinned her, no longer crushing. She could take a full breath.

"Thank you, God," Laura said. "She's not dead. Hang on. We've got to get this stuff off you."

"Ok." She could hear her own voice, feeble but there.

Another crash, Ronon throwing an ice block aside.

The light wavered. William had climbed up on a block, stripping off his gloves as he reached down to touch her, his fingers against the side of her neck. She smiled into his hand. He had warm skin, and she could feel every bit of roughness.

"Good pulse," he said. "Eva, can you talk to me?"

"Yes," she said. "Yes."

"Don't try to move her!" That was Laura, somewhere out of sight. "She may have spinal injuries."

The blocks were lighter now, Ronon and Laura still lifting.

"Can you feel your legs?" William asked.

"Yes. They hurt like hell."

"That's good." The lines at the corners of William's eyes crinkled as he smiled encouragingly. "Just hang in there. We're going to get you out and back to Atlantis in a jiffy."

"How?" Talking to him was distracting, just as he intended. Ronon and Laura were still moving ice.

William frowned. "Ronon is going to go get the jumper and…"

"Ronon…can't fly the jumper," she said. A weight lifted off her legs and she gasped.

"You leave the rescuing to us," William said.

The last piece. She could breathe, she could move her arms.

"Careful," Ronon said.

Laura knelt down beside her, her face pink with exertion. "My God, Eva. I'm so sorry. I didn't realize when I threw that grenade…"

"It's ok."

Ronon squatted between her and William. "Ok, let's have a look." His voice was calm, snow clumped on his beard. "I knew you'd be hanging in here. Can you move your legs?"

"Maybe," she said, and tried. Stabbing pains in the left one, but the right moved. She sucked in a breath and tried not to scream.

"Ok," Ronon said. "No spinal cord injury, no broken neck. Looks like you've got a busted leg here. I'd guess it's the left femur right above the knee."

His hands hurt like fury patting down her leg, feeling the wrongness, and it was all she could do not to yell. Eva bit down on her lip hard.

"Maybe some busted ribs. Not coughing blood and you seem to be breathing ok." Ronon gave her a lopsided grin. "You're a tough old bird. How are the arms?"

"Ok, I think…" She flexed her hands, surprised that they worked.

"I think that big block that was sitting across her legs took the full weight off her head," William said. "Ronon, how are we going to get the jumper down here? She's the only one who can fly it and we're out of range of Atlantis with the radios."

"We're going to go up and use the communicator in the jumper to call for backup," Ronon said. "Get Kusanagi to bring another jumper out here." He looked around. "There's probably a place down here flat enough to land." He looked down at Eva. "We'll have Keller out here in less than half an hour. So you just chill and it'll be good."

"I'm on it," Laura said, leaping to her feet. "William?"

"I'll come with you," he said. "If Ronon is staying here?"

"I'm staying," Ronon said. "Cadman, tell Control that we need a second jumper pilot to get our jumper back, and a full medical team."

"Got it." Laura and William took off, presumably to retrace their steps upwards through the base.

"Thanks," Eva said quietly. It hurt a lot.

"No problem," Ronon said. He put his hand to her throat, checking her pulse. "I've done this before."

"This?"

"Not exactly this." He was keeping her talking, keeping her alert. Eva knew that. "Got trapped in a collapsed building with Sheppard once. He had a pipe in his side, real bad bleeding." Ronon shrugged. "You just got to keep working at it, is all."

"Did you…dig out?"

"Nah. Carter dug in. One of those sucks to be us moments." He looked up toward the sky as if he expected to see the rescue jumper already. "No complaints. It worked." He took her hand. "How're you doing?"

"Hurts," Eva said.

"You busted that leg pretty good." Ronon nodded. "But not a pipe in your liver."

"Sheppard had a pipe in his liver?"

"Oh yeah." Ronon grinned. "Had Keller put transport sutures

in and then he went back after Teyla. I thought Keller was going to kill him herself."

Eva winced. Talking. Keep talking. The part of her that was professional applauded Ronon. He knew just how to do this. Keep them calm. Keep them talking.

"Didn't Carter mind? A guy with a pipe in his liver…"

Ronon shrugged. "Carter's ok." Ronon looked up at the sky again. There couldn't be anything there yet. The sky arched blue over the island, and Eva wondered how it had looked through barred windows.

"Hell of a place," Eva said.

Ronon nodded. "Yeah."

"The Count of Monte Cristo…"

"This place was a prison," Ronon said. "Marking the walls like that. It's how you measure time when you're afraid you'll forget it. Guys in isolation cells." He shrugged. "I guess the Ancients had prisons too."

"They…closed it down."

"That's what I figure." Ronon was still scanning the sky and cliffs above. "Who knows? They might have closed it down hundreds of years before the war. Would make sense why it wasn't in Atlantis' database if it had been closed for a long time. They sure didn't leave anything useful."

"Looks like," Eva said.

Ronon frowned. "I don't get the bears though. They didn't act right. They should have scattered when we started shooting, not rushed us. That's the way humans act, trained humans who have a place to guard."

"Guard bears," Eva said. It was hard to stay distracted from the pain.

"Maybe so." Ronon looked at her seriously. "Genetically engineered to guard this place."

"That's pretty creepy," Eva said.

There was a clatter, and Ronon jerked up, energy pistol drawn.

"We have a problem," William said.

"The explosion brought down the ice and snow over the doors," Laura said, her breath coming in gasps as though they'd run back down. "We're cut off from the jumper."

Ronon didn't swear. That was one of the things Eva had noticed about him. No matter what the pressure, he just didn't. Maybe the words didn't translate, or maybe it was more of a taboo and Ronon was too polite to use them. But he didn't swear. Even now. He looked at Laura with an expression that spoke louder than words.

"We can't get through the doors," William said. "There are thousands of pounds of ice and snow in front of it. I don't think the jumper is actually buried, because it was parked further away from the cliff wall, but there's no way we're going to get those doors open without heavy equipment." He looked at Laura. "And don't even say we could blow our way out. I have no idea how structurally sound the hangar bay is. We could bring the stonework down."

"I wasn't going to say it," Laura said quietly.

"What now?" William asked. "We've got to get Eva out of here soon."

Ronon glanced up at the cliffs as if trying to figure out another way to get to the jumper. It was seventy feet or more up to the plateau, and all of it nearly sheer rock coated with ice and snow. They had no climbing equipment. And Eva was willing to bet the Ancients hadn't left a pile of rope sitting around somewhere for thousands of years.

"They'll send a backup team eventually," Laura said.

"Eventually is the word," William replied. "We weren't going to do anything particularly hazardous and we weren't even off world. It's probably hours before anybody notices something's wrong, and we can't leave Eva lying in the snow with a broken leg for long. At the very least we're going to have to get her indoors and keep her warm."

"Oh good," Eva said. The idea of being moved didn't particularly appeal, especially not before Dr. Keller arrived with drugs.

Ronon frowned. "It's going to be hours."

"She might have broken ribs," Laura said. "We don't know if she's bleeding internally. I don't think we can afford to wait hours. We're not even due to check in for two more hours, and they're not going to worry until we're significantly overdue."

"Ok." Ronon squared his shoulders, looking at Eva. "We're going to have to move you. We need to get you off the ice and into somewhere we can keep warmer. It's easy to get hypothermia when you have a serious injury. Some of the environmental controls inside are working. Dr. Lynn, see if you can figure out how to turn up the heat in one of the barracks or living quarters. We'll move in there and wait it out. Carter will send a second team before long."

Laura had a distinctly skeptical look about the last. Eva wondered how long it would be. Two hours overdue? Four? That would be four to six hours from now at least. Probably they'd send a second jumper if they were out well past planetary nightfall.

"Ok," William said. "I'll see what I can do. How are we…?"

"I'm going to carry her," Ronon said. "Cadman, we need to tape up that leg as much as we can to keep it from shifting around when we move her."

It hurt, of course. And being carried in hurt worse, though it was good to at least get out of the wind. They went back to the lab with the working terminal on the theory that was the best chance of getting environmental controls working. It wasn't nearly as cold in there, probably not quite freezing, which was a big improvement from out on the ice.

Laura tried to make her comfortable in a corner, propped up with Laura's jacket for a pillow. "I'm so sorry," she said again. "Eva, I…"

"It was an accident," Eva said. "You didn't mean to."

"I know, but I should…"

"Yes, you should," Ronon said sharply. "And next time you will. So put it away. Not a priority."

"I've got the basic first aid kit," Laura said. "I could give you some painkillers, but you might be a little loopy."

"I'll take that," Eva said. "Give me a half dose. I don't want to be out cold." It might be comforting to just drift off and leave it in everyone else's hands, but somehow she didn't think it was going to be that simple. Something was nagging at her, as though an obvious solution was just out of reach. She closed her eyes and leaned her head back, waiting for it to take effect, feeling her pulse beating hard in her damaged leg. She felt like one gigantic bruise. But it was good to close her eyes a moment, listening to the voices of William, Laura and Ronon huddled over the terminal, William translating Ancient while Laura and Ronon tried to figure out the environmental controls.

It might have been that she dozed. Wishful thinking, to dream she was back in Atlantis, safe in the infirmary with Dr. Beckett in the background instead, talking to Marie Wu about some routine thing. She could hear their voices quite clearly. They were going over a chart. It was Dr. McKay's chart. She caught the name.

That was good then. She was safe in the infirmary, and somehow Dr. McKay was back. They'd rescued him.

Only there was a problem. He was in medical isolation, ranting and raving. That was Jennifer's nightmare, that they would get him back but not be able to restore him. That he'd be a Wraith forever, or stuck in some limbo between, half transformed. She'd told Eva so. It was nothing but Jennifer's fear.

There was a Wraith behind the glass of the first isolation chamber, screaming and clawing at the one way window, his face contorted, McKay and not McKay. Dr. Beckett was taking notes, talking quietly with his nurse. And in the second isolation chamber…

Eva sucked in a breath, cold horror running through her even as she knew it couldn't be true.

Desireé looked up from where she sat in the corner, her knees drawn up to her chest, her thin arms about them. Her black hair was faded to ashen white, her brown skin gone sickly green, but her eyes were the same. They met hers watchfully, seething with something as deep as the seas…

Eva jerked awake.

"…this is not about the environmental controls," William was saying. "I think there must have been some kind of weapons testing going on. I think it's quite possible that some of the material…"

"The other jumper!" Eva said.

Ronon and Laura turned to look at her.

"How are you doing?" Laura asked, coming over to kneel down beside her. Behind her the glass gleamed darkly, one way glass over two cells…

Distraction. "The other jumper," Eva said. "The wrecked one in the hangar. We didn't look inside it. It's quite possible that the communications equipment could be working, right?"

Ronon broke into a slow smile. "Could be," he said. "And if so, we can call Atlantis. Lynn, Cadman, go find out." They clattered out the door as Ronon came over and sat down beside her. He'd taken his heavy jacket off in favor of the heavily woven long sleeved tunic beneath it. "Good thinking," he said.

"I hope it works," Eva said.

Ronon looked at her sideways. "You know you're going to have to initialize it if it does. That's going to mean carrying you all the way up there again."

Eva nodded. "I know."

"Painkillers helping?"

"Some." There was no point in telling him that it gave her bad dreams. Their meaning was transparently obvious. Jennifer had been sharing her fears about Rodney's transformation, and she was visualizing Desireé like Teyla, disconcerted on some inner level by seeing Teyla as a Wraith Queen among them. "I think I'd rather get out of here sooner though. This place is creepy."

"Tell me about it," Ronon said.

CHAPTER FOURTEEN

Command Decisions

SAM LEANED back, letting the water run through her hair, her eyes closed. The *Hammond's* biggest drawback was two minute showers, and one of the nicest things about being in Atlantis was the constant supply of fresh water. The locker rooms were open around the clock for her crew, and there was always enough hot water for anyone to spend as long as they wanted in the shower. Which was a good thing. It was one of the places she did her best thinking.

Way back in her first year at the SGC, Daniel had turned it into a running joke. Every time there was a serious technical problem, you'd find Sam in the locker room with her head under the shower. Somehow wetting her head made her brain turn on. Very funny, but there was something to it. The sound of the water and the way the heat relaxed her did make her think better.

But it wasn't something she could do on the *Hammond*. Yes, nobody was going to yell at the captain for taking more than two minutes in the shower, but she could hardly make a rule and then abuse it. If the rule was fair you had to follow it, even if you thought you ought to be the exception, no matter what the price was. Jack had taught her that, and exactly how expensive it could be.

But there were always compromises. At least there were ways to obey the spirit if not the letter. The rule was about conserving water on the *Hammond*, where wasting potable water was very nearly a crime. Atlantis had no shortage of water. There was a whole ocean of it. And so if she wanted to spend half an hour in the shower in Atlantis, that was ok. At least it was forgivable, one amusing quirk of a well-liked captain. She had a few of those. She hoped they caused amusement, not resentment.

She leaned her head back, letting the water run down her hair. It was hard to keep it clean on the *Hammond*. Maybe she ought to cut it off again, but it had taken so long to grow. Eyes closed, she still half expected her old team to stick their heads in the locker room door, laughing at her. *"Still soaking your head, Carter? General Hammond said if you'd like to join us sometime today..."*

Instead it was the voice of a very hesitant airman. "Colonel Carter, ma'am?"

The Ancients had apparently believed in clear glass doors, and Airman Ayesha Salawi was looking at the ceiling, walls and floor with the visible discomfort of an Airman First Class who has been sent into the women's locker room to retrieve a colonel who isn't wearing clothes.

"Yes?"

"Dr. Zelenka sent me to get you. He said tell you that Teyla Emmagan has returned with the Wraith ship." Salawi seemed to think she was up there on the ceiling somewhere.

Sam turned the water off. "And Colonel Sheppard?"

"Colonel Sheppard is with her, and she says he's fine. But they need to talk to you about some important intelligence."

Sam let out a breath she hadn't realized she was holding. "Ok. I'm on my way." She reached for her towel. "Tell Dr. Zelenka I'll be up in five minutes."

John wasn't sure whose office it was. Theoretically Woolsey's, but Woolsey had been on Earth for the last month. Which made it his, temporarily. But while he'd been gone Sam had been using it, just as she had for the year before Woolsey arrived, even though actually it should have been Radek. The uncertainty seemed to be resolving itself by all four of them standing around, Sam with her back to the desk, Radek opposite her with his back to the door, his arms crossed over his chest, and John and Teyla at the other two points of the diamond.

Outside in the control room technicians kept sneaking glances. Some of them probably didn't know it was Teyla. For all they could see, he and Carter were meeting with a Wraith queen. He had to admit she was pretty scary looking, which possibly accounted for the way Radek was shifting from one foot to another while she explained. It did take a little getting used to.

Sam just listened.

"This is policy," Radek said at last. "I am not a policy guy, and I have no idea whether or not this retrovirus might hypothetically work. That is a question for the doctors, not for me."

"None of us know if it can work," Sam said.

"The issue is if we're going to work with Todd," John said. "Let's be clear on that. We don't know if this thing can work, and we don't know if he's on the up and up."

"I thought the issue was whether or not it is desirable for it to work," Teyla said. "If we do not want it to work, then we should not assist him further."

Radek shook his head, his glasses reflecting the overhead lights. "People fed upon and then what? Released to go make babies? So that they can be rounded up again later?"

"That is already the case," Teyla said. "Except that those who are rounded up do not return. And there are worlds of Wraith Worshippers as we know, humans who have traded the safety of some for the lives of others. If it were possible for them to trade only what is theirs to give, only their own life force…"

"And how would these things be decided?" Radek asked frowning. "Some would be prey and some would not be. It would come down to what side of a line you were born on."

"Maybe," Sam said. "Maybe not. There's too much we don't know." She took a deep breath. "But we do know that something like this worked in the Milky Way. The Jaffa were dependent on the Goa'uld for their longevity and health, because without the symbiotes they carried they would cease to be what they were. But once Tretonin, a chemical substitute, was synthesized they no longer needed to be subject peoples. It was, ultimately, a medical solution." She looked at John. "The Jaffa wouldn't have given up being who they were to be rid of the Goa'uld. People won't do that. That was the problem we had with the previous retrovirus."

"That, and it did not work," Radek pointed out.

"And that," Sam said.

"We do not know if this will work either," Teyla said.

"And the only way to find out is to trust Todd." Radek spread his hands. "I cannot say I am enthusiastic about this plan."

Sam was looking at him, and John realized with an ugly lurch in the middle that it was really his call. He was the commander of Atlantis. Sam wasn't going to step on him here. It was going to come down to him.

"Let's put it to the doctors," John said. "See what Beckett and Keller think. If they think it's plausible, let's see where this goes. We're a long way from having a working inoculation. And in the meantime we need Todd as an ally against Queen Death, particularly if Teyla thinks she can undermine the alliance and get Rodney back."

There was a hesitant knock at the door, and John and Sam both said, "Come," at the same time.

Airman Salawi stuck her head in. "Sirs, Banks said to tell you that Ronon has just missed his check in."

John frowned. "Check in?"

"Ronon took a team to investigate some Ancient ruins on one of the islands in the large archipelago," Sam said. She glanced at her watch and winced. "That was eight hours ago."

"Missing check in isn't Ronon," John said.

"He must be in trouble," Teyla agreed.

"I cannot imagine what," Radek said. "He is right here on this planet. There is nothing arriving that we would not detect with the city's sensors."

"Unless there were something already here," Sam said. "Ancient installations…"

"I'll take a jumper to check it out," John said. "Who's he got with him?"

"Cadman," Sam said. "The new archaeologist, Dr. Lynn, and Dr. Robinson went to fly the jumper."

John grimaced. Cadman was a good choice, but Lynn was new to everything and Robinson could fly the jumper on a good day, but had no combat skills at all. "Ok," he said. "Teyla, you talk to Jennifer and Carson and fill them in. I'll be back in a few."

Night was coming swiftly over the sea, the lights of Atlantis shining out into the darkness from every tower. For a change it wasn't snowing, though the instruments showed it was getting bitterly cold, eight degrees Fahrenheit and dropping. A couple of time zones westward the sun hadn't set, and John flew into daylight as he made periodic radio calls. "Ronon? Come in, Ronon."

Nothing. Of course it had looked like whatever was left of this Ancient installation might be underground, and if they were inside they might not be getting radio signals. John frowned. That was the most likely explanation. And yet he had a funny feeling about it. In his experience, things were rarely easy.

"Ronon, come in." There was the island, and John rolled the jumper in a neat maneuver to lose altitude, dropping down for a close air pass. The setting sun glared in his eyes and then he dropped beneath it, the shadow of the planet's curvature plunging him into shade.

There was the other jumper parked neatly on the plateau over the sea, alone in the midst of a field of snow.

"Ronon, come in." Something was wrong. He should be answering the radio unless he was far underground, but for the life of him John couldn't see any door or entrance to anything. "Ronon, please respond."

"Colonel Sheppard?" Captain Cadman's voice was full of utter disbelief.

"Cadman? What's going on?" John asked, coming around for a second pass.

"Is that you?"

"Yes, it's me." John shook his head. "Cadman, where are you?"

"We've had some trouble, sir," Cadman said. "We're underground and our radios won't reach you."

"I'm hearing you loud and clear."

"We're using the comm system of a wrecked puddle jumper," Cadman said. "It's a long story. But Dr. Robinson is injured, and an avalanche has blocked the entrance to the Ancient hangar that we came in."

"Ok," John digested that for a second. "Is Ronon there with you?"

"Yes. Let me put him on." There was a momentary silence.

"Ronon?"

"Hey Sheppard." Ronon sounded relieved. "Thought you were captured."

"Yeah well, Teyla rescued me." John scrubbed his hand through his hair. "Cadman says you're stuck."

"We're stuck," Ronon confirmed. "Robinson needs medical attention as soon as possible. And there's no way we're getting out that door."

"All right. Hang in there," John said. "Back with you in a minute." He switched frequencies, calling Atlantis. "Atlantis, this is Sheppard. Put Colonel Carter on if you would."

She must have been standing right there, because it was only a second before Sam came on. "What's the problem, John?"

He sketched it for her quickly, ending with, "So is the *Hammond* up to atmospheric flight and are the Asgard beams working?"

"They are," Sam said. "And we can about manage atmospheric flight. I don't think the hull is up to hard vacuum at this point, but we should be good for a little low altitude cruise to come get our guys. Tell them I'll be there in fifteen minutes."

It was twelve and a half, actually. John stayed on station, talking with Ronon and Cadman, until the *Hammond* arrived. At that point it was the work of a moment to beam them straight to the *Hammond's* infirmary.

"Off into the sunset," John said, turning the puddle jumper for home and following the *Hammond* in, Atlantis glowing ahead of them like a star resting on the sea.

Radek folded his hands, casting a quick look at William, who had at last subsided into silence. "I agree that the Ancient ruins are interesting," he said.

John nodded. "Yeah, but is that really a priority right now? With everything we've got going on?" He looked around at Ronon and William. "You guys found some stuff, and it's great if there's more down there, but is that really where we need to focus our best efforts right now?"

"It appears that this was once an Ancient prison, and perhaps also a weapons testing laboratory," William put in. "Some of the database seems functional, beyond the environmental systems. It's quite possible that we could retrieve information on the research that was undertaken here, and that some of it could be germane. I think we need to go back."

Carter winced. "You said that the entire entrance was blocked. That's going to require a lot of work with heavy equipment and a lot of time to dig back in. And a lot of expertise. A squad of engineers at least and somebody with the ATA gene to activate things."

"Yes, well," William began.

John shook his head. "I appreciate that it's interesting. And that it might be worthwhile. But we've got a lot on our plates right now. We can't pull people off the *Hammond's* repairs or off other critical functions. In a couple of weeks, when Kusanagi's team is free, then we'll think about it."

"It is really Dr. Kusanagi you need," Radek put in. "She has the ATA gene naturally expressed, and she is a fine engineer. I would recommend Dr. Kusanagi and the Marine combat engineers, and perhaps Captain Cadman, when the time is appropriate. But Miko is occupied with the *Hammond*, which I was given to understand is the first priority."

"It is the top priority," John said. "The *Hammond* is pretty much our only defense right now. Getting all systems fully restored is critical." He glanced around the table. "So we'll talk about the Ancient installation next week." He looked down at his laptop as if he had a to do list there. Which, Radek thought, he probably did. He knew what was coming and John making it so casual, in the midst of a biweekly meeting, made it seem less frightening and bizarre. And it was bizarre. "Next up, Todd."

Ronon shifted in his seat, not looking at Teyla who sat across from him.

"Todd wants a deal," John said. "Let's talk about it."

Carson leaned forward, his blue eyes grave. "First, let me say that I am skeptical that this idea of his can work without serious side effects. He's taking the track of strengthening the human victim during the feeding by tinkering with the makeup of the Wraith enzyme that is injected at the inception of the feeding process. We've seen with Lt. Ford what the effects of a mega dose of the enzyme are. And we've seen how drastic the physical and psychological changes are as a result. It might be possible for humans to survive the feeding, but the cost to them would be enormous."

"You're saying this would turn them all into Ford?" John asked.

"It very well might," Carson said solemnly.

Jennifer cleared her throat. "I don't think that's necessarily true."

John looked at her, his eyebrows rising. "Yes?"

"That's one of the possibilities," Jennifer said, biting her lower lip. "But certainly not the only one. I think it's a pitfall we should be aware of. But there are less drastic modifications that could be made."

"Not that wouldn't have some effect on the human in question," Carson said sharply, and Radek wondered if he were not thinking of the disastrous side effects of the Hoffan retrovirus, rather than strictly speaking the fate of Lt. Ford.

Carter put her head to the side keenly. "Do we actually know what side effects we're talking about when we're not discussing an exact formulation? Isn't this all hypothetical at this point?"

"Yes," Jennifer said, and Carson sighed but did not contradict her.

"Then how can we decide whether or not the side effects are too severe if we don't yet know what they are?" Carter asked. "Isn't that a question for on down the line?"

John sat up straight in his chair. "Look, we don't know if this will work, and we don't know what the side effects might be. The question is whether or not we find out. What's the harm in getting some more information before we make the decision?"

Ronon stirred, uncoiling like a sleepy cat, but there was nothing lazy in his movements. "That's not the question. The question is whether we work with the Wraith." He looked around the table. "How many times now have we decided we're going to make some deal with the Wraith? And every single time we've gotten screwed. Michael was a great idea. And then there was this hive we were going to ally with. And then there were Todd's deals. The question is how many times we're going to keep beating our head into the same wall before we get smart." His eyes met John's. "They're Wraith. We can't trust them. Every time we do, people die."

Carson blanched.

Radek cleared his throat with a quick glance at Ronon. "I am not sure I am comfortable with this either. Ronon has a point that this has not worked well in the past. Over and over we have been sold on a medical solution, but it does not work or it makes things worse." He thought he saw Ronon relax a tad. He had not expected anyone to back him up. He should have known better with Radek.

Teyla said nothing, just looked from one to another with her golden eyes.

"And if we don't do this?" Jennifer asked. "If we just let this opportunity pass by? What does that get us? We need to find out if this is possible. Just because we have a retrovirus doesn't mean we have to use it."

Radek sighed. "That is the Oppenheimer argument. We will

develop a nuclear bomb to see if we can. The problem is that once you have developed something you no longer have control of it. Once it exists it will be used. It will not be your decision, nor Colonel Sheppard's. It will be the decision of the Air Force or the IOA, and your opinions will no longer carry any weight. There are times it is best to leave the genie in the bottle."

"The genie doesn't stay in the bottle once anyone knows it's there," Carter said. "A number of governments were working along parallel lines toward the bomb. It was just a question of who got it first. When something is possible, someone will figure out a way to do it. And if you're lucky it's you before it's someone else." She looked at Radek. "Would you rather it had been Hitler who got there first? Or Stalin?"

John cleared his throat. "That's a point. Todd knows this is possible."

"Thinks it is possible," Carson corrected.

"Thinks it's possible," John agreed. "He may be right. If he is, and if this thing is viable, we're better off having a piece of it than having no idea what Todd's up to or how far this thing has gone. We can't prevent him from doing this work without us."

"We could kill him," Ronon said. "Say we're going to do the deal, get in close, and don't make a mistake."

"He is our ally," Teyla snapped.

"He's a Wraith," Ronon said. "In case you're forgetting."

"I remember it well," Teyla said, leaning forward in her chair. "But he has come to us in good faith. And you suggest we repay that with treachery. I am surprised you suggest something so dishonorable."

"People!" John cut off Ronon's reply, and he subsided into his chair in silence. "Right now we need Todd. We need the intelligence, and we need the shot at finding McKay. Assassinating Todd is not on the agenda."

"Put it on there for next week," Ronon growled.

John ignored it manfully, Radek thought. Instead he looked at Jennifer. "Dr. Keller, do you think this is worth pursuing? It's you he's asking for."

"I do," Jennifer said, though her face was taut and pale. "I'm willing to return to Todd's hive ship as he asked and see if this line of research is promising."

"And give the Wraith one more hostage," Ronon said under his breath.

"I am perfectly capable of looking after Dr. Keller," Teyla said pointedly.

"Ok," John said. He didn't look away from Jennifer. "It's your mission and your call. Take a look at his research and see what you think. And we'll go from there." He glanced at Carson. "You'll stay here. We need you if Dr. Keller is gone, and with your arm messed up, you're still out of the field."

Carson sighed. "If that's how it is," he said.

"It is our best chance," Teyla said.

"I hope we do not regret this," Radek said.

CHAPTER FIFTEEN

Quicksilver

THEY had moved the ZPM from the lab to the hyperdrive compartment, were slowly rewinding the cables that would knit it into the hive's systems. Rodney watched as Stone and Nightheart brought another cable into play, looking from them to the power displays and back again. Everything was working as it should, the lights steady blue, the indicators that marked the new cables fading from the first white heat of the connection as the load evened out. There was only so much he could do to slow down the work, at least not without arousing suspicion, though it made him twitch to see how far they'd come already. It was a good thing that Ember had always urged caution; Rodney merely let himself be persuaded more often, or led them further down paths he knew would be dead ends. If —when— he got out of this, he would know more about hive ships than any other human — more even than Jennifer, and she'd almost become one.

He blinked at that, blindsided by memory. Jennifer. He could almost see her face, her dark blonde hair, the way her mouth tightened as she considered a problem — her eyes wide with fear as the hive seed engulfed her. Not the ideal frame, he knew that now: better a male, both for size and bone mass, and to preserve the breeding stock. The collision of memories, real and false, Rodney's and Quicksilver's, rocked him back on his heels, and he put out a hand to steady himself.

Quicksilver? That was Salt, his tone uncertain, and Ember came quickly to him.

Are you all right?

Fine. Rodney managed a snarl, felt concern flicker through Ember's mind.

When did you last feed?

The question made his stomach roil, threatening dry heaves that would betray him. His feeding hand ached sharply, and he closed his fingers tight, waving the question away with his free hand. Ember's frown deepened.

You must not —

The door of the lab slid open, interrupting him, and Rodney bared his teeth again in a snarl that he didn't feel. The Old One came all the way into the lab — a blade among clevermen, unescorted, a sight to raise hackles as well as to inspire fear. Rodney straightened his spine. He was Quicksilver, brother of Dust, chief of the queen's clevermen.

Well? He put all the impatience he could muster into the thought, and the Old One smiled.

Our queen wishes a report on your progress.

It would go faster if I weren't being interrupted, Rodney said.

The Old One tipped his head to one side. *Are you well?*

I'm fine. Rodney thought his snarl was more convincing this time. *And, as you see, we progress. It's not easy to mate an Ancient device to our own technology.*

No, the Old One said. *They did not intend for anything of theirs to be of use to others.*

Well, not to us, Rodney said. If he could lose himself in the problem, that was his best defense. *There must be some humans native to this galaxy who have the gene that lets them use it — it's much more common in the Milky Way —*

Not a gift they wished to share, the Old One said. *Perhaps it did not go so well, with those other humans.*

I don't know, Rodney began. Focus on the problem… He was aware, suddenly, of the Old One's golden eyes fixed on him, of the Old One himself, his face smoother, less harshly molded than the other blades and clevermen. Older, certainly, you could see the age in him, in the thinning hair, but different, too, as though he'd been made to a different pattern — He felt the Old One's mind on his then, pressing gently, subtly, drew his false memories around him like a shield: Quicksilver, brother of Dust.

My lord, Ember said, and the pressure vanished.

The Old One turned, lips parting in a snarl. *You neglect your responsibilities, cleverman. Quicksilver hungers.*

Ember dipped his head, and Rodney said, *I'm busy. I'll feed later.*

The Old One shook his head, his attention still on Ember. *The queen charged you with his care. I am displeased.*

I am sorry, Ember said, though the tone of his mind suggested otherwise. *The queen has also bade us hasten the work at hand.*

And I am not a fruit-fed child, to be managed by him, Rodney said. *I have work to do.*

The Old One looked back at him, expressionless, the touch of his mind barely a whisper. "Nonetheless. It has been the queen's thought for some little time that you, Quicksilver, are not as well cared for as she would wish. And Guide has made it known that he needs his chief cleverman returned to him someday.*

No, Rodney said. Ember hissed softly, and the Old One tipped his head again.

Do you defy our queen?

I've spent ages getting him used to my methods, Rodney said, groping for an excuse. If he lost Ember— He killed that thought, hurried on, hoping the Old One had not seen his fear. *Him and his men. I don't want to go through that all over again. It's a waste of time.*

It is the queen's will, the Old One said.

But— Rodney bit off the rest of the thought, seeing Ember bow his head.

As the queen wishes, Ember said. His tone was tightly controlled, showing no more than the barest respect. *I and my men will return to Just Fortune. At once.*

And what am I to do for assistants? Rodney demanded. He was shaking, clenched his fists on the nearest console, and tried to project anger rather than the terror that seized him.

Nighthaze will assist you, the Old One said. *Perhaps he will make better progress.*

I doubt it, Rodney snapped. *I told you, I've just got them trained—*

The queen commands, the Old One said, and Rodney bit back the rest of what he would have said. He could feel again the touch of the Old One's mind, the subtle memory of Death in her glory, beautiful and compelling and now completely terrifying.

Quicksilver, Ember said.

Rodney gasped and turned to see the other man bowing deeply.

It has been an honor to work with you. Behind him, the rest of his men were bowing with equal respect, the murmur of their minds startling.

And I am honored to have worked with you, Rodney said. It occurred to him that there were others he needed to say that to as well, and pushed the thought aside.

One by one, the clevermen filed from the lab, men whose minds he'd come to recognize, whose strengths and weaknesses he knew too well: Salt, Stone, Whiskey, Crossroads, Ember last of all. Ember paused beside him, his body blocking the Old One's gaze for an instant, as he drew his off hand across Rodney's wrist. Words trailed with the touch, more secret than a whisper.

Forgive me, he said, and then was gone.

Rodney forced himself to glare at the Old One. *You have taken more than half my men! How am I supposed to finish this without them? And with our queen urging haste.*

I will send Nighthaze to you, the Old One said. *But I am sure you will manage.*

Oh, yes, Rodney said. *I'm sure I will.*

The Old One showed teeth in something that was almost a smile, and turned away. Rodney watched the lab's door slide shut behind him, tightened every muscle in his body to keep from shaking. He was alone. Ember — well, he might be a Wraith, but at least they were on the same side, more or less, and that counted. That counted a lot, when there wasn't anybody else. Sheppard will come, he told himself. They'll come for me, the team will, and all I have to do is stay alive…

He was aware, abruptly, of the last three clevermen standing silent and uneasy in their corners, turned on them with a snarl. *Well? What are you waiting for? We'll have to work three times as hard to make up for that piece of folly—* He only hoped they could not feel the stark terror behind the words.

CHAPTER SIXTEEN

Home Truths

RONON got up last, following Radek toward the door. He didn't look around.

Crap, John thought. But what he said was, "Ronon."

Ronon stopped, letting Radek leave ahead of him. John saw his shoulders square before he turned back. "Yeah?"

"You got a problem?" John asked quietly.

"Yeah." Ronon met his eyes solidly. "I do. I think you've stopped making good decisions about this."

"We've been over every angle," John said. "You've said your piece." He sat down on the edge of the conference table. It might be a good idea to make this look a little more casual.

"Yeah." Ronon nodded. "And you're wrong. You're talking about trusting the Wraith. You're talking about helping the Wraith!"

"That's not…" John began.

Ronon lifted his chin. "It is, and you know it. It's about making some kind of treaty with them instead of killing them all. It's about saying it's ok for them to keep on feeding on people."

John shifted on the table. His sidearm was digging into his leg. "Ronon, we don't have a way to kill all the Wraith."

"You're not looking for one, are you? We ought to be. We ought to be looking for a way to get rid of them forever. That's the only answer in the end. It's them or us." Ronon's eyes were level. "I used to be sure whose side you're on."

That felt like a body blow. But he'd taken lots of those. John's voice didn't even change. "And now you're not sure."

"I think this thing with Teyla is screwing up your judgment," Ronon said. "You're not thinking straight and you're making bad decisions." Ronon leaned back against the wall, almost too casually, as though he were trying not to make it a fight. He hesitated, lowering his voice. "You do that, Sheppard. You know that. You get too emotionally involved and you start making mistakes. I'm saying it as a friend. That's why I didn't say this in the meeting. You know you do it, and you know it's a problem."

John didn't say anything. He didn't have any wind.

"This thing with Teyla's messing up your mind, man. Pull the plug on this operation, get her back to normal, and take a deep breath. When Teyla's herself again it will all look different."

"Teyla's herself right now," John said quietly.

Ronon shook his head. "It's like a deep cover op. Sometimes they turn, sometimes they get confused."

"Teyla's not confused," John said sharply. "This is Teyla. She always has the telepathy."

"Yeah." Ronon straightened up. "And that hasn't always worked out. Remember the time the Wraith queen took over her body and she didn't even remember anything she did? She wrecked half the installation and kicked the crap out of me. How do you know this is Teyla? The things she's saying aren't normal, Sheppard. They're Wraith. They're not people."

Sometimes it hurts enough that you hit back, even if you're not going to. "Are you sure you're not just picking a fight with Keller?"

Ronon's jaw tightened. "Yeah."

"Listen," John got up from the table, not moving too fast. "The decision's made. If you're going to be the team leader, you've got to get with the program. And that means following orders and doing your best. If you can't do that, tell me now. Because if you can't, I need you off the team and somebody there who can."

Ronon's voice was very controlled, which was probably worse than if he'd been yelling. "I know how to follow orders, Sheppard."

"Then do it," John said, and very deliberately turned his back to pick up his laptop, tensed for the blow.

There wasn't one. Just the sound of Ronon's feet walking away.

John walked down the narrow corridor aboard the *Hammond*, an airman flattening himself against the wall to let him pass. John acknowledged the courtesy offhandedly and knocked on the door. This day was going from bad to worse, and right now he didn't think he could stand another conversation with Jennifer and Carson about the retrovirus, or for that matter with anybody about the retrovirus.

"Come." Sam was sitting at her desk in the light of the desk lamp, her hair half falling out of the French braid at the back of her neck. She looked up, startled.

"Sorry. Is it too late?" John asked. It was evening, but he'd hoped for one friendly conversation today and Teyla was too perceptive. She'd ask about Ronon, and he'd tell her. And then she'd feel like it was her fault. Or worse, she'd be furious and go start something with Ronon. Teyla had a temper.

"No. Come on in. Shut the door." Sam turned away from her desk. She had an mp3 player going, little speakers belting out the end of Madonna's *Crazy For You*.

John gave the door a shove. "Bubblegum pop," he said. "Not quite what I expected."

"Hey, it's a vice," Sam said. "I'd offer you a chair but I don't have room in here for two. So pull up a corner of bed."

John sat down on the end of the bed as the song changed, feeling vaguely weird about it, but this was Carter.

"I've got some *Grateful Dead* on here too," she said, swiveling the chair around to face him.

"*Touch of Grey*," John said, recognizing the opening bars. "That's more like it." He was starting to get a headache and pinched the bridge of his nose. "Listen, I wanted to talk to you about something before I left."

Her smile faded. "You're not going anywhere, John."

"I'm going with Teyla and Keller to meet Todd," he said.

Sam shook her head. "No, you're not." She leaned forward, her elbows on her knees. "You're in command in Atlantis, John. You can't just leave."

"Look, Teyla and Keller are going into this thing…"

She cut him off. "Yes. And that's their job. Being here, running Atlantis, is yours."

"You're here."

"The *Hammond* is my job," she said. "Atlantis is yours." Sam shook her head, but her eyes were kind. "You're not company grade anymore. You're not a captain who's supposed to run around shooting bad guys. You're a lieutenant colonel, and you're in charge of everything that happens in this city. Safeguarding Atlantis is your job, and that means being here and making the big decisions, not going off for two weeks on a mission where nobody can reach you." Sam's mouth quirked in a sideways smile. "I know that's a rough transition. The first time we walked through that gate on a mission without Jack after he was promoted I thought he was going to come running and screaming up the ramp after us. But he didn't. That wasn't his job anymore."

"If Todd double-crosses," John began.

"If you think he's not on the up and up, you've got to call it off," Sam said. "And if he is, then Jennifer and Teyla don't need you." Her eyes were very blue and met his firmly. "This is her job, John. It's her mission, not yours. You've got to let her take her knocks and learn to live with that, or call it off with her. That's the price of a relationship with a comrade in arms. And for a lot of people it's too high."

John swallowed, seeing again in his mind's eye the cold night sky over the desert, the Milky Way like a ribbon of light. "It's real high," he said quietly.

"I know." Her eyes didn't evade his. "You're the only person who can decide if it's worth it to you. But you have to let her go. Teyla's a grown woman. She's smart, competent, talented, the whole package. And she's the one who can do this. You can't hold her back because you want to take care of her, and you can't tag along to hold her hand. You've got to trust her."

"I do trust her," he said. "More than anybody." John looked down at his hands, at Carter's email open on her computer. "Teyla's level headed and she's tough. She doesn't wander off like McKay or get fixated like Ronon. She's always exactly where she's supposed to be, doing the thing she's supposed to be doing."

"And if it weren't Teyla you'd wish her Godspeed," Sam said thoughtfully. "There's no regulation against it because she's a civilian contractor. But that's what the rules are for, John. Because emotions get complicated."

"They get complicated whether or not you do anything about them," John said. Desert sky spreading from horizon to horizon, a cold night wind blowing.

Sam snorted. "Tell me about it."

John took a deep breath, lifted his head. "You've seen my record, right?"

She didn't look away. "Yes, John. I've seen it. When I was appointed CO in Atlantis."

He swallowed hard. "Well."

Sam glanced quickly at the speakers, still blaring the *Grateful Dead* loud enough to cover conversation. "For what it's worth, I'd have gone after him too. Not that it means anything."

"It does," John said. His mouth was dry.

"Sometimes you lose," Sam said. "You do the best you can, and you lose people anyhow." She glanced over at the pictures held to the wall over the desk with magnets. "You know that. It takes a certain kind of fool to raise the stakes when you don't have a very good hand." The wrinkles at the corners of her eyes deepened as she smiled. "But sometimes you win the jackpot."

"Yeah," John said ruefully. "A certain kind of fool."

"If you're not going to fold, you have to learn to live with it," she said. "It's one of those compromises with life."

"Like the anti frat rules," John said.

"Yeah." Sam pursed her lips. "Like that. They're there to protect women, every woman in the service down to Airman Salawi. They're there to keep people from abusing authority, because you can't give officers unlimited power without checks on it. When you break a rule like that, it's bad for every woman in the service. You can tell yourself that this situation's different and that you're special, but you know it's wrong. It's still wrong." She looked at him and shrugged. "Unlike some other regs that are just plain stupid. Just in case you didn't know I thought that."

"I kind of figured," John said. He swallowed hard again. "You know Mel Hocken is a good friend of mine from way back…"

"Don't tell me anything I don't want to hear," Sam said, straightening up in her chair. "I'm her CO while Caldwell has her flight attached to the *Hammond*, and I don't want to hear anything I can't say under oath."

"Got it," John said.

"I don't ask, and they don't tell. If I never heard it spelled out, it's not perjury to say I don't know," Sam said.

"I won't put you in that position." John nodded. "I get that. Believe me, there have been plenty of things around here I sure don't know anything about. I don't ask either."

Sam pushed her chair back and put her feet up on the edge of the bed. "Teyla will be fine," she said. "I've got a lot of respect for her. And she can handle Todd better than anybody else. Teyla and Keller will do this, and we'll find out if this idea even works. If it doesn't, there's no point in going through all the convolutions."

"Right," John said. "No point in borrowing trouble."

"That's what I always say," Sam said.

Jennifer watched Teyla where she stood at the controls of the Wraith cruiser, trying not to distract her from whatever course adjustments she was making. Her head was back, eyes closed, hair falling like black silk to her waist. The way her face was tilted to the ceiling, absolutely serene, hands outstretched on the control grips in front of her, she looked like a statue.

Jennifer shifted on the control room's only chair, wishing a little of that peace would rub off on her. It was perversely always easier for her to find it in the middle of a crisis than when all she could do was sit around and wait. It didn't help that Teyla was lost in concentration flying the ship and not talking.

She felt it as the ship changed course, Teyla shifting her weight as it did, maybe in reaction to the ship's motion or maybe as encouragement. The curtain of her hair swayed gently from side to side as if she really was bending her head in prayer, as if she was moved by the spirit Jennifer had never felt, even when she'd wanted to. She'd thought that medicine was going to be that for her, a calling, a vocation, and in a lot of ways it was, but she still wished that something would transcend all, would make it all fall into place for her. She'd thought maybe she'd find that with Rodney…

"We have arrived," Teyla said, her eyes opening at last, her shoulders relaxing as she stepped away from the controls.

Jennifer nodded and stood, shouldering her bag. "Well," she said. "What now?"

Teyla turned to the wall, and it shifted as Jennifer watched, forming a door that parted before Teyla like veils of flesh drawing back. "Now we pay a visit to my hive."

Guide met them himself, alone. He could have come before her guarded by drones and loyal blades, but there was little point in that. He suspected no treachery from Teyla Emmagan, and suspected that a gesture of trust would make her soften to him. He told himself that it was not that any part of his mind flinched at the thought of coming armed against his queen.

When the walls of the ship parted he was glad of his decision. Her mind leapt for his and tightened without a word, as clear a threat as any weapon, or perhaps just a reminder of the natural order of things, as unnatural as the present situation was. He inclined his head as if she were what she pretended to be, the barest reverence possible in courtesy.

"My queen," he said, and he could feel her flash of pleasure at the words. For a moment it was hard not to think of her as an adolescent girl-child who has gotten away with playing at queen, commanding her mother's drones. Then she strode forward, promise and threat in her every move, and it was impossible to imagine her a child.

"I am pleased to see my consort again," she said, a hint of amusement in the touch of her mind, although there was none in her words. He nodded and shifted his gaze to Dr. Keller, hesitating halfway down the ramp, clutching the strap of an oversized her pack. This one he would have to handle more carefully if he was not going to frighten her into uselessness.

"Dr. Keller," he said. "Come, we have work to do." He extended his off hand to her when she seemed reluctant to descend the ramp. "I will escort you."

*If you hurt her — * Teyla began, giving him a warning look. He met her eyes with a wry shrug.

What would it serve? I am in need of a biological scientist, not an easy meal.

You would not find it easy, Teyla said, and her mental voice was sharp enough that again he thought Steelflower was well-named.

The threat lingered as he kept his hand extended, and sharpened as Keller laid her fingertips gingerly on his. He couldn't tell if her expression was fear or the fascination of a prey animal touching a predator's claws. It was so hard to tell with humans.

"I'm glad you asked me to come," Keller said, letting him help her down the ramp, although her fingers were tense against his. "That you … well, that you trusted me enough, after last time. I really am sorry that didn't work out."

Guide inclined his head, acknowledging the apology without pausing to question what it meant for her to offer or for him to accept. "Perhaps we can learn from past mistakes. Come," he said, releasing her hand as she reached the bottom of the ramp, "let me show you."

CHAPTER SEVENTEEN

Challenger

THE INFIRMARY was quiet and empty except for Eva Robinson, who was sitting up in the near bed with her leg in a cast propped up on two pillows, her laptop across her middle as Colonel Sheppard came in and looked around, his hands in the pockets of his black BDUs. Eva closed *Plants vs. Zombies* quickly. If she couldn't maintain the professional demeanor of make-up and nice looking clothes while stuck in the infirmary, at least she could pretend she was working. "If you're looking for Dr. Beckett, he's in the back doing an MRI on Lance Corporal Hernandez," she said helpfully.

Sheppard came over and perched on the visitor's stool beside her bed. "What happened to Hernandez?"

"He slipped on the ice and fell down the outside metal staircase. Laura…Captain Cadman said he had to have an MRI to make sure he didn't have a concussion since he's got a big lump on his head." She closed her laptop. "I expect Dr. Beckett won't be too long."

"Actually, I was looking for you," he said.

Eva felt her eyebrows rise. "Why?'

Sheppard's hazel eyes were steady. "To see how you are," he said. "You got injured in the field, a pretty nasty break from what Sam's medical officer said, and you still did what you needed to do to complete the mission. I came to see how you were getting along."

"Oh," Eva said. His team, his responsibility. She supposed that made her his people. "I'm doing ok. Dr. Beckett said he'll let me out of here on crutches tomorrow. I'll be in this cast for six weeks, and then he'll take that off and put on a removable brace for another four weeks."

Sheppard shifted on the stool, getting comfortable. "Ever break a bone before?"

"I broke my arm falling off my bike when I was a kid," Eva said. "I don't remember it being this much of a pain, though."

"They say kids heal quicker too," Sheppard said.

"At least I don't have a double compound fracture like Major Lorne," Eva said. She looked down at her cast with some satisfaction. "This one's just a plain old broken leg."

"Yeah, Lorne's still off that leg for another eight weeks," Sheppard said. "And then he's got a month or two of PT before he's on active duty."

"Wouldn't it make sense to send somebody home when they're going to be out for four or five months?" Eva asked.

Sheppard grinned. "Do you want to go home?"

"No." Eva glanced down at her laptop quickly. "Besides, my job's mostly talk. As soon as I can get around on crutches I can get back to work."

"And you'd never get back." Sheppard shrugged. "We only send home the people we can't safely treat here. Right now we can only send people home on the *Daedalus* or the *Hammond*, and so we just evacuate serious injuries. *Daedalus* took Sam's people who had third degree burns. We're not equipped as a burn center. We sent Conrad because he needed a second surgery on his intestinal tract, and that's out of Carson's league. And we can only send them when they're stable. Anybody fragile stays here, rather than six days down to the first Milky Way gate on *Daedalus*. Then they go through to the SGC, and from there to the Air Force Academy hospital."

"I'm glad not to do all that," Eva said.

"No point in it," Sheppard said, propping his foot up on the bottom of the bed rail. "You'll be up and around and back to work, like you said. It's driving Lorne crazy to be stuck behind a desk for months, but there's plenty for him to do, especially with Woolsey gone."

"I'll bet," Eva said. Sheppard didn't strike her as an administrator, though; from what she'd seen his paperwork was unremarkable. Still, there was a huge amount of it to run the city, and if the redoubtable Lorne could take on some of it, no doubt it would be a help. "Do you think Mr. Woolsey is going to come back?"

She didn't really expect an answer, but Sheppard leaned back as though considering thoughtfully. "I don't know," he said. "It depends on a lot. On how pissed the IOA is about Atlantis leaving Earth. On how high O'Neill's cred is with the President. On a bunch of stuff we don't even know about."

"And if it isn't him, will it be you?" She couldn't help but ask, inappropriate as the question no doubt was. After all, this was just for her curiosity. Well, and to satisfy her anxiety about what would happen next.

To her surprise Sheppard grinned. "Not on your life! I already turned it down once. I asked to be taken off the final list before Sam was offered the job."

"You did?"

He nodded, ducking his head and adjusting his earpiece over his ear. "I'm not cut out for that. I've filled in before, after we lost Dr. Weir. And I'm fine with that, if I have to do it." Sheppard shook his head. "But I'm not a politician. And that's what about half of the job is. I'm no good at that, and just smart enough to know it." He grinned again, a surprisingly candid expression. "I'll leave that to Sam and O'Neill and Woolsey and Teyla. Just tell me what to shoot, and I'm good."

Eva couldn't help but smile back. There was something about Sheppard that left you with confidence in him, even when he was telling you his shortcomings. "And yet right now this whole thing with the Wraith is on you."

His smile faded. "We've all got to do some things that are out of our comfort zones," he said. "You're not a jumper pilot, right? Or part of an exploration team. But now you have been."

"That's true," Eva said. There had been a moment, trapped under the ice, that she had been pretty certain she wasn't going to get out. She'd wondered who would tell her daughter and what they'd say had happened to her. She'd wondered, in an almost detached kind of way, how they'd explain to Desireé what had happened on a nice, safe job as a contract psychologist. And then she'd heard the voices above, Ronon and Laura and Dr. Lynn, Dr. Lynn calling out, "It's ok! We're coming for you." The leg hurt a lot, but not as bad as having Desireé. And that was worth it too.

"You did a good job," Sheppard said. "Who knows what's in that Ancient installation? It's going to take a lot of work to get it cleared out, and we may find things that turn out to be critical." He uncoiled from the stool and leaned over and squeezed her shoulder. "So hang in there, feel better, and in a couple of days you'll be back to head shrinking."

It was on the tip of her tongue to say that he was good at his job too. But that might be way too frank. "And I'll see you in my office, right?" she asked, her tone leaving it half a joke.

Sheppard gave her a sideways smile. "When hell freezes over," he said.

"I've got my ice skates."

"Save them for Rodney," he said, and winked as he turned and left.

Eva leaned back on her pillows. She hoped he felt as much better as she did.

John slid his tray onto the lunch table opposite Sam. "Anybody sitting here?"

"I think they're afraid to," Sam said, a look of amusement on her face as she glanced around the half empty mess hall. "The loneliness of command."

"Ok, yeah," John said. "The airmen don't exactly eat with me either."

"Then I guess we get to be the geek table," Sam said. She glanced at him keenly. Rodney was captured and Teyla gone. Ronon… Who knew where Ronon was? There had seemed to be a certain amount of tension between him and John lately.

"Suits me," John said, pulling his chicken sandwich apart to put mayonnaise on the bun. "You think we're going to get Woolsey back?"

"I don't know."

John looked at her, his head to the side. "What's the problem between you and Woolsey anyway, Sam? I get the feeling it's more than you being relieved in Atlantis. That was the IOA, not him personally, and he didn't want this job anymore than you wanted to go home."

Sam sighed. "Yeah, it's more than that." She picked up her sandwich. "About six years ago he led an investigation of the SGC, an investigation of a mission where one of my best friends was killed. You didn't know Dr. Janet Fraiser. She was before your time. But she was killed in action in the field, trying to medevac an enlisted guy who'd been wounded."

"I'm sorry," John said quietly.

Sam shrugged, her eyes on her sandwich. "He did a report, basically putting a dollar value on all of our lives. The airman's life wasn't worth the expense and risk of getting him out."

"Bull honkey," John said.

"Yeah, that's what I said too." Sam looked up. "Less politely, I think. And then a couple of years later when Daniel was compromised by the Ori he wanted Daniel put to death so that he wouldn't pose a security threat. Not very efficient, to keep him alive and hope it would turn out ok."

"We don't do things like that," John said frostily. "Do we?"

"We do." Sam pursed her lips. Of course she knew he was thinking about Rodney. "Apparently we do."

"What happened?"

"Jack laid down the law, of course. They'd preemptively execute one of his people over his dead body. And it's worth running the risk to extract your people, no matter what." She took a drink of her iced tea, raised it in mock toast to John. "Turns out, just a few weeks later Woolsey had an object lesson in being on the other end of the stick. Nice of you not to leave him to the Replicators!"

"That wasn't about Woolsey," John said. "Or O'Neill. That was about Atlantis."

"Yes, well." Sam shrugged. "I still owe you for that one."

"I figure not getting court martialed again was thanks enough," John said. "But I'm glad it worked out ok for O'Neill and Woolsey." He took a bite of his sandwich and chewed carefully. "You know, maybe being out in the field has helped. He's not a bad guy, really."

"I know." Sam glanced up at the soaring ceiling, the windows far above letting in bright snowlight. "And I've got a better understanding of why we have to have those kinds of investigations, that kind of oversight, even if I don't think that you can put a price tag on a life. It's a different mindset. Governing is made up of those kinds of compromises. It's just that it doesn't sit very well with me, even if I get it." She picked up her sandwich again. "It's always hard to lose people. But that doesn't mean that it's not worth it."

"Yeah," John said. His eyebrows twitched. "I'm hoping that they don't start thinking the price tag for Atlantis is too high."

"That worries me too," Sam said. "You can't accomplish anything without risk. We don't have a very high national tolerance for risk taking. Remember after *Challenger* how there were calls to end manned space exploration?"

"Oh yeah," John said. "I remember *Challenger*. I was in my high school English class. The principal came on the PA system." He swirled a French fry around in the ketchup. "Where were you?"

"In the White House," Sam said.

"You were not," John said. "What were you, some kind of seventeen year old prodigy advisor to the President?"

"No, but I really was in the White House."

John leaned back in his chair. "Ok, this has got to be a good story."

Washington was cold and snowy that week, the week she'd been waiting for. Sam was doing Presidential Classroom, one of the government up close special programs for gifted high school juniors and seniors. She was rolling into the last semester of her senior year already accepted to college, ready for the last five months without a lot of pressure that she'd have in a long time. All she had to do was not screw up and she was set. So she could take a week out of school to go do a special program.

Of course it snowed buckets the entire week. She was coming from Florida, from Tyndall Air Force Base, and all her clothes from when they'd been posted in colder places were long since outgrown. So Sam pretty much froze to death the entire week.

"It'll be a great experience for you," her dad had said. *"A little taste of the best and brightest from all across the country, just like the Academy will be next year."*

If that was so, she hoped the Academy would have more science people. Presidential Classroom was full of social studies people, debate team captains and kids who read the Atlantic Monthly. Debate had never been her strong suit, and she felt distinctly outclassed. There were lots of structured discussions where you signed up to present one side or another of a topical issue and argued it to your peers, or where a group was assigned to come up with a position paper or a solution on something thorny. Thankfully, you could kind of steer what task forces you wound up on. Sam was a lot happier with strategic missile arms control than she was with migrant farmworkers.

Fortunately, her roommate, Sib, was one of those social science people, though she was way into space too. She also owned sweaters in a size that fit Sam, a definite plus since she was freezing her buns off. She was a good four inches shorter than Sam, with long brown hair all the way to her waist, and she talked incessantly. Not that it was bad. It made it easier to make friends.

"Sib is short for?" Sibling was all Sam could think of, and that was kind of a weird nickname.

"Sibyl," her roommate said, *throwing herself down on the bed in her blue and purple painted jeans. "That's not my real name either, but one of my friends started calling me that in ninth grade and now everybody does."*

"Because you see the future?" Sam asked.

"Or the past." Sib curled her legs up under her. *"So we're on the same team to present the pro position for the Strategic Defense Initiative at the session tomorrow night. Got anything nice you want to say about Star Wars?"*

"Well, obviously a missile shield will be very expensive," Sam said, carefully mustering her thoughts. "The number of payloads required to launch it is going to be extraordinary, even if many of them aren't space shuttle missions. Even if they're good old Titans launched from Vandenberg."

"So they're going to say it's too expensive," Sib said.

"How much is too expensive?" Sam asked. "Bigger than the entire budget of Strategic Air Command? Because that's how expensive it would have to be not to be worth it. If we can spend the money on parallel weapons systems to create parity, we can spend the money on anti-missile systems to reduce threat."

"How big is SAC's budget anyhow? And how much are the Vandenberg launches?" Sib deferred to her on things military in a very gratifying way, having discovered she was an Air Force brat.

"Big," Sam said. "And the Vandenberg launches are pretty affordable. I can call my dad and ask him first thing in the morning. He'll know and then we can provide an exact budgetary comparison."

"Cool," Sib said. "We've got the White House tour in the morning, and then in the afternoon it's small breakout sessions. Which one are you going to?"

"I don't know yet," Sam said. "I haven't decided. How about you?"

"The one on Solidarity," Sib said promptly. "The speaker is a Polish dissident who defected in Norway. It sounds pretty interesting."

Sam flipped open her schedule. "I was thinking about the one with the Russian Air Force officer from the Russian embassy."

"That would be smart for you," Sib said. "It's always a good idea to know your enemy."

Sam had never been in the White House before. It was big and had lots of gilded things. They'd only gotten as far as the East Room when Secret Service agents came pouring out of the woodwork, herding all the kids together and talking quietly with their group leader, hands on the headsets in their ears.

"We've got to leave," the group leader said. "We don't know

why." She looked worried. She wasn't a teacher. She was with the Department of the Interior, doing this as a special assignment for a few months. And so they hurried back out into weak sunshine, to their bus waiting a block away on 16th street.

"What do you suppose that was about?" one of the guys in the group asked Sam, possibly by way of making conversation.

"No idea," she said, concentrating on not slipping in her summer dress shoes on the icy sidewalks.

She didn't have winter dress shoes. Her old ones had been outgrown a long time ago, and it wasn't the kind of thing her dad noticed. If she said anything to him about it, he'd just boggle at her. "Holy Hannah, Samantha! Buy some shoes! You've got the Master Card."

And she did. She was seventeen. She could drive. She could go to the mall anytime and buy herself some shoes, or whatever else she wanted. Her dad would never notice or complain, not unless she spent a thousand dollars or something. She could buy really expensive Outback Red, or any kind of makeup or accessories she wanted. He wouldn't tell the difference and it would be ridiculously easy to hide anything from him. He had no idea what girls' clothes cost and he'd never notice if she left the house with her belly button showing.

But she didn't. Sam was responsible. She was really, really responsible. And her mom wouldn't have liked it if she'd done that, taken advantage of Jacob's ignorance and inattention. After all, it wasn't easy for him, trying to raise two kids by himself. Mark had only been nine when it happened. He was fourteen now and an athlete. Sam made sure he had lunch money and always took his cleats to school on the right days, that his gym clothes were clean and that his laundry was done. She wasn't sure what was going to happen next year when she was gone. But Mark would be fifteen. He could maybe do his own laundry.

Also it hadn't occurred to her she'd need winter dress shoes. And her dad would frown at that. "Samantha, it's DC in January! What were you thinking?"

Well, she wasn't. But she'd better start, because nobody was going to do her thinking for her.

They went to McDonalds at the corner of New York Avenue. Their group leader couldn't think what else to do with them for about two hours, but they could hang around McDonalds while she called people and tried to find out if she was supposed to take them back to the Shoreham or what. Sam sat in the window munching on a sausage biscuit, looking out at the late morning business people rushing by in the dress for success uniforms of professional DC. She might be here for real someday, assigned to the Pentagon, working on a top secret project. That would be pretty cool.

Sib was scribbling in a notebook she carried everywhere in her purse, her head bent over her sparkly purple pen.

"What are you doing?"

"Notes about SDI," Sib said. "For the debate tonight. I'm trying to get the main ideas down to three points. What's the biggest reason you support SDI?"

Sam folded her hands around her coke. "Because it's inevitable."

Sib looked up. "Well, it is. But we've got to do better than that. Elaborate."

"I guess…" Sam considered. "It's not like nuclear weapons are going to go away. I mean, unless we do nuke ourselves back to the Dark Ages, it's not like the entire field of nuclear physics is going to be forgotten. There are always going to be nuclear weapons, and there are always going to be situations where somebody thinks it's a good idea to use one. The only way, in the entire history of warfare, that we've ever gotten rid of a weapon is to render it obsolete."

"Ok," Sib said. "That's point one. The only way to get rid of nukes is to render them obsolete."

"A missile defense would do that," Sam said. "I mean, eventually. What's the point in building dangerous things that are really expensive if you know that whether you launch them on missiles or use strategic bombers they can be shot down from space before they can deliver their payloads? They become like fortifications — big,

expensive, clumsy things that don't give you a tactical advantage. We don't build castles anymore because they don't do any good. They're a waste of money and time. If nukes were just a big waste of time, there would be no reason to maintain an arsenal."

"That works for me," Sib said, scribbling away. "So why SDI? They're going to say that a space based missile defense system is impossible. It's sci fi. And that this is just a big bonus for the defense contractors, since it doesn't work."

"It doesn't work yet," Sam said. "No technology works the minute you think of it. It may take fifty years to work completely. Dramatic changes in the balance of offensive and defensive weaponry tend to take a while."

Sib looked up. "I totally see why you're going to the Air Force Academy."

Sam shrugged. "I think this stuff is fun."

"So do I."

"You guys!" A guy at another table stood up, a geeky guy with longish hair who looked totally out of place in his dress code blue blazer. He had a walkman on his head, holding the earphones against his ear in the loud restaurant. "You guys, the space shuttle just blew up!"

"Yeah, right Darryl!" One of the guys at his table laughed. "Way to put us on."

"No, for real." Sam twisted around in her seat, a sudden cold in the pit of her stomach. No. It wasn't a joke, not with that expression on his face, not with that look in his eyes. "It really blew up."

"Was there a launch today?" Sib said quietly as four or five people started asking questions.

"Yes," Sam said. "The one with the teacher in space. It was supposed to be about forty five minutes ago." She always watched the launches if she could. She'd known she was going to miss this one, with Presidential Classroom and the White House tour. "Oh my God."

"What?"

"That's what happened at the White House."

Sib looked at her, and Sam thought her face must have the same stricken look.

"It's on the radio," the guy said, as all around him the restaurant went still, construction workers with their thermoses frozen at the counter, business people stopping in their tracks. The woman on the register drew a deep, shaky breath. "About two minutes into the launch," he said, repeating what he was hearing. "The booster tanks separated. They don't know what happened."

No one spoke. No one said a word. Not anybody in the McDonalds. Everyone stood as though turned to stone, listening to this geek with his walkman, repeating word for word what he was hearing, his voice firm and unshaken as Edgar R. Murrow reporting from London.

"We have to see." They went straight back to the hotel. Sam ran through the lobby as fast as her summer heels would allow, Sib right behind her, through the silent Edwardian lobby with its chandeliers and parquet floors, past rooms where people had danced for Teddy Roosevelt's inaugural ball. Up the elevator. So slow. All up and down the hotel halls doors were banging open, televisions going on.

She sat on the bed, watching the clip replaying over and over, booster rockets looping wildly in the bright blue sky, the anchor's voice going again and again to shock and dismay.

And then back to the beginning again. "Good roll program confirmed. Challenger heading downrange. Engines beginning throttling down now. At 94%."

Sib reached over and squeezed her hand. "Oh my God," Sam whispered.

"Altitude 4.3 nautical miles."

"Roger, go at throttle up."

And then silence.

Rockets streaking soundlessly across a blue sky. Over and over and over.

"This is the end," Sam whispered.

Sib shifted on the bed, tears rolling down her cheeks. "I mean, maybe not. You know, for them. If you believe in God…"

"Not for them. For us." Sam felt her face flaring with shame even as she said it. "It's the end of space. This is the end. It will be years before we go back into space. We may never go again in our lifetimes. People won't risk it. We won't take the chance, not with more lives. Even if there are plenty of people who would do it."

"Would you?"

Sam nodded, her jaw hard. "Yes. I'd get out there tomorrow and say light the candle. But I'll never get a chance now." She lifted her arms, the heels of her hands against her eyes. "I'll never get the chance." Tears were choking in her throat, but she wasn't going to cry. She never cried.

There was the sound of Sib shifting on the bed, hunting through her bag. Sam took her hands away. "What are you doing?"

Sib pulled out the blue notebook, scrubbing the tears off her face with one hand. "We have to work on our SDI presentation."

"There is no SDI," Sam snapped. "There is no space. Don't you get it? We're done. We're through. The shuttle program is over. There won't be any national will for it. You can forget about a missile shield or an international space station or any of that stuff. It's like my dad says about Vietnam. Once we lose the national will to do something, it doesn't matter if we could do it."

"Who makes the national will?" Sib lifted her chin. "Who besides us?"

"We're kids."

"No, we're not," Sib said gently. "In six months you'll be in the Air Force and I'll be at college. We haven't been kids for a long time. We just didn't know it. We make the national will." She looked out the window at the trees in Rock Creek Park below, the city somewhere beyond. "That's the real debate that's going to be going on all over town. What does this do to everything? We have to hold up our end of it."

"Nothing hinges on this stupid debate tonight," Sam said. "It's just a bunch of kids arguing abstractions. And like we can convince

anybody that we need space based systems? Today?"

"We have to learn to," Sib said. "It's just a different kind of impossible fight. You want that future in space? Then we've got to sell it. We've got to sell it to the people who matter, the people here who are going to remember this day for the rest of their lives, who are going to be the voters and the decision makers. We don't get but one shot. It may not be the big one yet, but we can't know that. We can't know that it isn't. We can't know that we're not convincing somebody who will be president. This might be the big thing, the thing we're meant to do, the whole point of our lives."

"You think?"

"Why not?" Sib shrugged, opening her notebook. "Maybe you're the one who will convince people that the price tag is worth it."

John Sheppard bent his head over his coffee, a rueful smile on his face. "Yeah, I see that," he said. "I remember that day. Though I never thought I was going to another planet. I figured I was going to law school."

"I didn't dream this was possible in 1986," Sam said, looking up again at Atlantis' soaring windows. "If you'd told me then I'd be here, I wouldn't have believed it."

"Me neither," John said. "How'd we get here, anyhow?"

"One step at a time," Sam said. "A lot of luck and a little faith."

"And a whole ton of hard work," John said. He touched his mug to hers in a mock toast. "Which I should get back to."

"Me too," Sam said, pushing back from the table.

John picked up his tray, half turned to leave. "Nice pep talk, Carter."

"I aim to please," Sam said.

CHAPTER EIGHTEEN

Osprey

TEYLA dreamed, and in her dream she stood in the woods of Athos. It was early spring, and frost silvered the morning grass, clouds of mist rising where the sun struck ice, transpiring in a gray, soft blanket that clung to the hollows around the trees. In her dream she passed through the woods, insubstantial as fog herself. Her heart pounded tight in her chest. They were coming.

And then it was not the woods of Athos, but that planet where Ellia had dwelled with the man she called father. They hunted her through the woods. She could hear them coming. She could hear them coming as she fled, alone and on silent feet. She could hear them coming after, the faint whine of the puddle jumper, the voices of the hunters behind. They were coming.

Mist wreathed her. It surrounded her. It hid her. She vanished, insubstantial as a dream. One passed close by, gun in hand, his black boots leaving footprints in the dew, his head bent forward over his weapon, dark hair and muddy green eyes, intent upon his prey. He did not see her. She was a pale shadow, a trace of cloud across the moon.

Closer. Closer. There was the rattle of gunfire, and he ran toward it, toward the shore of the lake. It was only a water bird startled from its nest, white wings beating against the morning sky.

Osprey.

And then she sat in the tents of Athos, her fingers stabbing at a difficult piece of handwork by the fire, while Charin's hands moved smoothly, her voice weaving in and out of an old tale. "Once there was a girl who was transformed into a white bird, and the Ancestors hunted her because she was a changeling…" She sat by Charin's knee, bright patterns of thread shimmering in the firelight, half dozing. "She had become a revenant, and she returned at night to drink the life from her kin, but by day no man could find her, because they sought a girl, not an osprey."

The flap of the tent stirred in a cold wind, the flames wavering. Teyla looked up. Elizabeth Weir stood in the doorway, the flap stirring behind her between the doorposts. She wore a red shirt and dark pants, and her eyes met Teyla's firmly. "Once, in the City of the Ancestors," she said.

"Once in Emege," Charin said serenely.

"I was in this village once," John said, looking up from beside the fire. "I was drinking tea with this guy, and he had exactly your eyes."

"Exactly your eyes," Todd echoed, moving the gaming piece on the board between him and John. "She had exactly your eyes. The Osprey queens are the strongest."

"Cordelia," Elizabeth said. "It all came from Lear's cruelty."

"I do not know this story," Teyla said, stretching out her hands to Elizabeth, but she smiled and stepped away. "Tell me."

"I'll need a blood sample," Jennifer said, putting on her latex gloves.

"You know the story," Elizabeth said. Her eyes slid to John and back. "You are the story."

"Once, when Arda ruled in Emege," Charin began. "Long ago and far away."

"Do you need that much?" John asked, holding up his right arm where blood ran in long rivulets from claw slashes. Jennifer bent to catch them in a vial, his blood dripping on the floor with a sound like thunder.

"I need all of your blood," Jennifer said. "I need it all."

"Don't be greedy," Todd said. "If you drink it all today there will be none tomorrow. There will be none for Osprey."

John's eyes met hers over Jennifer's head. "It's for you," he said.

"No," she said, and took a step back in horror. Her hands were a Wraith queen's, Steelflower's hands. Only the feeding slit was open. She could feel her pulse pounding in it, lips engorged with hunger, aching with need.

"They fed upon the children of Emege," Charin said.

"Once in the City of the Ancients," Elizabeth said. "Once, in the Lost City."

Teyla's hand stretched out, reaching for him, and John lifted his chin but didn't flinch.

Todd smiled. "White ghost," he said. "Wraith."

Teyla wrenched awake, her heart pounding. Around her, the soft shiplight of Todd's hive ship came up, adjusting to a rosy daylight glow. She lay in her chamber, in the queen's chamber. There were no sounds other than the soft purr of the ship's systems. No alarms sounded, and the merest mental touch assured her all was well. Guide and Jennifer were at work in one of the labs.

Teyla clasped her hands together, trying to still them.

"Elizabeth," she whispered. "I do not understand…"

Jennifer closed her eyes against the glare of her laptop screen, still seeing formulas and graphs swimming behind her eyelids. She sat back, releasing shoulders sore from being hunched for hours, and reached up to cup the back of her neck, trying to knead out some of the knots.

It felt every bit as late as it was which, a glance at her watch told her, was almost three in the morning, Atlantis time. She vaguely remembered Teyla saying goodnight several hours ago before heading to her quarters, but at the time she'd been busy fiddling with the Wraith version of a microscope and some slides and, after that, setting up another round of cultures, hoping that this time one of them would do something.

At least they were making some progress, she thought, even if it wasn't as fast as she would have hoped. But she did think — finally — that they were getting somewhere. With a yawn, she sat up a little straighter and put her fingers back on the keyboard, trying to focus.

Twenty minutes later, notes finished, she leaned over one of the workbenches, watching behind plastic goggles as the newest biochemical compound turned blackish purple in the vial. Once its color was uniform, she carefully measured out three drops onto the waiting culture dish.

She yawned again and tried to cover it with her sleeve, then stood there for a moment with one hand braced on the workbench, hoping for a second wind. Across the room, Todd looked up from his own workstation and took her in at a glance, seeming amused.

"I would not advise falling asleep so near the prototypes," he said mildly. "If you require rest, go."

Jennifer had to swallow before she could speak. "No, I'm fine," she said, trying to ignore how good the word 'rest' sounded. "Just need a minute."

Todd rose smoothly and crossed the room with long, purposeful strides, looking as fresh as ever. Absently, Jennifer noted his good color, the sheen of his skin and the way his hair gleamed in the soft light. He looked like the picture of health, for a Wraith anyway, and she tried hard not to think about what that meant. Tried not to wonder who his last meal had been. The thought made her lips press together with distaste, and she looked down at the cultures, willing the retrovirus to work.

"Come, then," he said, at her shoulder, and Jennifer was proud of herself for not jumping. She looked up, and he gestured elegantly, inclining his head and turning over one long-fingered hand. He could have been a character from a romantic novel, some dangerous and courtly gentleman with his carriage waiting outside. It was that that left her so off-balance, she thought. It was hard to remember that he thought of her as food.

"I need to stay at this."

"If you are to function, you will need food and drink," he said, shrugging and not quite meeting her gaze. Maybe this was weird for him too, dealing with humans as something other than meals. She wondered if he pretended that they were Wraith, if that was easier than admitting to himself that all humans had personalities and interesting ideas and got tired when they'd been working too long.

"Maybe you're right," she said.

Todd led her through the twisting corridors of his hive, still enough of a labyrinth after several days that she would have been hopelessly lost alone. She suspected that it hadn't remained entirely unchanged, anyway; more than once she'd thought she caught walls shifting out of the corner of her eye. The room he took her to looked a lot like the one where she'd first met with him, the first time she'd ever seen a hive ship or been up close with a Wraith. It seemed like a thousand years ago.

He sat with her and must have called telepathically for food, because after a moment, a drone came in with a tray. The food was only fruit, but at this point in the day she was happy to see it, and there was a cup that when she took a cautious sip contained water, flat and entirely tasteless. She wondered if the ship distilled it somehow, if she was drinking part of what ran through the ship's veins.

"Thank you, Todd," she said, and then realized that couldn't be his actual name. Colonel Sheppard had started calling him that, because none of the Wraith had ever given them a name, or been willing to speak to them much at all. "Your name's not really 'Todd,' is it?"

In the dim light, the star-shaped tattoo stood out in sharp contrast to his skin, and his eyes seemed to flicker as he moved and the light shifted, like golden embers from a flame. Rodney had eyes like these, now. He tilted his head, hair spilling over his shoulder, a trail of silver against the dark leather. "It is not."

She wasn't sure if his lack of elaboration was simply a statement of fact, or an indicator that he didn't want to have this conversation with her. Talking with Todd about anything except their research made her feel all too sharply how alien they were to each other. "You do have them, though, right? Individual names?"

Jennifer wondered for a moment if the question was somehow offensive, but Todd barked a laugh, showing sharp teeth. "We do, little one," he said. "All of the thousands of Wraith who live, each of us has our own name, and a name for our lineage, and our ships have names, and our planets. We are not nameless beasts."

She looked at him, his face still again, his features standing out sharp in the dim light. "So, what is your real name?" she asked. "I'd rather not keep calling you Todd if there's something that would be more polite."

Todd frowned. "That...is a harder question than you realize. A Wraith is named from the shape, the sense of his mind. The images and sensations others feel when they speak to him. It is a difficult thing to capture in a word."

She nodded. "So, not like us, then. Not just a name that really doesn't mean anything, like Jennifer."

He looked confused. "But your name has meaning, does it not? Pale, or perhaps fair. Fair One is how you are known to us."

"I — " Somewhere between flattered and bemused, it took her a moment to get it. "That's what my name means, but it's not why I was given it. I mean, I was born in 1981. There were two other Jennifers in my class."

"Ah." Somehow, she thought he seemed offended by that idea. "Yes, I suppose we are quite different."

"Still," she said, reaching out impulsively to touch his sleeve, as if he were a patient. Establishing rapport, that was what they'd called it in med school. "If you can say that you call me 'Fair One,' there has to be a way for you to tell me your name, right? Something that sort of sums the telepathic stuff up."

He stared at her hand, looking white and washed-out against the black leather, then at her face, strangely and deep, as if seeing her for the first time. "My name," he said at last, "my name is one who goes alone, ahead. One who is sure-footed and certain, capable of finding a way for others who follow behind. Leader might come close, but not a ruler."

"Scout?" Jennifer tried, but he shook his head.

"No, for a scout is solitary, but I am..." He freed his sleeve from her hand, his own fingers moving on the table, as if trying to find the shape of something. "Guide. Guide is what you may call me." The smile he gave her was sharp and strange for a moment. "I give you my true name, Fair One."

"Guide," she repeated, and tried to smile in return.

The conference room at Homeworld Command was once again in use by the IOA.

"Dr. Daniel Jackson." S.R. Desai steepled his hands thoughtfully. "That is different."

"I thought you might think so," Jack O'Neill said.

"He is one of the best of the best," Konstantin Nechayev said, nodding seriously. "I must say that my government would strongly support Dr. Jackson as head of the Atlantis expedition. We have worked with him for many years, and he impressed us a great deal when he assisted us in the matter of our development of gate technology some years ago. A man of towering intellect!"

Jack gave him a look as if to say, don't overdo it.

"That he is," Desai agreed. "With the kind of broad humanist perspective the job demands. Which," he shrugged, "has been sadly lacking since Dr. Weir's death. I think Dr. Jackson is an excellent candidate."

Shen and Strom alike looked speechless.

"I do not know Dr. Jackson personally," Aurelia Dixon-Smythe said, glancing over the curriculum vitae before her. "But unless the PM has some objection, he seems a reasonable choice."

"SG-1," Strom said, making it seem like some sort of epithet. "Dr. Jackson has a long history."

Nechayev beamed. "He does indeed. If I understand your position correctly, Mr. Strom, it is the position of your president that the head of the Atlantis position must go to an American. Understandable. You are paying the bills, and so you expect to call the shots, to put it bluntly. Some of our other esteemed colleagues are determined that it should not be a member of the military. I, myself, had no objection to Colonel Carter, and voted against her replacement as you may recall. So. Name me an American more qualified than Dr. Daniel Jackson." He looked around the table with a smile.

"Jackson is…" Shen began, and then lapsed into silence. Whatever he was, it could not be summed up immediately.

Dick Woolsey opened and closed his mouth. He didn't look at Jack, and for a second Jack felt sorry for him. But this was just like the business with the Replicators. Dick had to play this naturally.

Nechayev was doing the heavy lifting as he'd promised. "I am very pleased with this suggestion," he said into the silence. "Very pleased indeed. I know that the President had the warmest possible feelings toward Dr. Jackson after the incident where he assisted Dr. Markova. His personal thanks, as I recall."

Desai's brows twitched. He knew this was a set up, but he also knew Jackson. "I think this is certainly an avenue we should explore," he said.

LaPierre looked entirely blindsided and glanced at Nechayev with scarcely concealed astonishment. "I thought a few years ago you wanted to execute him?"

Nechayev shrugged. "That was when he had been compromised by the Ori. Obviously that situation resolved itself."

"You mean I resolved it," Woolsey said.

"If you consider allowing yourself to be overpowered and transported away while the prisoner stole a starship to be resolving it? Yes," Nechayev said. "Come now, Mr. Woolsey. Your interactions have not always been successful, or in fact competent. Allowing yourself to be captured by the Replicators?"

"That was…"

"Unavoidable, yes." Nechayev waved a hand. "And yet the fact remains that you, and Mr. Strom, and Ms. Shen, and some of our predecessors who are no longer part of this body, decided on a disastrous course that nearly lost us not only Atlantis but also nearly caused a Replicator invasion of Earth. Had Atlantis remained under military control…"

"Now also recall I opposed that decision bitterly," LaPierre put in. "As did Mr. Desai."

"Yes, it was the three of us," Nechayev agreed. "I do not recall, what was your role in that, General O'Neill?" He all but winked at Jack.

Jack looked as innocent as possible. "Me? I nearly got nuked. Oh, and then we defeated the Replicators and took back the city."

Roy Martin, the new American representative, choked on his coffee. "You, personally, General?"

"Me, Dr. Weir, Colonel Sheppard and his team," Jack said. "With the invaluable contributions of Mr. Woolsey, who volunteered to be interrogated by the Replicators in order to give them false information."

Woolsey looked at him sharply, and Jack saw understanding dawn. Daniel Jackson was a poison pill, and a sufficiently plausible one that Woolsey's detractors would panic.

"Very admirable, Mr. Woolsey," Martin said.

Woolsey did his best to look modest. "Thank you, Senator."

"Dick never asks someone under his command to do something he wouldn't do himself," Jack said smoothly. "He's a hands on kind of guy."

"Even when that means being interrogated by the enemy?" Martin's eyebrows rose.

"I, um," Woolsey began.

"He's very modest about his role in it," Jack said. "But I can't say there is anybody in the world I would rather have had in that cell with me." A lot of people he would rather have had out of it, but that was beside the point. Why Sheppard couldn't have brought Sam and Daniel and Teal'c along was beyond him. The more the merrier.

"I see that it's nearly two o'clock," Shen said. "And unfortunately I have another meeting this afternoon. If we might try to end on time?"

Bingo, Jack thought. Poison pill swallowed. Let's pull the plug.

Desai frowned. "It's only quarter till…"

"We must respect Ms. Shen's time constraints," Strom said quickly. "I think that we should go ahead and recess on that note rather than moving on to the next agenda item. Does next Thursday suit you all?"

"I don't know yet," Dixon-Smythe said. "I'll have my assistant contact you."

"I don't know either," LaPierre said.

Nechayev smiled expansively. "I am at your disposal at any time."

CHAPTER NINETEEN

Snow

HE WAS beginning to think he should plan his own rescue — maybe steal a Dart, or, since he wasn't sure he could actually fly one, maybe a lifepod, they were designed for incapacitated passengers. He was fairly sure he'd located the ones nearest his own lab, and he kept track of when the hive came into orbit around a habitable planet. Like now: they had stopped to Cull, on a world with a Stargate and a reasonably large population — except he could imagine himself landing, and then what? He'd have to dial out — not to Atlantis directly, that would be too risky, because he'd have to spend time convincing them he was himself, and not a trick, so to some safer world where Sheppard could meet him — if he'd go for that again, after the last time. Not to mention all the people who'd be trying to kill a lone Wraith… Maybe New Athos? He could dial that address in his sleep, and he could probably convince Halling not to kill him right away. Maybe he could say he had a message from Todd? There was a certain perverse irony in that.

Except that he was never alone. Not that Ember had ever left him for very long, and why he hadn't noticed that until now, he couldn't have said, but now either Nighthaze or Heedless was in constant attendance. Heedless was Nighthaze's chief assistant, whose tone of mind was strangely sober for such a name — but then Rodney overheard some of the other clevermen joking about the number of times Heedless had regrown fingers in the wake of his experiments, and thought he understood. Wraith humor wasn't all that different from, say, Marine humor, when you came right down to it. If one of them had ever left him, he might have been tempted to try it, although he knew that failure meant not only that he'd be killed, but that in the process the Wraith would learn everything he'd been trying to keep from them. And that, he realized, was the key. If Sheppard didn't come, he would not only have to escape, but he would have to do it perfectly the first time. Or die trying.

The thought was like a blow, and he glared at his screen, at the golden waterfall of data, as though it could somehow help. Succeed or make sure he died: that was the sort of thing Sheppard would say, or Ronon. He was the one who found ways to survive…

Dice you for your thoughts, Nighthaze said, and Rodney bared teeth at him.

I am thinking that we have taken a wrong turn. As I told you two days ago. One of the watching clevermen snarled at that, but Rodney ignored him. *I need to think. I'm going back to my quarters.*

I will go with you, Heedless said.

No, no, Rodney answered. *Continue your work.*

Heedless and Nighthaze exchanged a quick glance, and then Heedless dipped his head. *Your pardon,* he said, *but the Old One has given orders…*

For a moment, Rodney was tempted to protest, to see how far he could push things, but better sense prevailed, and he contented himself with another snarl. *Must he interfere in everything? Very well. But if time is lost, it is not my fault, or yours.*

They walked back to his quarters in silence, Heedless a respectful pace to the rear. If he were going to try to escape on his own, Rodney thought, this would be the moment. Heedless was strong, but not particularly young or quick, and Rodney thought he could at least knock him down, and maybe out. But the larger problem remained, and he sighed, letting the door of his quarters slide closed behind him.

It was strange how he remembered the hives as dark and dank. The lights were pleasantly bright, and the mist that curled out of the corners was cool and soothing, balm to the senses. Probably some of the difference was fear, of course, and equally of course they'd never had any reason to go into the parts of the hive where the Wraith actually lived. He snarled at his own stupidity. Carson had answered that question long ago: the Wraith saw a slightly different spectrum of light than humans did. And now that he was Wraith, he saw the hive as they did, light and pleasant and comfortable — home.

Heedless had left a game of habitats set up, a problem laid out on the overlapping circles, and as he reached for it, Rodney couldn't help noticing that the fingers of his off hand looked somehow different, the skin more shiny than the skin of his wrist.

Is that story true? he asked, and Heedless blinked.

Story, lord?

Rodney waved his hand in the general direction of Heedless's own. *The one your men were telling. About fingers.*

Oh. There was a distinct sense of embarrassment in Heedless's mind. *That.*

Yes, that.

Partly true, Heedless said. The embarrassment was stronger now. *I was working to develop an explosive that we could grow quickly. My queen then was Starfire, and among our hunting grounds was one where the humans hid themselves in caves — natural and artificial, great runs of tunnels beneath a mountain. They would barricade themselves, and it cost time and effort to dig them out, so I thought, perhaps if we had a directional explosive, it would help us, and not kill so many of them to be impractical.* He shrugged. *I am fond of explosives.*

So I gather, Rodney said.

Heedless looked away. If he had been human, Rodney thought, he'd be beet red by now. *So I developed a formula, which was quite effective. But it wasn't as stable as I'd expected, and there were… accidents. I did have to regenerate my off hand twice as a result. But it should have worked, truly.*

Really, Rodney said. He held up his hand to forestall any further comment. *Just tell me you're not working on this any more?*

No, lord, Heedless said. *Nighthaze forbade it.*

Which, frankly, seems like a good thing, Rodney said. The

mere idea of testing explosives on a spaceship made him cringe.

Heedless ducked his head again, and Rodney turned to his own chamber. There was no door, just the curve of the hive wall itself to shadow the sleeping nest, and he put his back to Heedless as he stripped off his outer clothes. Heedless reminded him of someone, though he couldn't quite think who — but, yes, he could. Zelenka. Heedless reminded him of Zelenka, and with that realization came the memory of the last time he'd seen Zelenka, sprawled ungainly on the floor of the ZPM room with Ember bending over him, feeding hand outstretched.

He caught himself against the chamber wall, handmouth flattening painfully against the hive's inner skin. He flinched back from that, from the sensation that burned like ice in his palm, and felt Heedless's attention sharpen.

Quicksilver? Are you well?

Fine, Rodney snapped. *Just fine.* He wrenched his mind into order, made himself straighten, continue removing coat and undercoat as though nothing were wrong. He'd nearly killed Zelenka — well, Zelenka had nearly killed him, too, but it had been a closer thing the other way around… He had killed others, and even if he didn't know them, not like he knew Zelenka, it still mattered. And some of them he might know.

He hauled his mind away from those thoughts, from the memory of attacking Atlantis, of the puddle jumpers colliding as he dropped into the gateroom and headed for the event horizon. Right now, he couldn't think about it, couldn't afford to think about things like that. He had to concentrate on staying alive and finding a way to get himself off the hive. He set his coat in its place, the hive closing gently around it, and eased into his nest, drawing the quilts around his shoulders. He had never felt so alone.

Jennifer seemed refreshed when they returned to the laboratory, more alert as she bent again over their work. Guide returned to his own workstation, coaxing a dozen different simulations at once from the machine, scanning streaming data that read insufficient, unacceptable, unlikely, one probable abysmal failure after another.

With a soft snarl, he leaned closer and entered the information for another dozen compounds, watching green numbers chase one another down the screen. Across the room, peering at her own datascreen, Keller seemed to be faring little better, murmuring to herself beneath her breath as her fingers danced over the keypad.

Hours passed before Guide isolated a promising compound, and his breath hissed between his teeth with pleasure as he quickly keyed in the sequence to upload the relevant information to his portable datapad. He reviewed it as he strode to the workbench, checking for any possible errors, anything he might have missed, but this time he could find none.

"Oh, hey, do you have something?" Keller asked. Without waiting for an answer, she came to join him, tilting the datapad in his hand without so much as a by-your-leave. Of course the words were beyond her, but the formulas were universal, and he didn't miss her sharp intake of breath as she studied the screen. "Wait, I was just thinking—"

She caught up her own computing device, cradling it in one arm as she pointed excitedly at the screen. "Here, look at this—" He saw what she meant in an instant, and an unbidden smile bared his teeth.

"Very like indeed," he murmured, pleased. He set his datapad aside in order to tap a finger to her screen. "Though, this—?"

Keller nodded as she moved past him to place her datapad on the bench beside his own, shoulder brushing him in passing. "Yeah, I know. But it makes sense for the ratio to be a tiny bit different if you think about it, you know? I was thinking more human, you were thinking more Wraith. But let's run both. The other numbers match, and …"

Guide watched her hands as she talked, soft and unscarred, pale as some soft fruit. He was coming, grudgingly, to respect their skill and even their strange alien grace, as unfinished as they seemed. His gaze traveled upwards, taking in her long neck and smooth cheeks, still rounded with youth.

There was no fear in her, not now, at work. She reached for a slide, and her wrist brushed the knuckles of his feeding hand, and while he shivered instinctively, she did not even seem to notice. He marveled at that, as one waits with a thrill when prey picks its way close, stumbling into the trap of its own choosing.

And yet he had no desire to feed. He told himself it was because she was too useful too him at the moment, but he could not quite believe that it would be any different if he came upon her trussed for feeding. That was what came of knowing their names, he thought, with bitter amusement at his own foolishness, but it was not only that.

Unbidden he remembered a young queen at his side, gazing up at him raptly as he explained his work. Her hair had been the color of the sun, crimson as the blood of humans, exactly like her mother's. Guide remembered her mental voice racing as she demanded answers, sought them with an understanding as quick as any cleverman's.

"Guide?" Jennifer said, and he blinked. She was frowning at him, concerned. "I said, are you all right?"

He felt very old, suddenly, the memory like the ache of a long-healed wound. "I...sired a daughter, once," he said, looking at the workbench as his fingers shifted slides, their glass edges sliding together with precise, faint clicks. "It is a great honor to be chosen to father any child, but to father a queen..." He trailed off, not sure she could grasp such a thing. Humans bred like animals, with no care taken in the choosing.

"I didn't know you guys actually— I mean, I suppose new Wraith have to come from somewhere, but—" Obviously discomfited, she fumbled with a slide. "What's her name?" she asked, in an entirely different tone.

"Her name *was* Alabaster," he said after a moment. "Pale and strong as stone. Very much like our idea of you."

"I'm sorry," Jennifer said. It sounded like sympathy, but he told himself it was only that humans were softhearted toward the young of any kind, even nurturing baby animals as though they were their own kind. Their young were born so helpless, coming forth to shiver in the air when Wraith young would still be cradled in the shipwomb, coming forth only when they were ready to be weaned and to learn more than what the constant hum of the hive taught them.

"It was long ago," he said.

Keller nodded, looking away. "Right," she said. "Okay. I want to get these set up, and then I'm going to bed."

"Very well," he replied, and set to work. In his mind, however, as his hands kept busy, he kept remembering the touch of that young mind, as bright and unscarred as ice, or stone, or snow.

CHAPTER TWENTY

Croatoan

IT WAS good to be home, Steven Caldwell thought, back to the Mountain where the guys on the guardpost didn't even blink when you and three or four other people appeared out of thin air. Of course, they were expecting him. He'd called in and been ordered to Cheyenne Mountain, but since there were now precautions against beaming down through twenty six levels of substructure, he had to beam to the outside guardpost.

"Colonel Caldwell, sir," the sergeant on duty said, snapping to attention. "General Landry requests that you report immediately."

"On my way," Caldwell said, making his way inside and toward the elevator, followed by his exec. Their *Daedalus* flight suits were a badge of honor and got quite a few glances among the blue-clad SGC personnel.

He wasn't surprised that the moment he stepped out of the elevator the first person he saw was Richard Woolsey. Nor was he surprised that right behind him was Lieutenant General O'Neill. And Major General Landry. And Brigadier General Pellegrino.

"Welcome back, Colonel," O'Neill said.

"Glad to be back, sir," Caldwell said. He hadn't expected all the brass from Homeworld Command, but he supposed that he ought to have, even though he'd sent his report ahead. No one with the IOA except maybe technically Woolsey. That would account for debriefing at Cheyenne Mountain. Whatever was going on in Atlantis, O'Neill wanted to keep it a purely Air Force matter as long as he could. Which said something right there.

"If you gentlemen will come this way," Landry said, shaking his hand, "I've got a nice comfortable conference room just over here. Steven, I see your exec there is waving hard copies of your report, but I think it's safe to say we've already read it. I think we'd like to go straight to the Q and A, if that's ok with you."

"Of course, sir," Caldwell said. *As though he'd say, no, that's not ok. I can't actually answer questions to my boss and my bosses' boss.*

There was the usual muddle as everyone tried to sort themselves out in an unfamiliar conference room by rank, with Landry bumping someone else down the table because O'Neill was standing in front of the end seat like he owned it, and there was a civilian who wouldn't budge, Dr. Daniel Jackson. Caldwell wondered what the hell Jackson was doing here, but it wasn't his call.

Eventually everybody settled. Caldwell wished somebody would offer coffee, but nobody did.

"So." O'Neill steepled his hands on top of the hard copy of the report. "Tell me about Queen Death." He glanced down the table. "Catchy name. How do they come up with these things?"

Jackson looked over the top of his glasses. "I've been saying for years we should rename ourselves Infinitely Evil Space Superiority Command, but nobody listens to me."

Woolsey cleared his throat. He wasn't driving the conversation, and that said something important about how things had been going politically on Earth. "Colonel Caldwell?"

"I think we have a serious problem," Caldwell began.

Jack had come straight from Peterson Air Force Base to Stargate Command, but Daniel hadn't been needed until Caldwell's briefing, so he had his car there. Jack thought Daniel waited with admirable patience through the pleasantries afterwards, waited all the way through the familiar ride up in the elevator and the check out through the guardposts. He waited until Jack actually closed the car door.

"When were you planning on telling me?" Daniel said.

"Telling you what?"

"That you'd put my name in to replace Woolsey in Atlantis." Daniel gave him a sideways glance as he craned his neck to pull out of the narrow parking place.

Jack spread his arms on the broad leather armrests. "Never thought you'd get an SUV. I thought you cared about saving the Earth and all."

"It's a hybrid." Daniel hauled the steering wheel around expertly, managing to get out with at least an inch to spare on Jack's side. "And you're not going to get me off topic that easily. What were you thinking, Jack? The IOA hates me about as much as they do…"

"Carter?"

"I was going to say you," Daniel said. "And she has a first name. You could use it."

"Force of habit," Jack said. "And now who's getting off topic? Look, I know you hate the IOA…"

"What? Because they tried to have me executed a couple of years ago?" Daniel threaded his SUV through the parking lot.

"And you just hold a grudge over a little thing like that."

"Where to start?" Daniel put on the brake and stopped in the middle of the row. "Janet's death? Sending agents to dig up dirt on Sam's private life? Wanting to leave you frozen in stasis forever? Turning a blind eye to Kinsey's bullying?" He looked at Jack sideways. "I'm a poison pill, aren't I?"

"Not to Desai," Jack said. "He loves you. So does Nechayev. For that matter Dixon-Smythe could care less."

"But you think the rest of them will panic and want Woolsey back." Daniel shook his head. "Because they think they can't push me around."

"They know they can't push you around," Jack clarified. "If you were in Atlantis they'd have Elizabeth all over again."

"She did a fine job," Daniel said quietly.

"I know."

Daniel started the car moving again. "It's not that I mind you using me in your game with the IOA. But I wish you'd tell me first. I'd rather not hear about it from Landry."

"Sorry about that," Jack said. He probably should have mentioned it to Daniel. There was no need to play his cards that close to his chest. Force of habit, he supposed, to tell no one anything that wasn't essential.

Daniel looked mollified. "So do you want to know what I think?"

Jack tilted his head back and closed his eyes. "Ok, Daniel. What do you think?" If he really hadn't wanted to know, he wouldn't have agreed to let Daniel give him a ride home. The motorpool had cars.

"I think the Atlantis expedition is screwed." There was the squeal of brakes somewhere behind, but Jack ignored it. It wasn't as bad as Sam. Daniel drove absentmindedly. Sam drove suicidally. "There's no will to put into it what it requires, either here or internationally."

When Jack didn't reply, Daniel went on, the sound of his window going down as he leaned out to swipe his card to get out of the parking lot. "Croatoan."

There was a long pause, and it got the response he wanted. Jack opened his eyes and looked over. "What's a Croatoan?"

"A Native American tribe related to the Pasquotank," Daniel said. "But it's also a mystery."

Jack straightened up in his seat, fishing in his pocket for his sunglasses. The late afternoon sun was coming straight in through the windshield and his eyes were starting to water. They'd been photosensitive for a long time now. "Ok, I'll bite. What about it, Daniel?"

"Let me tell you a story," Daniel said, turning onto the expressway. "In 1587 a group of British settlers led by a man named John White, and financed by Sir Walter Raleigh, landed on the island of Roanoke just off the North Carolina coast. They were following up on a previous expedition, also led by White, which had established a temporary camp and begun friendships with the Native Americans who used the island as a summer hunting place. There were no permanent native settlements on the island, for good reasons, as the colonists would learn. These were not the kind of settlers who came later, not the adventurers of Jamestown or the fanatical religious separatists of Massachusetts Bay, looking for a place to practice their strict religion without the fetters of secular law. They were natural scientists, skilled craftsmen, skilled farmers, soldiers. Men and women too who were driven more by the relentless curiosity of the Elizabethan age. Some of White's papers and drawings survive — beautiful sketches of plants and animals, carefully measured and catalogued according to the best data collection of the day. Translations from the Algonquin language, accurate and sympathetic portrayals of the people they met there, beautifully rendered pictures and stories."

"You have a point?" Jack asked, more for form's sake than anything else. Of course Daniel did, and he'd get to it in his own time.

"A few weeks later, White returned to England with the ship to get more provisions, but it was late in the year and they could not sail again until spring. And you know what happened then."

"I do?"

"1588. The Spanish Armada. When spring came every ship was needed to defend England. The hundred and some members of the Roanoke expedition were not a priority, not when faced with invasion. White hounded the Queen and so did Raleigh, but to no avail. No ships could be spared. By the time the Spanish Armada was finished, the last ships wrecked in the gales of autumn off Scotland, it was too late to sail again. The next year it was the same story. The threat of war kept ships close in, fearing a repeat of the previous year's battles. It was 1590 when John White and the resupply ship landed at Roanoke. To find the expedition gone."

"Gone?"

"Gone. The settlement had been abandoned. The absence of most of the goods the expedition had brought, as well as the dismantling of some of the buildings, suggested that the expedition had not been attacked, but had moved on for some unknown reason. No bodies, no spent musket balls, no signs of burning or violence. All the clue there was left was the word 'Croatoan' carved into a tree."

Jack looked over at him sharply from behind his sunglasses. "Which means?"

"It was the name of a Native American tribe that lived about fifty miles away on the mainland. They'd had good relations with them in the past." Daniel shrugged. "We don't know why they left. We do know that the hurricane season of 1588 was exceptionally active, and that the entire island is very low lying. In recent decades it's been ravaged by hurricanes several times, and structures near where the settlement was were badly damaged. We also know that the Spanish raided along the coast in 1589, searching for a British colony, and that they had already destroyed a French colony in South Carolina. In any event, the island was a very unsafe place to stay. It seems likely that it became untenable, and that they picked up and moved in with their allies."

"So you're saying that when we get *Daedalus* back to Atlantis, we're going to find the whole place deserted with no clue except New Athos written on a pillar in lipstick?" Jack winced. "That's comforting, Daniel."

"I'm not saying that," he replied tranquilly. "I'm saying that things well begun have been abandoned before because the nation that sponsored them lacked the national will to follow through. Because other things happened at home that made the well being of the expedition a minor priority. Because it simply wasn't important enough."

Jack twitched. "Some people would say it's better that way," he said. "That it would have been better if there had never been colonies in the New World."

Daniel glanced at him sideways, a giant truck roaring past him in the outside lane. "Contact between the New World and the Old was going to happen. It was already happening. It had been nearly a century since Columbus, sixty years since the Aztecs fell. There's no putting the cat back in the bag once it's out, Jack. You can't just sail away and forget about it. Do you think for a minute that if we turned off the Stargate and recalled our ships that we would be left alone? That we can ever go back to the way things were? We have to be realistic. We're part of a wider universe, and you and I have been places that makes those old sea dogs' adventures pale in comparison." He looked back at the road. "And you know as well as I do that we're not the biggest dogs out there. We're technologically inferior, and our population is a tiny percentage of all sentient species we've encountered. We'd like to think we're the conquistadors, but we're not. Compared to the Wraith, or to the Jaffa or the Tok'ra here in the Milky Way, we're some second rate power trying to act real big with a bunch of technology we kind of half understand that we got from the Asgard or dug up from the Ancients. We're not the Spanish Empire. We're more like…"

Daniel seemed to run down for a moment, out of an appropriate comparison. "Lichtenstein?" Jack supplied.

"I was going to say the Venetian Republic, or maybe Norway in this period, but that will do."

"So your point is that we can't give up." Jack thought this was a pretty long winded way of getting there.

"My point is that contact is going to happen. The question is what the nature of that contact will be."

Jack didn't say anything, which Daniel seemed to take as encouragement.

"Do you think it makes a difference that the predominant strain in the founding of our country was Puritan separatism rather than the broadminded and curious attitudes of the Elizabethan age? Do you think that it's irrelevant to our national pathologies that we were founded to be a haven for a bunch of nuts who wanted to opt out of secular law and society and create a theocratic state?"

"Why don't you tell me what you really think, Daniel? An unbiased opinion," Jack said, his lips twisting in a half smile.

Daniel gave him a dirty look. "I'm not saying I'm unbiased. I'm saying that it was a tragedy for the entire world that the Roanoke colony was not the one that took root. I'm saying that if we drew our heritage from Roanoke instead of Plymouth that we would be a better country and a better people. If our guiding principles were based on the naturalists of the age of Shakespeare, rather than the manifest destiny of a bunch of Calvinists, the entire history of the world from that point on would be much improved."

"You can't know that," Jack said. "Daniel, if there's one thing we've learned seeing all these quantum realities and alternate timelines, it's that we have no idea how our actions will affect the future. We can't play that game. We can't hedge our bets based on some kind of mega end on down the road. We have to play the cards we have, right here and right now. We can't get into the whole 'ends justify the means' based on social theories of what will be better in three or four hundred years."

"All right, how's this for the short term?" Daniel glanced at him sideways again, apparently oblivious to the dump truck riding up on his back bumper. "The *Austerlitz* will launch in eighteen months. You know India's research ship is right behind them. The Russians want more Stargate access, and they're going to get it because they're chipping in money we can't afford. Meanwhile, our budget is flat for the next fiscal year and the Pentagon is planning a surge in Afghanistan. Your point about Atlantis?"

"My point is that we can't determine whether or not humans from the Milky Way have contact with the Pegasus Galaxy. That's out of our hands. What we can determine is what the guiding principles of these first contacts are. Who goes and what do they do? How do we respond to the peoples already there? How do we deal with the Wraith? What do we do about the rogue Asgard already in Pegasus? How do we safeguard the legacy of the Ancients so that it is available to all their heirs?" He shook his head. "We can't abrogate that responsibility, Jack."

"I never said we should."

"You said…"

"I said I don't make the budget. That's the President and Congress. And I don't determine the military priorities of the country. That's way above my pay grade."

Daniel snorted. "I thought that third star was good for something."

"It occasionally gets me drinks with pretty girls." Jack glanced out the window at the exit coming up. "Look, I can't control the IOA. I can't make them invest in Atlantis in the middle of an international economic crisis. All I can do is deal with our starships. Such as we have. As few as we have. Right now, 25% of our force is sitting in Atlantis. *Daedalus* will be on her way back as soon as she's repaired. That's what I've got, Daniel." His voice was harder than he wanted it to be.

"I know," Daniel said more gently. "Believe me, I know you're doing everything you can."

CHAPTER TWENTY-ONE

The Gift of Life

"WELL?" Guide asked, looming over her.

"Just a second," Jennifer murmured as she scanned the results, her lips forming the numbers soundlessly. "Almost done..." She ignored his quiet hiss of impatience, unwilling to rush. At last, she waved the datapad away and swiveled on the weirdly organic stool in order to look up at him. She could feel her heart pounding. "I think we've got it."

He bared his teeth slightly, either amusement or derision or both. "You *think*."

"Well, we won't know until we really test it. But at this point..." She nodded. "Everything adds up. The simulations and lab tests have gone perfectly. So ... I can safely say I *think* it will work."

Guide snorted. "Such confidence."

"Easy for you to say. You're not the one who's going to die if it doesn't," she said. It had been easy to throw herself into this project. Easier than usual, actually, to lose herself in numbers and results, because the implications of success were so much harder to think about. But now it had to be faced.

To her surprise, he barked a laugh. "Your jest is not in the best of taste."

"It's not a joke," she said, shaking her head. "The next step has to be a trial on a human subject. We can't just assume it works from the simulations."

"Of course it must be tested," he snapped. "But it would be wasteful to test it on yourself. There are humans in the feeding cells. Use one of them."

She stood, wishing he weren't quite so tall. But then, Teyla somehow managed to project utter bad-ass from all of five foot three, so maybe it wasn't height that she needed. "You want me to give someone who's waiting to be eaten a drug that, in itself, could kill him. And then you want me to watch while you feed on him and take notes," she said, putting as much anger as she dared into her voice. "And *then*, if it doesn't work, are you really going to tell me that you would do what you did for Colonel Sheppard and give this random human his life back? He's only food to begin with, right?"

"*You* were only food to begin with," he snarled, stalking closer. He held up his feeding hand, close enough for her to see the slitted mouth pulsating. She shivered but didn't step back. "Feeding is excruciatingly painful for the human, Fair One," he said, and his name for her sounded almost like a curse. "It burns, and you will feel it as your body shrivels, as the life drains from you and I consume you. It is not some gentle sleep."

Jennifer drew in a shaky breath. "Which is exactly why I'm not going to let you do that to anybody else as an experiment," she said. "Experimenting on an unwilling subject, on a prisoner... that's wrong. Beyond wrong. Which would narrow the choices to me or Teyla, and she wouldn't be as reliable a test subject with her Wraith DNA. Which... which leaves me."

"Leaves you for what?" Teyla asked, her boots clacking softly on the floor as she entered the lab. Guide bowed his head to her as if she really were his queen, before replying.

"This one wishes me to feed upon her," he said, still sounding angry. "I have expressed my reservations about this plan."

Teyla smiled thinly, after a moment, as if he'd added something else with telepathy, and for the hundredth time, Jennifer kind of wished she could hear what they were saying. She turned to Jennifer, her hairless brows furrowed with concern. "To test your retrovirus?"

"We have to know if this works. You know as well as I do that we don't have a lot of time here. It's like every time Rodney has tried something that would either do what it was supposed to or blow up." Her voice shook on his name, but she pushed on, thinking of all the times he'd given her that triumphant, *I'm the smartest man in the universe* grin. "Sooner or later you've just go to flip the switch."

Teyla shook her head. "But to risk your life for a test…"

"You're risking your life," Jennifer said. "Both of you. Teyla, I have to do this. We need to know. It's a risk someone has to take, and I can't ask anyone else to do it in my place."

Teyla nodded, making the ebony curtain of her hair sway. "Guide?"

"We require a trial," he admitted.

"Then let's do it," Jennifer said, heading for the workbench where their various prototypes were arranged, neat glass vials in an intricate bone holder. "There's no point in putting it off. Teyla, I don't know if you want to watch…"

Teyla gave Guide a warning look. "I insist on it," she said.

Jennifer unzipped her jacket and peeled it off. Even in the warm air of the hive, once she was standing there in her tank top she could feel herself start to shiver. She'd never actually watched a Wraith feeding, only seen video, and heard people talk about it, about seeing it again and again in their dreams.

She drew up a dose of the preparation with shaking hands, and set it aside. "Let's do this intravenously," she said. "That should have the fastest effect."

He nodded and took the tourniquet she handed him, tying it deftly above her elbow and taking her wrist in his off hand, tilting her arm, before flicking the cap off the syringe. "Are you very certain?"

Jennifer took a deep breath. This was the most dangerous part, she reminded herself. If they'd built the retrovirus wrong, she could die right here, and Guide couldn't save her. So if she got through this, the actual feeding part shouldn't be so bad.

"I have a video for my dad," she said, as clearly as she could. "In my top desk drawer. If anything happens…"

Teyla nodded. "Of course."

"Tell Rodney… tell him I never stopped trying, okay?" She swallowed hard against the knot in her throat.

Teyla met her eyes, her gaze steadying. "I will tell those who love you of your death. I will be your witness, if it comes to that," she said. "But it will not."

Jennifer tried to smile. "I hope you're right," she said, and looked up at Guide, watching her with his unfathomable golden eyes. She closed hers and took a breath, steeling herself. "Do it."

The needle pinched going in, and worse as he pushed the plunger. Jennifer hissed when he withdrew the needle and clapped her other hand to her forearm as he tugged the tourniquet free. Pain seared through her veins, every beat of her heart like a knife in her chest.

"Jennifer!" Teyla's voice was sharp with fear, but Jennifer's teeth were gritted too tightly to reply.

And then, as abruptly as it had begun, the pain stopped, leaving only a vague tingle in its wake. Still panting slightly, Jennifer straightened, one hand splayed on the edge of the workbench for support.

"Are you all right?" Teyla asked. "What happened?"

"That just…ahh, really hurt," Jennifer said, trying to breathe. "We'll have to see if we can do something about that little side effect." She looked up at Guide with a sudden unexpected feeling of power. If this had worked, he couldn't harm her.

"Come," he said, stepping back into the center of the room, beneath the place where the ribs of the ship met and tangled, like branches in the woods. She was going to have to cross the room to him, she realized. He wouldn't come to her.

"I will be here, watching," Teyla said, and Jennifer couldn't tell if that was threat for Guide or reassurance for her.

"I know." Jennifer drew in a breath and made herself look at Guide as she walked toward him. He was standing rigid, his eyes on her, his feeding hand tensed at his side. "I trust him."

He reached out as she approached, and she flinched before she realized he was reaching for her with his off hand. He traced a finger along the curve of her cheek. "You should not trust so easily, Fair One," he said, very quietly.

"I don't," she said. She found herself studying his face. Even this close, he really did look like some older gentleman. Someone's father. She could imagine Rodney like this, with amber eyes and green-pale skin. Surely his exasperated look would still be the same. "But I trust you."

He shook his head, and then bowed it as he had to Teyla, silver hair falling over his shoulders. When he straightened, his eyes found hers. "Your faith is not misplaced. I promise it." He lifted his feeding hand, unbearably slowly.

"You can't hold back," she said. "You have to really feed on me, like any other human, or this will all be for nothing." Guide's jaw tensed, his hand arched with the effort of holding it still. Her knees were trembling, her heart fluttering like a trapped bird. "You know that, right?"

"I do," he said finally, his voice rough as stone. His hand inched closer to her chest. "Are you prepared?"

Jennifer took a deep breath and nodded, unable to speak.

"Know that I would not do this if it were not necessary," Guide murmured. He gripped her shoulder with his off hand, holding her in place, and pressed his feeding hand to her chest.

His sharp nails bit deep, and a gasp at the shock turned to an involuntary shriek. She'd thought she was ready, thought she understood what was coming, but nothing could have prepared her for this.

Fire. Fire worse than the drug, worse than boiling oil, seared through her veins, blooming out from her chest in a burst of pain so intense she couldn't even draw breath to scream again, tears flooding her eyes. It built unbearably, and then blossomed into even more intense agony.

Then the pulling started. It spread from her solar plexus to her toes, to her fingers, her face, her back, ripping something out of her, tearing it from her no matter how hard she fought, and now she could hear herself screaming again, every muscle in her body cramped and rigid, fighting the endless pain.

Her knees gave out, and only Guide's hand on her shoulder was keeping her upright, his claws digging into her skin. Her throat was raw, and the world was reduced to ripping and burning and wave after wave of pain. There was a heartbeat pounding in her ears, a frenzied drum, and she could hear a high-pitched, keening wail like something dying.

There were knives in her veins, razor blades, shredding her from the inside, and the world was only pain. There was nothing else, would never be anything else —

The screaming grew strangled; weak. Trailed off.

The drum was slowing. One heartbeat, and then another, her chest clenching, and then nothing but silence.

Oh, God. Help me, she thought, quiet and startlingly clear.

The pain stopped.

Then there was nothing at all.

Stop! Steelflower's shout echoed through Guide's mind, compelling and insistent. Almost, almost he would have stopped. The draw was slowing to a trickle, life flowing into him faint and pure, the rattle in her chest telling him that the end was close. *Stop!* she shouted again, and this time there was her knife at his throat, claws against his wrist.

Guide lifted his head, his eyes opening, and he felt her blade then against his hand, ready to plunge into the wrist of his feeding hand to make his claws open. *I must not,* he said.

It is not working. You are killing her! The point digging in, her mind voice harsh.

I know, he said.

The woman beneath his hand looked ninety, her hair pale as milk, her eyes rolled up in their sockets, agony beginning to leave her face for slackness, her pulse slowing to twenty beats a minute.

The point of the knife dug in, drawing blood.

If I withdraw now it will kill her, Guide said, and his eyes met the Queen's. *She cannot take the shock again. She is not as strong as Sheppard.* He saw him in his mind's eye, Sheppard shriveled like this, lying helpless on the grass, borrowed life to heal. Borrowed, and then returned.

Steelflower recoiled in horror, and in that moment he showed her what he would do, let her feel as he felt, the draw, the intimacy of it. What it was to feed, what it was to feel life flowing into his hand. Slower. Her heartbeat slowing. And now the reverse. It was not pain to return life. It was ecstasy.

To feel it wash from him, pure and sweet and true, flowing into the Fair One like light… No, nothing so simple as light. Life was not so fragile. It was darker and messier, emerald and a thousand other shades, rich and complex, to take and to give, salt and dark. The knife in the back of his wrist was a spur, and he put his head back, feeling the Fair One's body arch as she took a shuddering breath. Air rushed into her lungs, and her face flushed, wrinkles smoothing as Sheppard's had, as though years erased themselves, as though time ran backwards.

Steelflower felt it through him, mind to mind, her hand on him. To mingle life was a primal intimacy. So had the First Queens fed, mind to mind and heart to heart. So might any demand the life of their blades, life given back to favorites as profound sharing. So might brothers in spirit.

That was what he had given Sheppard — full life taken and restored, as brother to brother. That was what he gave the Fair One.

She coughed, and her body shook. Hair like ripe grain again, her cheeks full and pink. Her eyes opened. The memory of pain was in them even as life flowed through her veins, even as he withdrew his claws, skin closing to faint white lines against her flesh.

"Jennifer! Jennifer, can you hear me?" Steelflower's voice was low and urgent, her other hand rising to rest against the Fair One's neck, checking the pulse there. "Jennifer?"

And then knowledge flooded through her. She turned her head and coughed, sweat breaking out on her forehead, her face against Steelflower's hand. "It didn't work," she whispered.

"It did not," Guide said, and his voice was heavy.

"Jennifer?" Steelflower turned her face gently. "Can you see me?"

"Yes." Her voice was thready, but her eyes fastened upon

Steelflower readily enough. "It didn't work."

"That is not important right now," the queen said, and there was anger in her voice. "What is important is that you live."

"I…"

"I fed your life back to you," Guide explained. "As I did for Colonel Sheppard, time and again. Like him, you will live. And in time it will trouble you as little as it does him."

"It didn't work." She closed her eyes.

"It did not," Steelflower said. She turned her eyes to Guide. "What does she need?"

"Rest," Guide said. "It is shock. Nothing more. All the life that was hers has been restored to her, every year. I have kept nothing."

Steelflower's eyes were hard. "I see that you did not."

Guide spread his hands and let her see the truth in his mind. He had held nothing back, no more than with Sheppard. And yet this defeat was bitterness in his throat. He reached down again and saw the Fair One flinch.

What do you do? Steelflower demanded in his mind.

"I would merely carry her to her chamber," he said aloud. "So that she may lie down in comfort and rest." His eyes went to Steelflower. "Unless you would rather carry her." Queen she might be, but she had only a human's strength, and the Fair One was taller and heavier.

"Carry her," Steelflower said. "Come, Jennifer. We will put you to bed. You will lie down and sleep to regain your strength."

He half expected the Fair One to argue, but she did not, only closed her eyes like a tired child and he lifted her up as though she were one in truth. Steelflower went ahead of them through the halls, doors opening before her, to the rooms they shared as though they were sisters. He laid her on the bed and she curled into a knot, her face tight.

"Sleep," Steelflower said, and laid her hand against her hair. "I will not go away."

The Fair One nodded, but she did not speak, her eyes closed.

Come, Steelflower said mind to mind, and she drew him

away, to the other side of a fall of cloth that screened the sleeping chamber, her hand on his wrist.

I did as I promised, Guide said, for he did not like the anger he felt in her. *You know that I have not played you false.*

I know, she said, and her eyes slid away from his. *It is not that.* Her head dipped, and for a moment she looked like a young queen in truth, faced with first darkness as anyone will be.

What then? Guide asked more gently.

It is only that I had stopped hating you.

Only that. Guide turned his hand in hers, palm to palm. *That is a small thing.*

It does not work, she said.

It does not work this time, he replied. *It would be unusual if it did. These things take much work. Next time…*

"There will not be a next time,* Steelflower said, and her voice was sharp. *Is that what you propose? To do this to her again and again?*

I had suggested some other… he began.

You sicken me.

Yes. He willed her to meet his eyes and she did. *But tell me you have never killed, Teyla Emmagan.*

She turned her face away, and he knew it was not he she hated. *There will be no second trial,* she said. *I will not be a party to this. I will not let you kill her and revive her again and again, as though you were her torturer. I am taking her back to Atlantis to Dr. Beckett's care.*

He felt the diamond-hard edges of her mind and he nodded slowly, knowing there was no challenge that would persuade her. *As you will, My Queen.*

CHAPTER TWENTY-TWO

The Things You Leave Behind

RONON Dex was a tough guy. Mel had watched him knock down three Marines in the gym, and she was impressed. She thought pretty much everyone was. And so the last place she expected to find him was sticking out from under a couch in one of Atlantis' TV lounges, muttering and grumbling. She'd been looking for a place that wasn't in use to watch a DVD, seeing as how the poker game had lost its luster. She would have just moved along if it hadn't been for the muffled yelp. What in the hell was he doing?

"Is there a problem?" Mel asked.

Ronon righted himself, or at least looked up scowling. "It's Keller's cat," he said. "I told her I'd feed the thing while she was gone, but it got away from me. I can't get it out from under there."

"Keller's cat?" She hadn't known pets were allowed in Atlantis, and they probably weren't. But everywhere people went in the service they found pets. Iraq, Afghanistan, Somalia, Kosovo — there was always a stray dog sleeping under somebody's cot, a guy with a couple of raggedy kittens that he fussed over. Anywhere they were settled for very long there were pets, babies, or both.

"Yeah." Ronon glared at the couch. "It's name is Newton." There were deep scratches on his left forearm, evidence of previous attempts to extract the cat. Probably some rough old mouser Keller had started feeding, mostly feral and untrusting.

Mel put down her DVD. "Let me have a try," she said. "I'm kind of a cat person."

"Watch it," Ronon said, stepping back. "It goes for the eyes."

Mel lay down on her stomach, turning her head sideways to glance under the low couch. Right in the middle, unreachable from both sides, a half grown Siamese kitten looked at her appraisingly, sitting like a tiny sphinx with its paws neatly folded.

Ok, not an old mouser. A kitten with too much energy to stay shut up all day.

"Hi Newton," Mel said. "You about ready to come out from under there and play?"

The kitten meowed back discontentedly. Yep, a Siamese all right. Ready to talk about its woes.

Mel fished in her pocket and produced a ball point pen. "Hey Newton. Look. Shiny thing!" She wiggled it back and forth in front of Newton, just out of reach of its paws. "Shiny, shiny, shiny thing!"

Newton looked at her with an expression that stated louder than words that he was much too smart to fall for a trick like that. And then did anyway. He batted at the pen, missing as Mel pulled it back.

"Not quite. Try again."

Four or five tries, four or five times the pen retreated, and then she had her hand on the scruff of its neck and backed out, standing up with Newton dangling from one hand. "Got him."

Ronon looked astonished. Even more so when she grabbed him with the other hand, holding him against her chest while he chewed on the end of the pen, which didn't turn out to taste good at all. "How'd you do that?"

"I always had cats," Mel said. She sat down on the couch, stroking Newton's silky fur. Sleek and healthy, the muscles in his shoulders sharply defined. Dr. Keller was taking nice care of a good cat.

Newton rolled over purring in ecstasy, displaying furry white belly to be scritched in an undignified way.

Ronon shook his head, the kind of admiration in his eyes that she'd expect for shooting something really important, or maybe kicking a guy twice her size, as she rubbed Newton's tummy, all four sets of claws flailing in the air, some of them sticking on her flight suit cuffs as he writhed. "I figured you had guts since you were a friend of Sheppard's."

Mel shrugged. "Yeah, I've known John a long time. Since we were teenagers, actually. He's a good guy."

Ronon sat down on the other end of the couch, keeping a

wide space between him and Newton, who he eyed suspiciously. "Was he always like this?"

"Sheppard?" Mel looked down at the purring kitten, now chewing playfully on her cuff with all four legs wrapped around her arm. She rubbed it under the chin, and it yawned, displaying a full set of nice clean needle sharp teeth. "He was a really sweet kid. A nice guy, kind of awkward." She shook her head, remembering. "Trusting. Kind. The guy you go to when you have a problem because you know he'll be there for you. He always had his heart on his sleeve."

"Sheppard?"

"Yeah. Kind of a prep, but not snobby. He could have rushed, but I don't think he cared about it. And then his dad messed his mom up over the divorce, and he had to work really hard to stay in school." Mel stroked the cat's little flat head. It had the long Siamese nose alright. "That's why he joined the service. He took his mom's part, and he had to have a way to pay for school. So no frat for him after that." She gave Ronon a quick smile. "The detachment's better than any frat."

Ronon probably didn't know what a frat was, but he nodded all the same. The concept worked, even if the exact words didn't. "He's not like that now."

"Who is?" Mel shrugged. "I bet you're not the guy you were when you were eighteen either."

Ronon looked startled, then his face relaxed. "No," he said.

"John said you were former military?"

Ronon nodded. "Yeah. When I was eighteen I was in my second year in examination school, getting ready to join the Immortals after the third year. I'd do three years there enlisted, then get my commission."

"Did everybody have to do a tour as enlisted first?" Mel thought that sounded like a pretty fair idea.

"Yeah. You learn everything from the basics up. How can you command troops if you've never been commanded?"

"Makes sense." Mel looked around at the lounge, at the windows opening onto night. "I've been in nineteen years. I might retire next summer. I don't know." She hadn't said anything about it to John, or to anybody else yet. Saying it to someone Air Force would be like promising to do it.

Ronon's eyebrows rose. "Don't like it?"

Mel shrugged. "If I didn't like it I wouldn't have stayed in nineteen years. But I've got some other stuff I want to do in my life, stuff I've put on hold for a long time. I don't see any way to do it without getting out." The kitten purred, writhing on her lap. "For a long time the scale balanced the other way, either/or. But now it's not." She gently extracted a stuck claw from her flight suit. "I've done a lot of things that I really wanted to do, a lot of amazing things that I'll never be able to tell anybody about. But I've done it. And now I'm wondering if it's time to do something else."

"Like what?"

"I don't know yet." Mel shook her head. "I'm not sure a commercial airline job would cut it for me. I like training. I like teaching kids how to stay alive and make their kills. I like being somewhere new, dealing with different people." She glanced up. "That's one way John and I are just alike."

Ronon put his head to the side. "So stay here."

"That simple?" Mel frowned. "I don't think so. I'm pretty sure the Air Force isn't going to let me stay here if I retire."

"Why not?"

"For one thing, it's classified all to hell," Mel said.

Ronon shrugged. "You've already got security clearance, right?" He leaned forward, putting his elbows on his knees. "Look, the way I understand this contractor thing, I'm Satedan but I work for the IOA as a contractor. I do my thing, they pay me for my skills. Right?"

"That's usually how it works, yes."

"So why can't you stay here and be a contractor here? For, say, Sateda?"

Mel blinked.

"One thing this business with the Genii showed us is that if we want our world we're going to have to show the Genii we can hold it. And that means reforming the Citizen Brigades. It means we need experienced officers who can train, and most of ours are dead. The ones who aren't have gotten settled somewhere else by now. We need to get the Satedan Band back, and we need to have a plan. If the Earthlings or Taur'i or whatever you call your-selves can hire a Satedan as a contractor, why can't Sateda hire you?" Ronon looked down at the claws hooked around her wrist. "I think we'd like you. And I expect you'd like us."

Mel blinked again. A door had opened in a blank wall, one she'd never thought was there. Maybe she'd want to go through it and maybe she wouldn't. But there it was. And maybe it was right. Maybe it could be the door into summer at last, the door to the place where she belonged. Her eyes hazed unexpectedly, and she looked purposefully down at the cat, smoothing its soft fur. "I'll think about that," she said. "I'll think about that a lot."

"No hurry," Ronon said, standing up. "But do you think you could do me a favor?"

"What's that?"

Ronon shifted from one foot to another. "Carry that animal back to Keller's quarters for me?"

"Incoming wormhole!" Banks shouted, and John came tearing out of the office, one hand automatically checking his pocket to make sure he had extra clips. "We're receiving a digital signal." She turned her head, the change in posture telling him a second before her voice. "And an IDC. It's Stargate Command."

John let out a breath he didn't know he was holding. "Put them on," he said. "And call Carter and ask her to get up here. Tell her the SGC's managed to get their hands on a ZPM and is calling in."

The static on the screen resolved itself into General O'Neill's face, looking somewhat relieved. "Sheppard? So you're still in the land of the living."

"I am, sir," John said, and couldn't help breaking into a smile. "We're just hanging out here. How about you?"

"When Caldwell left you were missing."

"I'm found," John said. He sobered. "But we've had some serious problems, as I'm sure you've heard."

"I have," O'Neill said. "What's the situation with McKay?"

"The same," John said. "The mechanical iris is holding, and we've had no further computer disruptions. They haven't found us yet, but when they do we're still screwed without a shield."

"The status of the *Hammond*?"

"Colonel Carter's on her way up," John replied. "She'll be able to tell you the details, but the *Hammond* is spaceworthy again."

O'Neill nodded. "Good to hear."

"Is Mr. Woolsey…" John began.

"We don't know yet." O'Neill shrugged. "His final hearing with the IOA is day after tomorrow. Supposedly either he'll be on his way back to you, or someone else will be."

"I see," John said tightly. That was not good news. John would be relieved to have Woolsey back, but the idea of getting some unknown quantity decided upon by the IOA…

"Eventually. They probably won't name someone immediately."

Sam came bounding up the steps, a huge grin on her face that she wiped off almost immediately, replaced by professional demeanor as she stepped in front of the cameras. "General."

"Colonel Carter. Good to see you in one piece." O'Neill's voice had a vaguely inappropriate mocking edge in it, a little too sarcastic for the situation. "Sheppard says the *Hammond* is spaceworthy."

She nodded. "We've done some repairs. I won't say we're in tip-top form, but we're battle ready."

"Woolsey may not be back," John said to her under his breath.

"Understood," she replied, her eyes on the screen, O'Neill in the control room of the SGC.

He glanced at someone they couldn't see behind him. "Colonel Mitchell, you can stand down. You won't need to go charging in right this minute." He looked back at the camera. "But I will need some reports. These are twelve days old."

"A lot has happened in twelve days," John said. "We've got an op running right now you'll want to know about." He scratched his head. "Banks, can you route this into the office? Sam and I will take it in there."

"Sure," Banks said. She switched it over and her screen went blank. She looked up at John. "It's good to hear from home, isn't it?"

Ninety-six emails in the upload from the SGC. Sam turned her speakers down, Billy Joel's *This is the Time to Remember* on too loud. That song always reminded her of Daniel, which was maybe why she opened his email first.

Hi Sam,
I'm glad you're ok.
That was Daniel, straight to the point.
Once again you've screwed up my trip to Atlantis! We were standing on the ramp. Vala was bouncing up and down and Mitchell had his steely-eyed hero thing going on, and Teal'c was…Teal'c. And Jack was pacing around the control room getting all over Landry's nerves. We were going to come charging in to rescue you, and just incidentally be in Atlantis for weeks until we could get back.

But no. You had to be fine! You had to not need rescuing. I swear Jack sounded irritated when he told Mitchell to stand down! Certainly we were disappointed. Mitchell wasn't going to get to take on the Wraith all by himself and Vala wasn't going to loot the City of the Ancients. And me and Teal'c… We were worried about you, Sam.

And that was Daniel straight to the point too.

Beside her on the desk Billy Joel was singing about walking on a beach beside an old hotel. It had been a deserted Goa'uld pleasure palace, not a hotel, but there had been a cold, windswept beach. They'd been stuck there for nearly two weeks, detoxing from an alien addiction, days and days of pacing up and down that beach with Daniel, listening to him tell stories. She had no gift of storytelling, but she'd certainly appreciated Daniel's that time.

I won't tell you to be careful, because I know you will be unless you can't. And I won't tell you to feel guilty or worry about us, because

I know you already do. I know you would trade anything for this opportunity. I know you have traded things for it. I mean, I'm a couple of years older than you, but men don't have a window of opportunity about having kids the same way women do. Command of the Hammond *at forty-one for how many years? Four or five probably? Believe me, Sam, I know the trade you're making, the door you're closing to be one of Earth's four starship commanders, to be, for these short years, at the pinnacle. To make the difference.*

And then it will be time to get out of the field. I'm not quite there yet, but I'm feeling it. I'm forty-four, Sam. I've been "Combat Archaeologist" for fourteen years now. I'm not done yet, but I can see it on the horizon. There's going to be a time when "we retreated to the Stargate under fire" stops sounding like fun. Ok, it's already stopped sounding like fun, but I can still do it. Jack knew when it was time to get out of the field, and he was wise enough to do it. I guess I'm saying there's a time to leave the table when you're winning, and you may have a bunch of hands yet to play, but I'm starting to look at the chips and wonder how many I've got left.

"Oh, Daniel," she said quietly.

I'm losing the edge the way Jack did. All of which is a round about way of saying that if the IOA relieves Woolsey, Jack's put my name in for command in Atlantis. It's a poison pill in some ways. He knows they know they can't push me around, and I figured I'd play. Why not? But now I'm starting to hope it happens. Which surprises me, because I didn't think I'd want that. But I think maybe…I do. I wasn't prepared for how let down I felt on the ramp that I wasn't coming to Atlantis.

"You know, you could just come," Sam said out loud. "You don't have to be rescuing me or taking command. You could just come." Of course it wasn't that simple, but maybe it would be. Maybe they could make it that simple.

I've wanted to come since the original expedition left, and my two brief(!) trips haven't turned out very well.

Which is one word for being electrocuted and nearly dying, Sam thought.

Anyway, what I'm trying to say is this: this is your moment in history. Seize it! Don't worry about us. The only thing we really want is to be there with you. Not to have you home one minute before you need to be. There is world enough, and time. Or at least we must live as though there were.

Love,
Daniel

"Oh, Daniel," she said again, glancing up at the pictures on the wall over the desk. That picture was more than ten years old, Daniel in his floppy hat and wire rimmed glasses, Teal'c looking impassive beside him without a hint of expression, on some alien world or another. It kind of said something that she couldn't remember which one, or exactly which mission that picture was from. It was after the one where they'd found Cassie traumatized and mute, the sole survivor of a bioengineered plague that had killed her family. It was after the one where she'd given her father to the Tok'ra. But it was before the one where they'd all lost their memory and toiled as slaves in underground factories. Daniel had had different glasses then.

"Such a strange life," she said, touching the picture with her fingertip, which was nothing like touching Daniel.

Sam hit reply and lifted her chin, squinting at the screen where the words wavered just a little bit.

Damn. Some things were horrible, yet unavoidable. She slid the drawer open a furtive inch and pulled them out, balanced the drug store reading glasses on her nose. Better. The letters were all crisp now. They were a terrible compromise, but you've got to do what you've got to do.

Dear Daniel,
Come to Atlantis. It's time.

"I know it is not the tensile strength you want," Dr. Kusanagi said, "But we do not have any of the 640 plating left. We used the last of it on the mechanical iris. I have some of the 440, which is enough to hold in vacuum, but…" She spread her hands apologetically.

Enough to hold in vacuum if it never had to take fire. Which made it problematic for hull repair. Still, it was less problematic than a gaping hole. And there was no point in griping at Miko about not having things she didn't have.

"Ok, if it's the 440 you've got," Sam said. "It will have to do temporarily."

"Until you get back to Earth," Kusanagi agreed, looking relieved that Sam wasn't going to do what Rodney would have done and demanded the impossible. Like that she conjure 640 hull plates out of thin air.

"Whenever that is," Sam said. It wouldn't make her sleep better to know she had a big dorsal patch that would blow wide open if anything got through the shields. They'd have to plan to keep the compartments behind it closed off and remove anything important. Fortunately, it was the secondary water filtration systems, which could be rerouted to the deck above if they moved the tanks. That would be a piece of work. And the space it would have to go into was the gym. Sam didn't have to look at the *Hammond's* specs to know that. She knew every compartment like the back of her hand.

Well, they could do without a gym for the twelve day trip back to Earth eventually, and while they were here they could use Atlantis'. "Tell Sergeant Manuel that he'll have to move the secondary water filtration tanks as soon as you get done with the hull plates. No sense having both your teams in there at the same time bumping elbows."

"I'll do that," Kusanagi agreed. "We will start on that section tomorrow."

"Great." Sam said. "I'll schedule a crew to collect the plates from wherever you've got them stored and bring them down so they'll be ready for your team in the morning. Weather report says it's supposed to be fair tomorrow after this rain clears out."

"Which is better than snowing," Kusanagi said. She and Sam

were both getting tired of crawling around on the *Hammond's* hull in a snowstorm.

"That it is." Sam gave her a pleasant nod and headed out of the lab. She'd have to tell Franklin to get the third watch crew to go get the plates. It would take them a couple of hours, and they'd definitely need the bobcat.

"I was wondering if I might have a word with you, ma'am," Major Lorne said.

Sam turned around to see him hopping up the hall behind her, his leg in its cast swinging freely as he plied the crutches. "Of course, Major," she said. It wasn't like Lorne to be quite so formal. After all, they'd been at the SGC together before he'd served with her in Atlantis.

"In private, if you have a moment," Lorne said.

Ok, that definitely rang trouble bells. "We could step in Dr. McKay's lab," Sam said. "I don't believe anybody is in there right now." It was only one door away, and wouldn't make Lorne hop all over the city to keep up with her.

"Yes, ma'am," Lorne said, falling in behind her as Sam keyed open the lock and turned on the light. Everything was neat, pristine, left spotless by Jeannie Miller after she'd gone over the last of Rodney's work and transferred it to her computer. She said she'd rather work in the main lab, and Sam couldn't blame her. It would be a whole lot less depressing to look for Rodney's loopholes in a room that didn't constantly remind her of his absence.

Lorne's mouth was set. Either his leg was bothering him a lot more than he let on, or this was a conversation he wasn't looking forward to.

"What's on your mind?" Sam asked, perching on one of the lab stools and gesturing for him to do the same.

"You probably know that last night was poker night for some of the guys," Lorne said.

"I do." The poker night had been going since she'd been in Atlantis if not before, the senior grade poker game that was all military and free of young lieutenants, distinct from the Girls'

Night which was organized by the female scientists.

"Some of the Daedalus' 302 wing have been playing, Lt. Colonel Hocken and Captain Grant. We asked the *Hammond's* folks if they'd like to join us, and Major Franklin came along."

"Nice of you to ask them," Sam said. Of course she hadn't been asked. She and Sheppard were off the top of the list as the captain of the *Hammond* and the military commander of Atlantis respectively. Nobody could relax if either one of them were around.

"Yes, ma'am," Lorne said. He looked a little abashed. "It's pretty laid back. A few beers, some good conversation."

"Sure," Sam said.

Lorne's eyes met hers. "I understand Major Franklin served with Colonel Sheppard in Afghanistan."

"I believe he was at the same base for a few weeks," Sam said carefully. "I don't think he knew him well though."

"That's good to know," Lorne said, looking as though he were choosing his words with equal care. "He was mentioning to Colonel Hocken that he was there when Sheppard was court martialed. He had a lot to say about the charges and about a bunch of rumors current around the base at the time. Seemed to think Colonel Hocken might be interested. Or that other people might find it interesting."

"I see," Sam said, and her voice was ice.

Lorne nodded. "I didn't think you'd want those kinds of rumors being repeated. Doesn't do much for morale, digging up old stories about stuff that might or might not have happened seven years ago. Sleeping dogs, and things like that."

"Yes indeed, Major," Sam said in a voice that sounded to her a hell of a lot like Jack. "I appreciate you bringing this to my attention. I wouldn't want the crew of the *Hammond* to cause any offense or misunderstanding on Atlantis."

"That was my thought too," Lorne said.

The cruiser *Eternal* returned to Atlantis on a day of rain. For once the temperature had risen above freezing, and gray drizzle sheeted the towers, darkening the concrete of the pier to the color of old steel. *Eternal* landed neatly on the north pier, settling onto her new landing gear with grace. Guide's men had repaired that for their queen, which was a very convenient thing for everyone.

John stood in the shadow of the cruiser's belly, watching Carson's team wheeling Dr. Keller down on a gurney, Carson holding a black umbrella incongruously over his patient.

"I'm fine," Dr. Keller protested weakly, one hand rising to shade her eyes.

"Not until I say you are, love," Carson said, keeping pace beside the gurney. "It's a traumatic thing, and Teyla was right to bring you straight home." His face was grim, and John knew he was seeing the ghost of Perla, that other dedicated young doctor who had killed herself with her own retrovirus trials.

John slouched over to Teyla, his hands in his pockets. She stood by the ramp, her Wraith face impassive as she watched Carson and Jennifer go inside. "What happened?" he asked quietly.

"It didn't work." She shook her head. "I do not know what else to tell you, John. Jennifer insisted on testing the retrovirus on herself rather than on one of Todd's prisoners. It was not effective. When he fed on her she would have died, had he not reversed the process as he did with you once."

John swore softly under his breath.

"He kept his bargain," Teyla said. "And he says she will have no more effects in the long term than you do. But…" Her voice trailed off, and he wished he could put his arm around her, but she wouldn't appreciate that, not on the tarmac in full view of half the city.

"Ok," John said. "Well, it was worth a try."

"I do understand why she will not permit it to be tested on someone else," Teyla said. "It is not that I disagree. But…"

"Yeah." John rubbed his forehead. "Let's go tell Carter

what happened. We had some good news while you were gone. The SGC managed to get their hands on a ZPM and they've dialed in. So we're not cut off anymore."

She fell into step beside him, her boot heels loud on the rain slicked pavement. "Is Mr. Woolsey back then?"

"No. The IOA are still having hearings," he replied.

"Poor Dick." Teyla stopped just short of the door, the rain falling around her. "He knew this might happen. He knew that bringing Atlantis back would be likely to cost him his career."

"He wouldn't be the first," Sam said, appearing in the doorway. She shrugged sheepishly. "It's not that I go around eavesdropping, actually. I just thought I'd come down and see how the mission went."

Teyla laughed. "We were on our way up to you, so you would not have missed much."

"I was saying Woolsey's in hot water," John said. "I wish we could have just thrown the IOA out the window and kept O'Neill in charge."

Sam's eyebrow quirked. "Do you? I don't. It's not his Air Force, John. And I could tell you some stories about the VP in the last administration. At least having more hands in the pot provides some accountability. We obey any lawful order, but most of the time we have no way of knowing how those orders were arrived at or what their consequences are."

"Any lawful order," John said with a mirthless smile.

"That doesn't contravene the Constitution of the United States." Sam stepped back inside, giving Teyla room to get out of the rain. "That's what our oath is to. That's what we promise."

"Try giving that as a defense at a court martial," John said.

"People have. People should." John fell into step beside her as they walked down the hall to the transport chamber. "There's a book called *Dereliction of Duty* you should read. About Vietnam."

"There's a winning topic," John said. "The elephant in the middle of the room. The thing you'd better not talk about. Thanks, but no thanks. I'm happy to be about a zillion light years from that argument."

"The questions aren't any different here," Sam said seriously, her back to the wall of the transport chamber.

John's face sobered. "I know that," he said.

CHAPTER TWENTY-THREE

Original Sin

"I HATE this," Sam said to no one in particular. She'd been on her way down to the Hammond when the *Eternal* had landed, and she hadn't been unhappy to be sidetracked by Teyla's return. She hadn't figured out quite what she'd say to Major Franklin.

Now, as the transport chamber doors opened again in the empty corridor, she figured she'd better work it out. Her crew was just starting to come together as a team, and now Franklin had to rock the boat. She was going to have to land on him like a ton of bricks. Being the disciplinarian didn't come easy to her, but over the years she'd learned how to do it and this was one of the situations that called for it. She couldn't afford the tensions within her crew this raised, and the last thing any of them could afford was a problem with Sheppard or the Atlantis expedition. Or, for that matter, with the *Daedalus'* 302 wing. Thankfully, Lorne knew her and trusted her enough to bring it to her before it got out of hand.

The doors to the pier slid open ahead of her, and here was Franklin coming toward her. Which begged the question of waiting. Better to get it over with.

"Major Franklin," she said. "Just the man I was looking for."

"Ma'am?" Franklin looked surprised. That wasn't her usual tone of voice. She sounded like she was channeling Jack. He could kick somebody's butt between their ears in the most thorough way she'd ever seen without ever raising his voice.

"I understand you have a problem with Colonel Sheppard," she said. Spit it out and see what he said.

"Ma'am?" He looked bewildered, not guilty. That was a good sign, if it was genuine.

"Telling stories on his record at the poker game last

night." She didn't wait for him to deny it. That was a General Hammondism — if you know it's true, never give them a chance to sidetrack the conversation onto how you know it. "I'm very disappointed in you, Major. That's unprofessional. Digging up rumors seven or eight years old about the commander of the base you're visiting and repeating them to his subordinates is absolutely out of bounds."

"Um," Franklin gulped. Ok, not guilt or hostility. Franklin could be a motor mouth. She'd already figured that out. Maybe this was nothing but that, gossip to make himself sound important when trying to fit in with people he didn't know. But Hocken would read it as a threat, and Lorne as an attack on someone whose back he was watching.

"Sheppard is a fine man and a good officer," Sam said. "Moreover, he's the commander of this base, where we are guests. Guests do not muddy the water for their hosts. Is that clear?"

"Abundantly, ma'am," Franklin said, drawing himself up. If she'd been him, her cheeks would have been flaming.

"Right now we are enjoying the full liberty of the city. It wouldn't be very pleasant if the crew of the *Hammond* or any individual were to lose that liberty and have to stay aboard the ship for the remainder of our stay." Atlantis' mess served fresh food. They had unlimited showers and a full gym, movie nights and poker games and pick up basketball. Franklin being stuck aboard the *Hammond* for several weeks would be a pretty severe punishment. For the entire crew of the *Hammond* to be stuck aboard the ship because Franklin had insulted the base commander would make his life utter hell.

Not that Sheppard would do that. He wouldn't punish the whole crew of the *Hammond* by placing the city off limits. But Franklin probably didn't know Sheppard well enough to know that. And Sam would certainly require Franklin to stay aboard if she thought he was going to make trouble.

"Yes, ma'am." Franklin's voice was very precise. He saw the event horizon looming there too.

"I do not want to hear any further stories about you spreading old rumors," Sam said. "Gossip is unprofessional, and doubly so when it reflects poorly on your ship and your command. I am sure this is the last of this incident."

"It is, ma'am." Franklin brought himself to attention.

"Good. Now go get a crew together to get the hull plates that Dr. Kusanagi will need for repairs tomorrow. Ask her which bay they're stored and move them to the tarmac next to the *Hammond*. You'll need the bobcat, because the plates are large and very heavy." Franklin had probably been on his way to dinner, but it wouldn't hurt him to wait a little while. A couple of hours' work loading hull plates would serve as a reminder of how very unpleasant his life could become, but wouldn't be severe enough to get his back up. That was the other thing she couldn't afford. She needed a first officer who was on her team, who was 100 percent bought in. She could strangle him for making this necessary. But it also wasn't the kind of thing she could afford to let pass.

"Yes, ma'am." Franklin opened his mouth and shut it again, as though deciding what to say. "Ma'am, I want you to know that I don't have anything personal against Colonel Sheppard. I barely knew him in Kandahar."

"Good," Sam said. "Then I'm certain we won't need to speak of this again."

Teyla dreamed, and in her dream she knew she was in Atlantis. She rose up from her bed and left John sleeping, left her rooms and walked the halls sleeplessly, through silent echoing corridors, past windows that opened on night.

She made her way to the control room, hearing even before she entered the comforting soft sounds of the machines, the voices of the duty crew. Chuck was at the ops board, and gave her a smile as she passed. The office door was open, and Teyla was unsurprised to hear Rodney, to see him pacing back and forth, explaining something to Elizabeth, who sat at her desk, her laptop open before her.

"Of course it's a problem," he said testily. "90 percent of the females died in the initial trials. But those who lived were more radically transformed than we anticipated. I don't think we had any idea that we would be creating those kinds of mental powers, far beyond anything we have previously experienced."

Teyla stood in the doorway, hesitating, but Elizabeth raised her eyes and beckoned to her. "Come in, Teyla," she said. "This concerns you."

"It's a big problem," Rodney said.

"The mortality rate?"

"No, no, no." Rodney shook his head. "We knew that might be an issue."

"What are you talking about?" Teyla asked, and thought she saw Elizabeth nod almost imperceptibly.

"What to do about the Asurans," John said, slouching in the visitor's chair.

"Michael," Carson said, standing by the window, looking out into the gateroom below. "What do we do with Michael? We should never have begun this."

"How else were you going to get this off my neck?" John asked, turning his head. The Iratus Bug was clamped on his throat, teeth in the vein.

"I think we've got a problem here," Rodney said. He turned and looked at her, Elizabeth's eyes following him. "We have to kill Osprey."

"It's too bad," Carson said mildly.

"Yeah," John said, and got to his feet in one swift move, leveling the P90 at her.

And then she was running, diving behind the control board as the shots followed her, rattling off the metal, throwing sparks from the Ancient systems. She was running and they were behind her, the gateroom floor dancing with tracer fire as she sprinted toward the open event horizon, John's voice behind her, calling in Marine teams on the radio. She felt the bullets touch her, once, twice, but miraculously she was still on her feet, still running through the pain, plunging into the wormhole.

And out the other end.

She stood in the gatefield on Athos, and a low moon was setting behind scudding clouds. Across the water the ruined city rose cold and stark.

Elizabeth stood before the gate, lifted her chin. "Where are we?" she asked.

"Athos," Teyla said, looking around. The wind whispered over the dry grass. "This is Gatefield. My mother was Tegan of Gatefield. My people came here in the spring each year of my life. We spent the winters in the valleys where the weather was less harsh, but we returned here every spring, to Gatefield and Emege That Was." She looked at Elizabeth, her heart still pounding. Guides came but seldom in dreams, but she knew one when she saw it. And of course it would take the form of one she had known and trusted. "Elizabeth," she said respectfully, "What is it I am supposed to know? What are you trying to tell me?"

"You already know," Elizabeth said. "You have all the pieces, Teyla. You just have to put them together."

"You will not tell me?" Teyla asked, though she did not expect an answer. If it were so simple, there would be no need of the rest of it.

"I can't do that," Elizabeth said, and Teyla thought she heard real regret in her voice. "But you have all the pieces now. It's all there. You should ask Kate to help you put it together."

"Kate is dead," Teyla said, and her voice broke on it. "She is dead these two years."

"Janus knew," she said. "But he did not tell me. Perhaps he told Dr. Jackson. I don't know. If so, he does not remember."

"I do not know what you mean," Teyla said. "Elizabeth, what use is there in asking people who are dead or who do not remember?"

"You remember," Elizabeth said. "It's in your blood, in your lineage. You remember. And you are free to act."

"And you are not?" Teyla asked sharply, her head rising like a hunting dog's.

Elizabeth shook her head. "Wake," she said. "And remember."

Eva Robinson had just put her cup of coffee down on her desk and switched on her monitor, ready to begin her day, when there was a soft knock on the door. She looked up and suppressed a shudder.

Teyla stood in the doorway, Teyla and not Teyla at the same time. She understood that the physical transformation into a Wraith queen was grueling, and of course it didn't make any sense to undo it when presumably Dr. Keller would only have to redo it again in a few days, but it was still eerie. For now it seemed that a Wraith queen was walking freely around Atlantis.

It didn't help that Teyla dressed the part, still wearing the black skirts and dark emerald bodice of the Wraith queen rather than her usual clothing. Maybe her regular clothes looked too strange on a Wraith. Maybe that was worse, or at least more confusing.

"Do you have a few moments?" Teyla asked politely.

"I have lots of moments," Eva said, glancing down at the calendar up on her computer. "I have all the moments until 11 o'clock." She shrugged. "I'm still not the most popular person in Atlantis."

Teyla came in, her skirts whispering against the door as it closed behind her. She lifted her chin. "I would like to talk to you about my dreams. This is something that I would have brought to Kate."

Eva smiled, picking up her coffee cup. It was snowing again, big moist white flakes swirling around the towers. "Come on in and sit down," she said. "I can be a pretty good ear too." She handed Teyla her coffee. "Can you hold this for me for a minute? I'm getting pretty good on the crutches, but I can't handle them with a full cup of coffee yet." Teyla took the cup and she pushed up, coming around the desk to one of the chairs by the window.

"I am happy to," Teyla said, handing her cup to her once she was sitting and had arranged the crutches close at hand. She settled into the other chair, shaking her hair back from her face. "Elizabeth said I should bring this to Kate, and since I cannot, I bring it to you."

Eva's coffee grew cold in the cup while the story unfolded. At last Teyla sat with her hands in her lap, silent. "That's pretty incredible," she said.

"I do not expect you to believe that I have really spoken with Elizabeth," Teyla said tightly.

Eva shrugged. "Why not? Many people have the experience of speaking with friends or loved ones who are dead."

Teyla looked at her keenly with sharp golden eyes. "You are different," she said.

"It takes a certain kind of arrogance to dismiss the experiences of thousands of other people because they don't jibe with your personal beliefs," Eva said. "I don't know what happens after death. But I do know that many people have very profound experiences dreaming about or talking with the dead." She put her coffee cup down. "It's not my job to change people's beliefs, Teyla. My job is to help people find solutions to their problems within the framework of their beliefs."

"I am asking you," Teyla said. "What do you think this is about?"

Eva sighed. "Well, at a glance the glib answer would be that you're deeply disturbed by this masquerade. You find yourself identifying with the Wraith, and that makes you question your relationships with the people in your life."

"I know that," Teyla said. "Believe me, I am aware that I make people uncomfortable."

"You would make people less uncomfortable if you wore your regular clothes," Eva said. "And you don't."

Teyla smiled, and it was a Wraith queen's smile. "Perhaps I think it is good for people to be a little uncomfortable. It makes them uncomfortable to see a Wraith as a person. It is always uncomfortable to see the enemy as people, and yet that is the truth of it."

Eva nodded. "That's a hard thing for people to do when they're engaged in battle. There's a school of thought that it's one of the primary reasons for PTSD. It's the people who have the strongest empathy, the people who are the most culturally flexible and have the strongest sense of responsibility for others who are the most vulnerable. They can't turn it off. They can't stop caring."

"And yet they are the best ones," Teyla said quietly, her eyes on the falling snow outside. "Who would want to entrust the lives of people to someone to whom they were nothing? I would not follow such a leader. Nor would I give responsibility to someone who did not feel the full weight of it."

"There's the bind," Eva said. "Empathy and flexibility are important in a leader. And yet it's those very qualities that mean that events cut them to pieces." She reached for her cold coffee. Cold was better than none. "So they've got to have something firm to stand on. They need good skills and a supportive network to get through it. With the right kind of platform to stand on, people can thrive in the most difficult situations." Her eyes met Teyla's. "But you know that," she said. "Coming from a world where everyone lives under that kind of shadow."

"Yes," Teyla said thoughtfully, "And no. Because there is no responsibility. The Wraith come, inevitable as weather, but also equally without fault. No one is to blame. Tragedy strikes, but no one is expected to do anything about it. It is no one's fault." She shook her head. "I am dreaming about old stories," she said. "I never liked the story of the changeling girl, never, not even as a child." She gave Eva a rueful smile, strange in a Wraith queen's face. "I felt sorry for her. A girl who was transformed into a monster, into a revenant, but who even the Ancestors could not catch, because she could shift her shape into that of a white bird. And so she haunts the forests still, disguised as a patch of mist or as a water bird, waiting for the unwary." Teyla shrugged, rearranging her sleeve along her arm. "I expect this is the sort of tale that all peoples have, to prevent children from wandering off into the forest. Do as your parents tell you and be home by dark or the changeling will get you!"

Eva smiled. "A lot of cultures have cautionary tales like that. It's true. But sometimes there's a seed of truth in stories."

"You do not dismiss them?" Teyla's forehead rose, what would have been eyebrows if she had them.

"Stories are the frame we give our lives," she said. "They teach us what to believe about ourselves and the world around us, give us touchstones. Give us ways of seeing ourselves that are either productive or not." Eva took a sip of cold coffee. "A few years ago I was working with kids who had been in a natural disaster, a terrible hurricane. Many of them had lost their homes, their schools, everything they had. Some of them had lost their parents or brothers and sisters. Very hard stuff. And so one of the frames we were working with was encouraging them to write their stories as superhero origin stories." Teyla looked quizzical. "Like in comic books," Eva said. "A lot of superheroes became who they were because of something terrible that happened when they were a child. Their parents were gunned down in front of them. Their world was destroyed. They were pursued and hunted when they developed mutant powers. All kinds of things. But in the stories, it's the origin story that makes the superhero who he or she is. So when we encourage the kids to frame the terrible things that have happened to them as part of a superhero origin story, what we're doing is giving them a way of looking at themselves as someone who will transcend the tragedy. They're going to be super. They're going to come out of this aware of their special gifts, strong people who have a brilliant future."

Eva took another sip of coffee. "In a very real sense, we become who we dreamed of becoming. We inhabit the story we tell about ourselves. But beyond that, myths and legends often are a way of passing down things that happened in the distant past."

"You're saying the changeling story may be true?" Teyla asked.

"I'm saying there may be a seed of truth in it. And you know that on some level, and your subconscious is trying to help you put the pieces together."

"And when I do?" Teyla asked.

"Then you tell the story."

Teyla was silent, and Eva rested her chin on her fingertips. "Let me tell you a story," she said.

"Truly?" Teyla smiled again, odd and fleeting on a Wraith face. "I will hear your story, Dr. Robinson."

"This is a story about both of us, and as far as I know, it's true." Eva marshaled her thoughts and began. "Once, a long time ago on the steppes of Central Asia, there was a woman. Her people were nomadic like yours were, pastoral people who followed their herds on the open seas of grass. They lived in tents and yurts built of animal hide, and they left no buildings."

"One day, in the last years of the war between the Ancients and the Wraith, the Ancients came among them and took her away. She came here, to the Pegasus Galaxy." Eva took a deep breath. "We don't know if she came alone, or with many of her people. We don't know if she came willingly, as an ally or a soldier or an explorer. Maybe she came as a wife or a lover. Maybe she came as a daughter. Or maybe she came as a drugged captive in the hold of a cargo ship. We'll never know how she came. We just know she did. And we know one other thing about her."

"What is that?" Teyla asked.

"She had a baby, a little girl. Maybe she had more than one. Maybe she had ten children. But she had at least one daughter, because through her daughter her mitochondrial DNA comes down to you. It passes through the female line, and like twenty percent of the people here that Carson has tested, yours comes from Earth. Yours comes from the steppes of Central Asia." Eva laced her hands around her coffee cup. "We know something else. When Atlantis fell, when the Wraith destroyed their civilization, she lived. Somehow, in everything that happened, she wasn't killed. She and her daughter survived. We know they did, because you are here, you and Torren who carry her mitochondrial DNA. She stands among your foremothers as surely as the Queen who gave you her Gift."

"You are the story," Teyla whispered. "It's in your blood." She looked up, her eyes meeting Eva's. "And what happened to her kin?"

"The ones who stayed on Earth went in many directions," Eva said. "There are people all over the world who have the same type. Some of them went east, and the type shows up in Siberia and northernmost China. Some went west, to the very edge of the known world, to Ireland and Cornwall and Brittany. And some went south, the most of them. The type is most common among the Pashtun peoples in Iran and Afghanistan." Eva smiled. "Our mitochondrial DNA tells a powerful story. We are all, every person on Earth, descended from a single foremother an incalculably long time ago, and all our DNA is a variation on hers. We call her the African Eve, and you're her daughter as much as I am. Once, a long time ago, there were two sisters and they said goodbye to one another. My foremother stayed in Africa, and yours began a long trek northwards, the first step on a journey of millions of lightyears." She leaned forward, meeting Teyla's eyes. "But the important thing is that it began with two sisters."

"No," Teyla said, and her eyes were hooded. "It began with three sisters." She lifted her face and shook her head. "I am standing on the edge of something so enormous and so terrible that I do not even know how to phrase it." She let out a long breath, her face inscrutable in its mask of plastic surgery. "I think I begin to see what Elizabeth meant, and it is a story so dark with blood that I recoil at it. I do not know what to do with this story."

She got up and paced to the windows, stood with her hands against the glass, looking out at the snow. "I will give you a story," she said at last. "Not the dark one, but the one everyone knows. The one all of my people know." Teyla paused, her long green claws against the falling flakes outside. "Once, long ago in the beginnings of time, there were the Ancestors, and they dwelled in paradise. There was no hunger and no war, no danger and no illness. And yet they were discontent. And one among them said, 'Let us make children in our own image, that we may joy in them, and in their precocious follies delight.' And so they did.

Ten men and ten women they made, each in the image of one of the Ancestors, tall and short, dark and fair, blue eyed and brown eyed. And they awakened them in paradise, and took them to their hearts."

Teyla did not turn from the window, swirling snow half obscuring the towers outside. "This is what we believe of our origins. We were conceived in love by the Ancestors. We were nurtured as any baby beloved by its parents, sheltered from the storms until we were grown. We were the children of love." She raised her head, her long black hair falling down her back, and Eva could not see her face. "We Athosians say that our first foremother was Amitas. It was not until I came here that I learned that her name has meaning in Ancient." Teyla turned. "Her name is Beloved." Teyla shook her head. "I do not know how to carry this story."

"I can't tell you that," Eva said. She met Teyla's eyes. "Except that I expect you'll tell it at the right time, to the right person."

CHAPTER TWENTY-FOUR

Compromises

CARSON shifted the sling on his shoulder, trying to find a comfortable place for its strap to rest. The thing was really beginning to get tiresome, but he knew well enough that he should give it another week at least. As things were, it seemed that all he was going to take away from their disastrous desert mission in the long run was a nasty scar and a good story to tell about fighting off killer reptiles. There was no use in straining his healing arm and going back to worrying about whether he'd have the full use of it.

Still, it would be good to be able to use both hands again. He peered at the computer keyboard, hunting and pecking left-handed to type.

"Carson?" Jennifer said from the doorway of the laboratory.

Carson stood at once. "You shouldn't be out of bed yet."

"My vital signs and my blood work are all normal," Jennifer said. "I'm not saying I feel great, but I'm also not planning to run a marathon or anything. I won't even take the stairs. Transport chambers all the way."

He looked her over. "How are you feeling? And at least sit down."

Jennifer didn't argue with that, sinking into a chair, her hand going to her hair as if worried that it was coming down from its severe ponytail. "I feel tired," she said. "And I ache all over, but I suspect that's from tensing up so much when — when I was being fed on. I took some ibuprofen, so I'm, you know, good."

"It's a tremendous shock," Carson said. "And, before you say it, I know Todd healed you, but I also treated Colonel Sheppard when the same thing happened to him. It can be a difficult experience in more ways than just physically. It wouldn't be a bad idea for you to schedule some time with Dr. Robinson."

"I will if it bothers me, but…" Jennifer shrugged. "I mean, I'm not saying it wasn't pretty awful, but I wanted to do this. I knew…well, maybe not exactly what I was getting into, but I knew what was going to happen, and I knew it was going to hurt. It was my choice. I think that makes it a little different from being tortured." She shrugged again, and looked away. "There were only a few moments where I really thought I was going to die."

Carson let out a breath. "That's the problem with doctors as patients," he said. "They're every bit as stubborn as these great strapping soldiers."

Jennifer's mouth twitched in a smile. "Oh, we're not that bad," she said.

"Worse," Carson said. "I'm so tired of this bloody sling that I'd have come down to complain about it if I weren't trying not to add to your stress."

"I'll take a look later, but I'm not expecting miraculously rapid healing," Jennifer said. "Unless you can get Todd to arrange that for you."

Carson repressed a shudder. "I'll pass on that," he said. He still remembered all too clearly having Michael close enough to touch him, and had no desire to be that close to any of the other Wraith. "Anyhow, I've had the Hoffan drug, remember? I can't be fed on without the Wraith dying of it."

"I know," Jennifer said. "That's why the next trial has to be me again."

"Oh, no, you don't," Carson said. "You can't imagine we're going to let you do this again."

"Nothing's changed," Jennifer said. "We still need to know if there's any way to make this work. I have some ideas about what went wrong, and, believe me, I'm going to run all the simulations I can, but at some point we're going to have to test this again. And I can't ask anyone else to go through being fed on as a test."

"Well, to start with, we know that your best try at a prototype didn't work," Carson said. "For all you know, this could be just one more blind alley."

"If we always gave up the first time something didn't work—"

"We'd have saved ourselves no end of grief trying to genetically modify the Wraith," Carson said a little sharply.

"And let a lot of other people die," Jennifer said. "Come on, the answer can't be 'we should always give up every time we have problems.'"

Carson shook his head. "Knowing that you might go through exactly the same ordeal again, that your life may depend on Todd deciding to heal you—"

"That's why it has to be me again," Jennifer said. "First, because now that I've experienced this, I can't ethically let anyone else consent to go through it for research purposes."

"I thought you were fine," Carson said.

"Yes, fine except for having been in agonizing pain, which is the part that– I just don't think we get to inflict agonizing near-death experiences on people. As a doctor, I have a problem with that."

"I do, too."

"But the main thing is, I know now that Todd will revive me, even at a point where I'm essentially clinically dead. I don't know how much of that is that he really wants to make this work, and how much of it is that he's scared of Teyla—"

"We're all a little scared of Teyla, love," Carson said with a smile.

"And I was starting to get the impression that I remind him of…" Jennifer hesitated, as if not sure whether she should repeat something a patient had told her in confidence. "Somebody who used to be important to him. Anyway, for whatever reasons, I'm confident now that if we try this again, he's not going to let me die. I can't put someone else's life in his hands, not when I wouldn't be as sure."

"Show me what you're thinking," Carson said reluctantly. He tried to think entirely rationally as Jennifer talked through the changes she wanted to make to the retrovirus, to focus on the genetic puzzle pieces rather than on the faces of patients he'd watched die after being fed on. It was hard not to remember all the young Marines he'd sent home with the faces of old men.

"I see what we did wrong," Jennifer said. "It's a simple adjustment. We just need permission to do one more test."

Carson shook his head. "I can't recommend it," he said. "Not when we're no more certain this time than we were last time. And not when I still have grave doubts about whether making this thing work is going to be good for anyone."

"It may be the only way we can save Rodney's life," Jennifer said.

"You're not thinking—"

"Yes, I am," Jennifer said, her voice rising in frustration. "What else are we going to do when we get him back? We've run a hundred simulations and none of them work. I don't know how to turn Rodney back into a human permanently. Do you?"

"The original retrovirus we used on Michael—"

"Causes global amnesia at any dose high enough to keep the physical changes from reverting," Jennifer said. "That's not an acceptable long-term solution. You know Rodney wouldn't think it was."

"It's better than dead," Carson said. "He could relearn what he knows—"

"A PhD in astrophysics and a couple of decades of incredibly specialized experience? There's no way, and you know it. Not to mention not even remembering his sister, or… or anyone else who's important to him. He'd hate that."

"He'd hate being dead worse," Carson said.

"I'm not sure you're right," Jennifer said. "But, okay, that's our best idea right now. So what if we try it, and Rodney isn't strong enough to survive the process? If he hasn't fed recently — and I can't really bring myself to hope that he has–"

"It could kill him," Carson said. "I know."

"I looked at your notes on the original experiment," Jennifer said. "Your suggestion if the first research subject didn't survive the transformation was for Sheppard's team to go out and get you another Wraith."

Carson closed his eyes for a moment, his good hand tightening on the lab bench. This was part of the reason he'd wanted to spend his time out in the field, not doing this kind of research anymore. It all twisted together in his stomach, the experiment on Michael that the first Carson Beckett had done but that he could still remember, the experiments on the hybrids, the ones who hadn't survived, who'd been disposed of as wasted materials—

"Carson?" Jennifer said, sounding concerned.

He made himself take a deep breath and focus on Rodney. Rodney, who God willing would be their patient soon, and who deserved to be well and whole again if anyone did. "We can put him in stasis," he said. "Take the time to come up with a solution that isn't as risky—"

"And eventually we'll have to test it," Jennifer said. "His best chance of surviving that is if he's fed recently. Tell me it isn't."

"I can't tell you it isn't," Carson admitted after a long moment. "But I can't imagine that he'd want you to endanger yourself this way just to make his chances better. And if you think he's just going to be willing to feed on you to survive, even if you know it won't kill you—"

"If it won't kill me, then it's like... like if he needed a kidney transplant or something. It's an acceptable risk for the donor, even if the process isn't very pleasant. I'd be willing to do that for Rodney, if it was what he needed to stay alive. Wouldn't you?"

"A kidney is one thing," Carson said. "Letting him feed on you—"

"We're hoping the process won't be nearly as painful if we get it right," Jennifer said. "And even if it is, wouldn't you do it if it would save Rodney's life? Wouldn't Colonel Sheppard, or Teyla, or... Okay, maybe not Ronon, not after what the Wraith have done to him, but you get my point."

"I suppose I would," Carson said.

"This is not going to kill me," Jennifer said. "If the worst thing that happens is that I go through what just happened to me again, I can accept that."

"We've seen that being repeatedly fed and revived causes significant side effects," Carson said. "When you treated Ronon after the Wraith brainwashed him, he was physically addicted to the Wraith's reverse feeding process. That wasn't easy for him to recover from, and I'm not sure I would say there aren't any lasting psychological effects."

"He said they did it to him over and over," Jennifer said. "I'm not talking about anything like that. Once more, maybe twice at the most. Colonel Sheppard survived more than that under worse circumstances, and he's fine."

"For a certain definition of fine," Carson said.

Jennifer spread her hands. "The one we use around here," she said. "I treat Marines and airmen all the time who've been wounded in action. Some I can patch up, and they'll be fine in a week. Some are going to carry the scars they got here for the rest of their life. Some of them have disabling injuries, or disabling post-traumatic reactions. I can't watch that every day and not be willing to do the same myself."

"You're not a soldier," Carson said.

"I know," Jennifer said. "And I don't want to be one, and I'm actually not sure—" She hesitated, and then went on more deliberately. "I'm not sure I want to be part of a program that does that to people for the rest of my life," she said. "But right now what's important is that this is what I need to do to save Rodney's life. Even if we never use this thing again, even if it never saves anybody else from the Wraith, if we can save Rodney, then I want to do this." She raised her chin. "Will you back me up on this?"

"There's no such thing as 'never using it again,'" Carson said. "You can't put the genie back in the bottle."

"Yes or no, Carson?" Jennifer said.

"Everything you're saying is true," Carson said. "I'll say as much to Colonel Sheppard. As to whether I think you should take the risk…" He shook his head. "I wouldn't do it to you as your doctor. But I want to help Rodney as much as you do, and if you're determined to do this to yourself, I won't stand in your way."

"Thank you," she said, her expression lightening.

Carson shook his head. "I just hope we won't both be sorry."

Sam ducked through the noisy gym to the small practice room in the back, dodging around four treadmills occupied by jogging Marines who were watching a long-ago recorded football game on the TV along the wall and arguing about every play. The door wasn't locked and it was quiet. Which was a good thing. She preferred not to try to concentrate on yoga with TV and football and loud arguments about 'You are so bogus, man!' Her Zen was a little harder to find than that.

Teyla stood in the middle of the room, bent into an incredibly painful looking pretzel pose, her green Wraith skin incongruous with her Athosian gym clothes.

"I'm sorry," Sam said, starting to back out. "I didn't realize this room was taken."

"You are welcome to come in," Teyla said, extending her arms to begin coming out of the posture. "It is very noisy in the main gym."

"Thanks." Sam put down her towel and bag on the bench beside the window. It was dark outside, and the stained glass looked muddy against the night. "I was looking for somewhere to do yoga without so much of a crowd."

"It is difficult to concentrate with the television," Teyla agreed, bending in another way that Sam thought seemed pretty much impossible. Teyla made it look easy.

"That, and I'm not sure I want some twenty year old commenting on my fat ass or saying, 'Hey, Carter can only bench press whatever.' I never used to be able to figure out why Jack started using the SGC gym at an ungodly time of morning, but now I get it."

Teyla looked at her critically, and also upside down. "I do not think your ass is fat," she said calmly.

"It's not as skinny as it used to be, and I do a lot of sitting on it on the *Hammond*." Sam sat down on the floor, taking off her shoes. "I have to be a lot more conscientious about going to the gym now that I don't have people chasing me and shooting at me on a daily basis."

"And you are not twenty," Teyla said serenely, inverting and stretching forward on her toes.

"That too." Sam started her stretches while Teyla leaned forward again, her back leg perfectly straight as she bent from the waist over her front leg. Sam was forty one. She couldn't have done that when she was twenty, and Teyla couldn't be more than a couple of years younger than she was. And she'd had a baby.

"I do not wish that I were," Teyla said contemplatively as she came up. "I was very foolish when I was twenty."

"I was very serious."

"I imagine that you were." Teyla looked at her, and her Wraith face was hard to read, though her voice was not. "Have you always known exactly what you wanted?"

"No." Sam put her right leg out, bending forward over it. Her forehead sort of touched her knee. Kind of. If she shifted off the hip bone. "I've made a lot of mistakes."

"I have too," Teyla said. Her voice was rueful. "That one's name was Jorrah, and I was unwise to marry him."

"Mine was Jonas," Sam said. She could definitely feel the pull in her hip. God, she was sick of that thing popping! Her hip was getting as bad as Jack's knees. "But at least I didn't quite marry him." She straightened up. "He turned out to be crazy."

"Jorrah was not crazy. Only manipulative." Teyla was on the other leg now, but there was a wobble in the pose this time. She wasn't holding it right. Left leg. The bone bruise she'd had a couple of months ago, no doubt. Those things took time to heal.

"Check," Sam said. "I dated one of those too. He wanted to get a dog and that was really the last straw."

Teyla didn't look up. "What is wrong with dogs?"

"Nothing is wrong with dogs." Sam switched legs, stretching her left one out. "If you like dogs. If you have the kind of life where you know you'll be home at a certain time and you can let the dog out and feed it."

"Of course," Teyla said. That hip was definitely wobbling, but she was determinedly holding the pose. "I thought perhaps it was some sort of Air Force taboo against dogs."

Sam snorted. "No. We've got some weird ones, but nothing against dogs. I was engaged to that one too."

Teyla's mouth twitched. "You seem to have had some close calls. You have been engaged how many times?"

Sam put her forehead to her left knee. That was easier. "Three," she said, only hesitating slightly. "Maybe I'm just hard to marry."

"That may be so," Teyla said seriously.

Sam stretched. "You know, when you live like this… Maybe the time will come when I'm ok with staying on Earth and getting a dog and being home at night. One day the *Hammond* will be somebody else's. But I can't imagine who I'd be if I didn't want to walk through the Stargate."

Teyla's voice was rueful. "Nor I," she said, coming out of the pose. "I am Teyla Who Walks Through Gates, and I cannot imagine that I would remain myself if I were content to always be in one world when there are so many to know. But it seems that my compromises do not have to be as cruel as yours."

"Don't they?" Sam asked, lifting her eyes to Teyla's Wraith face, feeding hand and Athosian clothes.

Teyla took a breath. "Perhaps they are," she said. "Only different."

"You have your son."

"Yes." Teyla sunk to the ground in one graceful move, her legs folding under her like some sort of water bird. "But I no longer have my rank and position among my own people. You have that. Athosians tolerate the Gift, unlike most of the peoples of this galaxy. But this…" She glanced down at her arms, her long emerald nails. "If I say that I am Steelflower? This they will not understand. It is too far and too much. I will be outcast." She shook her head, looking up at the darkened window above. "You have your starship."

"I do." Sam crossed her legs. "And that's not as smooth as I'd like it to be. I've always been the wonk, not the inspirational leader. I've always been part of a team. A starship crew has to be a team, but the captain has to stand a little apart. I can't be in there shooting the bull with Franklin and Chandler."

"I can see that." Teyla leaned back on her arms, arching her back. "What about Mel Hocken? Is she not officially part of the *Daedalus'* crew? It seems that the two of you have much in common."

Sam took a deep breath. "There are complicated reasons why that's not a good idea."

"I understand," Teyla said, and she thought she did. After all, she had lived among these people for more than five years, and she thought she understood their taboos, even if she did not understand the reasons for them. "Athosians are more accepting than many peoples because we have been repeatedly been culled to the bone. We live so close to the borders of the land of death that we know better than to reject any love that comes, whatever its shape or form. Who shall say that anyone should not care for another, or that a child should have one father alone when what is important is that everyone be part of the whole? Otherwise we will die." She leaned her head back, looking up at the beveled ceiling. "And yet if Kanaan saw me like this he would wonder if Torren were safe with me."

"You would never hurt Torren," Sam said sharply.

"Who knows what a Wraith would do?" Her smile was grim. "People would wonder. If Kanaan said, 'I do not want Torren to live with her because Atlantis is too dangerous, and because the new man she has chosen is not of our people,' Athosians would mock him. Kanaan is jealous, they would say. It is unseemly to be possessive of one who has moved on, problematic to upset the group with attachments which are not mutual. He would lose face, and none would listen to his complaints. But if he said, 'She is Wraith, and she no longer knows who she is,' that would be a different matter. 'Who can tell what she might do? It is too dangerous for a son of Athos, for my son.'"

"That totally sucks."

"So do your compromises."

"Yeah." Sam said. "They do."

"Which is not to say that Kanaan would do such," Teyla said. She sat up straight, her brow furrowed. "I do not think he would. But I have been wrong so badly before."

"Jorrah?"

"Yes." Teyla shook her head.

"At least he didn't try to set himself up as a god on a small planet?" Sam asked.

Teyla laughed, as she'd meant her to. "No. Did Jonas?"

"Oh yeah." Sam put the water bottle down. "Never can say I don't have taste."

"I think perhaps we will chalk it up to experience," Teyla said. "But John may be right that we are all a little cracked."

CHAPTER TWENTY-FIVE

Devils and Dust

IT WAS going to be close. Jack could see that. One vote, maybe two in either direction. A vote against sending Woolsey back to Atlantis was essentially a vote for Daniel. Now that they'd gotten in contact, it was obvious that someone had to be appointed immediately, and the crowd who didn't want Atlantis in the hands of the Air Force weren't about to leave it that way forever, with Sheppard in "temporary" charge that dragged on for months and months. If he'd really wanted to power grab, Jack thought, the smart thing to do would be just stall. Sheppard could run the show for the better part of a year that way.

But it wasn't Sheppard's forte. He'd gone into this intending to send Woolsey back to Atlantis. If that wasn't possible, Daniel was the best option, though frankly Daniel might kill him. Administration was not exactly Daniel's thing.

The swing vote was Roy Martin. And so Jack was surprised to see him by himself in the conference room a good fifteen minutes before the meeting was supposed to start. The IOA ran on diplomatic time, which meant the principals arrived fifteen minutes late. So Martin shouldn't put in an appearance for at least half an hour. Also, surely the other IOA members wanted to bend his ear one way or the other? Unless they were all sure of his vote.

All of that ran through Jack's head in the moment he checked in the doorway, an ironic smile on his face. "Senator Martin. Speak of the devil!"

Lieutenant Anderson, who was laying out the coffee service at the back of the room, started to attention, but he waved her down. She was furniture today, albeit furniture with sharp ears.

"Am I the devil, General?" Martin's eyes had a distinct twinkle. "I recall my honorable opponent did put cartoon horns on me in that ad back in '84. But then I expect he and the devil were old friends."

"As I recall you lost that election, Senator," Jack said.

"If at first you don't succeed…" Martin said. "You can't keep a good man down. And some other clichés." He laid his leather portfolio on the table before a chair with its back to the window. "Let me ask you one question, General."

"Anything," Jack said, opening his arms expansively.

"I'm not sure I want to know just anything," Martin said. "That's a dangerous opening to give me."

"I expect it is," Jack said.

Martin met his eyes. "Who's the better man?"

Jack swallowed. "Daniel Jackson."

"Who's the man for the job?"

"Richard Woolsey." Jack sat down on the edge of the conference table. "There are some jobs that don't call for good men. They call for men who can get it done."

"Who can handle this, you mean," Martin said. He leaned on the back of his chair. "Why do you think I have this job, here in my golden years?"

"You raised a hell of a lot of money," Jack said.

Roy Martin laughed. "A lot of people raised a lot more. I'll tell you why I'm here, General. I've been governor and I've been senator. I've lost and won and lost and I've served my time. Other than the importance of keeping active as a senior citizen, I'm here for one reason. I'm the President's man. I'm never running for office again and this is my last appointment. I don't owe anybody anything, and I'm not thinking about my career on down the line. I'm seventy-eight years old. I'm here because the President can trust me to serve no one's interests but his." Martin shrugged. "The President is satisfied with Richard Woolsey's performance. That's good enough for me."

Jack nodded slowly. "That's very clear, Senator Martin."

Martin sat down in his chair, beckoning to Anderson who was hovering with the requisite cup of decaf. "Hell of a thing," he said with a smile that might have been gamin sixty years ago. "Making decisions about other planets. But I suppose it was me or Dean Smith or Andy Griffith. You might do better with me."

"I don't know," Jack said easily, sitting down in his usual place. "Andy likes to fish. Do you?"

Lt. Colonel Davis stuck his head in the door. He was far too experienced to look surprised to see Martin already there. "Sir? Mr. LaPierre and Ms. Dixon-Smythe have arrived. Shall I bring them up?"

"Sure," Jack said. "Let's get this party started."

Dick Woolsey looked around the gate room with an expression of immense satisfaction. Winter sunlight streaked in through the high windows, the multicolored glass transforming it into patterns of light across the floor. Atlantis, just as it should be.

Except for the Wraith. It took him a moment to remember that Teyla was still in her disguise and not recoil when she hurried down the steps to greet him, her smile strange on the face of a Wraith queen.

"Welcome back to Atlantis, Mr. Woolsey," she said.

"It's good to be back," Dick said, and dropped his voice. "I didn't really expect to be."

"We are very fortunate that you are," Teyla said.

"I see you've been busy," Dick said, gesturing at her embroidered skirts and boots, the rest of the Wraith queen clothes.

"Very busy," Teyla said, "But I think it has proved useful."

Dick couldn't help a smile of admiration. "It's very convincing."

"Wraith politics is complex," Teyla said. "I should like to discuss it with you more fully at your convenience."

"I'd like that," Dick said.

Colonel Sheppard came down the stairs in his black uniform, an expression on his face that Dick was almost ready to call relief. Or at least thankfulness that they were getting no worse than

Dick Woolsey returning. "It's good to see you back," he said.

Dick nodded, lifting his head to the soaring ceiling. "It's good to be home."

Jennifer hesitated outside the door of Woolsey's office, straightening her jacket and taking a deep breath. She'd prepared her arguments and run through her reasons for why she needed to test the retrovirus again a hundred times in her head. The problem was, in her head she'd been arguing with Colonel Sheppard. She was pretty sure that Woolsey wasn't going to buy 'he's a member of your team, so we need to do whatever it takes' nearly as easily.

Still, now he was expecting her, and if she made some excuse to postpone the meeting, there was no telling when she'd actually get his undivided attention again. Her whole point was that they couldn't afford to wait. She squared her shoulders and went in.

"Dr. Keller," Woolsey said. "I'm glad to see you're up and around. I hear you had quite an ordeal."

"Actually, that's sort of what I wanted to talk to you about," she said. "You've read my report on the retrovirus, right?"

"I have," Woolsey said. "Although I admit I've been trying to get up to speed on a lot of things pretty quickly. It sounds like things have been busy around here while I was gone."

"That's one word for it," Jennifer said. "Okay, here's the thing: I'd like permission to conduct another trial of the retrovirus. I figured out what we did wrong the first time, and I feel really confident that this time it's going to work."

"Another trial," Woolsey said. He raised his eyebrows. "And by that you mean letting Todd..."

"Feed on me again," Jennifer said. "After I've taken a dose of the new retrovirus."

"I'm sorry," Woolsey said. "I think that's out of the question." He shook his head. "Even letting you conduct a human trial of the retrovirus at all at this point is a fairly severe breach of normal research protocols, and with the additional risk of being fed on — I can't authorize that."

"It may be the only way to save Rodney's life," Jennifer said. "We're not sure that he'll survive any attempt to restore him to human form without having recently fed. And it's not like we can let him just — just go out there and feed on somebody without this."

"No," Woolsey said. "But I'm also not going to let you risk dying — again — in an attempt to come up with a treatment that, at best, will benefit a single patient. I know weighing costs and benefits isn't very popular, but it has to be done, especially when the cost may be someone's life. Your life."

"Todd isn't going to kill me," Jennifer said. "He has every reason not to. After all, he wants to prove that this will work."

"You think it would be that useful to him to be able to feed on humans without killing them?"

"I think he knows what it could mean for both the humans and the Wraith," Jennifer said. "It would mean that we don't have to kill each other." She expected him to interrupt, but when he didn't, she went on. "As long as the Wraith have to kill humans to live, they have a problem. We're not going to stop fighting them until we entirely wipe them out. They can't entirely wipe us out, or they'll starve to death. So they just knock down any world that gets too technologically advanced, and then eventually people rebuild and start fighting them again. It's never going to end."

"Unless we find a way to destroy the Wraith," Woolsey said.

"Which we still might. I think we've convinced Todd that if we keep working on the problem, we will. Which leaves him two options." She shrugged. "Destroy Atlantis and wipe out technological civilization on Earth, knock us back to the Stone Age — well, that's easier said than done, and he'd still have to deal with the Genii."

"Not to mention that Earth isn't the only power in the Milky Way," Woolsey said. "I'm not sure the Wraith really want to take on the Jaffa and the Lucian Alliance."

"And the thing is, even if they could do it, it's still just a temporary solution," Jennifer said. "At least it is from Todd's point of view. He's thousands of years old. We'd probably all be dead by the time the survivors on Earth found a way to fight back against the Wraith, but Todd probably wouldn't be. Because they have to leave some of us alive, or they'll eventually starve to death. And we have to keep trying to kill them all."

"And Todd thinks this retrovirus changes the game."

"I think it does," Jennifer said. "If the Wraith didn't have to kill people... okay, it's disturbing. Believe me, having just gone through what I did with Todd, I'm disturbed. But the fact remains, there are already some humans who choose to live under the protection of the Wraith."

"As an alternative to being horribly murdered," Woolsey said.

"Which right now we can't prevent. Maybe eventually we can wipe out the Wraith as a species. I have a problem with that, but it's not going to be my decision. But right now, we can't defend every human planet in the Pegasus galaxy. We may want to, but we can't."

"No, we can't," Woolsey admitted. "Frankly, we're having enough problems right now just defending Atlantis and Earth. But that's a temporary situation."

"We hope," Jennifer said. "Look, we've stopped some Cullings before, right? When we happened to be in the right place at the right time. How many haven't we stopped? How many people have died who wouldn't have died if the Wraith could feed without killing?"

"How many would essentially be slaves aboard Wraith hive ships, fed on again and again?" Woolsey said. "Do you really think that wouldn't happen?"

"I don't know," Jennifer said. "Maybe it would, and I think that's as awful as you do. But at least there would be a chance of coming up with something better than having the same war keep going on for the rest of our lives."

"You're asking me to take an enormous risk for a very slim chance that this will actually work out well," Woolsey said.

"I'm asking you to let me find out if this works," Jennifer said.

"Here's a cost-benefit analysis for you: how many people in Atlantis have died from being fed on by the Wraith?"

"More than I'd like," Woolsey said after a moment.

"If this works, we could make our people immune to the harmful effects of being fed on. I wouldn't have to send anybody else home to die that way. I don't know about you, but I think that's worth a lot."

Woolsey looked at her for a long moment. "If we start down this road, there's no going back," he said.

"I don't think we can go back now," Jennifer said. "Todd's going to keep working on this retrovirus with or without my help. Unless we're talking about killing one of our only sort of allies among the Wraith—"

"That's probably a strategically bad idea," Woolsey said.

"Then he's going to figure this out. The only question is whether we'll have any control over how this first gets used, and whether we'll be able to use it for our own purposes."

"I'm probably going to get fired for this," Woolsey said.

"Didn't they just confirm that you were the best person for this job?"

"They're going to wish they'd hired Dr. Jackson," Woolsey said.

Jennifer felt her heart leap. "So can I do it?"

Woolsey closed his eyes for a moment. "You have my permission to test the retrovirus on yourself," he said. "We'll have to arrange another meeting with Todd to see if it's actually effective." He looked up at her. "You know, I've barely gotten back, and already I'm beginning to wonder why I wanted this job so badly."

"Believe me, I know how you feel," Jennifer said.

"Guide." Queen Death's tone was dulcet, but there was no mistaking the steel behind it, even through the subspace transmission, and he bent his head deeply in respect. "I should like to speak with your queen immediately."

"As it please your Graciousness," Guide said, feeling his heart leap in his chest for all that he knew there was nothing strange in his reply, "she is not aboard this ship at this time."

Queen Death did not seem to disbelieve him, but rather smiled. "I have indeed heard that she is traveling aboard a cruiser. Is that not so?"

"It is so," Guide said. If she had been captured…

"I understand she has met with young Waterlight," Death said. "And I am confused as to why she has not met with me."

"Waterlight is quite insignificant," Guide said truthfully. "I do not think she would dare to approach you as sister to sister."

Queen Death looked somewhat mollified, though her smile did not change, warm and dangerous as ever. "That is very respectful of her. Though I, of course, do not hold to such formality that I believe that only the elder may approach the younger! It is not such grave disrespect for the junior to speak first, provided her words are those of friendship."

He could but nod to that. "I am sure Queen Steelflower devoutly desires your friendship," he said cautiously.

"I am pleased to hear that," Queen Death said. "And since she feels that she must observe the niceties and wait upon my invitation, it is incumbent upon me to provide it." Her eyes flickered over his face. "I am sending coordinates at which I will wait for her, so that we may meet face to face as allies should, with no proxies or blades to stand between. If, as you say, your Queen does indeed devoutly desire my friendship, she will not let this opportunity go to waste." A slow smile spread across her face. "You may tell her so, Guide. Otherwise I will not believe that her desires are so sororal."

"Of course," Guide began, but the transmission ended before he could phrase another word.

Ember looked at him, a crease beginning between his fair brows. "And now?" he said in a tone studiously neutral of reproach.

It could not have lasted forever, Guide told himself. Sooner or later, Queen Death would insist on seeing his queen, and he could not deny her forever. It had come sooner rather than later. But perhaps all could still be turned to his advantage.

"Find me the nearest Stargate," he snarled. "I have a message to send."

CHAPTER TWENTY-SIX

Collateral Damage

"I DO NOT see that we have any choice," Teyla said. It was still weird to see her at the conference table like that, her skin tinted green and her face that of a Wraith, though not as weird as it used to be. John was getting used to it, and that was even weirder.

"How is that?" Woolsey said. It was kind of nice to see him back at the head of the table where he belonged, but nicer yet not to be there himself.

"If I do not show up for the rendezvous with Queen Death, this masquerade will be useless," Teyla said. "I will never be able to do this again, and any future intelligence we might have gleaned will be lost."

"And any shot at using it to get Rodney," John added.

Jennifer cleared her throat. She looked pale, but her voice was firm. "We owe Todd," she said. "And if we hang him out to dry about this we might as well say goodbye to our alliance."

Ronon snorted, not looking at her. "We never should have made a deal with him in the first place. I say we let him hang. Fewer Wraith to worry about."

Jennifer didn't look at Ronon either. "I don't think we can afford to do that."

"Not if there's still any chance of getting to Rodney," John said.

Woolsey steepled his hands. "Realistically, is that an option?"

Carter shifted in her seat but said nothing.

"I believe that it is," Teyla said, her skirts rustling as she moved in the chair next to John. "It is very difficult for ordinary Wraith to refuse to comply with my requests. A queen is a different matter, but I am able to gain access to information and people in this guise that we would never be able to otherwise."

"That's an important consideration," Woolsey said thoughtfully. "So far, this has been our most reliable source of information, and in the future could provide critical intelligence. I'm reluctant to lose that."

Ronon shook his head. "It'll be a double cross. You know that, right? There's no way this meeting is on the up and up even if Queen Death thinks you're Wraith."

"He has a point," Carter said from the far end of the table, leaning forward a little to be seen around Carson. "This smells to me like a trap for Steelflower. Queen Death can't be happy with her sapping off potential allies or setting herself up as a rival."

"So we double cross them back," John said. He put his coffee cup down on the table, looking up and back. "We know it's a trap. But she doesn't know that Teyla is with us. She'll be expecting treachery from Todd, but she's not going to expect anything from us. Let Teyla keep the rendezvous with Todd. And while Queen Death is occupied, we get a team in, grab Rodney, steal back our ZPM, and Carter shoots up the place."

"We tried that before and it didn't work," Woolsey pointed out.

"It didn't work for two reasons," John said. "We didn't know Rodney was a Wraith and didn't have any means to subdue him, and we didn't have an operative on the inside. This time we know what we're up against, and Teyla can get in ahead of us."

Woolsey and Carter spoke at once. "How are you planning to subdue Dr. McKay?" Woolsey asked.

"Won't Teyla be guarded and watched?" Carter asked.

"I can sedate him," Jennifer said with a quick glance at Carson beside her. "We've got a formula that will work on his metabolism. I can keep him unconscious as long as necessary."

"Of course I will be," Teyla said. "But if they are guarding and watching me, they are not doing other things. If Steelflower is their first concern, they will watch for treachery from us, and from the hive. They will not expect the Lanteans."

Woolsey's brow knitted. The way she had put it, the way she had phrased it, sounded as though she were really Steelflower, as though this were actually an alliance between her hive and Atlantis.

John jumped in. "This may be our best shot at stealing back our ZPM," he said. "If Queen Death has it aboard, there's a good chance our team can get it back. And then we'd be in a much better position all around." Not to mention, John thought, how much better a position Woolsey would be in with his superiors if he could say he'd gotten it back.

Woolsey swallowed. He looked down the table. "Colonel Carter, what is your military opinion?"

Carter leaned forward again, her eyes flicking over John before she replied. "The *Hammond* is no match for Queen Death's hive ship. If we get into a slugging match, we're going to get the worst of it. But, if you can get a team aboard in a cloaked jumper, we can certainly create a distraction for some limited amount of time. And if we had Todd's hive ship in it with us, we could take out her ship."

"Trusting Todd," Ronon said. He met her eyes firmly. "You're saying you're going to take the *Hammond* between two hive ships and trust Todd will shoot them instead of you. If this is a double cross, how do we know he's not in on it?"

"He is not," Teyla said.

Ronon looked across the table at her. "How do you know?"

"If Todd intends treachery, I can get that from his mind," she said.

"Yeah?" Ronon's eyes met hers, and John wished he could break that gaze. Something was breaking, tearing apart, and he had to stop it but he didn't have the words, didn't know how...

"I can get it from his mind," Teyla said levelly, "He will not be able to keep such a secret from me, not when we are face to face." There was no flush to her cheeks, only that icy Wraith voice, and her eyes did not leave Ronon's.

It was Carter who interrupted it. "If you're certain, then it's worth a try. This may be our best chance at getting both the ZPM and Rodney."

Teyla turned to her quite deliberately. "I am certain," she said.

Woolsey cleared his throat, glancing down at his laptop as

though it would somehow reveal something new. "There is one other thing," he said.

"What?" John asked.

Woolsey glanced at John, carefully not looking down Jennifer's side of the table at all. "The IOA has given me some very specific directives as part and parcel of my return to Atlantis. If we cannot recover Dr. McKay," he paused, taking a breath, "and of course we want to, but if we can't, we cannot continue to let him provide Queen Death with intelligence. Colonel Sheppard, your orders are to kill him."

He heard the indrawn breaths and his voice firmed. "Right now Dr. McKay is a threat to every human being in the Pegasus Galaxy, and a potential danger to Earth. If we cannot recover him, there is no next time. Is that clear?"

John felt as though ice had settled in his stomach, had frozen hard in his chest.

"Homeworld Command–" Carter began.

"Homeworld Command reluctantly concurs," Woolsey said. "But you are welcome to query if you feel it necessary." He looked at John. "This isn't a matter of politics, Colonel. Ask yourself if Dr. McKay would want to provide Queen Death with information that would lead to the loss of thousands of lives, including the lives of his family and friends. This is mercy."

John took a long breath. Ice, but he could breathe around it. He could move. It was true that Rodney would never want this. He would never want to remain a Wraith forever, or worse yet to give Queen Death the technology that would allow her to reach Earth. He'd rather die.

And this was it, the arithmetic of death. How much was one man's life worth? Everybody's?

"Mercy," Ronon said, but he was looking at Jennifer, not John. "There's only so much a man can take. There's only so much he should."

Jennifer bit down on her lip, her face white. "I know," she said.

Teyla was still and voiceless in the mask of her Wraith face.

Woolsey was looking at him. "Colonel Sheppard?"

"Understood," John said. "If we can't recover him, we'll do what we have to do."

"Ronon." John jogged toward the transport chamber. "Hey! Wait up!"

The doors closed ahead of him as though Ronon hadn't heard, hadn't seen them coming after. John put his hand on the closed doors carefully, not hitting them at all.

"Let him go, John," Teyla said quietly. "It is not you."

"I know." John turned back to her as the transport chamber doors opened again on an empty compartment. Even in the high heeled boots she wore in Wraith guise, Teyla hardly came up to his chin. But she was frightening all the same. Her black hair fell down her back from silver combs, and the veins in her throat stood out, a tracery of darker green against nacreous skin. She was terrifying. And beautiful.

Teyla stepped into the transport beside him but let him touch the map. Her nails made the Ancient interfaces awkward. It was hard to touch things directly with the pad of her fingers, and the momentary heat was what activated the touchscreens.

"Ronon has to get over this," John said.

"He is not going to," Teyla said as the doors opened on the corridor near her living quarters. "He cannot do this," Teyla said. "And such is my love for him that I cannot ask him to. It is too much for him to know this."

"It's you," John said stubbornly, following her into her rooms. "You're not a Wraith."

"John." She stopped in the middle of the floor, her arms at her sides. Behind her woven blinds covered the windows, opened to let in the dim winter sun, and a big plastic munitions crate held Torren's toys. Her laced black boots sunk deep into the white rug. "Look at me."

"I know what you are," he said.

"How much Wraith DNA does it take to make one Bloodtainted?

How much Wraith blood to be a Wraith?" She shook her head as he took a step toward her. "I am not fully human, John, even when I appear to be. I can still speak mind to mind. I looked human when I defeated Coldamber beneath the sea, and she was a great queen in her time."

"And if you hadn't we'd all be dead," John said. "I'm not going to complain about that." He reached for her hand and took it in his, drew her down to sit beside him on the couch. "You're a person."

"Is Todd a person?" she asked.

He'd known the answer to that in Kolya's prison. Which didn't mean he liked it. "Yes."

"Ronon has been hunted too long," Teyla said. "His scars run too deep. He cannot see the Wraith as people, John."

"No," John said. "No." He turned her hand over in his, his eyes on it. "That's the thing. You can't see the enemy as people. You can't afford to. The minute you do it, it's like slicing your guts up with glass every time you have to kill. You've got to turn it off. You've got to make it different. Otherwise you can't do it without going crazy." He didn't lift his eyes from her fingers, as though they held some answer. "Otherwise you get called in for an airstrike on some village that's harboring insurgents, and it turns out to be these guys you were drinking tea with last week, and you walk through the burned out houses afterwards and the smoke is blowing around you and you wonder if you got the insurgents but you got a lot of other people. You got that kid who was running around while you were talking with his dad, and he's lying there with his eyes open and no legs, and there's his grandmother dead beside the goat and Holland just keeps saying over and over that there were supposed to be Taliban here and…"

"John." She closed his hand in hers, dark green claws against his skin. "John."

He couldn't seem to stop, though he knew he should. He shouldn't say this stuff, not sitting on her couch with the verdigris walls of Atlantis about them and the snowlight coming through the windows unbearably bright. "And then two weeks later Holland's bleeding out on you and he says it's pay up time. Tit for tat. An eye for an eye. Those who live by the sword die by the sword. You can try to shut him up. You can make him shut up. But it's still true."

"John." Her voice was quiet, urgent.

And still he couldn't stop. "It's borrowed time, Teyla. Sooner or later the account is due."

Her eyes searched his face, as though she saw every mission there, every time the clock had been running out and he'd been willing. If someone had to go it ought to be him, the marked man.

"Very well," Teyla said gravely. "If it is borrowed time, then it is. You will do the best you can while you may, and when you must you will die. That will be the story of your life, and it is better than many. You will not die for nothing, and you will not die unmourned." Her voice cracked. "I will mourn you."

"I didn't mean to do that," he said. "I didn't mean to leave anybody who would be hurt."

"You do not get to make that decision, John," she said levelly. "That is my risk to take."

He bent his head again, looking down at her hand. It felt like a weight lifting, like something loosening within him. "Ok." One day it would be the last time. The reprieve would be over. Mitch and Dex and Holland had a few weeks. He'd had years. He'd had nearly seven years. It was more than he deserved. Nothing to complain about, really, when the time ran out.

Teyla watched him with golden Wraith's eyes and her voice was steady. "When the time comes I will mourn. But until then you will not deny me joy."

"I can never deny you anything," John said truthfully.

She lifted her hand to his cheek, purpled feeding slit against his skin. "I know," she said.

CHAPTER TWENTY-SEVEN

Disclosures

JOHN didn't think he would be able to sleep, but he did. And it was a good thing, too. Once the clock started running on this mission he had no idea when he'd sleep again. If he could rest before it started, he'd be in better shape all along. He'd hardly stirred when Teyla got up to go to the infirmary. Dr. Keller needed to touch up her work before Teyla left for her rendezvous with Todd — another round of injections of skin dye, a reapplication of a dental cap. He'd vaguely heard her leave and rolled over into the warm place she left behind, but hadn't awakened fully.

Now he did wake up, bright light coming in through the half opened blinds, glaring off the snow outside, and for a moment he lay there trying to figure out what the strange sensation he felt was. Nothing hurt. Right this second, nothing hurt at all. They had a plan and they were going to get Rodney and that was how it was going to be.

"Colonel Sheppard?" His headset crackled, and John flailed around for it, finding it on the floor in one of his shoes.

"Yes?"

It was Airman Salawi, but for a change she didn't sound stressed out. "Dr. Kusanagi has the watch, and she told me to radio you since Teyla was in the infirmary having a procedure. Kanaan's brought Torren back, and somebody needs to come to the gateroom and get him."

"Right," John said, scrubbing his hand over his unshaven chin. He'd been having a good day for about two minutes there. He wasn't looking forward to having a conversation with Kanaan. But he couldn't leave Torren stuck in the gateroom either. "I'm on my way."

Kanaan was talking to Kusanagi down on the floor by the gate, a couple of big boxes at his feet that John figured were the trade goods for the Athosians on their way back in exchange for the week's milk, Torren on his shoulder.

The sunlight through the stained glass made bright patterns across the floor, and Torren lifted his arms, fascinated by how the golden stripes rendered his hands yellow when he touched them. He twisted around abruptly when he saw John.

Kusanagi's eyes went wide. "I am very busy now," she said. "It was so nice to see you." She fled back up the steps to the control boards.

Crap, John thought, but kept his tone studiously nonchalant as he reached for Torren. "Hey, buddy."

Kanaan glanced over him, unshaved face and yesterday's uniform. "Dr. Kusanagi said Teyla was in the infirmary. Is she ill?"

"No, she's just having a procedure done," John said. None of the Athosians knew about Teyla's Wraith disguise, and she'd probably want it kept that way. It was hers to tell or not as she chose, not his. "She's fine. Dr. Keller's working on one of her teeth." Which was true. The dental cap that had come off was on one of her teeth.

"Oh." A bunch of the Athosians had had dental work done at one time or another, so it was an unremarkable reason. Kanaan looked him over again, a thoughtful expression on his face. He put the flat of his hand to Torren's cheek. "I will see you soon, Torren. Be well and whole."

"Bye-bye, Papa," Torren said cheerily. "Bye-bye soon."

"Yes, I will see you soon." Kanaan turned to pick up the boxes. "Tell Teyla I hope she is well."

"I will," John said, and looked up at Salawi at the board above. "Airman, dial New Athos."

Maybe it was that John was getting used to it, so much so that he didn't even think about it. Which said something pretty scary, actually, if you thought about it too hard, which he tried not to.

Or maybe it was that he was thrown by the whole thing with Kanaan in the gateroom and wasn't thinking at all.

In any event, John walked into the infirmary with Torren on his shoulder, not even thinking that Teyla would be in full Wraith drag, not even considering whether or not she wanted Torren to see her like that.

Jennifer was holding a mirror for her as she sat up on the edge of one of the beds, looking at the reapplied dental cap, her lips bared in a fanged grimace like something out of a nightmare. What could be scarier for a little kid than to see their mom transformed into the most frightening thing they could think of? This was worse than all the Wicked Witches of the West, all the bogeymen and chainsaw wielding freaks of John's childhood, because these monsters were real. Even though he probably hadn't heard that story yet, one day before long Torren would hear about his half brother, Kanaan's son who had been fed on by the Wraith when he was eight years old.

Teyla looked up, and in her expression of absolute horror John saw it all. She had never wanted Torren to see her this way, had no idea Kanaan was returning him today. She would never want this. Never.

And it was too late. John was already ten steps inside the door, Torren on his shoulder facing forwards. He'd already seen. Even if John stopped dead in his tracks, even if he turned around and sprinted for the door, it was too late.

Torren's forehead wrinkled, his face screwing up.

"Torren," Teyla began in a low voice.

"Mama!" Torren stretched out his arms, his face clearing as he recognized her, breaking into a wide grin. "Mama!" He nearly lunged out of John's grasp. John managed to put him down in time, flailing feet and all, and Torren dashed across the infirmary floor to plow into Teyla's knees as she slid off the bed.

"Torren." She went down on the floor beside him, her arms going around him as she clasped him tight.

"I gots frogs," Torren said happily, burrowing into Teyla's neck. "Papa said I could have them. So I gots them."

"Oh, good," Teyla said, burying her face in Torren.

"I'm sorry," John said belatedly. "I didn't think."

Teyla pulled her head back, looking at Torren's face beneath his mop of dark hair. "Torren, I don't want to scare you."

"Why be scared?" Torren said, his expression a study in perplexity. "It's you."

"General O'Neill, if you'll stay for a moment?"

Jack paused, letting the other officers file out of the Oval Office ahead of him. When the President politely asked you to stay it wasn't a request. "Of course, sir."

The President waited until the last one pulled the door shut behind him, then leaned back against the edge of his desk, his tall, lanky form and deep voice somehow incongruous together. "How does Richard Woolsey like his assignment?" he asked.

"I think he's pleased to be back in Atlantis, sir," Jack said neutrally, wondering what was coming. Surely nobody could have any complaints yet! Woolsey had been gone only two days.

The President read his body language. "No crisis, Jack," he said. "Just something I want you to start chewing on."

"What's that, Mr. President?"

"Disclosure."

Jack's mouth tightened, his cover under his arm. "Has there been another incident?"

"No." The President unfastened his starched left cuff and began to carefully roll his sleeve up in precise creases. "But there will be."

"Pardon?"

"How many people have been involved with the Stargate program in the last fifteen years? With the starships, or with the 302s? Counting support positions."

"I couldn't tell you exactly, sir," Jack said. "I'd have to get that number for you."

"Would you say 10,000 is in the ballpark?"

"Probably, yes," Jack said slowly.

"And how many abroad, counting the IOA, the staff and military personnel of allied nations, and of course the technical people who worked or are working on the *Korolev*, the *Sun Tzu*, the *Austerlitz*, or the still unnamed Indian vessel? Another 5,000?"

"At least," Jack said reluctantly.

The President unfastened his right cuff equally carefully. "There's no such thing as a secret that can be kept by 15,000 people. And that number is growing every day."

"We've had disclosure issues before." Jack frowned.

"Yes. But there's a big difference between one reporter on the scent, or a drunk soldier who tells his buddies about his tour of duty on an alien planet, and 15,000 people. Scientists, soldiers, doctors, politicians, psychologists, archaeologists and anthropologists, pilots…" The President spread his hands. "They're not all nuts. This is going to come out. Even if we closed it all down tomorrow." He saw Jack jerk, and raised a pacifying hand. "Not that we're going to. Not that we can. Ten or twelve years ago that might have been possible. But it isn't anymore. This is going to come out, the whole thing, sooner or later."

"If it does," Jack said slowly, trying to marshal his thoughts.

"When it does, it will change our society as profoundly as the Renaissance, or the discovery of the New World. It will alter our world forever. It will topple governments and scramble religions, create conflicts we can't even imagine yet. The era of integration of our world into a galactic society will make globalization look like a walk in the park. We will see brand new criteria for oppression, brand new reasons for violence, and the probable displacement of millions of people. It will redefine science, and challenge the beliefs of every human being on Earth." The President leaned back on the edge of his desk. "I've been thinking about it. A lot."

"We're not ready for that kind of thing," Jack said. "We've already got two wars…"

"We're not," the President agreed. "And my predecessors made the call to keep it secret. But that's not going to hold forever. So we have to get out in front of it. We have to start thinking about what we want. About how we want this to play out. We have to identify some best-case scenarios and think about how to get there. The worst choice is to just let it happen, however and whenever it does."

Jack let out a long breath.

"I want you to start thinking about this. I want you to put together some scenarios," the President said.

"Sir, that's not me." The words left his mouth before Jack was even aware they were there. The President's eyebrows rose. "I'm not the guy you need on this."

His eyebrows rose higher, if that was possible. "Then give me a name," the President said mildly.

"Dr. Daniel Jackson."

For a moment the President sat thoughtfully, mulling it over. "Who would have been Woolsey's replacement? I've heard he's shrewd. And he has credibility with the international community."

"He's a good man," Jack said, meaning it as a generic endorsement.

The President smiled. "Is he? Well, that's probably the most important qualification."

"Yeah." Jack smiled ruefully. "They used to call him my conscience."

"Ok." The President got up. "Put him on it. Get back to me in a couple of months with some thoughts. I don't expect quick answers or easy ones. But it's time to start talking about this." He took a few steps toward the door and Jack followed. "We need to approach this methodically and carefully. The last thing we want is to be putting it together on the fly when something happens."

"Yes, Mr. President," Jack said. It was how they'd always done things, but maybe that hadn't always worked as well as it might have. And Daniel ought to love this.

CHAPTER TWENTY-EIGHT

Steelflower

TEYLA stood by the Stargate. Above, the duty crew on control were trying to not stare at her. She did look impressive, in a very Wraith way. And yet perhaps Teyla would not take the stares for anything so friendly.

Radek put his hands in the pockets of his rumpled pants and shrugged. "It is just that it is another mission," he said. He gave her a sideways glance, a twist of humor to his mouth. "And perhaps that you are hot."

She laughed as he had hoped she would, turning about, her boot heels loud on the polished floor.

"We will see you soon," Radek said seriously. "We will get Rodney back, and then I can get out of the field."

"Yes," she said.

"Believe me," said Radek. "No one is more motivated than I to get out of the field." He scrubbed a hand through his hair. "Though if it does not go as planned and John…" He broke off and shook his head. "I do not know what will happen. If Rodney…"

Teyla regarded him with a Wraith's golden eyes. "If it comes to that, John will do what he needs to do." Teyla raised her chin, her voice low. "Though it will not come to that, Radek."

"You do not know that," Radek said.

"If it is necessary, I will do it," Teyla said evenly, her eyes on his face. "He will forgive me when he will not forgive himself."

Radek swallowed. He wasn't sure he trusted himself to speak. And so he squeezed her shoulder instead, black silk slick as water under his hand.

Woolsey came down the stairs, rubbing his palms against

his pants legs. "It's time," he said.

Blue fire kindled and the gate quickened, the honor guard standing well back of its opening. The surface rippled and a small figure stepped through, her black skirts billowing above tight-laced ankle boots.

Sable, Commander of the Honor Guard, went to one knee, his head bent. "My Queen," he said, a frisson running through him as he felt her mind sweep over him, clear and bright as a beacon beam turning through the night sky, calling the darts home to their cradles.

Sable, Queen Steelflower said, her eyes passing over those assembled. *Yarrow and Swiftripen, Elude and Gamester, clevermen and blades all. The best men.*

He rose at her touch, the perfume of her skirts brushing his face. "Your shuttlecraft is ready, My Queen."

"I have walked a strange road, my men," she said aloud, her eyes touching each in turn, bright as stars. "And you shall walk a stranger one still with me, perhaps. If any among you dare it."

"We are all your daring men," Swiftripen said eagerly. "And it is our honor to follow where our queen bids us."

Her eyes rested upon him like a caress upon his face. "I believe you are daring," Steelflower said, "and true as well. Sit with me on the shuttle, and we will speak further."

Gamester rolled his eyes behind Swiftripen's back, and Sable grimaced. How like Swift to manage to gather the queen's attention first! And now he would sit with her on the shuttle, a signal honor. Perhaps he would even be her first concubine.

"If you will come this way, My Queen," he said, bending low again.

"Of course."

Surrounded by her blades, Queen Steelflower went aboard her shuttlecraft, a fragile seeming figure among two tens of men.

The Consort was in the dart bay, of course. He went to one knee stiffly, but then Guide was not young enough for grace. "My

Queen," he said, and his voice was warm.

"My dear Guide," she said, and the caress in her voice was enough to send shivers down Sable's spine. All was as it should be. They were not queenless men, renegades with no hope for tomorrow. They served Steelflower and in her bright orbit were made whole.

"The ship is primed," Guide said, "and all the company is at your disposal. Will you walk its paths with me?"

"With great good will," Steelflower said, and put her hand to his wrist, her fingers resting lightly on his flesh. Sable thought that she spoke to him alone, some private words of tenderness perhaps, for Guide smiled and bent his head.

"This way, My Queen," he said.

The hive ship hummed through hyperspace on its way to a deadly rendezvous. And yet it did so with a sense of deep satisfaction shared with every man aboard. It had healed much since Guide returned, but now it was better still. Their queen was there as she should be, her mind a steady presence in its dreaming sleep. Even when she was not lost in shiptrance she was there, her mind on the edge of its consciousness.

Every man had seen her, every cleverman, and every drone. Every last one of the ship's company to the youngest fledgling barely out of the chrysalis had seen Steelflower, had felt her touch. It steadied them all. Some who had doubted she existed were now reassured while others were the butt of good humored jokes. There was no doubt she was real. There was no doubt she was a great queen. Even those who had seen Death were impressed.

As they should be Guide said as the doors to the Queen's chambers irised open before them.

Her forehead rose, but her mental voice was amused. *You have much more confidence in me than formerly,* she said.

Does that surprise you? Given what you have done?

With Waterlight? she asked.

Guide snorted. *Among other things* he said.

The Queen's Chamber was wreathed in fragrant mist, welcoming and cool, to soothe the skin and the senses alike. Cunning alcoves revealed strange compartments, boxes that might have been treasures or more utilitarian things, branching off one another so that first one charming vista and then another presented itself through half-walls of woven bone, grown that way as much for pleasure as use. Her bed was suspended from the ceiling on tendrils that looked like living vine, its covers of green silk piled high, each piece worked in thousands of fine stitches. Tiny lights were woven into the tendrils that might be extinguished at her thought, to light her or leave her in darkness as she preferred.

It's very... she began, and finished aloud. "Pretty."

Guide laughed, his voice loud in the small chamber. *We are not without aesthetic senses.*

I did not think that, she replied.

Did you not?

She did not reply, only walked over to the edge of the bed, the set of her shoulders dropping with weariness.

You should rest, Guide said more gently. *We have a full turn around of the watch to run before we leave hyperspace. There is no need for you to sit awake so long.*

Sleep? And make myself vulnerable? Her voice was skeptical, but she sat down on the edge of the bed.

I will watch over your sleep as a consort should, Guide said. *No one will disturb you. I shall be at your side.*

A shadow ran fast across her face, and though she did not speak he caught the sense of it — a swift and brutal fear of his body against hers, of relaxing in sleep only to awaken pinned beneath him.

Guide could not help but recoil in horror. *What do you think we are,* he asked, *that you imagine such bestial things of us?*

If you try anything, I will kill you, she said, and he heard the fear beneath the steel in her voice and did not doubt her.

What man would do such a thing? he asked. It was unimaginable. To defile a queen was worse than crime. It was sacrilege, unthinkable. The blade who even contemplated such would have no place in any hive. To take from all something so rare and remarkable…

She lifted her head. *It is common enough,* she said stiffly.

Among beasts, he said, and could not keep the distaste from his mind. What could be clearer proof that they were no more than animals?

And do such things never happen among you? she demanded.

Among blades, Guide conceded. *But to force oneself upon a queen…* He could hardly get the words out. *It is an unspeakable obscenity.*

Perhaps his distaste convinced her more than his words. She could, after all, sense the tenor of his mind.

Then you may stay, she said, and sat back upon the pillows, drawing her feet up before her like a young girl.

If it is your wish, he said, courtly as one should be, and sat down opposite her, his back against the tendril that suspended the bed. *Sleep. I will watch.*

She turned on her side, her eyes still upon him, pulled one of the large pillows so that a corner of it was beneath her face. *I have a knife,* she reminded him.

Think you that I want you so much? he asked. *I know what you are.*

And yet, she said, and he felt the humiliation burn through him like desire.

It is who we are, Guide said softly. *We are born to serve queens. Obedience and desire, courage and beauty and cleverness — they are all for her. It is an unusual man indeed who can defy a queen in word or deed.*

And yet you defy Death, she observed, the first of the tiny lights winking out. Her mental voice was cool, curiosity overriding all. That was always true of this one.

She is not my queen, Guide said.

Nor am I.

He leaned his head back against the tendril, looking up at the mist-wreathed ceiling. *My true queen is dead these many years. And yet her memory is a shield to me.* Snow in shiplight, soft washes of color playing across the skin of her shoulders, her eyes on his... He pushed the memory down, down into the darkness.

Not before she saw it. *You loved her,* she said.

Do you think we cannot love? Her mind was bright as fire, curiosity burning bright. *Anger and hope and fear, tenderness and desire and greed. Do you think we do not have these things?*

I do not know, she said softly. Another light winked out. She had sat thus once, years ago, watching through another night to another dawn with Sheppard, wondering if they would die that day. She had told him stories, and he had told her ones as well. The memory rose in her mind unbidden, vivid and crisp as any he held to his heart.

Old stories, she whispered, *Stories are powerful things.*

*They are indeed," Guide said.

She turned about on the satin pillows, her eyes on him. *Who is Osprey?* she asked.

A story, he said, only mildly surprised. *I will tell you if you want. It is no secret.*

Yes.

Guide put his feet up on the bed and began. *Long ago, in the first days of the world, there were the First Mothers. Osprey was one of them, nine in all. Nine queens and ninety-nine men, blades and clevermen alike, for that is how people were made. That is how we were born in the ice of the first world, beneath the light of the moon. To each queen were given certain gifts, no two alike, for no two lineages are the same. We all count our names from them, from the First Mothers, and each tells its own story. I am a blade of Night, that mother who took her name from the darkness between the stars, but I know Osprey's story well.

She is queen of mists and shadows, strong in mind, weaving illusions to hide and deceive. She is a white flower, a white bird, a fog rising among the trees. She is the shadow of clouds trailing across the moon.

Wraith, Teyla said quietly, her mind closed to him. *Revenant.*

Osprey queens are strong minded, Guide said. *And there is no illusion they cannot penetrate. Yet they are impossible to read if they do not wish it.* He looked at her keenly, a thought occurring to him. *Why do you ask?*

Her eyes did not leave him. *I have dreamed of her,* she said.

He nodded slowly. There was no sense in trying to keep his thoughts from her, not so close with her attention focused upon him. And yet he was not surprised. *We do not know what cleverman played with your ancestors' genes to such effect,* he said. *Nor whose genes he gave you. But it may be Osprey as well as any other.* He stopped, and at her silence went on. *It is part of being a queen,* he said. *To some extent lesser or greater, all queens remember. They share in some part in the memories of their foremothers, experience and knowledge the legacy of the blood they bear. For most it is a small thing, dreams and hazy memories without context. Some great queens claim to remember details, to recall with clarity things that happened to their foremothers. That is part of Death's allure. She claims to recall all that Coldamber knew, that Death in her time who led the first assault of the Great Armada.* His mental voice was dry. *Whom you killed beneath the sea, Teyla Emmagan. You killed her, Death who fed on Emege, who drank the blood of the children of Athos.*

He felt the flicker of her mind, and showed her Coldamber as he remembered her, when he was a blade scarce fledged, young and uncertain, expecting to die in the next assault, fodder for the weapons of the Ancients to screen the real attack. One look from Coldamber and he had gone to his knees, his face against the deck she walked upon.

And does Death remember? she asked quietly.

I do not know. Another light winked out, and he looked at her in the darkness, lovely and shadowed as any he had ever seen, the young queen with her mind like flame. *But you may well be of Osprey.* He did not want to add it, but it slipped between his reaching fingers. *Snow was.*

He could not stop the grief that welled, surprising as rising music, stark and pure as though it were hours old, and she caught it like a bird in her hand, held it to her chest. *I am sorry,* she said. And still her mind was closed to him.

They sat in silence in the darkness for a long time. He thought that perhaps she slept. Humans had to sleep so often. She could not go thirty of their hours without sleep and be sharp. It was best she sleep now. The last lights died. He waited. He kept the watch. The ship's ventilation systems breathed softly.

"I will tell you a story," she said aloud, and her voice sounded rusty in the soft air. "You have given me a story, Guide. Now I will give you one, a story to rend worlds and tear the veil from the stars."

"Tell me a story," he said.

She cleared her throat and began, her voice soft at first but gaining power as she spoke. "Once, long ago and far away, in the beginning of the world, there was a queen who had three daughters. She was a strong queen, but not a particularly good mother. She was inattentive, and over-absorbed with her own concerns, uninterested in nurturing her children."

"Her eldest daughter was born when she was very young, and for the most part she was left to her own devices. Her mother was often away, and when she did see her would set her tricky puzzles to solve, or try to teach her vast tomes of knowledge in a single night. And yet when this daughter had need of her mother, her mother was gone. But she was a resilient girl, and she learned to depend upon none except herself, to survive alone."

"As sometimes happens," Guide said.

"Indeed." There was a soft rustle in the darkness, and he saw the faint gleam of skin and satin as she moved. "The second daughter was the child of her choosing, and at first she was beloved, and her baby antics were her mother's delight. But time came when her mother grew bored with all that, and she was left more and more to the care of others and to her own private games. Having been doted upon, she missed her mother dreadfully, and she worshipped her and thought she could do no wrong even though now she was neglected."

Her voice hardened, strengthening in the dark, resonant and seeming to touch him to the bone. "The youngest daughter was unwanted and unwelcome, the bastard child of congress the queen did not wish to admit to, and she was cast out to make her own way. No one watched over her babyhood and no one guided her steps. Thus she grew full of bitter resentment for the matrimony that would never be hers, for her mother's regard and the full share that she should have had. And so in time this youngest daughter led a war against her mother and her sisters, and plunged all into disarray. Her mother she killed, and the favored middle sister she ground beneath her heel, wrenching from her sister all the tears and sorrow she could not gain from their mother. All the queen's vast holdings were hers, an empire uncountable. And so the eldest sister fled to a place far away, and there lived in obscurity, seeking to forget all that had been lost."

Her voice softened, and he could see what she saw, the pictures that she spoke. "The story begins as all stories begin, in the blue fire of a gate. A gate opened. A city rose from the sea, and legends walk. We stand in the time of story, my Guide. Blood binds to blood and like to like. Three sisters dwelt apart, one toiling in a distant land, one a slave, and one a queen. But that cannot be the end of the story, can it? How, Guide, shall this story turn?"

Like vast blocks beneath the earth moving in darkness, a piece fell into place soundlessly, like a deep subsonic shockwave spreading endlessly through the night. Stories too vast and too dangerous to tell, boxes with no keys, shadows cast by no light — all those things and more ran through his mind. Guide saw, and so did Teyla Emmagan.

"We are the story," she said.

Sheppard's blood running through his veins, bringing him to life in the depths of Kolya's prison. Sheppard beneath the sea, falling on his knees to Coldamber. Snow turning to see him, her eyes lighting in a smile like Steelflower's, warm and full of mysteries. The spires of Atlantis against the sky, the secret turnings of the hive, Earth's Stargate flaring deep within its concealing mountain.

Sheppard and Guide. Snow and Teyla Emmagan. Waterlight and Alabaster and Jennifer Keller bent over her work. Osprey vanishing like mist and Amitas clothed in white, and a woman from the distant plains of Earth going about her work with a weapon in her hand, her green eyes bright as Sheppard's.

"We are the story," she said. "We hold it all within us." Her voice choked and steadied. "And I do not know how it can end except in rivers of blood."

"I do not know either," Guide said, and reaching took her hand, as though she were his queen indeed, as though they were long lovers.

She did not flinch, only closed her small fingers around his. "I do not know," she said.

CHAPTER TWENTY-NINE

Two Queens

THE *GEORGE Hammond* cruised through hyperspace, serene and cool against the blue shifted blur. Eleven hours until time.

John lay stretched out on the lower bunk of one of the *Hammond's* empty crew quarters, halfway between sleeping and waking. The noise of the ship was soothing, the low key sounds of systems working normally. Best to sleep while he could.

There was no point in worrying about the rest of his team. Ronon and Cadman and Keller were probably sleeping too. On the upper bunk above him Radek Zelenka was snoring softly.

We're coming to get you, John thought, as though Rodney could hear it. I promise.

Nine hours until time. Jennifer Keller turned over on the narrow bunk, trying to get comfortable. Private quarters were scarce on the *Hammond*. Laura Cadman was permanently assigned to the *Hammond's* crew, however, and as a captain rated a single room the size of a closet. It had been nice of her to offer to let Jennifer take a nap there while she did whatever it was she did.

Jennifer didn't know her well, and she felt distinctly awkward around her. Laura had been a good friend of Katie Brown's, people said. She'd tried to play matchmaker for Katie and Rodney. How she felt about Rodney's next girlfriend was up in the air.

But it wasn't as though Rodney had broken up with Katie for her. They'd called it quits months before she and Rodney had even considered going out. And ok, maybe Rodney had dumped Katie really awkwardly, but that was just Rodney. It didn't have anything to do with her. He'd said it was because he didn't want to get married, but then he'd been the one in a hurry.

Maybe because he knew he didn't have much time left, some

part of Jennifer whispered, some part that was ruthlessly thumped and put away. But it refused to stay in the box no matter how hard she shoved it down. They'd had nearly a year. That was as much as some people got. If that was all there was for Rodney…

Down. Jennifer shoved the thought from her mind. She wasn't going to think like that. They were going to get Rodney back. And then everything was going to be fine.

Or was it, the treacherous little voice whispered. What if he was Wraith? What if he was crazy like Michael? Was that really what she planned to do with her life — nurse someone permanently insane? Was that what Rodney would want for her?

We'll cross that bridge when we come to it, Jennifer thought grimly. There was no reason to think that Rodney would be impaired that way. If he survived going off the retrovirus…

And then everything will be peachy? Her little internal voice just wouldn't be stopped. What if he wants to stay in Atlantis forever? What if he wants to get married? She could never bring up a child there the way Teyla was with Torren, never knowing if they were going to be attacked, never knowing what awful thing might happen. She felt a sick guilt over the cat! Children ought to be raised somewhere safe, with good schools and other kids and Little League teams and Girl Scouts and nothing worse that happened than cancer and car accidents. Not here, where any minute something might happen. How many gravely wounded children had she seen in the last three years on how many planets? There was no way she'd risk a child of hers that way. Never.

Rodney would understand that. And besides, Rodney didn't like children. He probably wouldn't want any, ever. He'd rather stay in Atlantis, living like he was in grad school forever, racing toy cars with Sheppard in the middle of the night…

Jennifer turned over, blinking. Laura Cadman's pictures regarded her solemnly from the wall over the bed, an old couple with their arms around her, one on each side, while she smiled from beneath her beret, impeccable in service dress and brand new lieutenant's bars. Across the bottom someone had written,

"We are so proud of you Laura!" She topped the old woman by a head. The man smiled into the camera, the corners of his mouth wobbly with emotion.

Did they have any idea what she did? Probably not. No more than Jennifer's father did. He didn't ask anymore.

Dad, I'm home to stay, in Nevada. Oh wait. Two months later and I'm gone again. I'm sorry. I can't tell you anything about it. I can't call. You can email me, and I'll reply in a week or two. That's all.

Jennifer put her head down on the pillow. They'd find Rodney. And they'd get him back to normal. And then there would be time to think about all the rest of this.

Seven hours until time.

Ronon sat down at the table in the *Hammond's* mess, realizing belatedly that he had a plate full of chicken casserole and no utensils. Maybe the bread, but that was going to get stares from the Hammond's people at nearby tables and comments about barbarians who don't know how to eat, an embarrassment to Sheppard and to Carter who had originally invited him to join the *Hammond's* crew.

A pair of chopsticks in a paper packet waved in front of him, and Ronon looked up. Captain Cadman smiled down at him from beneath her beret, a tray in her other hand. "Spare pair," she said.

"Thanks." He took the packet from her.

"Is this seat taken?" She gestured vaguely to the chair opposite. "No."

"Cool." Cadman slid into the seat and set her tray down. "Pretty busy, huh?"

"Yeah." Ronon tore the packet open and split the chopsticks carefully. "When did Carter start carrying chopsticks?"

"I dunno." Cadman applied herself to her chicken casserole with great gusto. In fact, Ronon wasn't sure he'd ever seen a woman eat so fast, not even in the Satedan guard.

He was staring, and she stopped and looked up at him.

"Something wrong?"

"No."

"I did a six mile run on the treadmill this morning," Cadman said. "Kind of worked up an appetite." She didn't look like she'd been running, her red-gold hair wound up neatly at the back of her neck. He supposed it did look wet.

"You like the *Hammond*?" he managed.

Cadman stopped, the food halfway to her mouth. "I do." She took a bite and swallowed quickly, then smiled. "Colonel Carter's a lot more of a hard-ass than Colonel Sheppard was. You'd better do it by the book and you'd better have an answer when she asks you, or you get the eyebrow and some scathing comment about being better prepared." Cadman grimaced. "I've never been very good at the book. You know. Lots of people say, 'Laura Cadman is really enthusiastic and she works hard.' But not so many say 'Laura Cadman is really smart.' So I get that look a lot." She grinned at Ronon, and it looked like the sun suddenly came out. "So I get questions like 'What would you do if you were in a shaft filling up with water and you could blow the door with C4 but you didn't have a fuse?' And most of the time I'm like 'WTF? Why would I be in a shaft filling up with water with a locked door and C4?'"

Ronon busted out laughing. "That kind of thing happens," he said, waving a chopstick at her.

"Maybe to you! Wouldn't it be better not to get stuck in a shaft filling up with water?"

"Yeah," Ronon said, still chuckling. "But it happens."

"So what would you do, Mr. Smarty Pants?" she asked.

Ronon took a long sip of his iced tea, as though carefully considering the problem. "Shaft. Water. C4." He grinned again. "I'd say, 'Teyla, how about getting us out of here?'"

Cadman laughed. "Oh that's a good one. That will sit well with Carter!"

"See, Teyla's got everything but a field kitchen in that backpack. Tiny little woman, but you get into anything and Teyla says totally calmly, 'It so happens I have a flare gun, an electric drill, four chickens and a spare Genii uniform right here.'"

"Seriously?"

"Seriously." Ronon took another drink.

"Major Lorne said that back when he did training at the SGC, O'Neill was the one with the final sign off and he was the hard-ass. Carter was the nice one. But Jesus H. on a pogo stick, she's the one washing people out now! There are four people with transfers pending as soon as we get back. They didn't cut it. In, like, three months." Cadman took a bite of her bread. "So I have to watch it. But it's really nice that Colonel Sheppard asked to borrow me while Major Lorne is on crutches. And that he said in writing that it was because he needed 'a Marine with a brain.' That helps a lot." She paused for another bite. "It sucks that Lorne broke his leg."

"It sucks a lot more for the people who got fed on instead," Ronon said.

"That too." Cadman looked thoughtful but uncowed, and Ronon remembered that she was, after all, the only Marine lieutenant in five years who'd served her whole tour and gone home without a stretcher or a body bag. Cadman was good at getting by. She was like the kids he'd grown up with, the best of them.

"Cadman, why are you a Marine?"

"Laura." She shrugged, her eyes on her plate as she took another bite. "Call me Laura. And I guess it was because that's what my school had. It was Navy or Marines, and I don't like boats." She looked up, her eyes very bright. "If what you're asking is why I'm not a graphic designer or something, it's a long story."

"Ok," Ronon said. He liked to hear her talk. And she did, pretty much nonstop.

"My parents are both flakes. I was in junior high when my dad went off to Arizona to find himself and my mom went to Miami with her boyfriend. So I moved in with Nana and Pops in St. Petersburg. Pops used to be in the Navy, so he talked about how much he'd liked it and all. But Nana and Pops didn't have any money for school, and they thought I ought to do better than the drive-thru, and my grades weren't good enough for any scholarships. Except the Marines. So they paid for my four years, and then I owed them four years." Cadman shrugged. "My four years are up, but I like it, so I'm staying in. How many mediocre graphic designers get to go to other planets?"

"Point," Ronon said.

"Besides," she said, "you meet some really interesting people. And some of them are pretty hot."

"What, like Rodney?" Ronon asked, remembering Cadman's whole mess with Rodney when she'd first gotten there, when a malfunctioning culling beam had left her stuck in Rodney's body.

Cadman laughed. "No, not exactly." Then she sobered. "I'm really sorry about Rodney. And I'm glad I get a chance to help get him back. He's an ok guy."

Ronon's eyes met hers across the table. "We may not get him back."

"It won't be because we didn't try," Cadman said.

Ronon looked away. Something weird like hope was crawling around in him. Maybe they could do this. Maybe it would work. And then everything could go back to normal.

"When we get into it," he said, "you watch out for Zelenka, ok? We've got to take him because we've got to have somebody to deal with Wraith tech if we need to, and we can't count on finding Teyla first. He can't shoot for shit."

"I'll watch out for him," Cadman promised. "He's a sweet old guy. Reminds me of Pops."

One hour until time.

Sam sat down at her desk and took a deep breath, looking up at the pictures held to the metal wall above with cheerful magnets in the shape of bright colored flowers. Cassie in her graduation gown. Daniel in a floppy hat and wire rimmed glasses, Teal'c looking inscrutable beside him in the light of some alien sun — that was an old one, that picture. Daniel didn't look much like that anymore. Jack in his baseball cap, sitting on the end of his pier with a fishing rod in his hand, looking straight at the camera with a sideways smile.

This was the email she never sent. But it was there, in case someone else needed to send it.

October 16, 2009
Dear Jack,
I'm not sorry. I don't regret any of it, not one minute, not one second. Not ever.
Your Carter

Her radio sounded softly. "Colonel, we will be dropping out of hyperspace in fifty minutes."

"Understood, Franklin. I'm on my way." She carefully hit the save button and closed the laptop, turned off the light and went up to the bridge.

Forty minutes.

"Be prepared to reopen a hyperspace window immediately," Guide ordered the helmsman.

The hive ship had not yet exited hyperspace, but Guide took no chances. Silent in the center of the control room, Queen Steelflower nodded her assent.

"We are ready, my commander," the helmsman said, his head bent over the console, half in shiptrance. "We are coming out of hyperspace now."

They slid through the window, blue streaked stars shifting to the speckled blackness of a normal starfield.

"We have a hail," the ship-master said, looking over his shoulder to his queen.

"One hive ship on our instruments," the helmsman said, "One and one only. It is Revenant, belonging to Queen Death."

"That is well," Guide replied. "All is as it should be." He looked at Steelflower. "What is your wish, My Queen?"

"Hail Revenant," Steelflower said evenly. "And inform them that I have arrived to speak with my sister."

Sable, the commander of the honor guard, winced inwardly. Let it never be said Queen Steelflower lacked audacity! She spoke as a superior queen to a lesser, or at least as one who would never acknowledge lesser status. Perhaps she would come as an ally, but not as a subject queen. And yet perhaps there had been too much bowing and scraping to Queen Death. She was, after all, not the only queen.

"Yes, My Queen," he said.

"Twenty five minutes to reversion," Major Franklin said precisely.

"Understood." Sam Carter settled back in her chair. "Raise shields five minutes before we exit hyperspace." She tapped her radio. "Colonel Sheppard? Is your team ready?"

"We're getting in the jumper now," Sheppard said clearly in her ear. "Me, Cadman, Keller, Ronon and Zelenka. We'll be ready to go on your mark."

"You're going to have a very narrow window," Sam said. "To get inside while they're launching darts."

"We've done it before." Sheppard sounded confident. "We'll cloak before we get out of the bay."

Franklin looked at Sam. "If they're cloaked our automatic systems won't be able to sense them. And …"

Sam nodded. "Sheppard? You'll have to do a purely manual departure. The moment you cloak we can't see you."

"Got it. Just open the bay doors for us and we're good."

Launch and recovery were the times the *Hammond* was most vulnerable. While her landing bays were energy shielded, those shields were incredibly fragile compared to her hull. And the bays were small. Thirty feet in height was nothing compared to the immensity of space. A pilot error of a few feet, of hundredths of a percent, would run a ship into the walls or into the delicate components within, which was why recovery and launch were generally done with the *Hammond's* systems providing constant data feedback to the 302s or jumpers. It took a very skilled pilot indeed to turn all the safeties off and do it on manual.

Of course, Cameron Mitchell had recovered her in a spacesuit on manual, aboard the *Odyssey*. Not that it was an experience she'd ever like to repeat.

But Sheppard was probably the most skilled jumper pilot they had, and he'd have the jumper's systems to assist. Sam didn't even blink at letting him do it.

"Open the bay doors as soon as we've raised shields," Sam said to Franklin. "Colonel Sheppard will take it out without assistance."

"Yes, ma'am."

The shuttlecraft mated neatly with Revenant, the door irising open in a series of cascading movements to reveal those within. Queen Steelflower stood straightbacked, her chin high, and no trace of trepidation showed on her face. At her back, her Consort loomed tall, his immaculate leather coat falling to his ankles, his expression impassive.

Steelflower's gaze raked the assembled blades. "I am Steelflower," she said.

Revenant's watch commander stepped forward, inclining his head deeply. "I am Iceseeker. It is my honor to escort you to the reception chambers where all has been made ready for you. My queen will join you shortly."

Steelflower hesitated a moment, her skirts swaying. She was not dressed formally, but rather like a warrior queen in boots and short coat, its emerald folds only reaching her knees, stiff with embroidery.

Her Consort read her movement. "Our shuttlecraft will cast off and return to our ship," he said. "Thereby to await Queen Steelflower's pleasure."

There was little the watch commander could object to in that. After all, they were two alone, as they had said they would be, and the crew of the shuttle would not figure in anything that came. "Of course."

"Then lead us, commander," she said, and her eyes fell on him like falling sparks. "We shall await your lady." She followed him with her head high, her slender hand set to her Consort's wrist in a gesture both graceful and courtly, as though she stood among her own kindred.

"Five minutes," Franklin said, frowning at the board. "Raising shields, ma'am."

Sam didn't reply to that. "Sheppard? You're good to go."

"Copy that," Sheppard said. "We'll be in and out before you get the paint scratched." He sounded high on adrenaline, ready to fight. Which was a good thing.

Sam opened the shipwide intercom. "Four minutes to reversion. All hands to battlestations. It's showtime, people."

It is a trap, Guide said, mind to mind, his hand brushing against hers as they stood within the reception hall.

I know that well, Teyla replied. Above, the low ceiling was arched with a tracery of supports scribing a perfect circle. At the center of it a low table held oath taking materials, while each of the six radial entrances was guarded by a drone in full battle gear, weapons at the ready. They carried formal pikes, not the more mundane stunners. There were of course no humans about, and for use upon another Wraith a bladed weapon would be more effective. Stunners could be shaken off and bullets survived, but severed limbs would not regrow.

I doubt Queen Death is even aboard this ship, Guide said, a pleasant smile on his face.

As long as Rodney is, and likewise the ZPM, she replied. "That, at least is true I think. These drones cannot hide such things from me.* She likewise gave him a courteous gaze. *And no, they do not yet plan to kill us.*

Yet, Guide said softly, a caressing note in his voice that was almost anticipation. He caught the hint of amusement in her mind. *Does that entertain you?*

You remind me of John, she said.

The *Hammond*'s bay doors slowly opened, revealing the blue of hyperspace. Outside the puddle jumper, in the landing bay, there would be claxons hooting warnings, but inside it was silent. Flashing yellow lights indicated depressurization.

"Coming out of hyperspace," Major Franklin said in his earpiece. "Good luck, Colonel."

"Thanks," John said, glancing over at Radek in Teyla's usual shotgun seat. "Here goes nothing." He moved the indicators to full cloak.

Outside, there was a brief flash as they reverted to normal space, sublight engines engaging with a flare of white fire. The *Hammond* had emerged ninety degrees to the ventral of the two hive ships, and now she pulled up in a climb vertical to her own plane of entry, forward rail guns opening up on the nearer of the two ships.

John wondered briefly how Sam had made sure she was shooting at the right one, but that wasn't his problem.

They rocketed toward the hive ship, looking for a moment as though they intended a collision, or at least a shield on shield pass that would strain every system, pulling away at the last second with only a few tens of meters between one shield and the other, rail guns spitting bright fire, the hive ship's shields flaring blue in the void. The *Hammond*'s gunners couldn't see them, so he'd have to dodge friendly fire too.

"Here we go," he said, and as the *Hammond* reeled away, diving beneath the hive ship, the puddle jumper leapt forward.

The hive ship screamed. There was no other word for it, for the alarms that rang out high and urgent in every room and corridor.

"What is happening?" Queen Steelflower demanded of the nearest guard.

"I do not know," he replied truthfully.

"Find out," Steelflower snapped, her Consort coming forward to her side.

The note of the alarm changed. Pilots to the dart bays. The ship was going to full battle alert.

A young blade of Queen Death's, his hair pulled back in a single white braid, came hurrying into the chamber.

"What treachery is this?" Guide snapped. "We have come aboard your ship in good faith, and now you are attacking our ship!"

"We have done no such thing!" the blade replied. "It is the Lanteans! It is the warship of She Who Carries Many Things."

"We will return to our ship immediately," Steelflower said.

The blade swallowed. "I cannot allow that," he said.

Steelflower drew herself up, her eyes fixed upon his. "Am I your prisoner then?"

His mouth opened and then shut. "No," he said. "At least I do not think…"

"Then you will stand aside and allow me and my consort to return to our ship," she said, and did not take her gaze from his.

Another blade approached, his steps swift on the floor. "Ardent, what are you doing?" His mind was hooded, his resolve firm.

"Queen Steelflower wishes to return to her ship, as the Lanteans are attacking us," the one called Ardent replied.

"That cannot be," the other said, and Steelflower felt a frisson run through her.

Guide, she said, a moment's warning as the blade drew steel.

CHAPTER THIRTY

Revenant

"I DO NOT see how we are to do this," Radek said quietly as the puddle jumper jinked, dodging madly around the fire radiating outward from the hive ship, trying to hug the surface of the shields as closely as possible.

"They'll open the bay doors to let the darts out," John said, his hands loose on the controls. There was no need to jerk a jumper. It moved like water, like his thoughts. Nothing had ever moved like it did.

The *Hammond's* rail guns spat fire, but the jumper rolled beneath it, friendly fire missing by a few meters. In the seat behind Radek, Cadman swore. "They can't see us," she said.

John didn't spare a breath to respond. He'd seen the dart bay opening, the first blue dots of launching flares. "There we are. Just like that, baby," he whispered. The puddle jumper slipped between the oncoming darts, rotating 180 as she slid through the gaps in their formation, straight into the maw of the dart bay.

Metal rang on metal as the blade drew a long knife, but Guide was faster. His arm rose in a lightning parry, catching it on a dagger of his own before his queen, a quick twist and disengage sending the weapon flying.

Ardent drew in a sharp motion but did not advance, his face a study in confusion.

Get them! the senior blade shouted, *In the Name of the Queen!*

So be it, Steelflower said, and with a sweep of robe she drew as well, back to back with her Consort, dropping into guard as gracefully as a blade.

The drones charged, pikes at the ready.

Guide took the first, grasping the pike in both hands. Closed thus, struggling for the staff, his knife slipped into the drone's chest. The drone staggered back stupidly, the knife standing out. The wound would heal, of course, but it would at least slow him down.

Guide brought the pike up sharply, the blunt end connecting with the second onrushing drone, sending him reeling, while the bladed back end connected with his legs, slicing through skin and muscle, dropping him to the floor.

Steelflower ducked beneath the first drone's pike, coming neatly beneath his guard with a series of flashing blows. In themselves they would not have been much to his might, but with short dagger in hand they were blinding. Literally. He stumbled, clutching his face, a wound that would take days to heal.

Ardent cried out something Steelflower did not understand in the heat of battle, pivoting to take the fourth drone who rushed against Guide from behind while he was engaged with the fifth. Her kick caught him neatly in the back of the knee and he fell, the blade of Guide's pike coming down across him.

Get her! the senior blade shrieked, and still Ardent hesitated. The last drone did not, but the butt of Guide's pike caught him full in the chest, sending him staggering backwards into Ardent.

You! Steelflower shouted, whirling to face the senior blade. *You are the one calling for my death, a treachery that only the least worthy of blades would consider! Will you not stand against me yourself? Must you stand back, coward, throwing drones at me in a man's place?*

His face was a study in dismay, and a slow green flush rose in it, but his hand was steady on a long knife

Yield to me or die! Steelflower said, her mind cold and tight as a vise. It closed around him like claws, like nails digging into his flesh, her will sharp and battle hardened.

I will not, he dredged from some part of his being even as his knees gave way, even as he dropped to the floor in front of her, the knife still in his hand.

Her eyes did not leave his.

His face contorted as slowly, slowly the knife rose, rotating hilt foremost. His hands shook. His mouth twisted. With an exhalation, he plunged the knife into his own chest, falling forward upon it.

Ardent let out some strangled sound.

Steelflower turned about, blood a darker emerald down her embroidered coat. *Will you yield?* she said, and her voice was iron.

I will, Ardent said, and dropped his dagger, his eyes glittering with admiration and desire.

That is wise, Guide said. His breath came heavily in his chest.

Are you injured, my Guide? she asked.

His mind voice was tinged with wry amusement. *No. Only old.*

If that is all, she said. Her eyes swept over Ardent. *Stand aside and hinder me no more.*

Yes, my queen, he said, and his eyes fell in rapt confusion as her hand lifted to his cheek, leaving a trail of blood along his jaw.

Very good, she said. With the whisper of leather on silk Steelflower swept from the chamber, leaving Ardent alone with the injured and the dead.

They were pinned down almost the second they left the dart bay. Bad plan, John thought. This was not working.

Blue streaks of stunner fire crisscrossed the corridor, flashes bright and solid enough to be almost blinding. There must be thirty or forty Wraith backed up. No matter how many they hit with gunfire, the Wraith could keep coming. John glanced back from where he crouched behind the farthest forward obstruction. Cadman was right behind him, covering Radek who could make himself very small and flat indeed against the wall, the reflection of stunner fire crawling in his glasses. Back, at the turn of the corridor fifteen feet away, now separated by a no man's land of open space, Jennifer sheltered in a doorway, Ronon at her back. He had pivoted, firing shot after shot down the hall behind them toward Wraith coming from the other direction.

"This is not going to work!" Ronon shouted into his radio.

"I see that!" John shouted back. "You get an opening of any kind, you take it." He glanced behind. "Radek, can you do anything with the wall panel there?"

The scientist was flat against the wall, an irised control panel almost under his elbow. "I do not know!" he said.

"Try!"

Radek worked his way around as John fired off another round of shots, scattering across the junction at different heights, Cadman covering him. Radek was swearing in Czech as he slipped a thin knife into the biotech circuits, prizing up a knot of fleshy cables like muscles. "I have no idea what these do," he said. Another stun beam hissed past him, plowing into the wall inches from Cadman. With an oath, he plunged the knife through, severing strands.

Down the hall, just beyond the juncture, a blast door irised shut, cutting all but two of the Wraith off from them. "Great!" John began, just as another irised shut between them and Ronon.

Cadman lunged out, P90 spitting, sending the two drones still on their side of the door spinning. She came up with her face tight, looking suddenly like Carter. "Now what?"

"Ronon?" John yelled into the radio.

"I've got a clear side corridor," Ronon said back. "But I can't get through this door. I think it's a pressure door."

In case the dart bay depressurized. It made sense that the corridors around it could be sealed against vacuum. They weren't going to get anywhere trying to shoot through that. "Radek?"

Radek looked up from the knot of fibers and shook his head, his glasses on the end of his nose. "I do not know what any of these go to. I am guessing."

"Ok." What he needed was Teyla, who could talk to the ship. But she wasn't here. Time for plan B. "Ronon, you and Keller go aft to the labs and go after Rodney. Keller's got the sedative, so you can stun him and she can keep him out. As soon as you've got him, have the *Hammond* beam you out."

"Got it." Ronon didn't sound particularly worried. "Where are you going, Sheppard?"

"Forward to the power hub where Zelenka said it was most likely they've got the ZPM. Don't wait for us, clear? As soon as you get

Rodney, beam out." John put his hand on Radek's shoulder. "Ok, leave those alone. Let's get to the power hub." Teyla would be with Todd. Like Ronon, she'd find her own way out.

This way, Guide said, moving unerringly through the dim corridors of the hive ship. About them alarms blared, the high pitched wail for pilots to the dart bay and the almost subsonic rumble of general quarters. Once or twice drones hurried into them, but none tried to hinder them. Steelflower was a queen, and to attack her without specific orders unthinkable. The merest touch of her mind on theirs assured it.

Where do we go? she asked.

You wanted McKay, he said.

Wait. Steelflower put a hand to his wrist, drew him back. *That is where the team goes, where they go already. I would find Death.*

She felt his surprise, though it did not show in his face. *You seek her out?*

That is the only way this will end, Steelflower said. *The only way. You know that, Guide. Queen to queen.*

His mouth opened and shut, as though he wished to say something aloud, but Guide did not, and he felt her will hard as iron against him, a fragile flower, yes, but wrought of steel. *Then we will go this way,* he said. *To her chambers.*

"Come on." Ronon led Jennifer through the maze of corridors that wound upon each other, twisting around until she had no idea where she was. But at least people had stopped shooting at them.

"Why aren't they after us?" she asked as Ronon slipped through yet another junction, pausing to look in all directions.

"After Sheppard," Ronon said. "Or Teyla." He looked back at her. "We get Rodney. That's the plan. They can take care of themselves."

"Ok." Maybe it was just the stress that caused the world to suddenly wobble in front of her eyes, and Jennifer paused, grabbing the wall. Her stomach rose. No. Absolutely not. She was not going to act like some green kid in front of Ronon. She'd been on missions before. She was not going to do this.

"You ok?" Ronon looked back over his shoulder frowning.

"Fine," Jennifer said. Step where the floor is, not where you see it pitching. Keep moving. It will all settle down in a minute. It's just nerves. Squaring her jaw, Jennifer followed Ronon through the maze.

It was only at the doors to her chambers that drones hindered them, four with pikes coming forward to bar the way into Death's chambers. "What business have you?" the blade who was the doorwarden asked, coming forward to speak with Steelflower. His name was Green, and Guide knew him only slightly, but before he could so much as phrase a polite question Steelflower's mind was on him.

Open the doors, she said, her mind voice echoing in Guide's own mind. *And tell these drones to stand aside.*

He resisted. Of course he did. But only a moment before he fell to his knees, his head bent, forehead almost touching the hem of her emerald coat, and a frisson ran through Guide. She was strong, almost too strong in her urgency. He should have known she was of Osprey. The mind touch, the flavor of it, was too familiar for it to be anything else. He should have known. This was brighter than Alabaster when he had last seen her, a child still, bright almost as Snow. Perhaps brighter, some traitor part of him said. She was stronger. Snow's mind had been versatile, clever as a cleverman, her thoughts whirling about like snow on the wind, this way and that as they danced in the air. Steelflower was all discipline. Her will did not waver.

She is not here. Steelflower spoke in his thoughts, releasing Green as though opening her hand. *Death is not aboard this ship, and has not been these many sleeps. It is a trap.*

So be it, Guide said, and let his satisfaction show through. He had thought it was. He had told her it was a plot to kill Steelflower. Let her know his wisdom!

We will take the ZPM, she said. *That at least we can do. And then we will find our way off.*

As soon as the shields drop, our men will have us out, Guide said, ready with a means as a proper consort should be. *They will lock on to the transmitters we wear, and they will do their part. We have only to wait for the Lanteans to drop the shields.*

That should present little difficulty, Steelflower said coolly. *But I would not have them bring us away empty handed. Show me where the power room is.*

The *Hammond* twisted, turning almost end over end as it dodged through a cloud of Wraith Darts, shields flaring blue almost to opacity with the volume of fire taken.

"Forward shield at 70%," Major Franklin said, "Holding steady, ma'am."

Sam Carter leaned forward in her seat, trying not to sway around with the weaving and bobbing targets outside. It was a side effect of the inertial dampeners — when you could feel nothing of your motion there was a true disconnect with the visual data. Past a certain point it was confusing. The body tried to compensate by moving in concert with the visual stimuli, even when it wasn't necessary.

But that was a scientist's impression, not a starship captain's. "Any change in the other hive ship?" she asked. She absolutely didn't flinch as the refuse of a breaking up Dart collided with the forward shield, shearing off harmlessly a few meters from the bridge viewport.

"Negative. They're just sitting there, ma'am."

Which was Todd in a nutshell, Sam thought. The *Hammond* and Queen Death's ship could go at it while he stood back waiting for a winner. And the last thing she could do was give them a run to provoke them, not with her hands full with the other hive ship.

"Leave them be," Sam said. "Concentrate on the Darts. Once their cover is gone we can open them up."

Alarms screamed in the corridors of the hive ship, but John

thought the resistance was actually lighter than it had been. Three teams on the loose were at least splitting the defenders, not to mention whatever havoc the *Hammond* was wreaking. Three of the big guys were guarding the power room, but a nice one-two play from him and Cadman put them down, enough bullets in them to sink them in deep water. Cadman wasn't sparing with the ammo.

"Ok," John said, making one more quick check around the room. "Cadman, we'll cover. Radek, get that ZPM out." He ducked around one of the festooned pillars that sheltered the consoles from the door, Cadman behind the one on the other side. They had overlapping fields of fire this way, but he could see further down the hall to the right.

Radek threw himself at the console, laying his P90 across the edge of it, his glasses sliding down his nose again. "I will be a moment," he said, peering at the alien interface. There was no need to tell him to get on with it as fast as possible. Putting the pressure on Radek didn't work the way it did with Rodney. All it would do would be fluster him and cause him to make a mistake.

For the moment there was no movement in the hall. John chinned his radio on. "Ronon?"

There was no reply. He'd like to take that as Ronon was busy. He would take it that way. For the moment.

"I cannot get it out," Radek said. "*Co s tím?*" he said, his fingers flying over the board of the interface. "Sheppard, I have a problem."

Footsteps in the hallway. Cadman sent a spray of bullets flying just at knee height, not really able to see what she was shooting at.

"Hold your fire!" It was Teyla's voice shouting back. "John, it is us!"

Cadman looked at him questioningly. Prisoner or not? Up and up or at gunpoint?

"Hold on," John said, and added for Cadman's benefit, "she'd have said Colonel Sheppard if she were a prisoner."

Cadman nodded. She was still learning the subtle things. "Ok."

"Come on in," John called.

Teyla hurried around the corner, Todd at her heels, a long bladed pike in his hands as he looked behind them.

"The power is fluctuating," Radek said. "This ship is seriously damaged."

"Good for Carter," John said. "Now pull that ZPM."

"I cannot! I told you." John took a step toward him, and he could see what Radek meant immediately. Long, vinelike tendrils wrapped the ZPM, its glowing surface seamed with green pulsing cables. "I cannot get it out. It does not obey an extraction order."

"What if you cut the cables?" John asked.

"Jen pøes moji mrtvolu," Radek said fervently.

"You will blow up the ship momentarily," Todd snapped, his coat flowing around him as he leaned over the screen. "You cannot pull it without turning it off unless you want to simply destroy us all."

"Then turn it off," John said. He looked around. "Teyla?" Surely a queen could tell it to disconnect.

"Let me see the interface," she said, sliding in beside Radek. "Perhaps…" She closed her eyes, her fingers on the tactile pads.

Todd looked back toward the door. "We do not have long," he said. "Sheppard, this was a trap for Steelflower as I thought. This is likely not the only ship of Queen Death's. We must get off this ship before reinforcements arrive. She would have anticipated that our hive ship would fight if Steelflower were ambushed. It is only that your Carter attacked first."

"Right," John said. He keyed the radio again. "Ronon? What's going on, buddy?"

CHAPTER THIRTY-ONE

Tiger by the Tail

"ALMOST there," Ronon said quietly into his radio. "I need silence, Sheppard."

"Ok. Check in when you're done." Sheppard's voice was worried. And why not, Jennifer thought. This was all crazy. Crazy dangerous. The world pitched around her for a second and then steadied.

"It should be just up here," Ronon said. He glanced at her, his brow furrowed. "You stay behind me. Once I've dropped Rodney, I need you to sedate him to keep him out. With this thing set on stun Wraith don't stay out long."

"I'm ready," Jennifer said. Her hypodermic was loaded, capped tightly in an inner jacket pocket. Even a Wraith would be out for a couple of hours with what was essentially enough anesthetic for major surgery. Rodney wouldn't be able to give them a fight while they were removing him from the hive ship and getting him safely aboard the *Hammond*.

The world steadied. Cold sweat still stood out on her face, and Jennifer shivered. She was getting a grip. Her heart wasn't pounding quite so fast. At least Ronon hadn't noticed.

Ronon slid up almost against the door to the lab, listening. Jennifer, behind him, couldn't hear anything, but apparently Ronon could because he smiled wolfishly. Here we go, it meant, and he looked almost happy as he activated the door, thundering through with a barrage of shots.

"Hey!" It might have been Rodney's voice, Rodney's voice utterly changed. She heard a shout, and then the shots ceased.

Jennifer peered around the door trying to see what had happened.

"Come in," Ronon said. He sounded satisfied as he keyed the door closed behind her. "Got him. He was by himself."

Rodney lay unconscious in the middle of the floor, one arm flung up over his face. Jennifer knelt beside him, rolling him carefully onto his back.

His hair was stark white but thicker than it had been, spiking up like an 80s rock star over a green seamed face, the sensory pits along the sides of his nose making his face look thinner and more pinched. His eyes were closed. The pulse at his neck was steady, his skin soft and a little oily under her hands. This was the first time she had touched him in two months, she thought. All the times she'd wanted to and touched empty air.

"He ok?" Ronon knelt down on the other side, carefully not touching Rodney.

"He's just unconscious," Jennifer said, nodding sharply. "Good job." She reached in her jacket pocket and pulled out the hypodermic, carefully rolled up his left sleeve and injected it into the vein. "We should have at least an hour or two with this, but I can't give him more."

"It's not going to take us an hour," Ronon said. He snapped a bracelet with a radio transmitter around Rodney's wrist. That would allow the *Hammond* to lock onto Rodney as easily as to them.

Once again the world wavered, and Jennifer clutched at the floor to keep from falling. Rodney's face swam before her eyes.

"Jennifer?" Ronon's voice was concerned.

Her vision darkened. What was this? This wasn't nerves. This wasn't a fear reaction. Jennifer opened her mouth but nothing came out. She couldn't speak. She couldn't see.

"Jennifer?" Sharper now. She thought maybe Ronon had grabbed her shoulder.

And then the world went entirely dark.

"I cannot remove the ZPM," Teyla said quietly, opening her eyes.

"You mean the ship won't take your orders?" John said, his hair dripping with sweat as he cradled the P90 in his arms.

"I mean that it cannot be removed," Teyla said shortly. "It has been completely integrated with the ship's systems. I cannot imagine who could have done this."

"I can," Radek said grimly. "Rodney."

John swore. He looked at Guide. "And if we pull the damn thing we'll blow ourselves up?"

"Immediately," Guide said. "Instantaneously."

"Ok, not a plan." John looked back and forth between Guide and Radek. "Can you set it to overload? That will take a while to build up, right?"

"It will," Radek acknowledged. "And yes, it can be set to overload."

"You will destroy the ship, Sheppard," Guide said. "And all else who are too near."

"It is what Steelflower would do," Teyla said. "To deny it to Death in revenge for her treachery."

Guide looked at her, and she felt his words as much as heard them in her mind. *You are Steelflower in truth.*

Yes, she said. *I am.*

"I will set it to overload," Guide said, coming around her to stand at the terminal. "We will have four minutes from when I am finished."

"Understood," John said, keying his radio on. "Ronon? What's your status? We need to get a move on."

The *Hammond* swam through a barrage of shots like a shark through a school of remoras, iridescent fire eerily beautiful as it danced around them, flaring blue off their shields. But the fire was less than before. Fully half the hive ship's batteries were disabled.

And yet it had not come without a price. "Forward shields at 40 percent," Major Franklin shouted over the din of equipment and people on the Hammond's bridge. "Dorsal shield at 70 percent."

"Understood." The captain was at the engineer's station, Lieutenant Mills having been removed from the bridge with serious burns on his hands when the relays overloaded and sent feedback through the control panels, shorting out with a massive electrical surge. It was the dorsal shield that Sam was worried about. The lighter hull plating Dr. Kusanagi had used for repairs wouldn't hold against a single shot if the energy shields failed.

The Darts still swarmed, but they were fewer as well. Hocken's 302s were doing a good job. But even as she glanced up, Sam saw one of them take a wing hit, shearing through the superstructure and clipping the entire wing off. The 302 spun out of control, plumes of gas venting into vacuum. From the wing tank, Sam thought analytically at the same moment that she turned to Franklin. "Beam that pilot out of there!"

"I'm trying, ma'am," Franklin said, an expression of concentration on his face as he bent over the board.

Sam looked back at the engineering board, toggling power. If she pulled it out of some other systems she could reinforce that dorsal shield…

"The infirmary reports they have Colonel Hocken aboard," Franklin said, an expression of momentary triumph on his face.

"Good job."

The helmsman put the *Hammond* hard over, looping entirely about some arbitrary center point, utter confusion for targeting aboard the hive ship. Every shot in the barrage was a clean miss. That took the stress off the shields for a moment, Sam thought. Good deal.

"Ma'am?" Franklin's voice rose above the noise. "We have hyperspace windows opening."

Oh not good, Sam thought, moving quickly from the engineering station to her own where she could get the other readouts. She could see the wavering, as though a fog had crossed the stars, then the northern lights shimmer as the windows opened not so far away at all. She could see for herself. She didn't have to wait for Franklin to say it.

"We have two additional hive ships and three Wraith cruisers coming out of hyperspace."

Queen Death's reinforcements had arrived.

"Sheppard, we're out of time." John's headset crackled with Sam's voice. "We've got six, repeat six, of Queen Death's ships out here. We've got to pull you out of there."

John looked at Todd bent over the interfaces that controlled the ZPM, still setting up the overload. "Roger, we've got you. Give us another minute here. We're setting up an overload."

"We may not have a minute." Sam's voice was calm, but she'd never say that lightly. "You've got until we get in range."

John looked at Todd. "How long?"

"Almost there," Todd said, his eyes still closed in the interface.

"Ronon?" John opened his radio again. "Ronon, do you have Rodney? The *Hammond* is going to have to pull us out."

"I've got a problem," Ronon said. "Keller's out cold."

"Keller?" John looked at Teyla, who seemed equally confused. "Did she get stunned?"

"No, just collapsed. She's having some kind of seizure." His voice sounded ragged.

It only took John a second. "Ok. We're going to work our way back to you. Stay where you are and we'll come for you. You've got the beacons activated, right?"

"Yeah," Ronon said.

"It is done," Todd said, lifting his head. The ZPM in its cradle was glowing brightly. "We have four minutes."

John opened his transmitter again. "Sam? Now is a good time."

"I can't do that right now." The *Hammond* twisted and dove again, trying to get through. The cruisers had engaged immediately, coming in to form a screen around the damaged hive ship. Each half and a bit the size of the *Hammond*, they didn't pack as much punch, but there were three of them. "The Asgard beams are short range."

"Ventral shield at 50%," Franklin said. "Dorsal at 60%"

Goddamn the dorsal shield. If Sam had been the type to swear on her own bridge she would have about that.

"We are losing the forward shield," Franklin said.

Sam shook her head. "Reroute the power." Which meant pulling it out of the others. Not good. She put her hand on the back of the helmsman's chair, looking out over his shoulder at the battle raging. "Get us in close enough to get our people."

"Ronon?" John spoke quickly, but his eyes were on the rest of his team and the ZPM now glowing brighter. "Ronon?" There was no answer. "Sam, pull Ronon out first. It's the cluster of three beacons, not four. He's got a medical emergency."

"Standby." Sam's voice was clipped and the frequency riddled with static.

"Perhaps we need to find another way off this ship," Teyla said.

"We will never make it back to the jumper bay in three minutes," Radek said, scowling at the ZPM. "And there is not much point in going anywhere else aboard the ship, as it will be entirely destroyed as soon as the ZPM reaches critical mass."

"Sam?" There was a sudden burst of stunner fire at the door, and John dove under a console, dragging Radek down with him. The Wraith had finally discovered they were in the ZPM room. Cadman had flattened herself against the far wall, while Teyla and Todd were behind the interface. The light of the ZPM grew brighter.

"Radek? Is it possible they could stop the overload if they got in here?" John yelled.

"Not a chance," Radek said from somewhere smooshed beneath him.

John hit the transmitter again. "Ok. Sam, now is a good time."

"I can't…" John heard her say, then felt the familiar prickle, saw the familiar shimmer in the air as the beams engaged.

"…get you right now," Sam finished.

The *Hammond* pulled up from an attempted dive between

two of the cruisers, shields shaking with the strain of a near shield on shield pass. There was the scream of instruments. They'd connected, ventral shield against the cruiser's shields, a bleed of power as the shields literally forced the ships away from one another, momentum blunted and deflected at the cost of enormous amounts of energy. The *Hammond* shook, inertial dampeners trying to compensate, and Sam was nearly flung off her feet.

"Damage report!"

"We've lost the ventral shield!" Franklin shouted over the screams of alarms. "Dorsal shield at 10%. Forward shield at 20%."

A massive hive ship rotated before the *Hammond,* weapons blazing at last, Todd's ship joining the fray. One of the cruisers was caught in its fire, incandescing as shot after shot plunged through the shield gap where the *Hammond* had damaged it. The shield on shield pass must have told on it as well.

"About time," Sam said, her hands flying over the engineering station. "That makes it two on five instead of one on six. Sheppard? Ronon?"

Nothing but silence on the frequency. The amount of EM transmissions flying around the battle site effectively acted as jamming.

"Franklin, can you lock onto the radio transmitters on the hive?"

"No, ma'am!" Franklin didn't look up from his instruments, sweat standing out on his brow, undistracted by the mayhem around him. "We are not close enough for a beam lock. And I am only picking up three signals."

Sam tried again. "Sheppard?"

Smoke wreathed him, choking him, filling his lungs. The ship was burning, fires eating up all the available oxygen. They'd go out soon. Vacuum would claim their fuel.

Ronon gave Rodney's legs a shove. Something had gone wrong. That wasn't a surprise. He couldn't raise Sheppard and he couldn't raise the *Hammond.* It was time to find his own way off the ship while there still was a ship. One more shove, and Rodney was inside the tiny escape pod, head lolling back to expose green veined throat.

Coughing, Ronon dragged himself to his feet. One more time.

The rush of atmosphere caught him with Jennifer in his arms, and he staggered, caught in a maelstrom of air rushing toward some distant hull breach. It was all he could do to hold onto her and a bulkhead at the same time. He couldn't make any headway. It tore away the smoke, but also the air. One deep breath, two. Overbreathe, because in a moment…

The rush stopped. Somewhere a bulkhead door had slammed shut, some crewman risking life and limb to seal a compartment. For now it held, but the ship was in its death throes.

The air was thin. Ronon held his breath, moving as slowly as underwater. The gravity was fluctuating too. Jennifer's hair floated out behind her, her eyes rolled up in her head, unconscious. Maybe dying. He had no idea what was wrong. But if they stayed on this ship any longer they'd all be dead.

His vision was getting spots. Not enough oxygen.

A few more steps. He thought it was to the left. Jennifer felt light as a feather. One hand of hers trailed along, as though she had drowned. Oxygen deprived, just as he was.

His vision darkened. He felt the gap with his left hand. Light as this it was easy to shove Jennifer in. Dark. The release must be here.

The door irised shut, self contained systems activating.

Ten seconds. Twelve.

Ronon drank down deep gulps of air. No time to check on Rodney or Jennifer, their bodies sprawled together, dead or living. No time. The hive ship pitched, inertial dampeners failing.

Ronon hit the launch switch, and in a blast of miniature thrusters the escape pod separated, blasting out into fire.

"What in the hell?" John said, the barrel of his P90 rising as he looked around the chamber of the hive ship. He'd felt the tingle of beams, had a moment's gratitude that somehow Sam had gotten close enough to grab them. Wrong.

Radek blinked owlishly, picking himself up from the floor, while Cadman drew in a breath of astonishment. Only Teyla seemed composed.

And Todd. He turned to a tall Wraith standing at a console, an expression very like pleased approbation on his face. "Well done, Ember."

"Where are we?" Cadman demanded. "What happened?"

The Wraith at the console didn't look fazed at all by Cadman being the one with the demands, and Teyla stepped forward, speaking formally to her as though they were barely acquainted. "We are aboard my ship. You have my gratitude for your part in combating treachery."

John felt like he was still a step behind, but Cadman looked like she was about three steps back.

Teyla turned to the Wraith at the console, and the other three who had hurried in.

"My Queen," one said, going to one knee. "We are relieved that you are safe."

"Through the good work of my cleverman, Ember," she said. "And the foresight of my Consort." She gave Todd an inscrutable look. John held his tongue. He knew better than to mess with her when she was playing this game.

Teyla turned and inclined her head a few inches to Cadman. "Blades and clevermen, gentlemen all, this is Wreathed in the Plants of Victory, a young kinswoman of She Who Carries Many Things. I tell you this day that my Consort and I should not have escaped from the treachery of Queen Death, whose blades attempted to murder me in the very Chamber of Oath Taking, beneath the most potent symbols of truce! I should be dead this moment were it not for her and the Consort of Atlantis, who had come aboard Death's ship as part of She Who Carries Many Things' attack!"

Her voice rang in the chamber. Radek was forgotten in the introductions, but probably he didn't rank enough to merit an introduction, some hanger on of Cadman's, who had now been inexplicably raised in status to Carter's heir.

"Such treachery is unthinkable!" the one kneeling before her said, his voice shaking and his eyes shining, a pretty understandable reaction to being at Teyla's feet.

"Yes, but it is not finished," Todd said. "We must go to the bridge. How goes it?"

The one they had called Ember nodded swiftly. "We came in close enough to get a lock. But there are three hive ships and two cruisers. The ship of She Who Carries Many Things has not fired on us."

"Nor will they with her kinswoman aboard," Teyla said, sweeping toward the door. "The bridge, gentlemen." Todd followed at her elbow as though he spent every day doing exactly what Teyla told him.

Cadman boggled at him. "Play it," John whispered as Radek came up beside them. "Just follow Teyla's lead. And let's find out what the hell is going on."

"Ma'am, we are reading no transmitters aboard the hive ship." Franklin's voice cut through the shouting on the *Hammond's* bridge. Something had shorted and a fire suppression crew were spraying foam while Sam leaned over the engineering station.

There it went. The dorsal shield was down.

"Pull us out!" she shouted to the helmsman. "We're naked!" She put one hand to her headset. "Blue flight, this is your recall order. Return to the *Hammond* immediately. Repeat, all 302s. This is your recall order!"

The *Hammond* spun about wildly, ducking beneath Todd's massive hive ship, open dorsal spot uppermost. Lt. Chandler deserved a commendation for this one. This was some serious flying.

"Sheppard? Sheppard?"

One of the 302s was coming in on one thruster, Captain Dwaine Grant. He'd never make it with the *Hammond* moving like this. Before she could say anything Chandler was on it. Behind the hive ship he could straighten out, let Grant line it up. She heard the line chatter as he slid in, inertial dampeners keeping him from being spread across the landing bay as the 302 touched wing first, skidding in a spray of sparks into the rigged barriers.

And then they were back out from behind the hive ship, rotating as they dodged fire intended for Todd's hive. The other hive ships had entered the fray, two on one, concentrating on the hive ship rather than the *Hammond*, remaining cruisers closing.

"Forward shield at zero," Franklin said calmly. Only the rear shield remained, and it was at 30 percent. All shots now would tell, and they could not take a dorsal hit.

"Sam?" Sheppard's voice cutting through the static.

"Where are you?"

Static from EM emissions bursting up and down the spectrum. "…on Todd's hive…" she thought she heard him say.

And then the massive hive ship started pulling back. Three Darts skimmed in, slipping through the closing maw of the Dart bay.

"Chandler, prepare to open a hyperspace window," Sam said, stalking toward the helmsman's station, sparks cascading from some overhead conduit.

"…Ronon?" Sheppard's voice cut in and out.

"Say again?"

"Have you got Ronon?" John asked, almost shouting into his radio as though that would somehow cut through the interference.

And then it was gone.

He spun around, absolute silence on the radio. "What just happened?"

"We have entered hyperspace," Teyla said, swinging around in a flurry of skirts. Whatever she was saying to Todd was telepathic, as was his reply. About them two dozen Wraith manned the bridge, way too many to take out as they stood, with no cover and Teyla in the middle of the room.

Radek visibly sagged, murmuring something in Czech.

"I don't understand," Cadman said.

Todd turned to her. "We cannot take on five ships, even with Colonel Carter as an ally. She was recovering fighters and her shields were down. It was time for us to retreat."

One of the Wraith, the one who had gone on one knee to Teyla, raised his chin. "And to carry word of Queen Death's treachery against our Queen to all who will hear!" His eyes shone as he looked at Teyla. "My Queen, this is war!"

"We are confirming the last of the 302s aboard," Franklin said.

Another explosion rocked the ship, the scream of alarms showing a solid hit. The inertial dampeners compensated, but not before it threw Sam sideways against the helmsman's chair. She grabbed at the backrest to stay upright. "Damage control?"

"We have hull breaches in A402 and A403," Franklin said. "Also B402. The compartments are open to space."

"Can you get an energy shield on it?" Sam snapped. The portside landing gear and the control matrices behind them. There shouldn't have been personnel in there, but…

"Negative," Franklin said. "We've completely lost the ventral shield."

One of the cruisers was closing in, ready to beam over boarding parties. Unshielded, they'd have Wraith all over the ship.

"Open the hyperspace window," Sam said. "Chandler, get us out of here." It might be too late. She might have already waited too long. She might have already waited too long getting the last 302s aboard…

The forward windows lit with unfathomable fire, the first shockwave shaking the ship even as the hyperspace window opened, Queen Death's hive ship exploding in a rain of visible light. Debris spread outward, propelled by the blast of the ZPM, gaining on the *Hammond* running before it like a skiff before a tidal wave.

The window was open, and the *Hammond* passed through.

ACKNOWLEDGEMENTS

More than any of the other books in the Legacy series, this one is a team effort. I do not have deep enough thanks for Melissa Scott and Amy Griswold, whose invaluable contributions have improved *The Furies* tremendously. Writing with the two of you is a pleasure!

I would also like to especially thank Gabrielle Lyons, who provided much useful advice, Mary Day, who gave me all of Eva Robinson's best lines, and Katerina Niklova, who translated Radek's lines into Czech for me. I'd also like to thank the advance readers who have added so much to this journey: Gretchen Brinckerhoff, Camy, Anna Kiwiel, Anna Lindstrom, Jennifer Roberson, Lena Sheng and Lena Strid.

Lastly, I'd like to thank my wonderful editor, Sally Malcolm, for giving me the chance to write these wonderful characters and continue the story of Stargate Atlantis.

Stay in touch...
Follow us on Twitter
@StargateNovels

Find us on Facebook at
facebook.com/StargateNovels

Sign up for our newsletter
at StargateNovels.com

THANKS!

STARGÅTE
SG·1.

STARGATE
ATLÅNTIS

**Original novels based on the hit
TV shows STARGATE SG-1 and
STARGATE ATLANTIS**

**Available as e-books from leading online
retailers**

**Paperback editions available from
Amazon and IngramSpark**

**If you liked this book, please tell your
friends and leave a review on a
bookstore website. Thanks!**